Step #1: Always leave him hungry for more.

How to Entice an Earl

Manda Collins

Author of *How to Dance with a Duke**

Don't miss the previous novels in this
delectable new series from
MANDA COLLINS

HOW TO DANCE WITH A DUKE

HOW TO ROMANCE A RAKE

Available from St. Martin's Paperbacks

How to Entice an Earl

Manda Collins

St. Martin's Paperbacks

This is a work of fiction. All of the characters, organizations, and events portrayed in this novel are either products of the author's imagination or are used fictitiously.

HOW TO ENTICE AN EARL

Copyright © 2013 by Manda Collins.

For information address St. Martin's Press, 175 Fifth Avenue, New York, NY 10010.

ISBN: 978-0-312-54926-8

Printed in the United States of America

St. Martin's Paperbacks edition / February 2013

St. Martin's Paperbacks are published by St. Martin's Press, 175 Fifth Avenue, New York, NY 10010.

10 9 8 7 6 5 4 3 2 1

One

"What about Lord Fortenbury?" Cecily, Duchess of Winterson, asked her cousin Lady Madeline Essex, her voice low so that the other attendees of the Wexford Ball wouldn't hear them.

As on so many previous occasions, Cecily, Maddie, and their cousin Juliet, now Lady Deveril, looked out at the dancers at a *ton* gathering without taking to the floor themselves. But this time it was from choice rather than a lack of partners—at least for the two married cousins. Both Cecily and Juliet had just released their husbands to find their way to the card room so that they could chat with Maddie, who had thus far been unable to remove herself from the ranks of the wallflowers.

It wasn't for want of a fashionable gown, she mused. The creation from Madame Celeste that she wore tonight might be a bit unusual, with its high waist and unembellished state, but there was no mistaking that the ocean-blue silk displayed her generous curves and ample bosom to advantage. And the color went well with her fair hair and coloring. It was a far cry from the sort of overembellished frocks and muted colors she'd worn at the beginning of the season. Although she'd never been one to mince words or back down from a challenge, her new wardrobe nevertheless gave Maddie a renewed sense of confidence when it came to the opposite sex. A confidence that would never allow her to grasp at the first gentleman who crossed her path.

"Lord Fortenbury is like a particularly eager puppy," she said, impatience furrowing her brow. "I like puppies, but I don't wish to be married to one."

Ever since her cousins had married, they had encouraged Maddie to make use of the dance card Cecily had "borrowed" from Miss Amelia Snowe, this season's unrivaled diamond. Shaped like a fan, the dance card's ivory petals marked with the penciled-in names of the *ton*'s most eligible bachelors could be easily "adapted" to conform to each new entertainment. For both Cecily and Juliet, the card had proven to be a good-luck token as well as a means of meeting eligibles, for soon after they acquired it they had each found their husbands. And while she was pleased for her cousins, she did not feel quite ready to follow them into matrimony. She had things to accomplish before she allowed herself to become enthralled by a husband and family. Like finishing her novel.

"Have you even used the dance card?" Juliet demanded, her auburn brows furrowed with suspicion. "I haven't seen you dance above three times this week. And twice were with Deveril and Winterson so they don't even count."

"You might try the 'smile–bat–tilt' method," Cecily suggested, referring to Amelia's penciled mantra on the back of the fan petals. "It worked for me when I was trying to find a gentleman to get me into the Egyptian Club."

Maddie refrained from pointing out that Amelia's advice had *not* in fact been what drew Winterson to

Cecily. "I do appreciate your concern," she assured both of her cousins, "but I do not wish to—"

She was saved from further discussion by the arrival of Winterson, Deveril, and their friend Colonel Lord Christian Monteith. Only now he was the Earl of Gresham, she corrected herself, thinking of Christian's recent elevation to the title upon the death of his uncle. It was difficult to think of him as Gresham rather than Monteith.

"I thought you were headed for the card room," Juliet said to her angelically handsome husband, Lord Deveril, who was dressed in the first stare of fashion, a ruby pin nestled in the folds of his pristine neck cloth.

"We were," Deveril said with a shrug, his golden curls glinting in the chandelier lights as he slipped a hand down to squeeze Juliet's, "but we ran into Gresham on the way there and lost interest."

"I do seem to have that effect on people," Monteith—or Gresham—said with a flash of white teeth.

As usual, his evening attire was more practical than fashionable, but his broad shoulders and strong thighs filled his coat and breeches impressively. Not that Maddie noticed such things. No, indeed.

"They are so overtaken by my charismatic personality that they can think of little else."

"Don't flatter yourself, old son," said Winterson, who had gravitated to his wife's side like a magnet to iron. "We came back," he told the cousins, "because we saw Amelia Snowe headed this way."

"And you came to protect us?" Cecily asked with deceptive sweetness. "It was gallant of you, darling. But you know that we are perfectly capable of handling her ourselves. We've done so for years now. Without assistance, I might add."

"I would trust you lot to dispatch with any number of villains on your own, my dear," Winterson said, unruffled.

"However, she has a friend of *ours* in tow, who is perhaps not so handy at defeating her as you are. And we thought we might linger nearby lest he needs a helping hand."

Before she could ask which friend was ensnared in Amelia's web, Maddie heard Amelia herself from somewhere behind them.

"You say the most wondrous things, Lord Fortenbury," the beauty, her voice as sugary-sweet as a confection from Gunters, cooed. "I have never heard my eyes compared to stars before."

Maddie shot a speaking glance at Cecily and Juliet. *This is the man you wish me to marry?* She'd remain a spinster before she subjected herself to such empty flattery on a daily basis. As someone who cherished language and words, she found his lack of imagination especially painful.

"Good God," Gresham muttered to them sotto voce, his expression pained. "I thought Fort had more imagination than that. Eyes like stars, indeed. I am surprised that Miss Snowe doesn't skewer him for such an affront."

But Amelia must be of the opinion that any compliment was better than none at all, and poor Lord Fortenbury blundered on. "Miss Snowe, I could compose an ode to your eyes and a ballad to your br . . . eathtaking lips."

At the pause, all of Maddie's party groaned—albeit quietly.

"I feel ill," Cecily said, lifting a hand to her midsection, "and it has nothing to do with my interesting condition. How can he degrade himself like that? It's appalling."

"A man will do a great deal to impress a beautiful woman," Winterson said, taking Cecily's arm and surreptitiously holding her hand.

Maddie averted her eyes and tried to stifle the pang of longing Winterson and Cecily's closeness made her feel. It wasn't that she was jealous of her cousin's happiness. But at times like this she was forcibly reminded that she still remained very much alone. Even Amelia, who was by far the most annoying young lady of her acquaintance, had managed to ensnare poor Lord Fortenbury. Not that Maddie wanted him for herself, but even so she wished for someone she could call her own.

Further conversation was forestalled when Lord Fortenbury, with Miss Snowe on his arm, approached them.

Maddie watched the pair with curiosity. Amelia was just as lovely as ever, though Maddie had long ago ceased to see her outer beauty as anything other than an empty shell. The real Amelia, if it were ever to manifest itself physically, would resemble a hideous gargoyle.

Fortenbury exchanged greetings with the gentlemen, while the ladies offered chilly acknowledgments to one another. It was evident to Maddie that none of them were particularly comfortable with the situation.

"Lady Madeline," Amelia said, breaking the silence first, her voice silky as it often was before she delivered a cutting barb. "What an interesting gown. I don't believe I've seen a waist like that since I was a girl. Never say that is one of Madame Celeste's creations. She is usually so *au courant*."

Since Maddie knew full well that Amelia frequented the modiste, she knew the remark had little to do with Madame Celeste, and everything to do with the woman wearing the gown. "Indeed it is, Amelia," she returned, not letting a hint of her annoyance show in her face. "Madame Celeste is so talented that I simply put myself in her hands without trying to second-guess her sense of fashion. She is the expert, after all."

Before Amelia could respond, Maddie was startled to hear Gresham speak up.

"I think Lady Madeline has never looked finer," the earl drawled, removing a quizzing glass, which Maddie had never once seen him use, from a hidden pocket in his waistcoat and surveying her from top to toes. Against her will she felt a blush rise from her neck into her cheeks. She would make him pay for this later. She could fight her own battles, thank you very much.

"You are too kind, Lord Gresham," Maddie said through her teeth, glaring at him. But Gresham, ignoring her pique, merely winked at her from behind the glass.

Amelia, who had never been one to argue with an eligible bachelor—even one who was friendly with her mortal enemies—simpered. It was not pretty. "I fear you misunderstand me, my lord," Amelia gushed. "I was trying to tell Lady Madeline how interesting her gown is. I feel sure that Madame Celeste has anticipated what will be the trend before much time has passed." Just in case her backhanded apology did not hit its mark, she extended her lower lip in a very pretty pout. As if she felt quite sad at having been so misunderstood.

"I'm sure Gresham understands his mistake, Miss Snowe," Lord Fortenbury soothed the beauty. "He's not at all the sort to hold a grudge." He turned to the other man with what on someone else would be a glare and asked with as much menace as a puppy could master, "Are you, old fellow?"

Maddie barely stopped herself from rolling her eyes at Fortenbury's protective display. What was it about Miss Snowe that turned men into fools in her presence?

Except for Gresham, she mentally amended. He was never one to follow the trend.

"Indeed I am not," Gresham replied to Fortenbury, though he made no move to step away from Maddie's side, for which she was surprisingly grateful. "I do hope, however, that Miss Snowe will attempt to make herself understood from now on. I should hate to hear of some young lady of lesser mettle than Lady Madeline having her feelings wounded by an unguarded word."

Her grudging gratitude to Gresham growing, Maddie watched as Amelia's eyes narrowed for a fraction of a second before she masked the annoyance with more simpering. Before there could be any more conflict, the sound of the orchestra tuning up for the next dance broke through the tension. Apparently deciding that they'd done their conversational duty, Lord Fortenbury and Miss Snowe left them to take their places in the sets forming on the ballroom floor.

"You are a very bad man," Maddie told her champion as the whole group burst into laughter. "I am perfectly capable of routing Miss Amelia Snowe, thank you very much. Even if you did raise her ire, I have managed quite well with Amelia these past few years and do not need a gentleman to ride to my rescue."

"No one said you did," Christian said with a small shrug, not contrite in the least. "I simply thought Miss Snowe might be more willing to take a dressing-down from a gentleman than from another lady. And it would appear that I was correct."

"She did listen," Maddie admitted grudgingly, "but do not think that she will forget it. You will be on her black list forever now. I'm not sure she is someone you wish to have as an enemy, my lord."

"I'm not afraid," Gresham said with a grin. "Are you, Lady Madeline?"

Mentally cursing him, Maddie shook her head. "It will take more than Amelia Snowe and her sharp tongue to frighten me. I may not have spent the last decade fighting Bonaparte, but I have a certain amount of skill when it comes to fighting drawing room battles."

The approval that shone in Gresham's blue eyes, or rather her stomach's flip in reaction to it, confused Maddie and she was grateful when Juliet broke in, saying, "I am tired of speaking of Amelia. We spend far too much time worrying about her and how she will affect things."

"She is certainly not my favorite topic of conversation," Deveril agreed, touching his wife lightly on the arm. "I think we should talk of something much more interesting." Turning to Madeline he said, "Juliet tells me that you are writing a novel."

Feeling the flush return to her cheeks, Maddie nodded. "I am, indeed, my lord. Though I pray you will tell no one else about it. I do not wish it to be generally known until I am finished with it and am able to sell it to a publisher."

"What is it about?" Winterson asked, his eyes alight with mischief. "Is it a roman à clef like Caro Lamb's *Glenarvon*? I should like very much to see certain people lampooned in novel form as she did with Byron."

They all laughed, though Maddie shook her head. "I'm afraid not, your grace. I do not think that I would wish to spend any more time thinking about Amelia than I already must. No, this is to be in the vein of Madame d'Arblay or Miss Austen."

"A love story, then?" Gresham teased, his green eyes alight with mischief. "I would not have taken you for a romantic, Lady Madeline."

"There will be a love story as part of the tale, yes," Maddie said, attempting to maintain her dignity even as his question sent an unfamiliar thrill through her belly. Perhaps she was coming down with something. Daring not meet Gresham's eye, she continued to the others, "The story itself will deal with a young man's inability to extricate himself from the ever more dangerous world of gambling and reckless life on the town."

"I beg your pardon, Maddie." Lord Deveril's blue eyes clouded with confusion. "How will a gently bred young lady be able to write of such things? I cannot imagine that you have ever visited a gambling hell or a house of . . . that is to say . . ."

"She knows what you're trying to say, dearest," Juliet said to her husband with a smile. "And I must admit, Maddie, to having wondered the same thing. Though I suppose you could use your imagination. Or ask someone—your brother for instance—for a description."

For a moment, Maddie debated whether to ask what she'd been intending to ask. After all, she did not wish to impose upon her friendship with her cousins' husbands. And yet, she did indeed need firsthand experience of a London gaming hell. Nothing ventured, nothing gained, she decided. "I don't suppose one of you would condescend to—" she began.

But before she could even complete the sentence, all three men nipped the idea in the bud.

"Absolutely not!"

"Never in a million years."

"Not for the wide world."

This last from Gresham, whose scowl reinforced his words. Looking from one to the other she saw that they meant what they said. "Very well," she said with a shrug. "You cannot blame me for asking. I did not think any of you would consider it, but I had to try. It is not a whim, but a necessary part of researching my novel."

"It's not that we do not wish to help you, Madeline," Winterson said kindly. "But it would be unconscionable for one of us to escort you to such a place. Even a gaming hell, which is the least objectionable of the establishments you named."

"Said like a man who hasn't spent much time in gaming hells of late," Gresham said with a frown. "Depending on the place they can be more dangerous than a br . . . house of ill repute. Mrs. Bailey's hell, for instance, is supposed to host an exclusive party tomorrow night that promises to include some very deep pockets. And you know how fraught things get when there is a great deal of money to be won and lost."

Maddie, who had been listening with half an ear as she tried to think who else might be persuaded to take her to a hell, stood straighter at the mention of Mrs. Bailey's. She had heard her brother speaking of a Mrs. Bailey last week, but she had assumed he meant a friend or acquaintance.

"Mrs. Bailey's?" she asked, careful not to sound too eager. "You wouldn't happen to know where her establishment is located, would you?"

But it was too good to hope that Gresham would not guess the reason for her question.

"No," he said baldly. "I will not put my neck at risk from your father and your brother by telling you how to get to Bailey's. Or any other hell for that matter."

"Very well," she said, lifting her head in a display of pride. "I will simply be forced to find another way to get there." Turning to Cecily and Juliet she asked, "Would you like to accompany me to the retiring room? If I cannot persuade these gentlemen to help me get to Mrs. Bailey's, I should at least ensure that my hair is still tidy and then see about making use of the dance card."

As the three of them wended their way through the crowded ballroom toward the ladies' withdrawing room, Maddie reflected that she would have to change her tactics. She would approach her brother about escorting her to Mrs. Bailey's. He, too, would protest, but having known him a great deal longer than Winterson, Deveril, or Gresham, she knew exactly how to persuade him. Her mind settled on a plan, she vowed to enjoy the rest of the evening. Because if she was lucky, she would begin researching tomorrow night.

"Never a dull moment with those three around," Gresham muttered to his comrades as they headed once again toward the card room. The glittering Wexford ballroom was filled to capacity, and it was with a sigh of relief that he stepped into the hallway leading to the parlor where tables had been set up. He'd never been one for crowds, and since the war he'd found them even less comfortable than before.

"They do add a certain spark to life," Winterson agreed. "Though I don't suppose you are required to take part in the festivities as we are, Gresham. I sometimes wonder if you do so out of loyalty or some other reason."

"A *tendre* for a certain golden-haired lady, perchance?" Deveril teased, elbowing Christian in the ribs. "She might take a bit of persuading, but I can think of worse matches for a newly minted earl."

Christian fought the impulse to turn tail and run. He knew it was inevitable for people to begin matching him and Maddie together simply because they were so often in company. But it was less about attraction than proximity.

At least, that's what he told himself, remembering how an errant curl of golden hair had brushed against her neckline as she walked away. He could not deny that she was an attractive young lady. And he admired her spirit—among other things. But he was not quite ready to enter into the matrimonial stakes. Perhaps when he was, he would consider her, but for now, he was content to look without touching, so to speak.

To his friends, he said, deliberately misunderstanding their hints, "Do you really think Amelia might be persuaded to have me? She is such a shy thing. I wouldn't want to frighten her with my strong feelings."

Deveril's snort was gratifying. It seemed that the earldom hadn't destroyed his comic timing, at least. Winterson, on the other hand was not put off the scent. "Prevaricate all you like, man, but I saw how you jumped to her defense earlier. Not many would be willing to lay their neck on the line for Maddie. Especially since she is more than capable of fending for herself."

Damn it. He had known it was foolish to protect Maddie from Amelia's taunts, but he had never been one to step aside while a bully was hurting one of his friends. And that, he supposed, was the operative word: "friends." What he and Maddie shared was friendship and it would be foolish to jeopardize that for something as fleeting as physical attraction. Or worse, marriage.

He kept an eye out for her because she needed someone to do so. Her brother, Viscount Linton, had shown little enough interest in protecting her from herself. And if Maddie reminded Christian of a certain other young lady, whose brother had also failed to protect her from the censure of the world, then he could hardly fault himself for feeling a certain responsibility toward her. He'd done little enough to shelter his own sister. If he were able, somehow, to see to it that Linton's sister didn't come to harm, perhaps he'd be able to forgive himself someday.

Aloud he said, "I was simply helping a friend. Either of you might have done the same thing if I hadn't done it."

"Not likely," Deveril said with a laugh. "I enjoy my bollocks right where they are, thank you very much."

"As do I," Winterson agreed. "Though I found it very interesting that Madeline did not protest your assistance overmuch. In fact, I'd almost say that she welcomed the assistance."

"Could it be that our Maddie is just as sweet on Gresham as he is on her?" Deveril asked in a bright falsetto.

Monteith fought the impulse to bloody the other man's nose. It was only for Juliet's sake that he refrained. "You are both as full of gossip as a school for young ladies. I shouldn't wonder if you took tea with the patronesses of Almack's on a regular basis."

"At least we'd be spending time with women, which is more than I can say for you," Winterson said, raising one dark brow suggestively. "You know if you don't use it, you're in danger of losing it."

"It," growled Gresham in a tone that would have sent lesser men fleeing, "is in perfect working order, I assure you. I've simply been too busy with other things, as it happens."

Remembering just what he'd been working on that was so important, he sobered. "Unfortunately, what I've been doing does affect Lady Madeline, but it's not good news, I'm afraid."

Sensing his shift in mood, Winterson and Deveril stopped abruptly. Gesturing for the other two to follow him, Monteith led them to an open terrace door. The small balcony was empty, and Monteith dug into his breast pocket for the cheroots he'd brought along for just such an emergency.

They went through the ritual of lighting and smoking for a few moments before Winterson said, "You may as well tell. You've piqued my curiosity, and no doubt Dev's, too."

Looking out over the Wexfords' back garden, Monteith said, "I told you that I've been doing a bit of work for Lord Leighton in the Home Office."

Leighton oversaw some of the government's investigations into threats against the crown. But only those that came from within, on English soil. Both Winterson and Monteith had worked with Leighton on the Continent during the war, and were confident that he would be quite effective in his new position. The war might be over, but they both knew that it didn't spell the end of attempts by those who were disappointed in the outcome to right the wrongs that occurred at Waterloo.

"Well, I've been charged to look into claims that Mr. John Tinker, and by association, Lord Linton, are involved in some capacity with the Citizen's Liberation Society."

Winterson whistled. "They were responsible for the assassaination attempt on the prime minister last year, weren't they?"

"I don't remember that," Deveril said, puzzled. "And what the devil is the Citizen's Liberation Society?"

"The authorities kept it quiet," Winterson said, the end of his cheroot glowing red in the darkness. "The only reason I know is because I keep in contact with the Home secretary."

"The CLS is a group of English citizens who adhere to the ideals of the revolution in France. They have been working underground in covert—and sometimes not so covert as in the case of the attempt on the prime minister—ways to bring about the overthrow of the monarchy."

Deveril blanched, "Are they unaware of the way the Revolution played out? Surely they don't wish for England to devolve into the kind of chaos that has reigned in France for the past few decades."

"They are convinced that their own attempts at egalitarianism will be more successful than those in France," Monteith said with a twist of his lips. "A triumph of optimism over experience, if you ask me."

"That's an understatement," Winterson said.

"So, Lady Madeline's brother is thought to be involved in this treasonous activity?" Deveril asked. "His father is an earl. Why would he do such a thing?"

Monteith leaned back against the wall, not caring if his evening coat was smudged. "I can't say whether Essex is involved in the society or not. I do know that Tinker is highly likely to be a member. He has always had leanings in that direction. His mother was French, and he lost a great deal of family in the war. But what I am supposed to discover is whether Linton has been persuaded by his friend to join the cause, or if he is simply maintaining a friendship that has stood him in good stead since university."

"That whole group, including Linton, Tinker, Tretham, even Fielding's widow," Winterson said, exhaling a cloud of smoke, "has been involved in questionable ventures for years now. Wasn't Linton blamed for Lord Fielding's death in that godforsaken curricle race?"

"Yes," Monteith said. "Though nothing has ever been proved." He shook his head. "Now, the Home Office wonders whether Linton, who is quite often short of funds, might have been driven to join his friend Tinker in a bid for money."

"Men have been driven to treason for less," Winterson agreed.

"Poor Maddie," Deveril said, tapping the ash from his cheroot. "She would be devastated to learn such a thing about her brother."

"Which is why you can say nothing to her," Monteith said sharply. "I mean it, Dev. No hint of what I'm doing, why I'm investigating Linton, can reach her ears. Not only would it endanger the investigation, but it might put her in danger. Lady Madeline might think she is perfectly able to take care of herself, but in this circumstance, I'd prefer that she not be required to."

"Of course," Deveril said. "I won't even tell Juliet, though she will make me pay handsomely should she ever learn I kept it from her."

"You have my word as well," Winterson said. "Though I hope you will let us know if you need help at any point in your investigation. Maddie is family and we will do what we can to help her. And Linton for that matter, though he has never struck me as a particularly admirable fellow."

"Nor I," Monteith agreed.

"At any rate," he continued, "the Home Office has intercepted a communication from the leaders of the CLS and it mentions a meeting at Mrs. Bailey's tomorrow evening between two of their operatives. I need to be there to see if Tinker or Linton do anything suspicious. If Linton shows no sign of involvement, then I can breathe a sigh of relief on that score at least."

"Good God!" Winterson said, hastily removing the cheroot from between his lips. "No wonder you were so adamant about not taking her to Mrs. Bailey's. I thought you were simply looking out for your own neck."

"Well, that, too," he admitted, remembering uneasily Maddie's response to their denial of her request.

"You don't suppose she'll try to go there without us, do you?"

"Surely not," Deveril said with a shake of his head. "Even Maddie isn't so foolish as to venture to such a place unescorted. She might resent having to maintain her reputation, but she would not carelessly put it in danger like that."

"I hope you're right," Monteith said, thinking of how determined she could be when shc wanted something. "I certainly hope you're right."

Two

$\mathcal{N}$othing you say will convince me," Viscount Linton snapped at his sister as he poured himself a glass of claret in the library of Essex House the next afternoon. Though the room was normally their father's domain, he was conducting business in Parliament today. Since their row earlier in the week, her brother had seemed careful to avoid Lord Essex, but that did not mean he would avoid partaking in his sire's best wine. "The pater would have my head, Mads."

To her annoyance, he was not proving as helpful as she'd have wished. "Papa need never find out," Maddie assured him. "Besides, any number of well-bred ladies visit gaming rooms. Your friend Lady Emily Fielding, for example."

The widow of James's good friend, Lady Emily Fielding, was one who cared very little for society's strictures. She did as she pleased and was unconcerned with the censorious glances she received from high sticklers when she deigned to attend a *ton* function. She had been thus even before her husband's death. But Charles's death had made her even more daring. As a result, she was not considered fit company for unwed young ladies.

All of which was immaterial to Maddie, who merely used her as an example of a gently born lady who was perfectly at home at gaming hells. But Linton was not moved.

"Lady Emily is a widow," Linton retorted, gesturing with his claret glass. "What's more, she runs with a faster set than you've ever done. If Mama and Papa thought for one minute that you aspired to model your behavior on hers they'd lock you in the attics and never let you come out.

"Why do you wish to go to Mrs. Bailey's anyway?" Linton asked. "It isn't as if you enjoy gambling. You can't even be bothered to pay attention through a hand of piquet."

Weighing her options, Maddie decided to tell him the truth. "Because I wish to write a novel that will take place in part in just such an establishment. So I need to see what one is like."

Linton rolled his eyes. "Is that all? Why don't you just ask me what it's like and I'll tell you."

"Because I need to see it for myself," she explained, beginning to lose patience. "Just as you would rather ride in a horse race yourself than hear about it second-hand from someone else."

As soon as she said the words, Maddie regretted them. Lord Charles Fielding had died in a curricle race that Linton had challenged him to. She hadn't been thinking of the issue at all, but her brother's sudden paleness alerted her to her blunder.

"Linton," she said, "I didn't mean to . . ."

"Never mind," he said, waving off her apology. "You can't go about refusing to mention the word 'race' for the rest of your life."

He seemed less angry than sad. And tired. He had, after all, been living with the pall of Charles's death over him for years now. Not only did Lord Fielding's parents blame James for their son's death, but Lord and Lady Essex had come to the painful conclusion that their son did indeed bear some responsibility for the other man's death. Unfortunately, rather than convincing him to curb his worst excesses, the death, and the subsequent social fallout, had only encouraged James to greater extremes of behavior.

Like gaming.

It was these extremes that worried Maddie so. She stopped pacing for a moment and paused to look, really look, at the younger brother she had always adored. With golden blond hair so close to her own color, and long, lean good looks, Lord James Essex should have been the most popular man in town. But thanks to his tarnished reputation, he was quickly becoming persona non grata among the society that perversely seemed to have rewarded his bad behavior when he was first on the town.

Maddie knew she had to do something to save her brother before it was too late. And perhaps by writing about the underworld where young men like him faced every temptation imaginable, she could learn what it was about that life that so fascinated him.

"You are perhaps not as popular with them as you once were," she said, referring to his lament about their parents, "but you must know that they only wish what's best for you."

"What's best for me now is to convince you to abandon this harebrained scheme," her brother bit out. "I will not take you to Mrs. Bailey's, Mads. No matter how prettily you wrap up your argument."

Maddie shook her head sadly. "I was afraid you would prove resistant," she said. "Which is why I decided to come up with an offer you cannot refuse."

"I doubt seriously that you have the wherewithal to come up with such a thing," he retorted, sitting back with an arrogant smile. "You forget that I have known you since you were a child, Mads. And I know all your tricks."

"Perhaps," she said sweetly, hoping with every bit of her being that he would not see through her bravado. "If you won't take me to Mrs. Bailey's," she said, "then I shall just have to ask someone else to do it. Someone who is more than willing to do it."

"What man in his right mind would take such a risk?" James demanded crossly, though Maddie was sure she saw a bit of unease in his eyes.

"Ah, brother," she said, wagging a finger at him, "there's where you've got it wrong. It is not a man I've asked to take me at all."

"What? What do you mean?" he asked.

"Just what I say. I will ask a lady to take me. Someone with whom I believe you are quite familiar," she said. "Lady Emily Fielding."

"You wouldn't dare," Linton said, the color draining from his face. "Mama would lock you in your room for a month."

"But," Maddie said, warming to her cause, "what Mama doesn't know won't harm her. And even so, who would Mama place more blame on for my folly? Me for taking the risk, or you for introducing me to Lady Emily in the first place?"

His jaw set, her brother finally surrendered. "Fine. If you are determined to go to Bailey's then I suppose I'll take you. At least this way I might be able to pass it off as a lark."

Thrilled that her gambit had paid off, Maddie clapped her hands, then threw her arms about her brother's neck. "Thank you, Jamie," she told him, using his pet name from childhood. "I promise you that Mama won't hear a word of our outing from me."

"It's not your tattling I'm afraid of, Mads."

Ignoring the little stab of fear she felt at his words, Maddie took herself off to prepare for her scandalous outing that night.

That evening, smoothing the skirt of a neckline-baring gown that would have sent her mother into a fit of apoplexy, Maddie gazed avidly about Mrs. Bailey's townhouse-cum-gambling-hell. It was both more than she'd imagined, and a bit of a disappointment.

The disappointment was that it didn't seem quite as scandalous as it had been made out to be. Yes, there were various games of chance set up throughout the parlors of the residence. And those engaged in playing the games seemed to be engrossed in them. But with a few exceptions, the attendees were the same sorts of people she might have found at any *ton* entertainment.

The difference was that the card parties Maddie had attended as part of the London social scene had never commanded the degree of attention that the whist and piquet tables did here. There was some indefinable air about the gathering that gave the rooms a hectic intensity that Maddie had never encountered before. It was this that she would try to capture for her novel.

"Stay close to me," her brother said in a low voice as he led her past a table where a passel of young lordlings vied for the attention of a lady—though that appellation might be questionable—whose scarlet gown made Maddie's feel demure by comparison. Tearing her gaze away from the tableau, Madeline followed her brother through the crowd toward a table at the far end of the room. She made a mental note to remember the color of the woman's gown for future reference, just in case she wished to portray a lightskirt in one of her novels.

"Lord Linton, how delightful to see you again so soon," crooned a tall woman who presided over the table where the brother and sister stopped. She was obviously Mrs. Bailey, their hostess. Maddie wasn't quite sure how she knew it. Probably because of the widow's proprietary air, which, to Maddie's annoyance, seemed to extend to her brother. "And who is your little companion?"

Maddie's spine stiffened at the description. She knew she was short, of course, but she disliked being reminded of her lack of inches. Especially by blowsy widows who ran gaming hells. Not that she'd ever encountered any before.

"Allow me to introduce m'sister, Mrs. Bailey," Linton said, giving Maddie a sharp look, doubtless because he knew of his sister's tendency to annihilate anyone with the temerity to mention her small stature. "Lady Madeline Essex, meet Mrs. Emma Bailey, our hostess."

"Charmed," Maddie said with a grudging curtsy. She was not pleased to see Mrs. Bailey's amusement at her annoyance.

"Welcome, Lady Madeline," the older woman said. "I'm so glad you were able to attend my party this evening. I do hope you will enjoy yourself."

If the widow suspected that Maddie had ulterior motives for visiting her home tonight, she kept her suspicions to herself. It was not at all unusual for ladies of the *ton* to seek out a bit of excitement by attending such parties, Maddie knew. They might tarnish their reputations a bit by doing so, but the damage was hardly irreparable.

"The pleasure is mine, Mrs. Bailey," Maddie replied,

mindful of her brother's warning not to draw attention to herself. "You have a lovely home." Which was not a falsehood. The row house on the outer fringes of Mayfair was tastefully decorated and but for the tables set up in the drawing room might have passed for any other modestly well-to-do home in London.

Something flashed in the other woman's eyes—shame? Maddie was unsure. Before her hostess could reply, a servant appeared at her elbow with a note. With a brisk nod, she excused herself, leaving Linton to lead Maddie to the hazard table.

To her surprise, she was already acquainted with several of the gentlemen who crowded round the table. Mr. George Vinson was losing quite badly, which didn't surprise Maddie in the least, since despite his affability he was not very bright. Lord Tretham, a friend of her brother's, seemed to be in good spirits despite his poor luck. But it was neither of these young men who drew Maddie's attention. Her gaze was immediately drawn to the Earl of Gresham on the other side of the table.

Was she to be exposed to him at every turn? she wondered in frustration. Meeting Gresham's eye across the table, she refused to let him see how annoyed she was. Instead she held her back ramrod straight and offered him a pitch-perfect curtsy. To which he responded with an elegant bow. Determined not to let him ruin her enjoyment, she moved closer to a table where a few gentlemen, and several ladies, were playing *vingt-et-un*.

Spotting Mr. John Tinker, whom she'd known for several years as a friend of her brother's, she took a place between him and Lady Emily Fielding.

"Hello, Mr. Tinker," she said, trying to cultivate an air of ennui rather than the excitement and curiosity that she felt. "Are you enjoying your game?"

As if startled to hear her, Tinker turned, his eyes widening. "What are you doing here, Lady Madeline?" he asked. "Never say your brother brought you."

"You needn't sound so astonished, Mr Tinker." Maddie laughed. "I enjoy the occasional social outing just as much as my brother does."

"You must excuse Tinker, Lady Madeline," Lady Emily Fielding said from Maddie's other side. "I fear he has rather shockingly traditional ideas about where ladies do and do not belong. It is an argument of long standing between us."

Maddie turned to look at the other woman. She had seen her from a distance at various *ton* parties, but had never really had the opportunity to look at her up close. She was every bit as beautiful as she was reputed to be. Her deep brown hair shone in the candlelight, and the crimson gown she wore fit her curvaceous figure like a glove.

"Yet you still remain friends?" Maddie asked, fascinated by the other woman's words. "That is quite a feat."

"I daresay it is because I cannot be bothered to maintain a grudge when Tinker is such a very good whist partner," Lady Emily said with a grin. "What can I say? I am easy to please."

Tinker bowed to acknowledge the compliment, then turned back to the baize table where a dealer called out the cards as he turned them over before each player.

As she watched the table, Maddie felt a male body step up close behind her. Startled, she jumped and turned to look up into a familiar green gaze.

"Lady Madeline," Gresham said, stepping back to allow her to turn. "I would like a word."

Annoyed, but knowing that she would have to speak to him sooner or later, Maddie excused herself to Tinker and Lady Emily. Grudgingly she followed the earl to an alcove on the edge of the chamber.

"What the devil are you doing here?" he demanded in a low tone that only she could hear. She could feel the frustration emanating from him in waves. "More importantly, what the devil was Linton thinking bringing you here?"

"You know perfectly well why I am here," she said in an equally low voice, trying to ignore the jolt of attraction she felt despite her anger. This is *not* how you are supposed to respond to Gresham, she informed her pounding heart. "I told you last night that I needed to be here so that I might write about a gaming hell in my novel. And what business is it of yours that my brother brought me here? I do not see you ringing a peal over the heads of the other ladies here."

"They are not related to my best friend's wife," he hissed, apparently unaware of the response his nearness was causing in her. "And their presence here will not somehow end up biting me in the—"

"Oh, do not be melodramatic," Maddie interrupted, annoyed both at herself and him. Leave it to Gresham to be attractive to her even when he was setting her back up. Curse him. "You are not responsible for my presence here. My brother is, and as he didn't seem to find the idea overly disturbing, I do not see why you should."

Gresham shoved a hand through his light brown curls. "You'll pardon me," he said, "if I do not use your brother's behavior as a guide for my own. He is not best known for his moderation or good sense."

At the slight against her brother, Maddie's attraction transformed into anger. It was all well and good for her to criticize a member of her family, but Gresham had no right to do so. "How dare you speak of my brother in that way, you . . . you . . . hypocrite!" Bristling with anger she continued, "If you are such a paragon of virtue, what are *you* doing here?"

Though they had started out speaking in undertones, both Maddie and Gresham had allowed their voices to rise a bit in their exasperation with one another. So much so that Linton, his luck at faro having run out, turned his attention away from the gaming table and hurried over to the bickering couple.

"Madeline," her brother said in a hiss, conveniently ignoring Gresham and addressing himself to his sister. "You are causing a scene. Do you not recall the terms of our agreement?"

The injustice of being taken to task by her brother, whose behavior—despite Maddie's defense of him to Gresham—*was* frequently outrageous, made Maddie's teeth clench. "Yes, I remember, but that was before I knew that I would be accosted by this interfering baboon."

Gresham raised his brows. "Baboon? Really?"

"Be quiet," Maddie ordered. She was thoroughly sick of both of them. There were reasons that ladies continued to press for emancipation from domination by men, and these two were prime examples.

Gresham, however, had not forgotten his quibble with the young viscount. "Linton, what do you mean bringing your sister to a place like this?" he demanded. "It's not as if her reputation is flawless to begin with."

"Oooh, you . . . you . . ." For once in her life Maddie found herself at a loss for words and had to vent her frustration by stamping her foot instead of shouting as she wished to do. *The nerve.*

"If you dare to ask me that," Linton said with a shake of his head, "then I'll wager you've never tried to convince Maddie to abandon a scheme. I'd have had more luck convincing the sun to rise from the west."

"Her persistence notwithstanding," Gresham said with a twist of his mouth. "Are you really claiming to have no control over your own actions? You could certainly have left this evening without bringing her along. I cannot imagine you've brought her with you all the other times you came here."

"Pardon me," Maddie interrupted, "but *she* is here and quite capable of speaking for herself." If she let them they'd make arrangements between them to have her home and she'd be in bed before the clock struck midnight. And she had only just got here.

"Yes, I know you are," Linton said through his teeth. "And you promised not to bring attention to yourself if I brought you along tonight. You were supposed to be quiet and to keep to the background as much as possible. You swore to me." This last he said with a pout in his voice that reminded her of their childhood tiffs.

"But I didn't know Gresham would be here scolding me like a disapproving governess," Maddie said hotly, angry that her brother cast the blame on her rather than on Gresham where it belonged. "I can hardly be expected to refrain from defending myself."

"Is there a problem, gentlemen?" Mrs. Bailey asked, stepping up to the threesome, her brows raised slightly.

"Not at all, ma'am," Linton told their hostess, masking his annoyance. "We were merely discussing an upcoming race at Newmarket and my sister became incensed. She does have strong feelings about the races."

"Especially when she's backing the wrong horse," Gresham said grimly.

Madeline, realizing that it might be best to remain silent before their hostess, said nothing.

"Interesting," Mrs. Bailey said, glancing from one

to the other of them. "I hadn't suspected that Lady Madeline was a racing aficionado. You must let me show you my stable one day, my dear. I think you'll find it quite amusing."

Somehow, Maddie got the feeling that Mrs. Bailey wasn't talking about horses. She would have asked for clarification, but just as quickly as she'd approached them, Mrs. Bailey left them again. Which was frustrating since Mrs. Bailey's use of metaphor was something that might work well in her novel. Yet another crime to lay at Linton's and Gresham's doors.

"If it would be all right with the two of you," Maddie told them, "I believe I will excuse myself to repair my coiffure." Never mind the fact that her hair was just fine; Maddie wanted to be away from her annoying brother and her equally annoying . . . annoyance, or whatever it was that Gresham was to her. Perhaps a few minutes alone would allow her to calm down and remember why she was here in the first place.

Not waiting for a response, she strode to the doorway and asked a lurking footman for the direction of the room set aside for the ladies.

Christian bit back a curse as he resumed his position at the faro table—watching, not playing. He might have known this mission wouldn't be as uncomplicated as Leighton had made it out to be.

When he'd agreed to keep an eye on Lord Linton and Mr. Tinker, he hadn't thought his acquaintance with Lady Madeline would turn out to be quite such a complication.

He'd known she would not be pleased, of course, to learn of his suspicions about her brother, but if things worked out as he hoped they would, she need never know about them. There was a fifty-fifty chance that the man who met with the Citizen's Liberation Society operative tonight would be John Tinker and not Lady Madeline's brother. He sent up a silent prayer that it would be the case, because if he had to face Maddie after he informed on her brother for treason, whatever one could call their relationship would cease to exist.

Aside from the problem of Maddie, he had also discovered, as he trailed Lord Linton and Tinker from gaming hell to gaming hell these past couple of weeks, that he no longer found that kind of life enjoyable. He wasn't sure if it was his recent inheritance, or a new-found sense of maturity, but whatever the case the sight of young men losing their family fortunes on the turn of a card made him slightly ill. Just this week, in between more genteel *ton* gatherings, he'd seen Lord Linton lose a small fortune at various entertainments. And the more he lost, the more fevered his gaze on the cards became.

He wondered if Maddie was aware of her brother's gambling obsession. Doubtless her parents were since no one could lose that amount of money without needing to apply to a parent for more. Recalling her defense of him earlier, he hoped that she was not. He would not like to see that sibling relationship jeopardized.

Even so, he wished that Linton had not been quite so easy to persuade when it came to bringing Maddie to Mrs. Bailey's tonight. He knew of course that Maddie could be determined, but he hadn't dreamed that she'd be able to convince her brother to bring her along.

Granted, it was mild so far as gaming hells went. Mrs. Bailey ran a tight ship, and was quite strict about what she did and did not allow to happen within the walls of her establishment. She kept the doors leading abovestairs locked so that amorous couples wouldn't be able to wander about in search of privacy. And she did not allow just anyone to enter the place. Entrance was by invitation only, and she was not above turning someone—even someone with pockets full of the ready—away should she dislike the look of them. Even so, he certainly would not have brought his own sister to such a place.

A familiar pain struck at the thought of Clarissa, but he dismissed it. This was about Maddie and *her* brother, not him.

Just as soon as she returned from the retiring room, he would suggest strongly to Maddie that she return home. If her brother chose to escort her, then he would know for sure that it was Tinker who was to meet the contact from the Citizen's Liberation Society. And that would reassure him on two fronts.

Three

$\mathcal{M}$addie was still fuming as she pressed through the doors of the chamber Mrs. Bailey had set aside for ladies. What right had Gresham to read her a scold? He was nothing to her. So what if he was concerned that Winterson or Cecily might chide him for her presence here? That didn't mean that the blame lay with him and not with Linton. Not that she was saying blame needed to be ascribed at all. She was perfectly capable of making her own decisions and she had chosen to come here tonight. Linton had simply agreed to be her escort. That her parents would be less than pleased should they learn of her visit here was beside the point.

And Gresham! Was there ever such a man for plaguing a young lady? One minute he was giving her looks that would scorch the paint off a fence, and the next he was reading her a scold. It was enough to make her wish to cut his acquaintance altogether.

She should have known he would be here tonight, she fumed as she removed her gloves and stared at herself in the cheval glass Mrs. Bailey had provided. Why was it that the only gentleman who roused her to any sort of passion was Gresham, of all people? She already knew from their time spent together this season so far that he was as stubborn as a mule. And he was constantly jesting and poking fun.

As the thought flitted through her head she met her own gaze in the mirror. So, this was what it had come to, she thought on a sigh.

She was siding against fun.

That was what attraction could do to a person, she thought wryly, tucking a wayward strand of blond hair behind her ear and surveying her low-cut gown in the mirror.

Deciding that she would have to do, Maddie turned to leave the retiring room.

Unfortunately the door was blocked.

Thinking that her brother or Gresham was playing a joke on her she called out, "You have amused me to no end! Now kindly remove yourself so that I may exit the room."

But there was no response from the other side of the door. Telling herself not to panic, Maddie considered the situation. If she were to shout, no one in the other part of the house would be able to hear her.

Taking a few steps back, she threw herself against the door—which hurt, dash it!—and was rewarded with movement. Squeezing herself through the small gap between the door and the jamb, gulping in air, she leaned against the wall, grateful for her freedom.

Looking about to see what had blocked the door in the first place, she saw a crumpled form pressed against the lower portion of the door.

"Good Lord," she gasped, squatting, and then kneeling to grasp the figure, whose features she recognized in the dimness of the corridor as her brother's friend Tinker.

"Mr. Tinker," she said, rolling him with some difficulty to his back. "John! Can you hear me?" She stared down into his face, noting his paleness and lack of consciousness.

Patting him on the cheek, she tried to rouse him once more, and was rewarded not by a response from her patient, but a trickle of blood burbling out from between his lips. It was then that she noticed the knife protruding from the man's chest.

She did what any sensible young lady would do when confronted by a dead man on the floor of a gaming hell.

Maddie screamed.

Christian was nearly ready to declare the evening a complete disaster, since Tinker had apparently left and Linton was engrossed in a game of whist, when he heard the scream.

Maddie's scream.

A rumble went through the room. The denizens of Mrs. Bailey's might be here for a brush with the dark side, but none of them was so jaded as to ignore a scream of terror when they heard one.

Along with several other gentlemen, Christian hurried into the hallway leading to the retiring rooms. There were gaslights on the walls, but they weren't nearly as bright as the ones in the main rooms of the house. Still, he was able to make out Maddie, kneeling on the floor next to the crumpled figure of a man.

He reached her first, and seeing that it was Tinker there on the floor beside her, a knife protruding from his chest, he glanced hastily around at the rest of the observers. One of them might be the operative from the Citizen's Liberation Society, and right now that unknown person was his prime suspect for the crime here.

Even so, taking in Maddie's ashen face, and blood-stained hands, he thought of another possibility. One that sent a chill through him.

"Madeline," he said in a soft voice that the others would not be able to hear, "did Tinker press his attentions on you? Were you forced to defend yourself?" He slipped an arm around her shoulders as she sat shivering on the floor.

But Maddie shook her head. "I didn't do it, Gresham," she said, allowing him to lift her up from the floor. "He w-w-was like this when I came out of the . . . the . . . retiring room."

Something in Christian's chest unloosed. Thank God.

The crowd who had come in response to Maddie's shriek had begun to press around them.

"Is he dead?" Lord Tretham asked, his normally sharp features flushed with fear.

"By Jove, I think he is," George Vinson said with something like wonder.

"I was just playing *vingt-et-un* with the fellow," Lord Fortenbury said, his voice cracking with fear, as if knives in the chest might be contagious.

"Ladies and gentlemen, please," Mrs. Bailey said, her voice calm, "return to your play. There is nothing to be done here. I will send for the authorities and we will soon have this righted."

There was grumbling but the gawkers began to disperse when Mrs. Bailey promised to offer refreshments to all of her guests.

"I will call the runners," she told Christian before she returned to the front of the house, discreetly leaving the two of them alone.

When she was gone, Maddie hid her face in Christian's shoulder. "If you don't mind," she said, in a voice more vulnerable than he had ever heard her use, "I should like to go home."

"You'll probably need to answer some questions," he said gently. "But I suppose the runner can come to you at your father's house tomorrow."

"I would prefer that, yes," Maddie said with a gulp. Her face was pale, and whatever bravado had propelled her into coming along with her brother tonight had dissipated. "Would you get James for me, please, so that he can take me home?"

Mrs. Bailey, who had returned with a sheet to cover the unfortunate Tinker, spoke up. "Oh, Lord Linton has already departed. He left as soon as you screamed. I thought he might have gone to fetch the runners but since they haven't arrived yet, I suppose he didn't."

At the news Linton was gone, Christian frowned. So did Maddie.

"He left?" she asked, incredulous. "Why would he leave when he is my escort? How am I supposed to get home? He knows I'm here!"

Christian heard a thread of panic underlying Maddie's tone and hurried to reassure her. "I'm sure he simply went to retrieve help as Mrs. Bailey suggested," he said, taking her hand in his.

He had no idea if their hostess's supposition was correct or not, however. There was no denying that Linton's disappearance was suspicious. What reason would he have to flee the scene if he were not somehow involved? Christian had supposed that it was Tinker who belonged to the Citizen's Liberation Society, but what if both Tinker *and* Linton were members? The possibility infuriated him mostly because Linton would then have knowingly brought his sister into the same quarters as traitors. The very idea made his blood boil.

Determined to see that Maddie was taken care of no matter what her brother's involvement in tonight's imbroglio, Christian took Maddie's arm. "I will see you safely home, Lady Madeline. Have no fear."

To his relief, Maddie, for once, did not argue, and allowed him to lead her out the back door of Mrs. Bailey's house and to his waiting carriage in the mews beyond.

Gresham's coach turned out to be a hackney he'd had one of Mrs. Bailey's footmen call for him. Which was fine by Maddie. She was just glad to be out of that house. Though she'd gathered up quite a bit of detail and description to make the gaming hell scene in her novel convincing, it was the circumstances of Mr. Tinker's death that would stay with her.

"Now we will see about getting you safely home," Gresham said, a little too brightly, as he climbed into the carriage with her and rapped on the roof to indicate that they were ready to depart.

Though Maddie was somewhat numb from her experience, she appreciated Gresham's attempt to bolster her mood. He could be kind like that, she thought, grateful that he had been the one to rescue her from the situation rather than someone less sensible like George Vinson.

Here in the closed confines of the carriage, she was painfully aware of him as a man. The interior was not so large that they were able to sit across from one another without touching. Indeed, his legs were long so that his knees brushed against hers every time the carriage drove over a bump.

They'd been in such a hurry to depart that there had been no time for the lamps within the carriage to be lit and moonlight limned the lines of Gresham's face, making his already rugged looks seem harsher somehow. Maddie was reminded that despite his noble lineage, this man was a solider—had spent nearly a decade fighting against Napoleon—and for once he looked it. It was difficult to remember when he was recounting an amusing tale, or poking fun at himself, that he was a trained warrior.

"Thank you for seeing me home," she murmured, the silence prompting her to say something, anything, to disperse the eerie quiet. "I don't know what I would have done if you hadn't been there."

"That's what worries me," her companion said. "What was your brother thinking to abandon you in such a place?"

Gresham's tone was curt, unlike him. And for a moment Maddie wondered if his anger could all be over Linton's hasty departure. Still, his implication that her brother had done the wrong thing set her back up. "He wouldn't have gone off and left me there alone without good reason," she said hotly. "I realize that Linton isn't always the pattern card of respectability, but he doesn't shirk his duty."

At least not when he can help it, she thought. In truth she was annoyed with her brother herself. She had known him to be reckless in the past, but never had he simply vanished when she needed him as she had tonight. It was unlike him. But worse, it reminded her that his behavior, which had been on a downward spiral in the past year or so, was getting worse.

"He certainly did abandon you tonight," Gresham said in a clipped tone. "Though I suppose he knew well enough that I'd look after you if it came to that."

"You make it sound as if I am a child in leading strings in need of a nanny," Maddie objected, disliking the idea she needed a keeper. "I am perfectly able to care for myself, thank you. Indeed, if you will just let me out in the next street, I will see myself home."

"You'll do no such thing," Gresham said with a frown. "Don't be ridiculous. I wasn't trying to insult your independence. The truth of the matter is that the streets of London are not safe for a young lady of gentle breeding. They are damned unsafe for every sort of person at one time or another."

Knowing he was right, Maddie still could not bring herself to back down from the issue. She folded her arms over her bosom, in a protective gesture. "I don't see you requesting an escort every time you venture out of an evening," she said sullenly.

"You don't see me every night," he said. "I could be requesting Winterson to see me from place to place every evening for all you know."

The mental picture of Winterson escorting a cowering Gresham from entertainment to entertainment surprised a giggle from her. As he must have intended, for he looked quite pleased with himself.

"I don't meant to be pettish about such things," she said carefully, her anger gone for the moment. "It's just that you can have no notion how frustrating it is to be unable to go about on one's own or make descisions for oneself."

"You forget that I spent the past decade in the military. I think I can understand the drawbacks of following orders," he said with a smile. "Though I did have some freedom, since I was an officer. I do understand your frustration. But the rules are not there arbitrarily." At her scoff, he amended, "Well, not entirely arbitrarily."

"I do understand the safety issues," she said. "It makes perfect sense. The only strictures that truly anger me are the ones that exist solely to keep ladies in their place. Like that ridiculous stricture against being seen at Mrs. Bailey's. For the most part it was not much more scandalous than many a *ton* ball. But because men have decided it's shocking for unmarried ladies to be exposed to gaming, I was forced to risk my reputation to go there tonight."

"But don't forget what happened there," he said, his eyes serious. "Mr. Tinker's death was precisely the type of occurrence that makes Mrs. Bailey's the sort of place where ladies should not go." Before she could object, he raised his hand. "No, hear me out, Lady Madeline."

When she had nodded for him to continue, he said, "The reason that Mrs. Bailey's is off limits is not, as you suppose, because men wish to keep young ladies away from gambling. If that were the case then card rooms at balls would be outlawed. The reason that Mrs. Bailey's is off limits is because gaming— especially at high stakes—raises tempers and makes it likely that violence will erupt as a result. That's all. Nothing more and nothing less."

Maddie considered his words. It made some sense, she supposed. "But I still don't agree that young ladies should be shielded from gaming. How are we to know what to avoid if we are never exposed to it and allowed to reject it in the first place?"

Gresham nodded. "I, for one," he went on, "am relieved that we can agree on something at least."

Deciding that their accord warranted a change of subject, Maddie said, "Do you . . . did you know anything about Mr. Tinker? I admit to not knowing him very well, but I can think of no one who would wish to see him dead."

"No," Gresham said after a brief pause. "I've met him socially before, of course, but I was hardly well acquainted with the man. I'll look into his background more closely tomorrow. Perhaps see if there is something to be done for his family."

"That would be . . ." Maddie paused, searching for the right word. "Kind."

There was a lull in the conversation, both of them lost in their own thoughts as the carriage bumped along through the darkened streets of the city.

"Are you well?" he asked, his voice carrying a note of compassion in it that Maddie hadn't even known he was capable of. "Regarding what you witnessed, I mean. It can be shocking to the system to see something like that. Even for a young lady as self-assured as you."

And suddenly she was there again, kneeling in the hallway of Mrs. Bailey's house, cradling a dying man in her arms as he breathed his last. She saw the pallor of his face, the burble of blood coming from his mouth, the knife protruding like something out of a nightmare from his chest. And she began to tremble.

Wordlessly, Gresham shifted to her side of the carriage and gathered her in his arms and held her as she wept. Maddie could do nothing to stop the tears. Her chest burned with them as she tried and failed to bring herself under control. She was aware of the sweep of Gresham's hands over her back, his touch oddly gentle. He said nothing, and neither did she. She couldn't. She was too overcome with horror for what she'd seen and felt earlier in the evening.

And then, just as wordlessly, it was over. The sobs that racked her body abated, and silently he handed her his handkerchief and she set about repairing the damage her tears had caused to her complexion. She gave silent thanks for the dimness of the carriage that would prevent him from seeing the worst of it.

Though Gresham no longer held her, he didn't move back to his side of the carriage, either.

"I'm sorry," she said sheepishly. "I don't know what came over me."

"There's nothing to apologize for, Maddie. Nothing," he said quietly, fiercely. "It changes a person, seeing something like that. I don't see how you can help it doing so. It's a monumental thing to see the life seep out of a person. And when that person dies by another's hand? Well, let's just say that I've seen war-hardened soldiers respond with less dignity than you just did. So do not apologize. Your reaction was honest. And real."

Unable to formulate a response that would do justice to his eloquence, she simply nodded.

When the carriage rolled to a stop in front of the Earl of Essex's town house, Gresham opened the carriage door and leaped down, handing Maddie out himself rather than making her wait for the driver. "Do you wish me to come inside with you? Explain to your parents what happened?"

"Good God, no!" That was all she needed, for her mother to learn that she'd ridden home in a closed carriage with Gresham on top of the fact that she'd gone to a private gaming house. One or the other would be shocking enough to her parents. Both together would likely give either or both of them an apoplexy. "That is, no, thank you. I couldn't ask you to do that."

The glint in his eye told her that he knew exactly why she was refusing his offer. But rather than push the matter, he gave her a brisk nod. And bowed very correctly over her hand as if they were in a drawing room.

"If you need to talk about . . . things," he said, his gaze meeting hers briefly, "you know where to find me."

"Thank you, my lord," she said, suddenly feeling a wave of gratitude that he'd come to her rescue tonight. "I do."

"Good night, then," he said, bowing slightly once again. As if he were unsure of what to do. Which wasn't really like Gresham at all, Maddie thought. Odd, that.

"Good night, my lord," she said, before hurrying up the walk toward her father's house. When she reached the steps, she turned and watched the carriage drive away. Her rescuer gone, she bolted up the steps to the entry door, grateful that her father's servants were elderly and did not keep a close watch on the front walk at night.

It was not until she was safely inside her bedchamber that she realized she still held the earl's handkerchief clutched in her hand.

Four

The next morning, his mind still occupied by the events of the evening before, Christian went in search of Winterson. He found his friend reading the papers and drinking coffee at White's.

Since the other man's marriage earlier in the season, he'd become a bit annoying in his blissful contentment. It wasn't that Christian begrudged his friend his contentment. After all, Winterson had done his bit for king and country, and had come home with a bad leg to show for it. And after that ugly business with his brother's murder, Winterson deserved some happiness. It was just that he was so bloody smug about it all.

"Morning, Gresham," the duke said, setting his newspaper aside to greet his friend. "You look like hell."

"Thanks," he said, dropping into the chair opposite his friend. Nodding to a nearby waiter, he indicated that he would also like coffee.

Winterson lifted his brows. Christian almost never drank coffee. "Late night?"

"You've not heard about the goings-on at Mrs. Bailey's last night, then," Christian said. It was a statement, and not a question.

Winterson shook his head. "Enlighten me."

In some detail, Christian related to his friend what had gone on at the gaming hell the evening before. Though he stopped short of telling him about Maddie's involvement beyond her finding of the dying Tinker.

The duke gave a low whistle. "Not what you expected to happen when the operative met his contact last night, I'll wager." He shook his head and leaned back in his chair. "So what had Lady Madeline to say of all this? I have difficulty believing she stood aside quietly while you questioned the witnesses."

Christian snorted. "Hardly." He thought back to her response to the goings-on last night, and sobered as he remembered her distress in the carriage after they'd left the scene. "She was shaken, of course. More than I had expected from her, I'll admit. I had been given to think that she was entirely fearless."

"One thing to remember about Lady Madeline," Winterson said, "is that she feels things deeply. She is so determined because she cares." He sipped his coffee. "Or so Cecily has given me to believe. They are alike in that, I think."

Not a bad assessment, Christian thought. "She did care very much when her brother disappeared as soon as she alerted the rest of us to Tinker's stabbing."

Winterson sat up straighter. "What? I knew Linton was a scapegrace, but I hadn't realized he was so far gone he'd leave his sister behind at a gaming hell, for God's sake. It's bad enough he took her there in the first place—I assume that's what happened. Maddie is headstrong but she's not foolish enough to visit a gambling den, even one that borders on respectable, by herself."

"No," Christian agreed, returning his coffee cup to the table, and toying with the handle. "She's not that foolish, though she was very determined to visit Mrs. Bailey's. I don't know what she used to force him to bring her, but he did not strike me as having acquiesced to taking her there willingly. Which makes it odd that he disappeared so soon after Tinker was found. She was holding the dead man in her arms, for God's sake, and he was gone."

"I know that his family has been worried about Linton for some time now," Winterson said with a sigh. "It would appear that he needs more than concern at this point. I have little doubt that his father will cut off his allowance after this debacle. Possibly more."

"One can only hope that it will do some good. As it was, I was forced to escort Lady Madeline home in a hackney. I am grateful that we weren't noticed." He waited for his friend's inevitable chastisement.

Winterson gave him a look.

"What?" Though Christian knew full well what.

"You took Lady Madeline home in a closed carriage?"

"Yes, what's so odd about that?" *Other than the fact that it's damned scandalous?*

"Aside from the fact that it's damned scandalous?" Winterson asked, as if talking to a small child.

"You exaggerate," Christian bit out.

"I think I do not."

"Well, there was little other choice." Christian sat up straighter. "She was stranded at a gaming hell. She was hardly going to walk home through the dark streets of London. Or accept the escort of Vinson or Fortenbury. I could not allow her to do that, even if she wished it. What if they'd taken a liberty? Do you really wish to see her married off to either of them?"

"And I suppose I should like to see her married off to you?"

"Better me than those fools," Christian said, his temper rising. "I did what was necessary—both for my conscience and as Lady Madeline's friend."

Winterson was silent as he watched his friend, his gaze assessing. Finally he said, "Interesting. I had no idea that was the direction of things."

"Don't be absurd," Christian said sullenly. "There is no direction of things. I was simply behaving as a gentleman ought. I have little doubt you'd have done the same thing in my position."

"Not if I wished to remain living," Winterson said wryly. "I have little doubt that Cecily would avail herself of my pistol if she caught me escorting another lady home in a closed carriage. Cousin or not."

His annoyance diffused by Winterson's wry humor, Christian said, "Then you should be grateful it was me there last night and not you."

"I suppose you're right," Winterson said. "How did Maddie endure her ordeal, do you think?"

Reflecting on her demeanor during their trip from the hell to Essex House, instead of recalling her trauma, Christian remembered what it had felt like to hold her in his arms and was disturbed by his body's immediate response to the memory. Damn it, he'd better get himself together or else Winterson would suspect he'd done more than simply offer the girl a ride home. And that *was* all he'd done. And offered a shoulder to cry on. Which was what any gentleman would do in such circumstances. He had nothing to feel guilty about. Not a thing.

In answer to Winterson's question, he said, "She was as strong as you'd expect. Though understandably upset by the experience, of course." He did not speak of Maddie's tears. That was something he knew she would wish to remain private. And he was unwilling to betray her trust in that way.

Changing the subject, Christian said, "Tinker's death, coupled with Linton's flight, makes it difficult to determine which of them was there to meet with the Citizen's Society. It might have been one or both."

"Linton's departure certainly does make him look guilty," Winterson said. "Especially when one considers that if they were both members of the society, Linton might have been instructed by his superiors to remove the other man."

"But if he were going there with the express purpose of killing Tinker, would Linton have chosen to do so in a manner that would ensure his sister be the one to find his body?" Christian demanded. "My opinion of the fellow isn't all that good, but I'm not quite sure I believe that he would do such a thing. I know Maddie certainly doesn't."

Winterson shrugged. "That's to be expected."

"True," Christian said. "But it does make me wonder if Tinker's death is even connected to the society."

"What, you mean it was simply coincidence that Tinker was murdered on the same night you were expecting him to make contact with the society?"

Now it was Christian's turn to shrug. "More or less. Simply because I was expecting there to be someone at Mrs. Bailey's who is a member of the society doesn't necessarily mean that they would be the ones to commit the murder. In fact, it seems uncharacteristic of them to waste their time and energy on such a killing when doing so would bring the attention of the government down upon them. More so than it is already, I mean."

"The way I see it," Winterson said, "is that no matter the motive for killing Tinker, your number one suspect is Lady Madeline's brother. Which is going to wreak havoc upon your friendship with her."

Unfortunately, Christian had to agree with his friend.

No matter whether Linton was guilty or not, Christian was in for a very uncomfortable few months.

Though exhausted, Maddie awoke at her usual time the next morning.

Checking with the butler at breakfast, she learned that her brother had not returned home the night before. Which was troubling, though he did from time to time stay with friends. She hoped that this was one of those occasions.

Of more immediate concern was the butler's news that her mother wished to see her before she left for the day.

Her appetite gone, Maddie laid down her fork and knife, drank a final gulp of tea, and headed for the stairs and her mother's small sitting-room-cum-office, where she managed the household business as well as her extensive social schedule. Lady Poppy Essex was as exacting as a general, and every bit as demanding. And though Maddie loved her mother, Poppy could be just the tiniest bit unforgiving when it came to her daughter's social stature—or lack thereof.

Cecily's stepmama, Violet, saw her lack of success as lamentable but not unexpected. Whereas Juliet's mama, Rose, saw her daughter's failure to take as something to celebrate, for reasons that Juliet had only recently become aware of. But it was Poppy who was the most displeased by her own daughter's continued spot among the wallflowers. And though she told Maddie again and again that it wasn't her fault, Maddie had long since come to understand that what Poppy meant was the exact opposite of what she said.

From Maddie's earliest years, her mother had found her wanting. Maddie was too loud, too short, too rambunctious, too outspoken. She was scolded for mussing her hair, for dirtying her pinafore, for playing soldiers instead of dolls. In short, whatever Maddie did, her mother found something about it to correct.

Only in the past few months had the Countess of Essex seemed to come to the conclusion that despite her unrelenting urgings, Maddie was not interested in becoming a social success, and was indeed quite happy in her current position. To Maddie's immense relief, her mother had chosen to leave her to her own devices.

Even so, it was with some trepidation that she climbed the stairs to her mother's parlor-cum-office. It wasn't that she feared her mother's wrath. At this point in her life she'd come to understand that her mother's scolds were less about Maddie herself, and more about her mother's attempts to control her own environment. But still, a dressing-down was never pleasant, and if her mother had learned of Maddie's adventure the evening before, then a dressing-down was exactly what she was in for. She might have decided to let Maddie remain unpopular, but she would hardly be pleased to hear she had risked her reputation in such an outrageous manner yesterday evening.

Squaring her shoulders as she stood before the door to her mother's study, she knocked briskly on the door, and entered.

Seated behind her massive though elegantly turned desk, the Countess of Essex was as fresh and lovely as ever. Her golden hair was dressed simply in an elegant chignon, and her deep rose gown brought out the pink in her cheeks. Only in the last couple of years had there been any hint of gray in her blond tresses, but even with that mark of her age she was still as beautiful as Maddie could ever recall.

"Hello, darling," the countess greeted her daughter. "Do sit down. Shall I ring for some tea?"

Answering her own question, Maddie's mother rose and gave a tug on the bellpull. "I find I'm quite thirsty and it's been quite a while since breakfast."

When Maddie only nodded, her mother took her seat again. "I daresay you've only just had breakfast since you had a late night last evening." The countess tilted her head and waited for her daughter to respond.

"Is that a question, Mama?" She had long since grown accustomed to her mother's use of indirection to begin her scolds. It was one of the reasons she so favored plain speaking. After a lifetime of hints and suggestions, she craved direct communication.

"Oh, do not be difficult, Madeline," Poppy said with a sigh, as if disappointed that she hadn't shocked her daughter. "It was merely an observation. Though now that you mention it, I did call you up here to discuss your visit to Mrs. Bailey's gambling house last night. Really, darling, what were you thinking to go to such a place?"

Maddie did not bother asking where her mother had learned of her escapade. She had spies everywhere.

"It is hardly as if I went to a bona fide gaming hell, Mama," she said reasonably. "And I went there with Linton. I don't see you scolding him for going there."

The countess pinched the bridge of her nose, as if warding off a headache. "We have been over this and over this, Madeline. There are some places where you will never, ever, be allowed to visit because of your sex. I know that your Mrs. Wollstonecraft, with her *Vindication of the Rights of Woman,* would disagree, but she is not your mother. Your cousins are able to see this fact, so I do not understand why it is so difficult for you to do so."

Maddie did not bother protesting that Cecily and Juliet had done their share of visiting unacceptable establishments before they were wed. Her mother was incapable of seeing their behavior as questionable as Maddie's.

"Oh, come, Mama, there were any number of ladies there last night, including, I might add, Lady Skelton, who I believe is a friend of yours."

"Be that as it may, Maddie, you should not have gone there and you know it. What made you wish to go there in the first place?"

"I was doing research for my novel," Maddie responded, preparing herself for derision. To her surprise, however, her mother seemed to brighten at the news.

"A novel?" she asked, her blue eyes wide with interest. "I was unaware that your interest in literature had moved from poetry to prose."

"I have had some success with poetry so I thought—"

"You thought you would try your hand at novel writing," her mother finished for her. "I think it's the perfect story to put about for your visit to Mrs. Bailey's. And if you plan to write about the evils of gambling so much the better."

"But I wasn't planning to—" Maddie began, only to be cut off by Poppy.

"No, no, don't tell me what your plans are, dearest," Poppy said with a smile. "I want to be as honest as possible when I'm questioned by the busybodies at the Marchford ball tonight. I'll take care of everything. Your visit to Mrs. Bailey's may make it into the gossip sheets, but by tonight all of the *ton* will know that your true reason for going there was in the interest of art.

Anyone who has ever read a novel will be unable to condemn you. It's perfect."

"So, you aren't annoyed with me for going to Mrs. Bailey's?" Maddie asked, shocked.

"Oh, dearest." Her mother shook her head. "Of course I am annoyed with you. Not only did you go to a gaming hell with your scapegrace brother, you also risked your reputation. Again. Annoyed is the least of what I feel."

"But you aren't going to punish me in some way?" Maddie looked suspiciously at her mother.

"I suspect that your encounter with that poor man, Mr. Tinker, was punishment enough."

Maddie closed her eyes as the whole grisly experience came rushing back to her.

Unexpectedly, she felt her mother's arms come around her. "I'm sorry you had to endure that, darling," she said. "I can't imagine how terrible it must have been. Please don't put yourself in danger like that again. I couldn't bear it if something awful were to happen to you."

And for the first time in a long time, Maddie felt at peace with her mother.

A short while later, having donned a pelisse and hat and called for the carriage, Maddie arrived at Winterson House to find that Juliet was already there.

"Dearest," Cecily said, wrapping Maddie in a warm embrace. "How are you? What an ordeal you had to endure last night."

Accepting a hug from Juliet, and allowing a cup of tea to be pressed into her hand, Maddie asked, "So, how did you learn of it?"

"Winterson, of course," Cecily said, reaching for a macaroon. "He had it from Gresham at White's this morning."

At the mention of Christian, Maddie felt herself color. "Oh," she said, trying to remain nonchalant. "What did he have to say for himself?"

"Only that you were the one to find poor, stabbed John Tinker," Juliet said, patting Maddie's hand. "And that Linton ran away and left you to find your own way home."

"If I see your brother any time soon," Cecily said grimly, "I will give him a towering scold. Not only did he leave his dying friend behind, he abandoned you. That is not the behavior of a solicitous sibling."

Cecily brushed the macaroon crumbs from her lap and rested her hands on her stomach. She was so newly *enceinte* that her condition had not yet begun to show, but Maddie had noticed that her cousin was often to be seen with her hands there. A pang of envy shot through her. Not that she begrudged Cecily her happiness. She definitely deserved it. And Juliet, who had endured a horrific injury and kept the secret of it for years at her mother's behest, was utterly entitled to her wedded bliss with the handsome Lord Deveril. She was happy for both of her cousins.

But there were times when she wondered whether she, too, would ever find a man who would love her as her cousins' husbands clearly loved them. Unbidden, she remembered what it had been like to be held against Gresham's chest last night. How safe she had felt then. How protected. There had never been any suggestion that he would push her for more. But instead, she'd felt as if they were a team of two.

Was that what Cecily and Juliet felt with their husbands? What must it be like to share one's burdens like that? She and her cousins had always been a team of sorts, struggling against the strictures that society placed upon them, and those members of the *ton* who found them wanting in some respect.

But since their marriages she had felt her cousins begin to pull away a bit. Which was to be expected, she knew. After all, they were part of their husband's families now, not just their own. She could not deny the fact that she felt some sadness at their new situation, however.

Recalling herself to the conversation at hand, Maddie said, "No. You are correct. Linton was perfectly dreadful to leave me behind as he did last night. Especially given that one of his oldest friends was lying stabbed on the floor."

"Why would he do such a thing?" Juliet asked, biting into a ginger biscuit. "I know that Linton has been a bit of a hellion, but I have never known him to be so lost to propriety and brotherly concern before."

"I must admit that I am disturbed by his disappearance, as well," Maddie said. "He didn't come home last night. It makes me wonder if there was more to Mr. Tinker's death than a simple argument over gaming losses."

Cecily paused, her voice gentle as she asked, "You don't suppose that Linton . . . ?"

Maddie felt her heart clench. She was disappointed in her brother, but she was not yet ready to assume him guilty of murder. Was she?

"I cannot imagine why he would," she said aloud. "As far as I know James was not losing badly enough last night to make him wish to do such a thing to his friend. And they were playing at different tables anyway. He could hardly have lost money to Tinker if they weren't playing with one another."

"It might have been over something that happened at another time," Juliet said glumly. "Perhaps your brother owed him from before."

"It's a possibility," Maddie admitted. "And I am not

so foolish as to believe that the authorities will look that carefully into their history together. The very fact that Tinker is dead and Linton is missing seems to indicate that he is responsible for his friend's death."

"I'm just glad you were unharmed," Juliet said with a shudder. She, too, had come into close contact with a killer recently. "It would have been just as easy for whoever killed poor Mr. Tinker to harm you, as well. After all, you were close enough to hear what happened."

"But I didn't hear anything," Maddie protested. "Or at least I don't believe I did. I was too busy adjusting the bosom of my gown in the retiring room after what Gresh—That is to say, after a comment by another guest."

"Gresham didn't approve of your gown?" Cecily asked innocently.

"He thought it was too low cut."

"That doesn't sound like our Gresham," Juliet said with a raised brow. "I have it on good authority from Alec that he is what is known among gentlemen as a brea—"

"As I was saying," Maddie interrupted, before Juliet could continue with what promised to be a very alarming revelation about the earl. "I was too busy adjusting my gown to hear anything that happened in the hallway. So there is little danger that the killer will come after me. And I will tell anyone who asks the same thing."

"That would be best," Cecily said. "In fact, I will put it about this evening at the Marchfords' ball. And you and Juliet will, too. You are both coming, are you not?"

"I wouldn't miss it," Juliet said with a grin. "I plan to dance a waltz with my husband."

"And it would seem that I have a rumor to spread about myself," Maddie said with a frown. She did so detest balls.

"Cheer up," Cecily told her with a grin. "I hear Gresham will be in attendance, as well."

That, of course, was what Lady Madeline was afraid of.

Five

After his conversation with Winterson, Christian made his way to the Gresham town house in Berkeley Square. He'd only lived there for a few weeks, and still had a bit of trouble realizing that it belonged to him.

He'd visited for family occasions before joining the army, but never with an eye toward inheriting the place himself. He still considered it a freak accident that his cousin had died before siring an heir who could have inherited the earldom.

Though he'd sent a note informing his mother of his intention to remove from his bachelor rooms at the Albany to the the Gresham town house, she had chosen to remain in Scotland where his two elder sisters and their husbands and families lived. Ever since his twin, Clarissa, had died while he was at war, the relationship between Christian and his mother had been conducted largely by post. And, to his regret, he preferred things that way. If he ever found himself in the same room with his mother again, he was unsure of how he would be able to keep from unleashing all the rage he felt over his sister's loss.

Shaking his head to clear the dark mood that threatened, he bounded up the front steps, the door opening before he could reach it. The butler, Yeats, had a penchant for correctness in all things, and had probably been watching for him.

"Good afternoon, your lordship," Yeats said as Christian stepped into the entryway.

Handing his walking stick and hat to the footman beside his reed-thin majordomo, Christian accepted a stack of letters from the butler.

"You have a caller, my lord. I have asked him to wait for you in the study."

"Curious," Christian said, "do you know who this mysterious visitor is?"

As if insulted by such a question, Yeats sniffed, then offered a card on a salver.

"Interesting," Christian said, reading the card. "See that we aren't disturbed."

Making his way upstairs, Christian opened the door to his study to find Lord Thomas Leighton, late of His Majesty's Army, sipping brandy and reading that morning's *Times*.

Upon hearing his host enter, Leighton raised a graying brow. "About bloody time, Gresham. For a new earl you spend very little time counting your stacks of gold."

Pouring himself a glass of brandy, Christian snorted. "That's because I am constantly being hounded by a demanding old blighter from Whitehall who thinks I've got nothing better to do than chase Bonapartists."

"You should tell that old blighter to leave you alone," Leighton said, sipping his own brandy. "Or to get another hobby."

"I'll consider it," Christian said with a wry smile. Taking a seat behind his desk, he leaned back in his chair and said, "I take it this isn't a social call."

"Hardly," Leighton said, sitting up straighter. "I

heard about the business at Mrs. Bailey's last night. I want to hear your version of events."

In detail, though without referencing his conversations with Maddie, Christian told the other man about the events leading up to Tinker's murder the night before.

When he was finished, Leighton whistled. "I wish you'd been able to see who it was that confronted Tinker in the passageway."

"So do I," Christian said with a frown, thinking once more of how close Maddie had come to stumbling upon the murderer at work. "Unfortunately I didn't see anyone leave the room with the exception of Lady Madeline, and I know she wasn't the one to kill the fellow."

"So you trust her?" Leighton asked. "Despite the fact that she's Linton's sister? We did have reason to think he might be the man the Citizen's Liberation Society might have been planning to contact. Now that Tinker is dead, I wonder if Linton might not have been the CLS operative who was planning to contact Tinker."

"You can trust Maddie, sir," Christian said, then winced inwardly. "Lady Madeline, I mean."

Leighton didn't miss the quick correction. "Maddie, is it? Just how well do you know this chit, Gresham?"

"We move in the same social circles," Christian said with what he hoped was indifference. "She is the cousin of my friend Winterson's wife."

"Is she, indeed?" Tretham asked. "I hope you won't let that friendship compromise your duty. You would not be the first man to be taken in by a pretty face, son."

"Lady Madeline is *not* involved in her brother's activities," Chritian bit out. "She was there to conduct research for a novel, for pity's sake. It was foolish for her to convince her brother to take her there, but hardly criminal."

Then, realizing he might have sounded less than respectful, he added, "My lord."

Leighton remained silent, waiting for Christian to continue. It was a particularly effective interrogation technique. One that Christian had used himself a time or two. Realizing that his superior was giving him a chance to make amends, he thrust his hands through his hair, ruining his valet's hard work.

"My apologies," he said finally. "It would appear that I am perhaps more involved with the young lady than I like to admit. But I do assure you that she has nothing to do with the Citizen's Liberaton Society. I don't really think her brother is, either, though his behavior last night is certainly not that of an innocent man."

"No, it isn't," Leighton said, rising. "I want you to find out one way or another, Gresham. And that might mean making that pretty face you're fond of look very sad. Are you prepared to risk that?"

Christian stood as well. "I won't like doing so, of course," he said, "but I will do what's necessary to ensure the country's safety."

"Good man," Leighton said with a smile. "If we're lucky, you won't need to make your lady weep."

Following his commander from the room, Christian sent up a prayer that he was right. Otherwise, he'd have to deal with a very angry, very distraught Maddie.

Fully prepared to spend the entirety of the Marchford ball sitting out every dance, Maddie was somewhat surprised to find herself in demand as a dance partner, thanks in no small part to her firsthand knowledge of what had happened at Mrs. Bailey's the night before.

True, she had been less wont to sit out dances since her cousins had married, but even so she was certainly no toast. And Amelia Snowe, still smarting from her own failure to bring someone, anyone, up to scratch, had done her part to make sure that Maddie did not benefit too much from her cousins' marriages. It was an open secret that Amelia had set her cap for the Duke of Winterson at the beginning of the season. And the fact that someone like Cecily Hurston, who, though a viscount's daughter, was considered firmly on the shelf, had caught Winterson's eye galled Amelia to no end.

Thus it was that Maddie found herself the recipient of Amelia's glare from the opposite side of the room as she took her place next to Cecily once more.

"Someone should tell Amelia that scowling like that can lead to wrinkles," she said to her cousin as she sipped the cup of punch Lord Dimsdale had brought her. "I should think someone as concerned with her appearance would know that."

"Well, you were dancing with Lord Dimsdale, dearest," Cecily said. "She's had to lower her expectations since both Winterson and Deveril defected. But I understand that Dimsdale has a healthy income. Certainly enough to keep her in frocks."

"I don't think you've sat out a dance all evening," Juliet said from her position next to Cecily. "You are certainly in looks tonight. Is that a new gown?"

"You know it is," Maddie said with a grin. "It's the one I bought the day that Deveril came with us to Madame Celeste's."

She was amused to see her cousin blush. That had been the day she convinced Deveril that he would need to take desperate measures if he wished to court Juliet.

Which had, apparently, worked because it wasn't too much later that the two had married.

"I was rather preoccupied that day," was Juliet's response. "But we were discussing you. That shade of rose is quite becoming. As is the cut."

"It's hardly my gown that accounts for the number of dance partners I've garnered this evening," Maddie wryly. "It's because they all wish to know what happened at Mrs. Bailey's and they are all kicking themselves for not being there to witness it themselves."

"They are a bloodthirsty lot, these gentlemen," Cecily said with a frown. "They cannot stand the idea of missing out on the least bit of excitement. It's quite sad, really."

"Well, they aren't hanging about Gresham peppering him with silly questions," Maddie said resentfully. It had not escaped her notice that Christian had not been among those gentlemen seeking her out tonight.

"Speak of the devil," Juliet said in a low whisper. "Here he comes now."

And true enough, Gresham was approaching them from across the ballroom. He was in looks himself tonight. His light brown hair was slightly longer than was fashionable, but was arranged in artful disarray. And his black coat and breeches created a sharp contrast with the white of his shirt points and cravat. A diamond and onyx pin winked from the folds of his cravat, which had also been expertly arranged.

"His man has obviously been speaking with Deveril's," Cecily said to her cousins. "Which is all for the better considering his own carelessness about such things."

"Yes, Deveril says that Gresham grew tired of being harangued over his appearance so he agreed to let his valet take instruction from Deveril's."

"It has certainly paid off," Cecily said. "Don't you think so, Maddie?"

But Maddie was preoccupied with the man himself, who was striding toward them like a jungle cat on the prowl. Good Lord, she thought, is this what I've come to? Clichés about jungle cats? She turned her attention instead to Gresham's expression, which was grim.

"Ladies," Lord Gresham said as he bowed to the cousins. "I hope you won't mind if I steal Lady Madeline for a word."

Yes, they do mind. Maddie didn't speak the words aloud, but she hoped that she conveyed the sentiment effectively. She wasn't ready to be in his company again. Last night's ordeal at Mrs. Bailey's gaming hell had been harrowing, and not only because of Mr. Tinker's murder. She'd seen Christian, or Gresham she corrected herself, in an entirely different light, and her newfound . . . awareness . . . was not at all comfortable or convenient.

"We don't mind a bit," Cecily said, breaking into Maddie's thoughts. Her sideways glance at Maddie indicated that she was ready to send her off with Gresham whether Maddie liked it or not. "I'm sure you both have much to discuss."

Maddie glared at her traitorous cousin. She'd deal with Cecily and her matchmaking schemes later.

Grudgingly she allowed Gresham to take her arm, and just as she had last night, she felt a thrill of excitement zing through her as she placed her hand on his arm. Trying to calm her senses, she realized that they were not headed toward the dance floor. But when she saw the direction in which he headed, Maddie had to fight the impulse to balk like a mule.

"It is quite warm here," Gresham said, as if he hadn't noticed his partner's reluctance to continue on. "Let's step outside for a breath of air, shall we?"

"Yes, let's," Maddie said, reconciling herself to the situation. Unable to stop herself, she reveled in the feel of hard muscle beneath his coat sleeve and his leashed power as he walked beside her.

Before she could succumb to temptation and inhale the scent of him, they arrived at their destination. For which Maddie was grateful.

The terrace beyond the dance floor was blissfully cool after the closeness of the ballroom. And though several other couples had also sought out the openness of the balcony, their conversation was a far cry from the loud chatter inside the house.

A kinetic silence fell over them as they walked, arm in arm, toward a small alcove created by a bower of spring peonies trained to grow tall and tower over a bench. Reaching the secluded nook, Gresham stepped back and allowed Maddie to take a seat while he remained standing. Her independent nature didn't much care for the asymmetry of the arrangement, but some traitorous impulse within her did.

"You are recovered from last night's ordeal?" he asked, his gaze boring into her.

There was an intensity in his question that puzzled her. He had seen her home last evening, after all, and assured himself that she was well. She had lain awake long after arriving home, unable to get the image of Mr. Tinker's face as he breathed his last out of her mind. But eventually she'd drifted off. Not that she would reveal any of that to Gresham, of course.

"Yes," Maddie responded. "Thank you for asking, my lord."

His curt nod indicated that he'd expected as much. But it was Gresham's next words that indicated to Maddie that her welfare was not his only reason for asking her here.

"I have heard from more than one source that you are claiming not to have witnessed anything about the man who killed Tinker last night," he said briskly. "Is that correct?"

Relieved, and a little disappointed that the charged atmosphere between them had disappeared, Maddie nodded. "It's nothing more than the truth. I didn't see the man who killed Tinker."

"How well did you know him?" Gresham asked. Then, perhaps realizing that it was an impertinent question, he added, "If you wish to tell me, that is." Though it was clear that the amendment was only for courtesy's sake.

Deciding that answering the question would harm no one, Maddie said, "I've known him as a friend of my brother's for some years. Mama did not see him as the sort of person a young lady should spend a great deal of time with, however, so we were never in the same company above a dozen times."

"It's not like you to back down from a parental dictate," Gresham said with a raised brow. "Did you obey her?"

Maddie bit back a huff of annoyance. "Of course I obeyed her. To be perfectly truthful, I found him a bit of a bore. All he talked about was horseflesh and racing. Not a favorite interest of mine."

"What do you know of his friendship with your brother?"

This question stopped Maddie cold. "Why are you asking about Linton?" she demanded, though she knew the answer without asking.

Gresham looked as if he wished to evade the question, but said, "I don't know if your brother had anything to do with his friend's death, but it is a possibility. His disappearance doesn't make him seem innocent."

Before Maddie could protest further, he lowered himself to the bench beside her. At eye level now, he said, "I didn't bring you out here to discuss your brother or his friends."

Maddie was disconcerted once more by those intense eyes. "I wanted to tell you," he went on, "that you are doing the right thing in telling everyone that you saw nothing last night."

He took her gloved hand in his. Maddie tried and failed to ignore the frisson of awareness that vibrated through her.

"The last thing you need is to draw the attention of a killer," Gresham said seriously.

"So you don't think Linton did it?" Maddie heard herself ask. It was a good thing, she told herself, that he didn't suspect her brother. A very good thing.

His lips tightened. "I didn't say that," Gresham admitted, making her stomach leap in fear for her brother. "I simply think that if the man who killed Tinker is not your brother, then you could do much worse than to let him know that you are not a threat."

"If?" Maddie demanded, pulling her hand from his grasp, looking Gresham boldly in the eye. "I know for a fact that my brother didn't kill his friend. He might be a gambler and an occasional drunkard, but he would never do something so reprehensible. Never."

"Easy," Gresham said, his voice soothing. "I know you love your brother. It does you both credit. But I must tell you that this is a more complicated matter than it appears on the surface. And until the authorities can learn just why Tinker was killed, you must prepare yourself for the cloud of suspicion to hover over your brother for a bit. If he is innocent, as you claim, then it will just as quickly move on to implicate the real killer."

"I don't understand," Maddie said, frustrated by his

lack of candor. What did Gresham know of the matter anyway? And why did he suddenly appear so grave? It was unlike him, she realized. He was always given to joking and laughing. She wasn't sure she'd ever seen him as serious as he'd been these past two days.

"I cannot tell you the full story," Gresham said, rubbing the back of his neck. "But your brother is involved with some very bad characters. Men who would think nothing of killing a man for any number of reasons."

"Then they are the ones who killed Mr. Tinker," Maddie said with what she hoped was convincing authority. "Not Linton."

"It's too early to say," Gresham admitted, leaning forward to rest his elbows on his thighs. Maddie couldn't help but notice how the shift in position displayed his muscles beneath the fabric of his evening coat. "What I do know is that you are well out of the business. And I would suggest that when next you speak to your brother that you caution him against the company he keeps."

"As if that would make a difference," she said before she could stop herself. Feeling disloyal, she went on, "That is not to say that James is stubborn, my lord."

Gresham laughed softly. "I'm afraid you won't fool me on that score. I know all too well that stubbornness runs in your family."

Since it was true, Maddie couldn't be too angry over the assessment. Even so, she wondered whether he was serious about her brother's intimates. "Do you really think that one of Linton's friends might have something to do with Tinker's death?"

"I do, indeed," Gresham said seriously. "And I would be pleased if you could find some way to keep out of the company of your brother and his friends until this matter is settled."

Christian watched as Maddie's brow furrowed with concern for her blackguard of a brother.

"Are you quite serious?" she asked, her color rising in her agitation. Feeling like a lecher for wondering, he speculated about whether the blush extended farther down than the bodice of her gown revealed. He hadn't even allowed himself to entertain those kinds of thoughts for Maddie in the past, but once the barrier in his mind against them had crumbled at the Wexford ball, he'd had the devil of a time controlling them.

"I cannot simply abandon Linton to whatever it is that these people mean to do to him," Maddie went on. "He's my brother!"

Which was the trouble, Christian thought. She was loyal to a fault and it was unlikely that she'd consider her own safety as a reason for keeping out of the killer's way. Whoever he might turn out to be.

In an effort to smooth things over, and to remind her where his own loyalties lay, he said, "I do not mean that you should abandon him, Lady Madeline. I only wish for you to protect yourself. Your brother is a grown man and can fend for himself should it come to that, but you are—"

But that was clearly the wrong tactic, Christian thought with an inward curse. If she'd shouted at him he'd have been less afraid than he was at hearing her softly angry tones.

"I am what?" Maddie asked with deceptive calm. "I am a weakling because I had the misfortune to be born a woman instead of a man? Is that what you're saying?"

"No, damn it!" Christian said, unable to keep the harassed tone, and the expletive, from his response. How did he manage to constantly be at verbal daggers drawn with her? "You're twisting my words," he went on in a calmer tone. "I only meant to say that Viscount

Linton is his own person and shouldn't drag you into danger with him."

"I am already there," Maddie said vehemently. "I was there. I held that man in my arms as he drew his last breath. If you understand anything about anything then you should know that such an occurrence has affected me deeply. And my brother's friendship with him only makes it more imperative that I do what I can to make sure that his killer is brought to justice."

Her words sent a jolt of terror through him. Lady Madeline Essex searching for Tinker's killer was the last thing he wanted to see. She'd already endangered herself enough with her visit to Mrs. Bailey's.

Careful to keep his fear from his tone, he said, "Lady Madeline, Maddie, you are not under any obligation to find this man's killer. Leave it to the authorities and I promise you that I will keep you apprised of any developments that might affect your brother."

He hoped the promise to keep her in the know would reassure her enough to let the matter go. He wasn't prepared for her next question, however.

"You just said that it should be left to the authorities," Maddie said, her eyes narrowed in suspicion. "And yet you say you will keep me apprised of things as they pertain to James. What do you know about the situation? Are you working for the authorities now?"

"No, I misspoke," Christian said quickly. *Damn it. Damn it. Damn it.* "I only meant to say that if I should hear anything about the business, I will share that information with you."

But it was too much to hope that she would be fobbed off with such a tale.

"I don't believe you."

Maddie's gaze was cool, self-assured. At any other time he'd have found it damned attractive. To be honest, he found it attractive now. But he also recognized that her expression spelled trouble for him one way or another for the next few weeks.

"I thought it was odd for you to be in such a place as Mrs. Bailey's last night," she said conversationally. "You aren't known for being much of a gamester. Even tonight you aren't haunting the card room like most gentlemen do to avoid the matchmakers."

"That doesn't mean that I can't have taken a recent interest in gaming," Christian said, though he knew she would not believe him. Her skepticism had shifted into certainty.

"You were there following my brother," Maddie continued, hammering another nail into the coffin of his peace of mind. "Or Mr. Tinker. It doesn't matter which, only that you were there when Mr. Tinker was murdered and now you're convinced that Linton had something to do with it."

"You can't know any of this," he said, still keeping up the pretense of denial. "I am a gentleman and as such am free to go wherever I choose. It is a mere coincidence that I happened to be there on the same night that Tinker was killed."

"You might even have killed him yourself," she said suddenly, standing up, her hands covering her mouth in dawning horror. "Oh, God. You didn't, did you?"

Leaping up from the bench, he took hold of her hands. "Maddie, you know that's not true. You know it. I cannot tell you why I was there, but I can assure you that I did not kill Tinker. For one thing, if I had, someone would have noticed me disappearing from the card table long before he was found."

To his relief, she seemed to see the sense of what he said. Christian wasn't sure just why he'd panicked at her accusation, but panicked he had. Doubtless it was because he'd come to appreciate her good opinion and he did not wish to lose it. Of course that was it, he assured himself.

"I suppose you're right," Maddie said, clearly unaware of the inner battle her companion was fighting with himself. "Though I still don't believe it a coincidence that you were there last night. Nor do I believe your interest in Linton's presence there last night is mere curiosity."

"At least you don't think me a murderer," he said with more honesty than he'd intended. "I can live with your suspicion on the other matters, but not that."

Maddie's eyes softened as she looked up at him. "I don't," she said gently, reaching a hand up to touch him lightly on the cheek.

And all at once Christian became aware that they were alone out on the Marchfords' terrace.

He wasn't sure when Maddie had developed charms—the very idea would doubtless make her laugh—but ever since he'd held her in his arms last night, he'd had the devil's own time trying to erase the memory of just how right she'd felt there. Not to mention the memory of her soft, spicy, floral scent. He'd noticed it immediately when he'd greeted her earlier this evening, as well, but he'd been able to file it away for later perusal. Apparently later was right now, he thought, as he leaned forward and brushed his lips against hers.

"What are you doing?" she asked against his mouth, more from surprise than anything else.

She felt him smile against her mouth. "I'm trying to kiss you," he said. "Now stop talking and kiss me back."

If any other man had said such a thing to her, Maddie

would have kicked him in that vulnerable place her brother had told her about. But to her surprise, she found Christian's masterful words arousing. So, she did what he asked, and kissed him back.

As if she were a priceless work of art, he cupped her face gently in his hands, letting his mouth make all the demands. Opening his mouth over hers, his tongue traced the outline of her lips, and Maddie, reading his silent query aright, opened her lips and invited him in. Stroke by stroke, he took possession of her mouth, until gingerly Maddie accepted his challenge and slid her tongue against his. Each time they touched, the fire between them burned hotter until Maddie was no longer able to tell which of them was in control.

She wasn't quite sure how it had happened, but what had begun as rather sweet and gentle turned hot and passionate. His body seemed to grow stronger, harder against hers, and his hands slipped down to wander over her back, her sides, even as her own grew impatient with the cloth that separated them from skin-on-skin contact. As she grew bolder, and allowed her hands to wander from his back to snake up the front of him, she felt Gresham groan into her mouth, the vibration reverberating through her in pleasurable pain.

"Madeline," he said aganst her chin, his mouth tracing a path down her neck and toward the exposed flesh of her bosom. "God, you have bewitched me."

Her hands stroking over his shoulders, she felt him tug gently at the sleeve of her gown, exposing her breast to the open air. The sudden coolness was a relief, but the feel of his hot mouth enclosing her nipple was utter bliss. Unable to stop herself, Maddie gasped at the sensation, feeling the pull in her belly and lower.

At her noise, Christian stilled. Then to Maddie's disappointment, he pulled back with one last reverent kiss for the top of her breast and began setting her gown back to rights. With a disappointed sigh she helped, though every time their hands touched she felt a jolt of sensation.

Her wardrobe returned to normal, Maddie shook her head in disbelief. "Unbelievable."

"My sentiments exactly," Christian said, his breathing slowing. "Though I mean it in a good way, of course."

Maddie's lips quirked despite the gravity of the situation. "Of course. A most excellent way."

He caught her eye and they shared a laugh. Christian lifted a hand to stroke her cheek, which to her embarrassment brought Maddie to blush. "I suggest we return to the ballroom at once before we are missed. I think we were lucky enough to escape notice until now, but it would be foolish to tempt fate."

"A good idea," she agreed. "I suggest that I go inside first, and then you follow in a few minutes."

Christian nodded, and gestured for her to leave first, which Maddie did, albeit in a daze of astonishment.

Six

$\mathcal{U}$nable to face her cousins' curiosity upon her return to the ballroom, Maddie instead made a beeline for the ladies' retiring room. Unfortunately, she encountered someone far worse: Amelia Snowe.

As she was already over the threshold, it was too late for Maddie to leave when she saw the icy beauty. Besides, she didn't wish to give Amelia the satisfaction of knowing her presence had rattled her.

"Why, look who it is," Amelia said from her usual position—before the looking glass, "it's Lady Madeline Essex, who was so unfortunate as to be caught in a gaming hell this week."

"Do tell us, Lady Madeline," she said, turning with what Maddie could only assume was great reluctance from her own visage to cast her gaze upon the other girl. "Was it worth ruining your reputation, this escapade of yours? For I doubt any gentleman of true social standing will look twice at you now."

Her constant companion, Lady Felicia Downes, tittered at her friend's words. "I do not think they would have done so before the gaming hell incident, Amelia. No offense meant, of course, Lady Madeline. But you know how unpopular you are with the gentlemen."

Since she knew good and well that her reputation was bruised rather than broken, Maddie knew better than to let them draw her into their discussion. She also knew better than to believe Lady Felicia's backhanded apology. Instead, she didn't speak at all, simply moved before an empty mirror and assessed her hair for disarray. If Amelia and Felicia but knew how she'd just spent the last quarter hour they would have real ammunition to use against her. But Maddie trusted Gresham implicitly on that score, so she knew they would never know about the interlude on the terrace.

"Cat got your tongue?" Amelia asked coolly, though Maddie could tell from the twitch in her nemesis's cheek that she was annoyed by Maddie's refusal to engage with her. "I would think that someone with a brother on the brink of ruin and two cousins who were forced to marry in haste would take every opportunity to prove her own innocence."

"How are your dear cousins, Lady Madeline?" Felicia slipped closer to Maddie, the proximity making her uncomfortable. Felicia had been a bully as long as Maddie could remember, often resorting to pinching and other underhanded bits of violence to exert her authority. Now that they were adults she could hardly inflict physical pain, but she knew as well as anyone just how discomfiting an invasion to one's personal space could be. "I vow I was never more shocked when we learned the true extent of your cousin Juliet's infirmity," she said. "It's a wonder poor Deveril didn't apply for an annulment as soon as he learned of it."

"Then, of course," Amelia said, picking up her henchwoman's thread of discussion, "there is Cecily. I suppose she must have been quite overset to learn just how . . . close her mother had been to Lord Geoffrey

Brighton. It's such a shame that he went mad like that. You don't suppose it runs in the family, do you?"

The rumors about Juliet's injury, and the speculation over Cecily's parentage had circulated through the *ton* for weeks now, and were laughable to those who knew her cousins. But even so, Amelia and Felicia were just the sort of gossipmongers who had kept the talk going. Her cousins were now happily wed and the rumors were given less credence every day, but even so there were still some people who could not let the gossip die.

"Still she is silent," Amelia continued. "I cannot warrant it, Felicia. I was given to believe that Lady Madeline was the least able to contain her temper of all three cousins. I guess the talk is wrong. Or Lady Madeline is a coward."

Maddie might be able to endure her fair share of derision, she might even be able to listen to Amelia mocking her. But she drew the line at being called a coward. If they were men, she would have been fully within her rights to challenge Amelia to a duel. Unable to demand satisfaction on the field, she would instead make her displeasure known to her enemy.

"Amelia," she said, shaking her head sadly, "you really must stop every once in a while to remove your foot from your mouth. I'm sure my cousins did not see fit to inform you of their situations, marital or otherwise. And it is hardly genteel for you to mention what is no more than rumor. But I suppose blood will out."

She felt a bit of conscience at alluding to Amelia's less than elevated parentage, but sometimes one had to fight fire with fire.

"Hmmph," was Amelia's only response. Then, "I don't know why you have to be rude. If I hear about certain things through the kindness of strangers, that's my affair."

"Well, when you use your knowledge to threaten harm against me and my cousins I believe my behavior falls less into the category of rudeness and more into the category of self-preservation."

Shaking her head with annoyance at Maddie's refusal to be led into an argument, Amelia tugged her friend's arm. "Come, Felicia, we have gentlemen waiting for us."

"Enjoy the dancing!" Maddie called after them, feeling an extreme sense of relief at being left, finally, blissfully, alone.

She really did resent Amelia and Felicia's hold over the *ton*. Not only because they so often used their social status for mischief, but also because they frequently got the facts wrong. So they were not only spreading gossip, but incorrect gossip at that.

Still, those were the least of her worries. Word of her visit to the gaming hell had spread through the *ton* as quickly as a head cold. But to her relief, most didn't see her behavior as all that shocking. Married women went to gaming hells all the time, and at a time when every dowager engaged in some form of gambling, a visit to what was essentially a weekly card party was not seen to be all that scandalous. The unfortunate circumstance of Mr. Tinker's death was the only element of the tale that gave people pause, and even then the reaction was less censorious than sympathetic.

Shaking her head at herself in the mirror, Maddie tucked a wayward strand of hair behind her ear, straightened her bodice, and stepped out into the hallway. As she made her way back toward the ballroom, she was startled to hear a familiar voice coming from an antechamber off the hallway. What on earth was Linton doing here?

"You'd better get your story straight before you start

telling tales," she heard her brother say from the little room.

Maddie was grateful that he was no longer missing, but from the sound of things, he was embroiled in something else untoward. She couldn't quite understand what her brother's companion was saying, but judging from his growl, it wasn't good.

"Who the devil would do this?" Linton demanded, his voice cold. Determined to learn just who he was speaking to, Maddie pushed softly on the heavy wood door of the room in question. Linton faced the door, while his companion stood with his back to the door. There was something about the cut of the man's coat and his hairstyle that seemed familiar. But even so she was unable to tell who he was.

"Someone with a damned grudge," the man said, his voice still too low for Maddie to recognize, "who thinks they know what really happened. Someone who makes good on their threats. Just as I will if you don't get me the funds soon."

When Linton's eyes met hers, Maddie inhaled sharply. Especially when she saw the set of his jaw. Clearly he was not pleased to see her. Or to know she'd overheard his conversation.

Before she could speak up one way or the other, the man facing her brother walked toward the fireplace in the small chamber and to Maddie's astonishment seemed to vanish into thin air. Which was not possible, she told herself. It must have been an illusion of some sort.

"Maddie, what are you doing here?" Linton demanded as she stepped into the room. "This doesn't concern you."

"Maybe not," she agreed, "but you concern me. Especially when someone goes so far as to threaten you."

Now that she was closer she saw that the fireplace pulled out, leading into a corridor beyond. Whoever had threatened Linton knew this house.

"Thank you for the concern," Linton said cynically, "but I am perfectly able to look after myself. I would just as well not have you getting involved in my business. Especially given the scold I received this morning from Papa regarding your escapade to Mrs. Bailey's the other night."

Maddie stiffened. "I find your chastisement to be completely ludicrous considering how you abandoned me to make my own way home that night. Not to mention the fact that you left me there to deal with the death of a man whom I thought you considered a friend."

To his credit, Linton looked abashed. Thrusting his hands into his hair, he said, "It was badly done of me, I know, Maddie. But you must believe that I didn't mean to leave you there without escort. It's just that when I saw Tinker there like that . . ." His eyes took on a look of desperation that Maddie had never seen in them before. "It was like Fielding all over again, you see."

His clenched jaw told Maddie that it had taken a great deal for her brother to admit such a thing to her.

Gathering him close to her in a hug, she said, "I'm sorry, dearest. It never occurred to me that Tinker's death would remind you of Fielding's. But it makes perfect sense. So you saw him there in the corridor before I found his body?"

Putting her away from him, Linton mopped his forehead with a handkerchief and nodded. "It was not the same situation at all of course. And I had no role in Tinker's death. But when I found him with a knife sticking out of his chest, I had to get out of there. I had no choice in the matter, Mads. I had to leave."

Remembering how distraught her brother had been

when his dearest friend, Lord Fielding, died, she nodded. His response to Tinker's death made perfect sense now. Even so there was the matter of the tête-à-tête she'd just interrupted.

"What did that man mean just now, Linton? About threats?"

Her brother winced. "That has nothing to do with Tinker's death. It's just something to do with a business matter. That is all."

Maddie frowned. "Gambling debts?"

His lack of response was an answer in itself.

"Jamie," she said, using his childhood nickname. "Why do you keep at it?"

Her brother shook his head. "You wouldn't understand. How could you when I barely understand it myself. I simply feel a . . . a compulsion to keep going. Even long after I know that luck has eluded me and there is no chance that I can possibly recoup my losses. There is just some small voice inside me that urges me to play one last hand, roll the dice one more time. And sometimes it works."

"And sometimes it leaves you indebted to men who think nothing of threatening you at a *ton* ball," Maddie said curtly.

He shrugged, acknowledging the point.

"I must ask you, Mads," he said seriously, "to please refrain from saying anything about this to Mama and Papa. And for God's sake, stay out of that business with Tinker. Whoever is responsible for his death has already shown himself willing to kill. I hardly think he will stop from harming you because you are a lady."

"I can't do that," she said bracing herself for his displeasure. "I held that man in my arms as the lifeblood poured out of him. The least I can do is try to find out who brought about his demise."

"Maddie," he said seriously, stepping closer to her, looking wearier than she'd ever seen him. "You don't know what you're saying. Tinker was involved in things you have no conception of. Just stay out of it and allow the authorities to handle it. Please."

Her brother's expression was pleading, but Maddie could still see that he was holding something back. Perhaps because of his own less than clear conscience? Or was it something far more selfish? An idea sparked, and she said, "I will stay out of the investigation into Mr. Tinker's death if you will promise to refrain from going to places like Mrs. Bailey's for one month."

But she could see as soon as he apprehended her words that she'd hit a nerve. Whereas before he was pleading with her, now his expression was one of fury.

"Did Mama put you up to this?" he asked, his mouth tight. "Or was it Father? I know they dislike the company I've been keeping, but I wouldn't have thought them capable of ruining your reputation to curb my behavior."

"They did nothing of the sort." Maddie almost stamped her foot she was so annoyed with the track their discussion had taken. "I went there of my own volition and for my own reasons. But I worry about you, Linton. We all do. If something good can come out of Mr. Tinker's death, then I'm going to try to make it happen."

"Well, you can stop worrying." His eyes were cold. Maddie could have wept at how quickly their discussion had devolved into an argument. "I am going away for a while. Somewhere that I can do what I please without the interference of overprotective parents or a busybody sister."

"Jamie, don't be this way." But it was already too

late. With one last baleful glance, her brother departed the small antechamber, leaving Maddie alone with her worries.

His thoughts still filled with Maddie, Christian made his way through the crowded ballroom toward the parlor where the Marchfords had set up the card room. He was not usually one for games—especially after the goings-on at Mrs. Bailey's—but he wasn't ready to leave yet, and also wasn't willing to dance with anyone else.

"Don't see you in the card room much, Monteith," Lord Lawrence Tretham said, appearing at his side. "I admit that the current crop of young ladies is less than enthralling, but what can one expect with virgins?"

Christian gave a mental curse. He had known Tretham since they were both in leading strings, and while they were friendly enough, he did not count the fellow as a friend. However, since he was a member of Viscount Linton and Mr. Tinker's set, he might prove to be a useful contact.

Monteith shrugged. "I simply did not care to dance any longer.

"Besides," he added, "I was barely able to play a hand before Mrs. Bailey's erupted the other night."

Tretham grimaced. "Bad business, that. Poor old Tinker didn't deserve that. From what I've heard the authorities still don't know who did it."

"You were close to him, weren't you?" Christian asked, accepting a brandy from a hovering footman. "You and he and Linton are in the same set."

"We were friends, I suppose." Tretham shrugged. "Not quite as much as in the old days, of course. Before Fielding died, I mean."

Sipping his brandy, Christian didn't respond, allowing the silence to stretch in the hopes that Tretham would fill it.

Which he did.

"None of us were really close to Tinker," Tretham said. "He was a bit of a radical politically. And he had a tendency to keep his own counsel. Though I suppose of the lot of us, Linton was his closest friend."

Before Christian could comment, Tretham changed the subject.

"Saw you with the little Essex chit," the other man said, sending a chill down Christian's spine. "The other night at Mrs. Bailey's, I mean. Wouldn't have expected to see her there. But it seems she's got a bit of fire in her, that one. Too bad she was the one to find Tinker, of course."

"I believe it was upsetting for her," Christian replied noncommittally.

He was saved from further commentary by a shout from the other side of the room.

"Damn it," Viscount Linton exclaimed, leaping up from his chair. "You did that on purpose, Cargill."

So, Christian thought, the blighter was no longer missing. He crossed to the table where Linton had been playing whist and took in the scene.

Mr. Edward Cargill, an aging dandy who had a tendency to lose heavily when he gambled, dabbed ineffectually at Linton's claret-spattered waistcoat and cravat. "I do apologize, my lord," the old man said with some distress. "It was an accident, I assure you. My elbows, y'know. They're always in the way."

"You're always in the way," Linton said, his voice rising, his words slurred with too much drink. "Ish bad enough that I've been losing all evening, but this is the last straw. Cargill, I wish for you to—"

Seeing that Linton had no intention of accepting the

other man's apology, and wishing to prevent further trouble, Christian stepped forward, and interrupted the younger man. "Linton, I know it is annoying to have your waistcoat ruined, but I feel sure Cargill had no intention of doing so. Let's go out onto the terrace for a cheroot and forget about cards for a bit, shall we?"

Annoyed by the interruption, but too drunk to formulate any real sort of argument, Linton tried but failed to pull his arm from Christian's grip. "Ish a damned nuisance, Gresham," he said with a shake of his head. "Ish a new weskit."

"No doubt, old fellow." Christian clapped an arm over Linton's shoulders, as the other man staggered. Exchanging a nod with a grateful-looking Cargill, Christian led his charge from the room, Tretham stepping in to hold up Linton on his other side.

"Did you come in your own carriage, Linton, or shall you ride in mine?" he asked as, instead of heading for the terrace, he led the two men toward the entrance hall of the Marchford town house.

"He can ride with me, Gresham," Tretham said calmly. "I've had as much wholesome entertainment as I can stand for one evening, anyway."

Christian didn't like the notion of leaving Maddie's brother in the tender care of Tretham, especially since he wished to question him about the business with Tinker the other evening, but there was little he could do without causing a scene. For the time being he was simply grateful that Linton hadn't called out a gentleman three times his age over a spilled glass of claret.

When they reached the entryway, Lady Emily Fielding was there waiting for her own conveyance. "Oh, dear," she said, taking in the sight of Linton flanked by Christian and Tretham. "I hope you haven't been too unwise, Lord Linton," she said, her brow raised in something between censure and exasperation.

"Heavens!" Lady Poppy Essex's tone was one of horror. "What on earth has happened?"

At his mother's voice, Linton tried to stand straighter. And failed. Christian dipped his knees to keep from dropping the other man.

"Mama, ish not wha' it looks like," Linton said, swaying between Christian and Tretham. "Jus' a li'l acshiden'."

Stepping closer to her son, Lady Poppy looked him up and down with an expression of disgust. "An accident, yes, I see."

Turning to Christian and Tretham, she said, "Thank you for seeing to my son's safety. I will leave you to it, then."

And to Christian's astonishment, she turned on her heel and returned to the ballroom.

"In for it now," Linton said morosely.

"Then we will have to ensure that you get a good night's sleep before you face the dragons," Tretham said cheerfully. "My carriage should be here by now."

Together, he and Christian walked Linton through the entryway and out the doors, with a bit of help from Linton himself, settling that gentleman into Tretham's carriage.

Turning to go back inside, Christian was surprised to see Lady Emily standing in the doorway, watching them.

"Before Fielding died he was never inclined to drink to excess," she said, a sad smile lighting her beautiful features. "He can be really quite lovely when he isn't in his cups."

Since Christian had been in the army then, he had no firsthand knowledge of Viscount Linton's behavior when he was younger.

"I hope that he will find a way to limit himself, then," he said to Lady Emily. "For his friends' sake, as well as his family's."

She nodded, then excused herself to climb into her own waiting carriage, leaving Christian to stare out into the night.

Seven

Despite a fitful night of dreams of Maddie in varying degrees of both undress and arousal, Christian awoke at a reasonably early hour the next morning. His years in the military had instilled in him a healthy respect for early rising, no matter what might keep him from his rest.

His first destination after breakfast was Lady Emily Fielding's town house. He might be wrong, but her interaction—or lack thereof—with Linton last night had hinted to him of a much more intimate friendship between them. He needed to speak to Linton today if at all possible. And he wished to avoid running the fellow to earth in his parents' home. There was far too much likelihood that Maddie would stumble upon their discussion and he wished to protect her from the matter if at all possible.

His brisk knock at Lady Emily's door was greeted by a dour butler who did not seem at all pleased to see him.

"Good day," Christian said, offering his card. "I was wondering if I might have a word with either Lady Emily or Viscount Linton."

The retainer's nose pinched in disapproval. "I don't

know to whom you are referring, my lord. This is the home of Lady Emily F—"

He was interrupted by a voice behind him.

"Don't be a stiff neck, Marsden," Lady Emily said from the landing above. "Let Gresham come in for a cup of tea and I shall see if our guest is receiving callers today."

With eyes that warned Christian not to get too comfortable, Marsden led him to a small but cozy sitting room that faced Half Moon Street. They exchanged meaningless pleasantries while waiting for the tea tray, which arrived soon enough. He'd just begun to sip his tea when Viscount Linton, his eyes bloodshot and his skin an unhealthy shade, entered the room as if the air were made of chain mail.

Without ceremony, Linton, his blond hair matted on one side, collapsed into a comfortable chair before the fire and asked Marsden, who hovered close behind, to bring him coffee.

"I hope you have good reason to raise me from bed at this hour, Gresham," Maddie's brother said, looking like death. "I've the devil's own headache this morning and I don't take kindly to being roused here at the home of my . . ."—he paused—"friend."

"I don't doubt it, Linton," Christian said, leaning forward to prop his elbows on his knees. "You were quite foxed last night as I recall."

"I don't remember seeing you," Linton said with a frown. Christian wasn't all that surprised considering the amount of brandy he suspected the other man had consumed. "And how did you know I was here, anyway? We are discreet, damn it."

This last he said with the injured air of a young lad defending his honor.

"I was there, nonetheless," Christian said. "As for how I found you here, it was a lucky guess. There have been whispers, you know. It's impossible to keep anything entirely secret in this town."

Linton rubbed his forehead with the heel of his hand. "I am fully aware of it," he said dolefully. "Doesn't matter how quiet I try to keep things, the pater always has a way of winkling out the truth."

Shaking his head at the other man's foolishness, Christian decided to get to the point. But before he could speak, Linton went on. "I suppose you're here about that business with Tinker the other evening."

"Quite perceptive of you, Linton, I am here about that business. I need to ask you some questions about it in my capacity with the Home Office."

The words "Home Office" made the younger man straighten a bit. "What the devil has the Home Office to do with old Tinker's getting himself killed over gambling debts?"

"What makes you think his death had something to do with gambling?" Christian asked, ignoring the question about the Home Office. "Do you know of someone who's been threatening him?"

The younger man shook his head, then winced at the movement. "No, but it stands to reason, don't it? He was killed in a gaming hell. It must have had something to do with gaming."

While Christian couldn't fault the fellow's logic, it didn't necessarily work that way. Deciding not to dispute the matter, instead he said, "What made you run away that night?"

He wanted to berate Maddie's brother for abandoning her, but he didn't wish to spook him at this point. They could discuss his bad behavior regarding her after this business was settled.

Linton rubbed a bleary eye. "I know it was wrong of me. I knew it when I did it. But I had to get out of there. As soon as I saw that it was Tinker who'd been killed, I knew that I'd be the one who got blamed for it."

"Why?" Christian asked. "Because you owed Tinker money?"

Linton's bloodshot eyes opened wide. "How did you . . . ?"

"It wasn't hard to guess," Christian said with an inward sigh. Was this man really capable of killing his friend? He doubted it. "You were in a gaming house, after all. And you were the only one there who fled the scene."

"Not the only one," Linton said, animating a bit. "Stands to reason that the one who did it also fled the scene." It was hard to argue with the triumph in the man's face. Especially when one considered just how hard his brain must have worked to arrive at the conclusion, no matter how false it might be.

"You know, of course, that fleeing the scene like that will make you the number one suspected culprit."

If Linton were worried, he didn't show it. "I did what I thought I had to do at the time."

Though he'd been prepared for Viscount Linton's pigheadedness—he was, after all, Maddie's brother—Christian hadn't quite guessed just how nonchalant he'd be over the possibility that he'd be found guilty of murder.

"I don't think you understand the gravity of this matter, Linton," he said firmly. "You are indeed at the top of the suspect list. And I do not wish to frighten your family, but you should perhaps ask your father for some guidance in the matter. His influence or perhaps that of your uncle Lord Shelby might be necessary to see to it that you are protected."

He already looked a bit ill, and now Linton's complexion went even paler. "You're serious?" he demanded. "How can this be happening? It was a silly gambling debt between us. That's all. Tinker was my friend, for God's sake."

Christian didn't bother pointing out that Tinker was the second of Linton's friends to die in a mysterious manner. Nor that his presence here in the home of that first friend's widow, having obviously spent the night in her bed, was damned suspicious, as well.

Probably because she'd been eavesdropping, Lady Emily herself stepped into the room and wrapped a comforting arm around Linton's shoulders.

"Do not despair, Linton," she soothed, all the while glaring at Christian. "No one with a jot of sense would ever think you killed Tinker."

Seeing that he wouldn't get much more sensible talk from the viscount, Christian rose.

"Thank you for speaking with me, Lord Linton," he said. "If you can recall anything new about that night at Mrs. Bailey's please don't hesitate to contact me with it."

Neither his hostess, nor her paramour, bid him goodbye. He was almost to the door when he paused. "For what it's worth, I don't think you are responsible for Tinker's death. Unfortunately, I'm not the one who makes the ultimate decision about who we hold accountable."

With that parting salvo, he left.

His meeting with Linton out of the way, Christian decided to pay a call on Tinker's widow. While it was doubtful she knew who had killed her husband, she might know about any threats the fellow had received in the past few months.

The Tinkers' home was nestled on a quiet street where those with social standing but without accompanying wealth could live in comfort without the stigma of an address outside fashionable London. It was notable among its neighbors because of the black crepe that adorned the door. And the golden-haired young lady who stood on the stoop about to lift the muted door knocker.

What the devil is she doing here?

Christian should have guessed Maddie's next move would be to question Tinker's widow, but he'd thought she would wait a few days at least before doing so.

Tossing the reins to a young lad who appeared as if from nowhere—likely he'd been waiting for just such an opportunity for ready coin—Christian leaped down from his vehicle and hurried up the handful of steps leading to the Tinkers' door.

"Fancy meeting you here," he said, coming up behind Maddie, and at once remembering just how good she'd felt pressed up against him last night. He'd better nip that line of thought in the bud if he wished to accomplish anything worthwhile today.

If she were unnerved at seeing him again she didn't show it, however. Turning to face him, she said, "Ah, Lord Gresham, this is a surprise. I simply came to pay my respects to Mr. Tinker's family. I was not aware you were acquainted with the man."

"Since you were only slightly acquainted with him, I do not see much difference in the wisdom of our respective errands," Christian returned.

While they waited for some response from the Tinkers' servants, he took the opportunity to study her appearance.

In deference to the Tinker family she wore a violet-colored gown. Her golden hair was neatly arranged in a simple chignon beneath a pretty but subdued straw bonnet. Her eyes, thanks to her attire, seemed more violet than icy blue today, though there were slight shadows beneath them. She might have gone home from the ball earlier than he had, he guessed, but she had not slept well. Doubtless she was concerned over Tinker's death and her brother's possible role in the matter. Still, as ever, she was lovely, her short stature belying what he knew was a strength of will that could outlast any soldier's.

"I thought," he explained, "to ask Mrs. Tinker some questions about her husband's activities these last few months. As is my prerogative in my work for the Home Office." He gave her a speaking look, but true to her nature, Maddie did not flinch.

"Well, I do not have the Home Office to hide behind . . ." Her brow lifted in challenge. "But as Mr. Tinker was a close friend of my brother's, I thought to offer my assistance to his widow, should she need someone to learn more about her husband's death."

"Do you often offer assistance to the widows of your brother's close friends?" Christian asked. "If so that must keep you quite busy."

At her glare, he relented a bit. "Maddie, you must know that as a lady, a peer's daughter in fact, you cannot uncover the same sort of information that I can. It's just a simple fact."

"Are you saying that just because I am a woman I don't have the mental capacity to—?"

Her question was cut off—thank God—by the opening of the door.

Before Maddie could elbow her way in, Christian spoke up.

"Lord Gresham and Lady Madeline Essex to see Mrs. Tinker."

"There's been a death in the family," the rawboned young footman said, attempting to shut the door on them.

"Please, sir." Maddie spoke up. "I was there the evening of Mr. Tinker's death and I would so like to pay my respects to Mrs. Tinker. We will only stay for a few moments, I promise."

Christian watched cynically as Maddie employed her lashes and dimples to good use. The footman, poor fellow, didn't stand a chance. He'd have to look out for that ploy himself in future, Christian warned himself.

"I suppose paying your respects would be all right," the young man said, ushering them inside the tiny hallway. "If you'll wait in the parlor, I'll get the missus."

He left them in a small but comfortable room, furnished with a sofa and two chairs arranged before the fire. An embroidery frame rested before one of the chairs, as if the lady of the house had been in the midst of stitching when she was called away.

"Do not think I have forgotten what you said earlier," Maddie said, turning a gimlet eye on Christian. Her anger lent her an air of passion that he would do well to ignore. Her cheeks were pink in her anger and her eyes sparked.

Oh, yes, he should definitely ignore her right now, he thought, even as he felt his body respond to her. Damn it, he was here to talk to Tinker's widow, not indulge in lascivious thoughts about Maddie.

"What?" she demanded, her hands on her hips, when he didn't respond. "Have I said something to amuse you? Why are you staring at me?"

If she only knew, he thought. "I will address your concerns later," he said, in what he hoped was an even tone. "It wouldn't be right for us to indulge in an argument in a house of mourning," he added piously.

His companion's snort revealed just how seriously she took his warning. Even so, she seemed to shelve her annoyance for later.

"This seems to be a smart enough little house," she said, changing the subject. "Do you suppose Mr. Tinker had family money?"

"My husband had a small inheritance from his maternal grandmother and my dowry," a voice said from the doorway. "Though I don't know what business it is of yours."

Christian turned to see a pale young woman with mouse-brown hair, dressed in all black, standing in the doorway.

"Mrs. Tinker," he said, bowing to her. "We apologize for the intrusion into your grief. But Lady Madeline and I wished to pay our respects."

Twin flags of color appeared in the widow's cheeks.

"Yes, well, you've shown your respects," she said stiffly. "Now I must ask you to leave."

"I am so sorry for your loss, ma'am," Maddie said, stepping closer to the other woman. "I was with your husband at the end, and I wished to assure you that it was peaceful. You may take that comfort at least."

Mrs. Tinker took a step back from Maddie. "I cannot see why you would think that meeting the woman who accompanied him to that shameful place could possibly be of comfort to me."

Maddie looked genuinely perplexed. "I don't know what you've been told, Mrs. Tinker," she said, "but I did not accompany your husband to Mrs. Bailey's. I was there with my brother, Viscount Linton. I believe he was a great friend of your husband's."

If anything Mrs. Tinker seemed more appalled than before. "Yes," she said with a bitter laugh, "Viscount Linton was a great friend to my husband. He led poor

John from vice to vice like a puppy. My husband was no saint, Lady Madeline, but he was not nearly so blind to propriety before he made your brother's acquaintance as he was after. Make no mistake, I place the blame for my husband's death squarely upon your brother's head. If he had never met Linton, my John would still be alive."

Her spleen vented, the widow seemed to crumple a bit. "Now, if you will excuse me, I would like to go lie down. I'll have Greeley see you out."

With those words their hostess turned and shut the door of the parlor firmly behind her.

"What on earth was that?" Maddie asked, looking as if she were going to burst into tears. "Could Linton really have been so detrimental to her husband's health?"

Though they had made no prearrangement, Maddie allowed Christian to hand her into his phaeton after instructing the maid who accompanied her to return home without her. She had been rattled by Mrs. Tinker's accusations against her brother. It was bad enough that Tinker had been killed, but added together with the bit of conversation she'd overheard at the Marchford ball, things were looking very grim for her brother, indeed.

"What's going on in that brain of yours?" Gresham inquired from beside her, where he expertly steered his vehicle through the streets of Mayfair. "I did find Mrs. Tinker's accusations troubling, but that doesn't necessarily mean that she knew what was actually going on in her husband's set. In fact, it sounded to me as if she knew very little about what her husband was getting up to."

Maddie appreciated his attempt to soothe her fears, but she saw it for what it was. She'd been concerned about the company her brother kept for a while now.

But Mrs. Tinker's accusations that Linton had led her husband farther down the road to ruin had stung. Because on some level she suspected that her brother *had* led Tinker astray.

"It is true that she seemed not to be overly familiar with Mr. Tinker's activities," she agreed, "but I cannot help but wonder whether she was not correct about Linton's role in Mr. Tinker's death. Not that I think he killed him, for I don't think James capable of that. But I would not be terribly surprised to learn that he accompanied Mr. Tinker to Mrs. Bailey's before that night."

"Even if that were the case, Tinker is . . . was a grown man. He did not seem to be impaired in any way."

"No," Maddie said seriously. "But perhaps he was just as much under the spell of gaming as my brother is."

A chill breeze made Maddie pull her pelisse tighter around her, a shudder running through her. There was far too much hiding in all of this business, she reflected. Which prompted her to ask, "Just what *is* your interest in all of this, Lord Gresham? What has Whitehall to do with gambling?"

"We have shared a kiss, Maddie," he said glancing at her mouth. "Do you think you could call me Christian?"

"Changing the subject will do you no good, my lord," she said pertly. "Christian," she added when he gave her a stern look.

"That's better," he said, his gaze intense for a fraction of a second before he looked away. "As for my motives for looking into this business with Tinker, I have my reasons. Reasons which I am not presently at liberty to divulge, but suffice it to say that some very important people have been watching Mr. Tinker for some time."

For the first time since that night at Mrs. Bailey's, a stab of real fear shot through her.

"I cannot like my brother's involvement in this," she said hotly. "I cannot. He is profligate, true, but hardly a criminal to be investigated by the Home Office."

"Do not fly into a pelter," Christian said mildly but not unkindly. "It likely has nothing to do with Linton and everything to do with Tinker and his other friends."

"What other friends? How am I to ensure that my brother doesn't somehow end up in trouble for this if I don't know who the true culprits are?"

"Maddie, much as I wish I could, you know I can't tell you that," he said, taking her hand in his. It was a gesture of friendship, she knew, and it calmed her a little. "I honestly wish you would trust me to deal with all of this."

"Why?" she asked, suddenly wondering if he was calming her with ulterior motives. "So you don't have to tell me anything about what you find? I think not."

Christian did not answer right away, turning his attention to the horses as he steered around a sluggish buggy.

Finally turning back to her, he asked, "Have you considered letting your brother handle his own affairs?

"Like Tinker," he said firmly, "he is a grown man and perfectly capable of handling his own affairs."

"Yes, you see how successful Mr. Tinker was at handling himself," she said bitterly.

Realizing that perhaps he needed further explanation for her zeal, she went on. "I do not expect you to understand my relationship with Linton."

Christian looked away. "I understand more than you think," he said bitterly.

Belatedly, Maddie recalled that Christian had lost his twin sister some years ago. The gossips had hinted at suicide, but she'd never heard the full story. Perhaps he did understand her need to protect Linton after all.

Gently, she said, "There is a certain bond between siblings. And an even greater one between siblings who are close together in age. Especially when you have grown up as Linton and I did."

Christian turned to look at her, his eyes searching. "I thought your upbringing was happy."

"Only after we reached a certain age," Maddie admitted. She was hardly comfortable discussing the matter, but she felt somehow that Christian needed to know. "When we were younger, and this is not generally known so I wish you would not repeat it . . ."

"Of course."

As she spoke, he had steered them into Green Park onto one of the lesser used carriage paths and drew the phaeton to a halt.

Turning to face her, he waved her to continue.

"When we were children, my father wasn't on very good terms with his own parents," she began, "because of his wildness, for want of a better word."

In fact Viscount Linton, as the current Earl of Essex was then known, had been all but cut off from his family. In part because of his carousing, but also because of his insistence upon marrying the penniless but beautiful Miss Poppy Featherstone. The Earl and Countess of Essex were well-known for their abstemious ways, in spite of the ribaldry of their generation, and when young Viscount Linton had defied them there had been rumors that he would be cut off altogether.

Christian knew the tale, of course. He also knew that when the elder earl died his son had turned over a new leaf and now led a life just as retiring as his father's had been. He'd always wondered what had caused the change, and now he suspected he was about to hear it.

"I have heard that, yes."

"Well, what is not generally known is that my father could be quite nasty when he was in his cups. And when his father cut off his allowance, my parents were forced into economies that were foreign to them—well, to my father at least. Mama, as you know, grew up quite poor and knew how to make a penny last. But Papa was bitter, and became even more so when they were forced to remove from the Essex town house and into a smaller one. And when he was angry he drank. And when he drank he became, well, violent."

Christian felt a knot of dread form in his belly at her words. "Violent how?"

"Well, you must understand that he was not himself when he drank. It was as if all the rage and disappointment he felt about their straitened circumstances came out when he was inebriated." She looked down at her clasped hands, not meeting Christian's eyes, which made him want to pull her close. "He shouted mostly. Though he never struck us, he did take out his anger on whatever inanimate objects were unlucky enough to be in his path."

"Thank God for that at least," Christian said.

"You would not say so if you were an eight-year-old little girl whose favorite dolly had just been smashed to bits," she said wryly.

He hated that tone in her voice, as if she had seen far more than she should. It made him want to gather her up in his arms and comfort her. Kiss away her tears.

"In any event," she continued, "Papa was quite volatile in those days, and as I was older than Jamie, I tried to look out for him. My grandparents made sure that we had a nurse and food and clothing. Grandpapa did not wish to punish us, after all, and I think he wanted to ensure that Jamie, as the heir, would receive a proper upbringing. I believe there was even some talk at one time that we would go to live with our grandparents but neither Mama nor Papa would allow that."

"Even if it meant that you two saw more than you should of your father's temper?"

"To be fair, we weren't often in Papa's company when he was in one of his moods. And I do not think either of us would have wished to leave Mama. We were a close-knit family despite our troubles. And when things were good, Papa could be quite entertaining."

"But . . ."

"But there were many times when we heard our parents arguing downstairs. And a few times Papa came up to the nursery to prove some point to Mama—I think to show her that we were suffering as a result of his parents' interference. And those times were quite terrifying."

Though he knew that Lord Essex was now the pattern card of respectability, some part of Christian wished that he could go back in time and thrash the younger version for what he'd forced his children to suffer through. Because though Maddie obviously wished to downplay the incidents, he suspected there was much more to the story than she was telling. The idea of her as a little girl, cuddling her brother close as they listened to their parents arguing, filled him with inexpressible rage.

"What did he do?" he asked aloud.

"Mostly he queried us about our well-being. Did we get enough to eat? Were our lessons enough? Did our nurse treat us well?"

"That doesn't sound too terrible," Christian said carefully. Perhaps he'd misjudged Essex.

"The questions themselves weren't awful in and of themselves. It was . . ." She shook her head as if searching for the words to describe the experience. "It was as if he were asking us questions that had another meaning altogether from the surface. Because he was trying to prove some point I think we knew instinctively that if we gave the wrong answer he might react negatively."

"And then what would happen?"

"He might shout at us, at Mama, at nurse."

"But you say that he never hit you."

"No, he never did," she explained, "but, and I can only say this from my own perspective, it always felt as if he might become violent at any minute when he was drinking."

"So this is why you keep such close watch over Linton?" he asked, unable to resist the urge any longer, and reaching out to take her gloved hand in his. He understood her need to look after her brother far more than she could know. He, too, had tried to protect a sibling once. And failed. Would he cause Maddie to do the same?

It was the most damnable coil.

"Yes, though I suppose it sounds silly to you," she said quietly. Not waiting for him to respond, she went on. "Papa stopped drinking almost as soon as his father died. I think he regretted losing the chance to mend fences with him. And Mama insisted, of course. I think she grew tired of remonstrating with him. And when he assumed the earldom, he finally realized that he needed to take his responsibilities more seriously."

Christian sensed that there was more to the story, but the inner workings of the Essex household were beyond him at the moment. All he cared about was seeing to it that Maddie did not come to harm, and that she never had to suffer the kind of grief and regret that he had. Surely he could do that along with his duty to the Home Office.

"So your brother has gone on to follow in your father's footsteps," he said finally. He thought back to the scene last night at the Marchfords', and was glad he hadn't informed Maddie of what he'd seen. The knowledge would only distress her further.

When she looked up, he saw moisture in her eyes. "I greatly fear he has. Which is why I have to ensure that he does not become any more involved in this business over Tinker's death than he already is."

Though he now understood her reasons for wishing to rescue Linton, remembering the man's inebriation last night and his sickly pallor this morning, Christian very much feared that it could be too late for Maddie to save her brother. From either his gambling or his drinking.

If he had a chance to do things over again, he would do his damnedest to shield his sister Clarissa from the danger that led to her death, and much as he wished to protect Maddie, he could not fault her for the worries for her brother that drove her to risk her own reputation.

"I'd better get you home," he told her, not meeting her eyes lest she see the approval there. He might understand her need to shield Linton, but he could not give her his support while she was intent on putting herself in danger.

He'd lost one woman he cared for, and he was damned if he'd lose another without putting up a fight.

When Maddie returned home it was to find that Juliet had called in her absence and was waiting for her in her sitting room.

"What brings you here?" she asked, pouring herself a cup of tea and removing her gloves. "I thought you were supposed to go shopping with Cecily this morning."

"I was," Juliet said, sipping from her own cup. "But Cecily wasn't feeling well this morning so we decided to postpone our trip. Which is just as well since it would be more fun if the three of us could go together."

"You know I would love to. I simply couldn't go this morning. I had an errand."

"Yes, that's what I heard," Juliet said, unable to conceal a grin. "I heard from Alec that he saw you with Gresham in Green Park."

"How the devil do you know that already? It hasn't been more than fifteen minutes since we left the park!" Really, was it too much to ask that she have one morning to herself without half the *ton* gossiping about her and with whom she was seen?

"Come, Maddie," Juliet chided, "you know better than to try to hide anything in this town. Someone is always watching. I wouldn't be at all surprised if our servants had a network of their own to carry tales to one another."

"I wasn't trying to hide it, precisely," Maddie groused. "I simply accepted a ride home with Gresham in his phaeton instead of taking a hackney."

"Interesting." Her cousin's green eyes twinkled. "Because it sounded to me as if the two of you were deeply engrossed in conversation in the park. *Alone.*"

Despite her efforts to school her features, Maddie was unable to prevent the blush from creeping into her cheeks. Even so, she tried to deny Juliet's implication. "We happened to be going in the same direction and he offered to drive me home. In an open carriage. We stopped in the park to discuss . . . um . . . Mr. Tinker's death. It was all perfectly innocuous, I assure you."

"Oh, I believe you," Juliet said with a raised brow. "Perfectly innocuous. Which is why you are blushing, of course."

"I wish you would stop teasing me, Juliet," Maddie said, unable to keep up the pretense any longer. "My relationship with Gresham . . . or rather this morning's encounter *was* innocuous. I went to visit Mr. Tinker's widow and unexpectedly met Gresham there."

Juliet's face lost all playfulness. "Oh, Maddie, I am so sorry. I had no idea. Why didn't you ask Cecily or me to come with you? We would have been more than happy to."

Feeling churlish for her pique, Maddie sighed. "I know you would have come with me, but I felt it best to go alone, since I do not even know Mrs. Tinker and I did not wish to intrude upon her more than was necessary."

"But you did go," Juliet pointed out. "You must know that you had nothing to do with that man's death. Don't you?"

"I do," she responded, shaking her head to clear the memories of that night from her mind. "But I did wish to see her and offer her my sympathies. And I thought perhaps that she would wish to hear more about her husband's last moments. I underestimated her anger about the whole situation, I fear."

"Anger?" her cousin asked. "Why should she be angry with you? You were hardly responsible for his death."

"She was angry at Linton," Maddie explained, remembering with mortification just how Mrs. Tinker had railed against her brother. "She holds him much to blame for her husband's death."

"Well, Linton can hardly have kept a grown man from going to a gaming hell. And it's not as if he killed Mr. Tinker, after all."

"True," Maddie said. "We don't know what sort of influence Linton might have had over the man. But I will learn it from him at the soonest opportunity. If for no other reason than to warn him that Gresham is looking into the matter for the Home Office."

"Gresham?" Juliet demanded. "Is that why he was there that night? I vow I did find it odd to hear that he was in a place like Mrs. Bailey's. It's no small secret that he hasn't much interest in gaming."

"Well, he was there investigating something," Maddie confirmed. "And he is definitely interested in Mr. Tinker's murder. That was how I came to ride home with him. He came upon me on Mrs. Tinker's doorstep."

"Really?" Juliet pulled the tea tray closer and took a macaroon. "So he was following you?"

"Hmm, that hadn't occurred to me," Maddie admitted. "I suppose I thought he was there for his own reasons."

"Well, perhaps his own reasons have something to do with looking out for you," Juliet said slyly. "Because he *likes* you."

"Lord spare me from happily married ladies hellbent on matchmaking," Maddie said with a sigh.

But her cousin only laughed.

"Changing the subject," Maddie said pointedly. "I have come up with an idea that I would like to get your opinion about."

At Juliet's nod, Maddie said, "It's just this. Since my brother was so foolish as to bring suspicion on himself by fleeing the scene, I would like to ensure that the blame for Tinker's death does not fall on him. Being foolish is certainly a bad thing, but it is not a crime."

"You can't think that Gresham blames your brother for Mr. Tinker's death. From what you've told me of who was there that night, it could have been any one of them."

"I don't know what Gresham thinks since he refuses

to tell me." Maddie tried not to sound as hurt over that as she felt. "And I would not wish him to compromise his position with the Home Office, anyway."

"It is a muddle, isn't it?" Juliet asked, her green eyes sympathetic. "So, what will you do?"

Her cousin's matter-of-fact acceptance of Maddie's decision to involve herself in the investigation warmed her heart. Juliet might be cautious, but she was always supportive and Maddie was grateful for it.

"I mean to become friendly with the same set that Linton and Mr. Tinker belong to."

"You mean the fast set?" Juliet asked, her eyes wide. "Your mama will have a conniption!"

"I know," Maddie said with an unrepentant grin. "I won't follow their every scandalous pursuit, of course. I will simply become friendly with them. Speak to them at *ton* parties. Perhaps secure an invitation or two to some of their more exclusive gatherings."

"What can I do to help?" Juliet asked, grinning herself.

"I would like you to go to Madame Celeste's with me," Maddie said, relieved that Juliet had agreed to help her. She would have put her plan into place without her cousin's help, but knowing she had an ally made the prospect less daunting.

"Of course," Juliet said with a decisive nod. "I suspect Cecily is feeling better by now. Let's stop at Winterson House on our way to Madame's."

Maddie gave her cousin an impulsive hug. "You are the best."

"I should certainly hope so," Juliet said, hugging her back.

They were on their way downstairs to call for the carriage when a footman met them with a note for Maddie. Recognizing her brother's handwriting, she ripped it open and quickly scanned the hastily penned missive.

At her muffled curse, Juliet gasped. "What is it?"

"It's Linton," Maddie said, her voice sharp. "The featherwit has left town until the investigation into Mr. Tinker's death has died down."

"What will you do?" Juliet asked.

"I will continue with my plan," Maddie said firmly. "He might be foolish enough to think that he can defend himself from afar, but I am not."

Eight

Oh, please do tell me again about the intricacies of the Waterfall," Christian said to Deveril, his eyes gleaming with mock enthusiasm. Letting his pose drop, he continued, "Really, Dev, when will you get it into your excessively thick head that I have little to no interest in fashion?"

"So long as you keep attending social functions in monstrous waistcoats like that," Alec gestured with a moue of disgust at Christian's blue peacock-embroidered waistcoat, "I will continue to attempt to teach you some kind of taste. It's the least I can do. As your friend."

"What's wrong with this one?" Christian asked, perplexed. He'd chosen it himself, against the judgment of his valet, because it reminded him of Madeline's eyes. Though he'd never tell her, or Deveril, that.

"If you don't know," Deveril said with a long-suffering sigh, "then I can't begin to tell you."

They'd been discussing Lord Deveril's favorite topic— or rather Lord Deveril was discussing while Christian affectionately mocked him, in that way that gentlemen have of ribbing one another—at the Harbaugh ball for some time when a prickle on the back of his neck alerted him to a ripple in the crowd.

"What's amiss?" he asked, turning to where the crush of guests had begun to accumulate at the entrance to the drawing room. "Has Prinny arrived at the last minute?"

Deveril frowned. "I don't think so. People would be falling over themselves to toady him rather than crowding round. Probably just some young lady trying to cause a scandal. There's one at every gathering, it seems. If they can't make their mark by behaving properly, they take it into their heads that causing a ruckus will get them noticed."

"When in fact it merely causes their mamas to tighten the leash," Winterson said, stepping forward. He'd been hovering over Cecily ever since they'd discovered she was with child. And this evening was no exception. "I suspect it's a tradition that's been around as long as there have been young ladies with mamas."

With his extra height, Winterson craned his neck over the crowd pressing forward. His soft curse sent a frisson of dread down Christian's spine. "What is it?" he asked.

"You're not going to like it," Winterson said with a scowl. "I'm pretty sure I don't like it, either."

"Is it Cecily?" Deveril asked, his blond brows drawing together.

"No," Winterson said, as the crowd performed a maneuver much like Christian thought the Red Sea must have done, and parted right down the middle to reveal the figure standing boldly in the entrance to the Harbaugh ballroom. "It's not Cecily."

No, it certainly wasn't. The air in the room seemed to evaporate and Christian felt the need to run a finger under his suddenly too-tight neck cloth. Standing at the head of the room, wearing a blue gown that was far more revealing than any debutante had the right to wear, her hair arranged in a fashion that seemed to evoke the bedchamber, was Lady Madeline Essex, flanked by her cousins.

"What the hell is she thinking?" he muttered, stepping forward, unsure if he was going to read her a thunderous scold or kiss her senseless in public.

A hand on his arm stayed him.

"Don't make it worse than it is," Winterson cautioned. "Right now, it's just a gown that's a bit too revealing. If you march over there with that look on your face it turns into a scene that will be talked about for weeks."

"They'll talk about this for weeks as it is," argued Christian. "What the hell is the matter with her? Does she mean to ruin her reputation entirely?"

"There is very little that Maddie does without careful deliberation," Deveril said thoughtfully. "I doubt that this entrance is any different. She probably has a reason, however misguided."

Christian felt his jaw clench painfully—though not as painfully as the tightening of his groin—as he watched Maddie slink toward them, flanked by her cousins. It was as if she were possessed by the spirit of a courtesan. A very skilled one, at that.

What had happened to the no-nonsense young lady he'd argued with yesterday?

"Gentlemen," Maddie said in a sultry tone that did *things* to him. "I hope you're having a pleasant evening."

"Interesting, certainly," Deveril said with a wry smile. "The gown is exquisite, Mads. If a bit . . . bold."

"I helped her choose it," Juliet said with a glance at her husband from beneath her lashes. "In fact, I ordered one just like it."

"Which you will not wear in public," Deveril said with what might be termed a growl. Then realizing his rudeness he added, "No offense, Maddie."

Maddie laughed, her tousled curls brushing against her bare neck in a way that made Christian wish devoutly to do the same. "None taken, my lord." In a low voice she added, with a flash of humor, "I marvel that I managed to wear it in public myself."

"Then why the bloody—" Christian said, his voice raised, before five voices shushed him. "All right, all right." He waved them off. "Why," he began in a lower voice, "did you wear it? Have you no care at all for your reputation? Every man in this room is staring at your . . ." He paused, searching for a polite term, and settled on, "Body."

Laughing loudly as if he'd been relaying a risqué anecdote rather than scolding her, Maddie said, "Oh, Lord Gresham, you are so amusing."

In an undertone, she added, "Because I needed to make a spectacle of myself in order for Lady Emily Fielding to let me into her inner circle."

"What?" Christian bit back a curse.

At his outburst, Maddie straightened her spine. "I told you I planned to find out who killed Mr. Tinker. Have you not heard the talk tonight? They all think Linton did it."

"I don't see how you could have heard any talk given that since your arrival you've been the topic on everyone's tongue," Christian bit out. He had the urge to cover up Maddie's form with his coat, toss her over his shoulder, and escape the Harbaugh house with her.

"Children," Winterson warned, "you might wish to carry on this conversation elsewhere. You are being watched."

Christian looked up to see that his friend was right. All eyes in the room were on them. Even the dancers seemed to watch them from the dance floor.

"Fine," he said, "Maddie, come with me."

"Certainly not," she said with a frown. "I am engaged for the next set."

"Then give me your dance card and I'll take the next dance," he barked. "It's a waltz, so we'll be able to talk."

"I am sorry," she said without any sort of remorse he could see. "I'm afraid I don't have a dance open all evening. I hope you'll excuse me."

And with that, she turned to young Lord Kenneth Upham, whose not-so-veiled glances at Maddie's prominently displayed attributes made Christian wish he'd brought his dueling pistols to the ball, and allowed him to lead her onto the dance floor.

"Damn it," Christian said under his breath. As if he didn't already have enough to worry about, what with Leighton breathing down his neck for information on Tinker's death, and Linton's abrupt disappearance from London, he also had to protect Maddie from her mad plan to clear her brother's name.

"If it's any consolation," Winterson said with a sympathetic clap on the shoulder, "I don't think her parents will stand for this one bit. So she might begin and end her notoriety in this one night."

And true enough, the Countess of Essex stood on the opposite side of the ballroom looking like thunder. Lord Essex was, as was his custom, in the card room. He would doubtless be informed of his daughter's behavior later.

"I wish I could believe that," Christian said, ignoring the avid gazes Maddie's cousins trained on him. Let them think whatever they wished. He had no intention of tying Maddie to him. But he'd be damned if he would allow her to ruin herself while he could do something to stop her.

The trouble, was, of course, determining just how to do that.

* * *

Maddie was still fuming over Christian's response to her attire as she walked on the arm of Mr. George Fullerton to the refreshment room. She'd managed to avoid him—and her parents—by dancing every set, which was an unusual occurrence for her. And though she'd chatted a bit with Lady Emily Fielding, she'd not, as yet, gotten close enough to that lady to exchange more than a few words with her. She had to figure out how to ingratiate herself without alerting Lady Emily to her scheme to determine if somone in her set was responsible for Mr. Tinker's murder.

"Here we are," Mr. Fullerton said, in his bluff, pleasant way. He was handsome enough, Maddie supposed, if one were interested in that brawny sort of fellow. For her part, she preferred a bit more wit than brawn, but Mr. Fullerton was a means to an end anyway. Besides, he'd not very subtly suggested several times over the course of their dance that they retire to one of the antechambers of the Harbaughs' town house and get to know one another a bit better. She wished to catch Lady Emily's notice, but not at the risk of her total ruination. A bit of scandal here or there would be all right. A total scandal, neither she, nor, she surmised, her parents, were willing to risk. "Ratafia. I don't know how you ladies stomach the stuff," Fullerton went on, handing her a glass of amber liquid, "but I suppose it's the thing, eh?"

"I don't believe Lady Madeline cares for the stuff, Fullerton," said a voice from behind them.

Drat. Maddie cursed her bad luck as she turned to see Christian standing behind them. She'd been hoping to avoid another scene with him tonight. She'd known he would not approve of her plan, but she had underestimated the degree to which he would show that pique in public. He'd very nearly ruined the whole evening's plan with his scold earlier in the evening. And it was none of his affair what she chose to wear. He was hardly a relative, and if Winterson and Deveril hadn't scolded her, what right had he to do so?

"Ah, Gresham," Fullerton said, completely oblivious to the cues of displeasure radiating from the other man. "Didn't know you was here tonight. I say, that's a dashed nice waistcoat." Taking out a quizzing glass, Maddie's companion surveyed the earl's attire with the air of a scientist observing a new specimen.

"Indeed," Maddie said, her brows raised in as haughty as manner as she could manage. "I believe peacocks suit you."

Christian, his expression grim, gave a mocking bow to acknowledge the hit. "Lady Madeline," he said, "There is an urgent matter we need to discuss in the library. I believe Lord Harbaugh has the very volume of Shakespeare's sonnets I was telling you about."

She was not interested in listening to a tirade from him. Nor would she leave the ballroom before she'd spoken more than a few words with Lady Emily, Maddie determined. "I'm sorry, my lord," she said, "but I'm afraid I am unable to go with you."

"Dashed pretty words, those sonnets," Fullerton said companionably, still completely unaware of the undercurrent running between his companions. "I think I like the one about the 'ever-fixed mark.' Do you know that one?"

"No," Maddie and Christian said in unison, neither one of them breaking eye contact with the other.

Undeterred, Fullerton went on. "You should look it up. It's good reading when you want a bit of culture. I'd prefer a nice long gallop myself, but you have to stable the horses sometimes, eh?"

"I believe you really must come with me, Lady Madeline," Monteith said through clenched teeth. "There is a message from your cousins that I need to convey."

"I do not see why they don't just tell me themselves," retorted Maddie.

"They have gone home," her nemesis said with a frown.

A flash of alarm gripped Maddie. "Cecily is all right, is she not?"

With a hint of remorse, Christian nodded. "Of course! I apologize for alarming you. Your cousin is well. Simply fatigued. And you know how protective Winterson has become. He whisked her away at the first hint of a yawn."

Despite her annoyance, Maddie couldn't resist smiling. "It drives her to distraction, his hovering."

Christian smiled back at her, and Maddie felt a flutter deep in her belly. "I imagine I'd be the same way. If I had a wife. With a child on the way."

The air between them grew charged and a thread of attraction seemed to draw them closer.

"Would you?" Maddie asked, feeling his gaze drop to her mouth.

The moment was interrupted when Fullerton spoke up. "Well, Gresham, if you're going to show Lady Madeline the Shakespeare, I'm going to toddle off to the card room. My lady, it was a pleasure."

Maddie struggled to pull her attention back to her escort. "What? Oh, yes, thank you, Mr. Fullerton, for the dance. I hope that you will . . ."

Then as if waking from a dream, she realized what was happening. "Wait, Mr. Fullerton, you mustn't . . ." But he was already gone.

And Christian now had a firm grasp on her arm. She could protest but it would draw unwanted attention to them. In addition, she reflected, it was probably best to have this discussion now rather than later. If she meant to make a concerted effort to infiltrate Lady Emily's social circle, then she would need to work in future without Christian's interference.

Silently, she allowed him to lead her down the dark-paneled hallway. As if he'd been here before, he unerringly found the library door, and stepping aside, ushered Maddie in, firmly locking the door behind them.

For a moment, Maddie gazed appreciatively at the floor-to-ceiling shelves filled with books. She had little doubt that the book of Shakespeare's sonnets they'd been discussing could be located on one of them. At least that part of the story to Fullerton hadn't been a lie.

"If you are finished drooling over Harbaugh's library," Christian said with a hint of amusement, "I should like to discuss your plan now."

She watched as he stalked forward, resting a hip against Harbaugh's desk, watching her with the lazy intensity of a lion sizing up his prey. Again she thought of jungle cats. Bad, Maddie.

"I do not know what business it is of yours," she said pertly. "I have decided to investigate the murder of Mr. Tinker and I plan to do so by getting closer to Lady Emily Fielding. There is no danger involved. It's hardly the same thing as wandering the streets of Seven Dials, after all."

"If you honestly believe that then you are more foolish than I imagined," Christian said, his eyes narrow with temper. "Did you not pay any attention to what happened to your cousins these past few weeks? They have been exposed to all manner of danger, and in the finest houses in London no less."

"Oh, do not be overly dramatic." Maddie put her

hands on her hips. "They were in the presence of mad-men. This person is hardly that. In fact, I suspect he's someone perfectly ordinary."

"And an ordinary person might kill someone just as effectively as a madman." He scowled. "I have seen both do so in the war. In fact, ordinary men kill more frequently than madmen, as there are more of them."

"This is beside the point," Maddie said with frustra-tion. "Whatever the danger or threat, it does not matter to me. I cannot allow my brother to be accused of a murder he didn't commit."

"No one has accused him of anything, Maddie," he said, with equal frustration. "He is one of several men we are looking at, true, but there is no reason for you to ride to his rescue just yet."

"It's only a matter of time," she retorted, "and you know it. Linton was there at Mrs. Bailey's with Mr. Tin-ker, and his disappearance that night—for all that it was innocent enough—cast the shadow of blame over him."

Christian thrust his hands into his hair, stopping just short of yanking on it in frustration. "Maddie, I am in-vestigating this for the Home Office. Do you not think I would tell you if there was a chance that Linton was in imminent danger of being arrested for this crime?"

"I don't know that you would do so," Maddie said honestly. "I know that your loyalty is to the Home Of-fice and not to me or my brother. And I don't blame you for it. Which is why I must discover for myself who killed Tinker. If you would just let me do so in peace, then we could both get on with it and one of us would learn the truth of the matter. As it is, you are just wast-ing my time by prosing on at me about my reputation, which is worth nothing if I cannot save my brother."

"Wasting your time?" Christian demanded. "Woman, are you mad? I am trying to keep you from losing your reputation before you make yourself completely un-marriageable. Do you wish to be tied to someone like Fullerton for the rest of your life?"

"I don't wish to be tied to anyone," she said hotly. "In fact, I don't wish to marry anyone at all."

"Do you not?" Christian asked, his eyes hot with anger. "No one at all?"

Maddie took a step back from the ferocity of his gaze.

"Then you'll miss out on this," he said with a growl, stepping closer to her, wrapping his arms around her, and kissing her.

Hard.

He hadn't intended to kiss her at all, but once he felt her soft lips under his and her arms snaked around his neck, he was a lost man.

There was no room in his mind for rational thought, only sensation, as he opened his mouth over hers and, instead of resisting, Maddie gave a little sigh and welcomed him in. Christian had wanted to do this all evening. As soon as he saw her crossing the ballroom, head held high, in this gown that left so little to the imagination. Now that he held her pressed firmly against him, there was no need for imagination, as he reveled in the feel of her every curve molded against him. They fit together like a lock and a key. And nobody was going to be turning her key but him.

Nobody.

With a groan, he slid his tongue against hers, tempting, teasing, thrusting into the sweet hotness of her mouth. His hands were everywhere, on her arms, her back, her backside. Anywhere that he could find purchase as he tried desperately to keep them both from falling under the storm of sensation.

Sliding one hand over her back, which had been left partially bare by the daring cerulean-blue gown, he slipped his other hand over the curve of her belly and up to cup her breasts, which pebbled beneath his touch like ripe berries. She gasped as he palmed, gently plucked at them, all the while continuing to ravish her mouth. He felt a surge of triumph mixed with pleasure as she rocked her pelvis against his arousal.

Perched as he was against the desk, Christian reversed their positions, boosting her up onto the thankfully uncluttered surface. With the added support, he did what he'd been longing to do all evening, and slipped the sleeves of the gown down over her shoulders, revealing her generous breasts to his gaze. Unable to stop himself, he dipped down to take first one, then the other, in his mouth. Maddie's gasps of pleasure, combined with the feeling of her hands in his hair, sent his pulse racing even faster.

"Easy," he soothed, "I'll make you feel better, sweet Maddie."

"Please," she gasped against his mouth as he leaned up to kiss her, sliding his hand down her leg to gather up the bottom of her skirts and petticoats. Slipping under her garments, he caressed her bare leg until he reached a pair of the sweetest little beribboned drawers he'd ever seen.

"Oh, Madeline," he whispered, looking down at them, "I very much like these."

But she was in no mood for compliments upon her wardrobe. And Christian didn't blame her. Kissing her again, he reached up and found the slit in the pantalets and touched her softly at the apex of her thighs. She was wet and hot and he longed with every fiber of his being to bury himself inside her. But he was damned if he'd deflower her in the Harbaughs' library. For now it was enough to feel her pant of need against his mouth, and the tightness of her soft body against first one finger then another.

Maddie hadn't expected any of this tonight, but as she moved against Christian's thrusting fingers, she couldn't think of expectations, only need. Sharp hunger that drove her to mindless passion as she welcomed his oh-so-gifted touch. Everything—his scent, his feel, his touch—everything about him fired her need.

"More," she gasped against him, knowing that she wouldn't be satisfied until he was joined with her in the most primal way. "Please, Christian."

"Shh," he whispered, touching the center of her arousal with his thumb, sending a jolt of sensation through her. Unable to control herself, she let the shudders of pleasure course through her, until with a sharp cry, she let the maelstrom consume her and she found release.

Panting, slowly coming back to herself, Maddie felt Christian carefully pull her bodice back up to cover her bosom. Still clinging to him, she felt him kiss her gently on the top of her head, and reversing their positions again, gather her up in his arms.

"We should not have done that," she said, resting her forehead against his shoulder.

"I disagree," Christian said. "Wholeheartedly."

Though she knew it would be better if she pulled away from him, she could not help but enjoy the feel of his arms around her. Even so, she pulled back a little so that she could look into his gaze. If there were any hint of triumph she'd have no choice but to disentangle herself. But she saw only warmth and affection in his blue eyes.

"Well, of course you say that," she said crossly, "you have nothing to be ashamed of."

He frowned. "Nor have you, Maddie. And if you think that what we just did was done only by you then you obviously missed out on the part where I put my hand up your skirt."

That brought her to the blush. "Don't be absurd. It's just that you're a man so you can do . . ."—she made a vague gesture with her hand—"that without any feelings of guilt. Whereas as a lady I am forbidden from such things while I am unmarried. I suppose now I'm just as fast as Lady Emily. I hadn't thought to actually begin behaving like her quite so soon. I had hoped to work up to it."

"You are absurd," he said with a shake of his head. "Do you know that? Utterly absurd. I don't wish for anyone to know we've been closeted in here for this long, much less what we've been doing. As far as I'm concerned, no one needs to know about this but us."

"Oh," she said, feeling her face flush in mortification. She hadn't thought that he'd consider her beneath his touch, but she was still an Ugly Duckling after all. And he was a much-sought-after earl. He could doubtless have his pick of ladies. She had thought she'd vanquished her foolish feelings of insecurity long ago, but the encounter with Christian had lowered her defenses in a way she'd never experienced before. "I see."

Pulling back from him, she stood and shook out her skirts. Turning away, she made sure that her bodice was straight, and patted her hair into place in preparation to leave.

"No, you don't see," Christian said, pushing off the desk. She felt his hands on her shoulders as he turned her to face him. "Maddie, look at me."

When she kept her eyes downcast, he gave her a little shake. "Look at me."

Knowing that if she refused it would just draw the thing out, she relented, infusing her glare with as much defiance as she was able to muster.

"I'm not ashamed, angel," he said. "Not one bit. Do you really think I'd hide my association with you? The only reason I'll keep this a secret is because it's nobody's business but ours. And to preserve your reputation, for all that you seem determined to ruin it. Not because I'm ashamed of you."

"Oh." She exhaled. "I'm sorry, I—"

"Don't apologize," he said, kissing her on the end of the nose. "I'm just surprised. I would have expected you—the most courageous lady I know—to draw my cork if I ever behaved so ungallantly, not go slinking off into the ballroom alone."

"Well," she said, flushing again at the compliment. "I suppose I was feeling a bit . . ."

"Vulnerable?" he asked, his eyes knowing.

"Trust me," he continued, pulling her back into the circle of his arms, "you have nothing to be ashamed of. I have little doubt that most of the men in that ballroom would be happy to have you grace their arm for the foreseeable future. And if you wish it, I'll parade you around the Harbaughs' ballroom myself, growling like a mad dog at any man who dares more than a glance."

"You're absurd," she said with a giggle.

He answered with a growl.

They rested in companionable silence for a moment before she continued. "Do you think that I might have turned some heads tonight? I mean enough that Lady Emily might welcome me into her set?"

She felt Christian sigh against her. "What?" she asked.

"I wish you would abandon your plans," he said, stepping back from her, thrusting his hands into his already disheveled hair. "I am quite sure your brother would not approve, and I very much suspect that you might end up ruined as a result of this scheme—more so than your attire tonight has done."

"I have to do something," she told him. "If not for Linton then for Mr. Tinker's family."

"No one has called him a murderer," he said in a harassed tone. "All that has happened is that he has been questioned about the murder."

"What do you mean questioned?" she demanded. "I hadn't heard that."

"I didn't want to alarm you," he said, his expression grim. "And neither did your brother. He wants you to stay out of the matter. And I do, too." He had no notion of whether Linton wished her to stay out of the matter or not, but he was comfortable speaking for him nevertheless.

"Well, you'll both need to learn to live with disappointment," she said, patting her hair into place. "For I mean to get close to Lady Emily and to figure out which of her set is responsible for Mr. Tinker's death."

Christian could hardly inform her that her plan was unsuitable not only because it endangered her reputation, but primarily because Lady Emily was Linton's mistress. God knew Linton didn't deserve it, but Christian was reluctant to strip away the last vestige of Maddie's affection for her brother by revealing that he was sleeping with his best friend's widow. Besides, despite her fears of being thought as fast as Lady Emily, he suspected the suggestion of stigma from a friendship with the other woman would erase those fears entirely. Any suggestion that, as a lady, she should avoid certain people tended to push Maddie right toward the forbidden.

"If you are so hell-bent on this course of action," he said, crossing his arms across his chest, "then let me come with you."

"No, I . . ." She paused as if just now hearing him. "What do you mean come with me?"

"I will be your partner in crime," he said simply. "When you are invited to a less than respectable party or to an outing with your new friends, you'll take me with you. I'll come along and be your watchdog."

And perhaps he might be able to protect her from the sort of situation that had led his twin to her death. Clarissa hadn't been nearly the force of nature that Maddie was proving to be, but he didn't want to test the limits of her strength by allowing her to move in such a crowd alone.

"Why would you do that?" Maddie asked, her blue eyes narrow with suspicion.

"Because I want to know who killed Tinker as well," he said simply. She didn't need to know about his sister and her own brush with a very fast crowd. All she needed to know was that he did not intend to allow Maddie to risk her own life as Clarissa had done. "And I know that Winterson and Deveril, not to mention your brother, would wish for you to have some sort of protection if you're going to jump headlong into this business."

She was silent as she thought over his offer.

Finally, curiosity got the better of him.

"Well? Do we have a deal?" he asked, already thinking of ways to persuade her if she refused.

"Yes."

Christian felt her relax against him as she gave him her answer. As if the decision had left her exhausted.

Rather than pumping his fist in the air, he gave her a quick hug.

There would be time enough for celebration when they were cleared of this infernal tangle.

Nine

"Lord Gresham! Might I have a word?"

Hyde Park was still fairly deserted because of the early hour. Christian, who was walking his gelding, Galahad, after a good gallop, looked up to see the Earl of Essex approaching him from atop his own mount, a glossy chestnut with more than a little spirit.

Lord Essex himself was rather like an older version of Viscount Linton. His blond hair was liberally threaded with gray now, and despite his age, he obviously had kept in good enough shape to prevent the sort of physical decline that beset so many older men.

It was difficult to see him and not think of the tale Maddie had told him of Lord Essex's behavior during her childhood. There was an intensity about the man that he imagined could be unsettling for a child. Especially if it was combined with intoxication.

At the reminder of Maddie, Christian felt a stab of guilt at facing her father. He'd already decided last night that he would marry her. He had wanted, however, to take things slowly. He knew how stubborn Maddie could be and he didn't think that having her father demand the match would be the best way of convincing her of its necessity. If anything, she might defy him merely on principle.

Squaring his shoulders, he nodded to the older man. "Lord Essex," he said, "I am at your disposal."

Not liking the disparity in their positions—Christian on the ground, Lord Essex atop his horse—Christian gave Galahad one last pat on the neck and remounted. He indicated with a tilt of his head that they would do well to remove themselves from the small crowd gathering in Rotten Row.

With an answering nod, Lord Essex agreed, and they made their way on horseback to a spot far enough away from the others that they might talk undisturbed.

"It has come to my understanding that you are investigating the murder of a Mr. Tinker," Lord Essex said without preamble. "And that my son is your primary focus. Is this correct?"

Christian felt a stab of relief at learning Lord Essex wished to talk about his son rather than his daughter. On the matter of Viscount Linton, at least, he could reassure the older man.

"It is true that I am looking into the matter for the Home Office," he said. "Though I would not say that Linton is my only focus."

Judging from his expression, this did not reassure Lord Essex. "What has the Home Office to do with a murder over gambling debts? Surely the government has more to do than pry into matters that might more easily be handled by the runners."

"I'm afraid I am not at liberty to disclose the reasons for the government's interest in the matter." Christian appreciated that the earl was curious, but especially given his relationship with Lord Linton, he could not reveal the details of Tinker's connection with the Citizen's Liberation Society. "Suffice it to say that there is good reason."

Lord Essex flushed. "Why the devil not? I am a member of the Lords and have the ear of the prime minister. I demand that you tell me what this is about. What has my son gotten himself involved in?"

"I appreciate your concern, my lord," Christian said firmly. "And for what it's worth, I believe that your son is likely innocent of Tinker's murder. Though I do know that he owed the dead man a considerable amount of money, the murder, was likely unrelated to that."

"But what can I do?" Lord Essex demanded, his color rising. "It is all well and good for you to say you think him innocent, but we both know that innocence does not always ensure freedom from prosecution." Christian could all but feel the frustration emanating from the man. "He is my son, my heir. I cannot simply stand back and allow him to be pursued like a common thief."

The chestnut, perhaps sensing his rider's agitation, grew restive and tossed his head. Essex, however, kept his hand firm and brought the animal under control.

"Then, with all due respect," Christian said, "perhaps you should have ensured that he did not run like one."

A flare of anger lit Lord Essex's eyes, but just as soon as it was gone, it was replaced by a naked bleakness that was difficult for Christian to witness.

"I know, damn it," he said, passing a weary hand over his face, his shoulders drooping. "If I could have done so I'd have locked the boy in his room. But he's an adult now and refuses to be led about by the nose. Or so he says."

Looking up at Christian, he continued, "I know I've not been the best example for the lad to follow. There was a time when he and Madeline were children that I behaved very badly, indeed. But I thought that I had convinced them that my behavior was not something to emulate but something to abhor." He shook his head. "Obviously I was wrong."

"And his departure from town?"

"That, I'm afraid," Lord Essex said, "was done without his consulting me. The damned fool should have spoken with me before he left at the very least. But he has been too much under the influence of that Fielding widow of late. I feel sure she is the one responsible for his absconding."

Thinking back to Lady Emily's proprietary air the other morning, Christian was convinced that Lord Essex was right on that score.

"At this point," he said, "it is suspicious, but not beyond the pale. We are investigating other possible connections to Tinker, so for the time being Lord Linton's absence from town is not as dire as it might be.

"I would, however," he continued, "suggest that you confide in your brother-in-law Lord Shelby, and perhaps the Duke of Winterson, and ask them to intervene with the Home Office on your son's behalf."

Essex frowned. "I thought you said that you were not at liberty to say what the Home Office's interest was in Tinker's death."

"I did," Christian said calmly, "but requesting their influence does not make it necessary for you to know that. All you need is to have them—and perhaps try yourself to—approach the Home Secretary and request that he intercede on your behalf."

Christian wasn't all that comfortable with how political influence impacted the way that justice was meted out by the government. But it was something that was done with great frequency at Whitehall, and he knew that removing the cloud of suspicion from Linton might encourage the man to return to London. Which would make it possible to keep a better watch on him.

"Why are you telling me this?" Essex asked suspiciously. "What interest do you have in seeing my son cleared?"

Christian shrugged. "I can claim friendship with your daughter."

At the mention of Maddie, Lord Essex's complexion darkened. "She is becoming quite a handful," he said. "She has always been headstrong, but she has become more so in the past few months.

"I wish to thank you," Lord Essex continued grudgingly, "for seeing that she returned home safely that night from Mrs. Bailey's." He mopped his brow with a pristine white handkerchief. "I hold Linton to blame for that occurrence, of course." He smiled conspiratorily. "We men must ensure that the ladies in our lives remain safe, even it means doing so without their consent. They can hardly be expected to make the most rational of decisions, can they?"

Christian thought about what Maddie's reaction to her father's statement might be, and decided it was probably better for the older man that she wasn't there. If Lord Essex didn't realize that his daughter, while rash at times, was quite a rational person, then he didn't think disabusing him of his misunderstanding would do much good at this point. And, for all that he understood Maddie's hypothetical anger, Christian himself was as guilty as Lord Essex of wanting to protect her from her own impulsive nature.

"I see," he said. He certainly wasn't going to say something that might get back to Maddie and put him in her black books. Especially since she'd agreed last evening to allow him to protect her as she went about her mad plan to prove Linton's innocence.

"I thank you for your suggestions regarding Linton," Lord Essex said. "I hope that if anything changes about my son's status, you will let me know."

Relieved that he was being dismissed, Christian nodded. "So long as I am free to do so."

"I suppose that's the most I can ask," Essex said, touching his hat in farewell.

But before he turned his horse away, he raised a gloved hand. "When you are next in public with my daughter, you might do a better job at concealing your interest in her." Christian felt his face redden. "We wouldn't want there to be talk about the two of you. Linton has created enough scandal for the family at this point."

With those parting words, Essex took himself off.

Christian stared after Maddie's father in astonishment. So much for thinking he was completely unaware of their connection.

He didn't deceive himself into thinking that her father's words had been anything less than a warning.

Guiding Galahad to the bridle path, he determined to heed it.

As much as possible.

Probably.

Damn it.

Maddie arrived at Felsham's Bookshop in midafternoon, having followed Lady Emily there in a hackney at a discreet distance from her house on Half Moon Street. She knew that Lady Emily was an avid reader of Minerva Press novels and had overheard her telling Amelia Snowe just the night before that she was desperate for the latest title that had just come out that month and would be purchasing it today. After waiting for the lady to exit her house for most of the afternoon, she'd been relieved when she finally spied her climbing into her carriage and departing at last.

If she'd had another destination in mind, Maddie would have extemporized, but she was grateful that her attempt to become friends with the other woman would take place somewhere that she felt at home.

Felsham's was not quite as fashionable as some of the other bookshops, mainly because it was situated in a less than fashionable part of town. It was also known—though Maddie wasn't supposed to be aware of it—for acquiring books of a scandalous nature published mostly on the Continent. She'd once overheard her brother discussing the fact with his cronies. The owner, John Felsham, didn't care who visited his shop so long as they had the money to pay for their purchases. And as a result he attracted a number of ladies who wished to purchase items without censure. Maddie herself had been a customer for years because of Felsham's eclectic selection but had never gotten up the nerve to buy the naughty books. She spent most of her money there on novels and philosophies.

The bell on the door jingled merrily as she stepped inside. In keeping with her new, faster persona, she'd worn another of her new gowns, a primrose walking dress with a deep green pelisse. It wasn't scandalous at all, but the way it hugged her every curve made her all too aware of the body beneath the clothes.

"Hello, Lady Madeline," Mr. Felsham greeted her from behind his counter. "I hadn't thought to see you again so soon."

She'd been in just last week to pick up a gift for Juliet's birthday—a book of Dante's poetry. "Good morning, Mr. Felsham." She scanned the room but didn't see Lady Emily or any of her hangers-on. "I was hoping to look through your collection of Madame D'Arblay's works again. No need to show me, I know the way."

And with that she wandered through the shop to the rear section where Felsham kept the novels. To her relief, she saw Lady Emily there, scanning the shelves where Maddie knew Felsham kept the Minerva Press novels.

"Lady Emily," she said, stepping forward, "what a lovely surprise. I did not know you were a customer of Felsham's."

The dark-haired beauty, who to Maddie's eye looked rather pale today, looked up warily. "Lady Madeline," she said, inclining her head, her dark eyes watchful. "I am perhaps not so famous for my intellect as you and your cousins are, but I do indeed know how to read."

To Maddie's disappointment, rather than engage her in conversation, the other woman turned back to her book. This won't do at all, Maddie thought in frustration. Trying again, she leaned over to see which of the three-volume sets the other woman had chosen. It was a particularly lurid gothic tale that Maddie had devoured in one sitting.

"I enjoyed that one," she said, feeling like an interfering busybody, but needing to keep the conversation going. "I particularly liked it when Melisande discovers that she is the long-lost daughter of the duke." Adopting a nonchalant air, she began her own perusal of the shelves.

From the corner of her eye, Maddie saw Lady Emily look up. "I've already read it twice," the widow admitted reluctantly. "It's one of my favorites."

Giving a mental huzzah, Maddie nodded. Trying to appear cool, and failing, she said eagerly, "I haven't read his other books. Have you? I think I might like *The Wayward Heart,* but it seems as if it might not be as good. It is difficult to compete with the secret daughter of a duke."

"I haven't, either," Lady Emily said, her countenance more animated now. "My sister says that it's good, though. There was one particular scene that she said made her sleep with the candles burning."

Abandoning the pretense that she was there to look at the books, Maddie turned to look at the other woman. "I wouldn't have expected you to be such a devotee of novel reading. Where do you find the time? I mean, your social activities alone must take up a great deal of your time."

"Simply because I attend a few parties I must necessarily be interested in nothing else?" Lady Emily asked, brow raised in gentle censure. "I do attend quite a few social functions, but that doesn't mean that I never have an evening where I stay home and do whatever I please. Your own brother, who is often at the social functions I attend, took a night to rest last night. Why shouldn't I?"

Maddie wondered if she knew that, far from taking an evening off, James had taken himself off altogether. "I didn't mean any insult, Lady Emily," she said sincerely, "I simply don't know how you manage it. It's all I can do to attend two or three social evenings a week and even then I find myself going a bit mad. I can't imagine having your social schedule and finding time to read, as well. It seems like a great deal of work."

"It can be," Lady Emily said, looking mollified, "but I grow restless if I spend too much time on my own. No matter how enjoyable I find a novel, I simply must get out among people. I am a social creature, I'm afraid. Fielding used to say—" Abruptly, she broke off.

Visibly reining herself in, she turned to the bookshelf, and pulled the three volumes of the novel down.

When she turned to Maddie again, her expression was composed, and perhaps lacking the enthusiasm it had when she'd pulled herself up short. Still, she clearly felt some interest in Maddie because she continued. "Perhaps you'd like to join a few friends and me at my house tomorrow night? It's not much, just a card party. We do play for high stakes so if you aren't interested, feel free to decline. I believe your brother has already been invited. Just ask him to bring you along."

Maddie frowned at the notion of James allowing her to tag along. It would have been an unlikely scenario even if he weren't out of town. Even so, she felt her heart quicken at the invitation. She had little doubt that some of the same men who had been in attendance at Mrs. Bailey's on the night of Tinker's death would be there.

"I'd like that," she said, trying not to sound too eager. It would not do to seem like a sycophant. "Though I don't think James will be able to attend. He was called away suddenly."

Lady Emily's eyes narrowed fractionally at the news. "Really? I was unaware of that. It isn't like Lord Linton to leave town without informing his friends."

The way that the other woman emphasized the word made Maddie wonder just what sort of friends Lady Emily and her brother were. Still, she could not let her brother's possible relationship with the widow affect her plans.

Remembering her promise to Christian to bring him along with her on any investigative excursions, she asked, "Might I bring another escort, perhaps?"

The other woman's eyes sharpened. "Really?" she asked. "Are you not a bit young for escorts?"

Maddie felt herself blush. Ignoring the implication that her escort would do more than accompany her to the entertainment, she said, "He's just an old friend of the family. And I shouldn't like to ruin your numbers by arriving as a lone female."

Lady Emily gave a brisk nod. "I don't worry too much about such things as numbers, but it would make things easier, I suppose. Bring your old family friend along, then."

When the other woman was gone, Maddie leaned her head against the bookshelf, heaving a sigh of relief. She'd been convinced that Lady Emily would see through her overture of friendship as soon as she opened her mouth, but she hadn't. And thankfully, she had been quite open to extending the invitation to her card party. Though she'd hoped for such an outcome, Maddie hadn't been sure she'd find success so quickly.

Remembering that she was supposed to attend a musicale at Juliet and Deveril's the next evening, she decided that a fabricated illness would be the most expedient means of explaining her absence to her mother. It would be difficult, but if she gave her maid the evening off, and slipped out after her parents left, she could manage it.

What would Christian say? she wondered. He was as concerned for her reputation as her own mother seemed to be, she thought with frustration, but she would simply have to explain to him why it was imperative that they attend this party. Reputation or no reputation, she had to figure out who killed Mr. Tinker if Linton were ever to be free of the veil of suspicion.

And he *had* agreed to assist her in her investigations. If he balked then she'd simply have to remind him that he'd given her his word.

Hurrying out to her waiting carriage, Maddie made her way home and began planning her attire for the next evening.

The next evening found Christian waiting impatiently in an unmarked, closed carriage for Maddie to approach. For discretion's sake, he'd asked the coachman to wait in the mews behind Essex House, so that Maddie would not be seen from the square.

She'd sent round a note yesterday afternoon informing him that they'd be attending a card party at Lady Emily's house. And though he'd wanted to send back a note inquiring whether she was possessed of all her faculties, he had instead sent back a hastily scrawled assent. Maddie was strong-willed enough to attend with or without him, and knowing just who Lady Emily counted among her close personal friends, he would prefer to take her there himself. He knew that he was willing to do the right thing by her should he compromise her reputation. He couldn't say that same for the Duke of Endover, Lord Phillip Bynes or Lord Tretham. Not to mention Colonel Sebastian Grant, whom he knew from his days in the army and disliked. Strenuously.

Thus it was that he welcomed Lady Madeline, wearing yet another gown that set his teeth on edge—this time in a deep gold color that brought out the highlights in her hair and offered up her bosom like the main course at a banquet—into the dark carriage.

"You're looking . . ." He searched for the right word to describe the gown. "Fetching" sounded too wholesome. "Ravishing" was too . . . something else. Delectable? True, but entirely inappropriate. ". . . well," he finished lamely.

As if she had heard his mental discussion with

himself, Maddie gave a laugh. "I must admit that it does make me feel quite scandalous," she said. "It's as if the gown affects my whole personality. Which is silly, I suppose, since I am still the same old Maddie. But it does give one a certain—"

"Yes, rather," he broke in before she could finish the thought. He was having a hard enough time keeping his hands to himself. Hearing her describe how the silk felt against her skin would send him over the edge.

Changing the subject to a safer topic, he said, "What do you know about this party?"

"Very little," she admitted, not commenting on the shift in topic. "Lady Emily didn't tell me who would be in attendance. Just that it would be a group of friends. I don't think it would be at all surprising should we find her usual crowd there."

"The other entertainments offered tonight," he said, watching the way the moonlight illuminated her face, "don't seem to be of the sort that would draw attention from her friends. Aside from Juliet and Deveril's musicale, there's the theater."

"Yes," Maddie agreed. "Of course, those are the respectable entertainments you mention. Lord knows what sort of other vices are available throughout London."

Mind on the mission, Christian reminded himself, though all sorts of vices he'd like to engage in with Maddie raced through his mind. "Lord knows," he echoed, giving himself a mental shake.

"Do your cousins know about this plan of yours?" he asked, suddenly wondering if Cecily and Juliet had informed their husbands and whether he should expect a request for pistols at dawn sometime in the near future.

He wasn't sure how he knew it, given the dimness of the carriage as it rolled through the streets of London, but he sensed she was blushing. "They know," Maddie told him after a moment. "At least, Juliet and Cecily both know that I plan to prove that Linton was not involved in Tinker's stabbing. They do not know that you have agreed to help me."

Christian wasn't sure whether to feel relieved or disappointed.

"Why not?" he asked.

"I do not want to worry them," she said simply. "Plus I know that they would want to help, and I don't want them to risk their own reputations because of something my brother did. He is my brother, and my responsibility."

He didn't point out the unconventional nature of her declaration. In polite society it would be the other way around, with her brother claiming Maddie as his responsibility. It did her credit that she felt so protective of him, but he found himself once again feeling no small amount of anger on her behalf. She should not be burdened with this matter. It should be handled by her father, or both her parents.

But Maddie had always been unconventional, and a bit of a mother hen for those she loved. It was one of the qualities that made her so . . . he deliberately made a mental diversion around the word "lovable" and chose "appealing" instead.

"So," he said aloud, "I will not find myself flayed alive by either of them should something untoward happen." He wished he could say the same of their spouses, but thinking back to the circumstances of their own marriages, Christian felt somewhat safe from persecution on that score as well.

"Nothing is going to happen," she chided. "We are simply looking into the matter of Mr. Tinker's murder."

"Yes," he agreed ironically, "nothing ever happens in the pursuit of murderers. 'Tis the safest pastime imaginable."

"Do not be glib, my lord," she chided. "I am not a simpleton. I realize there are certain dangers. Besides, I thought that was the reason I brought you along. For protection."

"Yes, of course that's why you brought me along," he muttered. "For protection."

They fell into an uncomfortable silence. Despite his promise to her that he would come along on this visit tonight, he couldn't help but feel as if he were leading a lamb into the lion's den. He did not know how much Maddie knew about the sorts of things Lady Emily and her friends—Lord Linton included—got up to, but he had a feeling she'd be leaving tonight's entertainment with a bit less innocence than when she entered. Which made him angry on some level.

Thinking to hint that perhaps she didn't need to protect her brother all on her own, he said, "I spoke with your father yesterday."

He watched her mouth fall open in surprise and, too late, realized the implication of what he'd just said.

"You did?" she asked in a high-pitched voice. "Wh . . . why would you do that?"

"He spoke with me, rather," Christian said hastily, feeling like a thousand fools. "He approached me in the park to ask what might be done to help your brother."

"Oh." The relief she infused into that one word was hardly flattering, but Christian could not blame her. It was hardly every young lady's dream to be proposed to in an unmarked carriage on the way to a scandalous card party. Or, he rather thought it wasn't Maddie's. Even so, he felt a pang of disappointment at her response.

Trying to move the conversation forward, he said, "I think you might have a bit more faith in his determination to protect your brother's reputation. In fact, I think if you were to abandon your plan, you might trust in your father to see to it that your brother is cleared in the matter."

But that was obviously the wrong thing to say. "I'm afraid you don't know my father as well as I do, my lord," she said. He did not like being "my lorded" by her. "He disapproves of Linton's every action. I know he might wish to see to it that my brother escapes the ultimate punishment for his association with Mr. Tinker, but he believes that Linton needs a dose of reality. What better way to give it to him than to allow him to be frightened into toeing the straight-and-narrow path?"

Christian didn't bother arguing. He'd only spoken to Lord Essex about the matter once. Doubtless Maddie knew her parents better than he did. Even so, he believed her father was not so willing to let her brother linger under the cloud of suspicion as she thought.

"He does control the purse strings," Christian said. "That might prove to be incentive enough for your brother to curb his habits."

"It hasn't thus far," she said with a weariness that made him wish to gather her close and comfort her. She shouldn't burden herself with this. "Linton had a small inheritance from our grandmother and he went through it rather quickly. He needs his allowance to make ends meet. I am actually quite surprised he is not deeper in debt than he is already considering his fondness for gambling," she admitted, "but I suppose he wins more than he loses."

Their conversation was aborted when the carriage came to an abrupt stop.

A sharp rap on the door, doubtless the footman's attempt at discretion, alerted them that they'd reached their destination.

"Into the breach," he said to Maddie, who suddenly looked very young and very vulnerable in the half-light of the carriage. Resisting the urge to kiss her on the forehead, Christian instead offered her his hand, and as the door opened and the footman lowered the step, he handed her out.

Ten

Maddie was grateful for the strength of Christian's arm as he led her into Lady Emily's drawing room. She counted seven couples seated around the room, some at card tables, and others lounging on chairs and sofas and divans.

Their hostess floated forward, her gown a deep crimson confection that brought out the roses in her cheeks and looked extraordinarily well with her dark hair.

"Lady Madeline, Lord Gresham, what a pleasure to see you," Lady Emily said, offering her hands to Maddie, and a short curtsy, which Maddie couldn't help but see showed her bosom to perfection. A jolt of jealousy ran through her as she watched Christian notice. Of course it wasn't as if he could help it, given that there was hardly anywhere else for the poor man to look.

"When Lady Madeline told me she'd be bringing an escort, I had no notion it would be you, Lord Gresham," the widow said with a half smile. "I've been trying to persuade you to attend one of my little social evenings for months now but to no avail." She turned to Maddie. "You must tell me your secret, Lady Madeline."

How different this Lady Emily was from the one she'd encountered in Felsham's, Maddie thought. Gone was the intelligent lady who loved to read, and in her place was this flirtatious siren. She'd known the other woman had a reputation for seductiveness, of course, but she hadn't counted on her practicing her charms on Christian.

Hands off, she thought as she smiled in what she hoped was a mysterious manner. "I don't think there is any great trick. If you wish to know the truth, we are often at loggerheads with one another. Perhaps you are simply too agreeable."

Something like respect flashed in the other woman's eyes before she nodded. "Yes, I might have guessed Lord Gresham is keen on verbal and *other* sorts of sparring."

Before Maddie could retort, Christian broke in. "We don't wish to keep you from your guests, Lady Emily," he said briskly, holding Maddie's arm in a firm grip. She was annoyed at his interference, though she supposed it would not do to tear out her hostess's hair before the party even began.

With a slight nod, as if she were ceding the point to Christian, Lady Emily went on. "I think the card tables are all filled up, so you'd be best with one of the parlor games. I believe the group with Lords Tretham and Bynes is about to begin a round of secretary." She gestured to a table in the corner where a mixed group of ladies and gentlemen talked. Waving in the other direction, she went on. "And Endover's is playing charades. I'll leave the choice between the two up to you."

With a curtsy, she left them alone to make their own decision. Maddie suddenly felt naked as the other party-goers watched them without bothering to hide their interest. She supposed it was unusual for new people to add to their numbers.

"Let's get started," Christian said in a low tone beside her. She was glad suddenly that she hadn't tried to attend this party alone. Gratefully, she clung to his arm, drawing strength from his presence.

"Which do you prefer?" she asked, looking from Tretham's group to Endover's.

As an aspiring author—though it felt like ages since she'd concentrated on her novel—she was quite good at wordplay so she would feel confident enough with the group playing secretary, a parlor game that involved making up stories. And Tretham had been there on the night of Tinker's murder. The Duke of Endover, however, was known to be a bit of a gossip, so he might be more forthcoming with details about Tinker's interaction with the rest of the group.

"Secretary," Christian said firmly. "It is unlikely that there will be any time for conversation during a game of charades."

Maddie couldn't argue with that logic, though she hoped that there might be time to speak to all of the assembled group before the evening ended.

"Secretary it is," she said, allowing him to lead her to Lord Tretham's group.

"I must warn you," she added, looking up at him from beneath her lashes, "that I play to win."

Patting her hand, Christian smiled. "I wouldn't have expected anything less."

"Before we begin, I shall go over the rules," Lord Bynes said to the partygoers assembled round the table.

Christian had taken the seat to Madeline's left, and she was flanked on the other side by Lady Mary Stokely, who was as silly a woman as ever he'd met. Still, he was grateful that Tretham was seated on the opposite side of the table from her at least. He was far too handsome for Christian's comfort, and his flirtatious manner with Maddie had begun to grate on his nerves.

"I shall give you each a pencil and a piece of paper," Bynes said, handing the sheaf of pages to Mrs. Lawless on his right. "You are each to write your name at the top of the page, and then fold it in half and place it within the hat, like so." He demonstrated, and placed his paper within a battered top hat that sat in the middle of the table. If the fellow meant to explain every last detail of play it would take an hour for the instructions at least, Christian thought impatiently.

"Once everyone has placed his page into the hat, we will pass it round the circle and each person will choose a page. It goes without saying that if you choose your own, you should put it back and withdraw another."

When everyone had received a pencil and written his or her name on the sheet, they set about folding them, and placing them into the hat.

Christian marveled at the ability of some of his fellow guests to write at all, much less their full names, given the amount of brandy they had already consumed. But he supposed writing while intoxicated was a skill needed for signing gambling vowels, among other things. Folding his own page, he dropped it into the hat, hoping that he was the only one who could feel the excitement emanating from Maddie. She'd been the first to put her own page in and now tapped her foot impatiently as she waited for the game to advance.

"Now," Bynes said, obviously taking his duties as game master much more seriously than his companions, who were giggling and in general not paying the man much heed. When they did not seem willing to stop their side conversations at his announcement, he cleared his throat and rapped upon the table. "Ladies and gentlemen, please pay attention."

"We're not in school, old chap," Tretham complained, "you needn't behave like a bloody prefect."

Christian inwardly winced at the curse, but none of the ladies—Maddie included—seemed to be offended.

"I thought he preferred the role of naughty schoolboy," said Mrs. Lawless, giggling, "caning and all that." She was a blowsy widow whose gown left very little to the imagination. And she had clearly had far too much champagne.

Christian saw Maddie redden at the loose talk, and cursed himself for agreeing to bring her here. She had no business here with this lot.

"I say, Mrs. Lawless," he said in an easygoing tone his soldiers would have known preceded a set-down. Reining in his temper, however, he let that be his only comment. It would not do to alienate the very people they hoped to get information from.

He had assistance, however, from an unforeseen ally.

"Indeed," Tretham said to the widow with a raised brow. "We mustn't let Lady Madeline think that we're savages. Young unmarried lady and whatnot."

Not taking offense, Mrs. Lawless merely giggled again, reinforcing Christian's assessment of her sobriety. Or lack thereof.

"As I was saying," Bynes continued, his annoyance at the interruption making him grow peevish. "Everyone should take a paper from the hat, and write his opinion of the person whose name is listed at the top of the page."

He paused for dramatic effect.

"You may begin . . . now."

If Bynes were hoping for a fevered rush of hands to

draw out their pages, however, he was doomed to disappointment. The hat was passed from person to person in a very civilized manner, until everyone had withdrawn a name. And then silence reigned as they set about writing.

Christian opened his page and was annoyed to see Mrs. Suzanne Newsom's name. He only knew her slightly and that was as a social acquaintance and not a friend. He could hardly say what he really thought, that she was pretty enough but had more hair than wit. Nor could he mention her tendency to carry on rather indiscreet flirtations with younger men. Frowning, he used the pencil to scratch the words "excellent dancer" beneath her name. Which was true enough.

He folded his paper back again and tossed it into the hat, his arm brushing Maddie's as she put her own paper in.

The zing of sensation between them almost made him jerk his hand away. He stopped himself from hiding his reaction to the rest of the room, however. He had no problem with the other men in the room assuming there was something between them. Indeed it would be better for Maddie if they thought she was under his protection. Not as his mistress, which would put her beyond the pale, even with this set. But his response would hardly do that. He simply did not wish them to think she was without protection. Especially now that Linton was from town.

"Now," Bynes said, drawing a paper from the hat. "The first name I draw is . . ."—he unfolded the paper—"Mrs. Lawless."

"Well, Kitty," Tretham said in an undertone, "you'd best prepare yourself for some scandalous flattery."

"Oh, you." Mrs. Lawless swatted Tretham with her fan. "I am prepared, Lord Bynes. Do your worst."

"Mrs. Kitty Lawless." Bynes read the paper to himself, and only the pinkening of his ears betrayed that the words on the page might be thought risqué. "Mrs. Kitty Lawless," he repeated, "vigorous and insatiable."

The men, except for Christian, guffawed, while the ladies tittered. Christian's jaw tightened as he felt Maddie shift uncomfortably next to him. Glancing over at her, however, he saw that she was looking on with amusement. He hoped that only he noticed that her smile did not reach her eyes. It would not do for this lot to find enjoyment trying to make her progressively more uncomfortable.

"It is true," Mrs. Lawless said with a wink at Maddie, "I do enjoy vigorous exercise. And am often quite famished afterward."

"Yes, of course," Bynes said, playing into the new game of indirection, his eyes going from Maddie to Mrs. Lawless. "Exercise. That's what it means. And appetite. I vow I have seen Kitty eat quite a lot at one time. She has a most healthy appetite."

But this only increased the laughter.

"Why don't you continue, Bynes," Christian said mildly, though he wanted more than anything to knock the other man senseless with his fists. "I believe we all know of the lady's legendary appetites."

With a shrug that indicated he thought Christian a spoilsport, Bynes nevertheless assented. "Yes, yes, of course," he said. Turning to Mrs. Lawless, he asked, "Have you any notion of who would write such a fine compliment to you, Kitty?"

A hush fell over the table as Mrs. Lawless looked at each of the men sitting around the table. Even, to his annoyance, Christian. Then finally she stopped at Tretham. "I believe it was you, my lord," she said with a firm nod.

But Tretham shook his head. "Sorry, old thing," he said with a hint of regret. "It was not I."

"Oh, pooh," the redhead said with a moue of annoyance. Turning to Mr. Corley, she asked, "Was it you, Niles?"

"It was, indeed," Corley said with a smug grin, leaving little doubt as to how he knew of the woman's vigor and appetite. Bussing her on the mouth, he said, "How could you doubt me, m'dear?"

They went through two more rounds with Mrs. Newsom and Christian—his compliment coming from Bynes who called him a fine shot—which he was more than happy for the other men to know, considering.

"Now," Bynes said, withdrawing another paper from the hat. "Lady Madeline, we come to you. Your compliment is"—he looked with a hint of fear at Christian before he began—"that you are a . . ."—he cleared his throat—"Tasty morsel."

The words hung in the air, and Christian literally felt a red haze descend over his vision. Who the devil had had the temerity to write such a thing, right in front of him? He braced himself to rise, but stopped at the feel of Maddie's hand on his arm. The table had erupted in a series of catcalls and giggles, and in an undertone she said to him, "Please do not make a scene. I need to make friends here."

He prepared to defy her, but her tug on his arm stopped him.

"You promised," she reminded him, and for that reason alone, he kept his seat. If he hadn't he would have leaped over the table and throttled Tretham with his own bare hands. For he knew it had been Tretham who wrote it. No one else at the table had the bollocks to do it while he was sitting here next to Maddie. Looking across the table, he met the other man's eyes and

Tretham silently raised his glass. He would need to keep an eye out on that fellow. Christian knew that now. He wished he'd known it before he agreed to bring Maddie here tonight.

"Who do you think wrote that about you, Lady Madeline?" Bynes asked, once the furor had died down.

Christian watched as Maddie bit her lip and turned from gentleman to gentleman. Finally, her gaze stopped at Tretham. "Was it you, my lord?" she asked, eyes narrowed.

Christian was pleased to see that she didn't blush as she said it. Didn't reveal for one moment that the other man's words had unsettled her. Because he knew they had. For all her boldness, Maddie was not so bold as she pretended to be. And he'd felt the tremble in her hand when she touched him a moment ago. But she wouldn't reveal that to the room at large. Which made him incredibly proud.

Christian prepared himself to hear the other man accept his victory, but to his surprise, Tretham said, "It was not I, Lady Madeline. Though I heartily concur with the sentiment."

Christian shared Maddie's puzzlement. Why would Treth lie? he wondered. There could be little doubt that he had been the one to write it. No one else made sense. Though he supposed it *could* have been one of the others. Which meant he would have more than one man to speak to privately about inappropriate interest in Maddie. Mentally, he cracked his knuckles in anticipation.

"Was it you, Lord Bynes?" Maddie asked, breaking into Christian's revenge fantasy.

"Wh-what, me?" Bynes asked, his eyes revealing that he was all too aware of Christian's eye on him. "No! No! Good heavens, no!"

"You need not be so vociferous, darling," Mrs. Lawless said. "Save the poor girl's dignity."

"So, Lady Madeline has guessed twice and was incorrect. The real author may now demand a forfeit," Bynes intoned. "Will the author please reveal himself?"

There was a long silence as the people seated around the table looked from one person to the next to the next. But no one spoke up.

"If no one is willing to—" Bynes began.

"No, wait," Christian interrupted the other man. "I did it. I said Lady Madeline is a tasty morsel and I demand my forfeit."

"What?" Maddie gasped. "Whatever are you talking about?"

"It was I, and I demand a forfeit," Christian repeated. He wasn't sure which of the fellows had written the assessment of Maddie, but he wasn't about to let the man claim a forfeit of her.

"But you already said you wrote the one for Suzanne," Bynes protested. "That's against the . . ."

At the death glare Christian leveled upon him, the other man blanched and broke off his objection. "My mistake. Carry on."

"Well, what's it to be, old fellow?" Tretham asked with a smirk.

Christian would be damned if he'd admit to the table at large that he was lying through his teeth, but this was Maddie he fought for. And he would not allow another man to paw at her while she was under his watch.

Turning to where she sat, astonished, Christian said, "I demand a kiss as my forfeit."

Maddie stared at Christian as he sat beside her, his eyes demanding that she go along with his ploy.

When she'd decided to come to this party tonight she'd known, of course, that her very presence here would put her reputation in peril. There was no mistaking the way that the matrons of the *ton* subtly averted their eyes when Lady Emily passed by them. As if her scandalous reputation was a contagion they might catch by gazing upon her.

Even so, she hadn't counted on behaving in such a scandalous fashion herself. And certainly not with Christian. Or rather, not openly before an audience with Christian. Yes, she'd already kissed him, but doing so in this decidedly unprivate setting would set them on a course she had little doubt would end in matrimony. Was she willing to make such a sacrifice on Linton's behalf?

The very thought of her brother and what it might mean should Mr. Tinker's death be laid at his door sent a shiver of fear through her. Of course she was willing to make that sacrifice. But she hadn't quite realized his freedom would come at the sacrifice of hers.

Still, she rationalized, the kiss would be no more scandalous than one taken beneath the mistletoe at Christmas. Christian would hardly subject her to anything terribly naughty in front of their present company. He was a gentleman, after all.

Placing her faith in her partner in crime, then, she squared her shoulders.

"Very well," she said to Christian, not daring to meet his eyes. "You may take your forfeit."

Offering her cheek to him, she was unsurprised when she felt his gloved hand upon her cheek as he turned her head and set his lips firmly against hers. She wasn't sure what made her do it, but at the feel of his mouth on hers, she opened her lips every so slightly and dared him to take the kiss deeper.

She felt his hands slide down her shoulders to grip her upper arms, and with a small groan he took her lower lip between his teeth then took full possession of her mouth.

Maddie felt her knees tremble as she clung to him, opening her mouth wider to allow him access. She met him stroke for stroke as he licked into her mouth, the heat of it sending thrills of sensation from her mouth, to her belly, and lower still.

When Christian lifted his head, both of them breathing heavily, she almost protested but the applause from their onlookers reminded her that they were not alone. For those few moments she had forgotten where they were and why they were there. She'd forgotten everything but the feel of his mouth on hers and the warmth of being held in his arms.

Despite her determination to be sophisticated about the matter, she felt herself blushing. Taking her seat once more, she was pleased to feel Christian's strong grip on her hand beneath the table. It might be craven of her, but she was glad for his support when she saw the speculation in the eyes of the other men.

"A poor showing," Tretham said with a shake of his head. "I could do so much better than that, old fellow." Maddie wasn't sure if he meant the words, or if he intended to rouse Christian's temper. She definitely knew that there was no way on earth she'd ever wish to engage in that sort of activity with Tretham. The very idea made her feel ill.

"Don't even think of it," she heard Christian warn the other man with a slight growl, which surprised and warmed her. "The lady is spoken for."

The public declaration turned Maddie's head in surprise. She'd known he wanted to protect her from the interest of the other men, but she hadn't expected him to be so bold. She found him gazing back at her, his eyes challenging her to correct him. Unable to protest, she turned away, feeling her heart beat faster.

"So that's the way it is, is it?" Tretham asked silkily, his eyes narrowed. "I might have known you'd pick the sweetest bloom for yourself, Gresham. You always did have excellent taste."

"See that you remember it, Tretham," Christian responded, his tone biting. Maddie had little doubt that if the other man did forget he would be more than happy to jog his memory.

Obviously made uncomfortable by the undercurrents of competition between the two men, Bynes cleared his throat. "If you are finished paying your forfeit, Lady Madeline," he said with a gesture to the stack of folded pages before him, "we shall continue with the game."

"By all means, Lord Bynes," Maddie said, trying to adopt a bored air despite her agitation. "Continue on with your recital."

With a nod of thanks, Bynes pulled the next folded sheet of paper from the stack. "Aha! Lord Tretham," he said with a touch of enthusiasm. Doubtless the man thought that Tretham's mere name was scandal laden and would lead to diversion, Maddie thought.

But Bynes's enthusiasm was quickly replaced with alarm. "Oh," he said, his Adam's apple bobbing up and down in agitation. "Oh, dear."

"What the devil is it, Bynes?" Tretham snapped. Even he seemed to know that if Bynes were unsettled then it must be something serious, indeed. Snatching the page from his friend's hand, Tretham read whatever was on the page, and Maddie saw him turn pale before he threw the page down upon the table.

"I know this is your idea of a joke, Kitty," he said with a curl of his lip, "but it's not funny."

Puzzled, Mrs. Lawless frowned. "I didn't have your name, Treth."

And one by one, the players denied having drawn Tretham's name.

Curious to know what could have so unsettled Lord Tretham, Maddie reached for the paper.

Her blood chilled as she read the words scrawled beneath Lord Tretham's neatly penned name.

"Murderer."

Wordlessly she handed the page to Christian. His expression grew speculative.

"It would seem, Treth," he said with deceptive calm, "that someone thinks you're a murderer. Would you care to defend yourself?"

Tretham, whom Maddie had never seen in anything other than urbane calm, thrust a shaking hand through his carefully arranged curls. "I bloody shouldn't need to defend myself, Gresham," he said with a defensive tone. "Though I suppose if it will help, I am not a murderer. I don't even know whom I'm supposed to have murdered."

"Of course you aren't a murderer," crooned Mrs. Lawless, "no one could believe such a thing."

"Obviously someone thinks it, Kitty, or they wouldn't have written it," Bynes said reasonably, not meeting Tretham's glare. "Would the person who wrote this please confess so that we can hash this out?"

But no one at the table seemed willing to admit to the accusation.

"By process of elimination, then," Tretham said with a frown. He took up the stack of pages that hadn't been opened yet.

But when they'd gone through all the pages, each was accounted for and matched back to its author—even the one about Maddie, which Christian was interested to note had come from Tretham. Any remorse he might have felt over taking someone else's forfeit was gone. Especially in light of the accusation against the man.

There was only one left over and it was the paper with Tretham's name at the top and the word "murderer" underneath.

"Whoever did this simply filled out two," Christian said with a glance round the table. "It was quite brilliant, really."

"I'm glad you think so, Gresham." Tretham had gotten past the astonishment at being so accused and had become angry. "I have little compunction announcing to the table at large that if I find out it was a man who did this, I will call him out."

"And if it was a lady?" Maddie couldn't help but ask. She had always been a bit diffident when it came to Tretham, what with his reputation. Despite his friendship with her brother, his quick temper unsettled her. But tonight she found him downright disturbing.

Her question must have brought him to his senses, however, for he collected himself and shrugged. "I doubt a woman would dare such a thing."

Relieved by Tretham's return to composure, Maddie turned to Christian and asked the question that had been hanging over the group ever since the offending note had been read aloud. "Why? Why would someone carry out their accusation in so public a manner?"

"Because he wants everyone to know what he suspects is true," Mrs. Frawley, a pretty matron who had been quiet for most of the evening, said softly. "It's the only explanation," she said to Tretham's questioning gaze. "Whoever did this is someone who doesn't have any way of accusing Treth to his face, so he has gone about it in the only way he knows how. Through subterfuge and indirection."

"You seem to know a great deal about it, Anita," Tretham said with a frown. "I hope this doesn't mean that you're the culprit."

But Mrs. Frawley shrugged her scantily clad shoulders. "It's not I, Tretham. I simply know what it's like to feel hemmed in by the constraints of society."

Maddie liked Mrs. Frawley the better for her honest admission. But one question still puzzled her. "Does this person mean to accuse you of Mr. Tinker's murder, Lord Tretham?" she asked. "I thought you were at the gaming table the entire evening when he was killed. Indeed, you were one of the only people at Mrs. Bailey's who most assuredly could not have killed the man."

"Why accuse him, then?" Bynes asked, puzzled.

"Because whoever did this wishes to divert attention away from himself," Christian said. "It's quite simple, really."

"Do you care to enlighten us, my lord?" Maddie asked him with exasperation.

"Well, the accuser either knows and cares for the person who is most at risk for being accused," he said, looking at Maddie in a way that made her spine tingle. "Or," he said, looking round the table, "he is the killer himself."

Eleven

*A*fter the accusation against Tretham, the party seemed to lose some of its vigor, and before long Maddie found herself in a closed carriage, alone, on her way back to Essex House.

She would have preferred to make the return trip with Christian so that they could compare notes from their evening's escapade, but he'd insisted that it was bad enough for him to accompany her to Lady Emily's, much less ride in a closed carriage at night with her. Alone. She supposed he was right, though she suspected that as soon as her presence at the party was learned, the gossips would not praise her for her restraint in riding home alone.

She'd been unsure what to expect from the evening at Lady Emily's house. The woman's reputation made it sound as if she would have a parade of nude footmen serving refreshments and an orgy every hour on the hour. In fact, though it had been a bit scandalous when the gentlemen took their forfeits, the party itself had been rather tame. It reminded Maddie of how disappointed she'd been when as a child she had insisted upon watching one of her parents' parties from the upper balcony of the ballroom, and though the ladies' dresses were pretty enough, it had seemed not unlike any other party. So far as she could tell, Lady Emily and her set were not so very different from any other group of friends.

Thinking back through the events of the night, she wondered for the hundredth time who had written the note beneath Tretham's name. He had clearly been rattled by it, despite his protestations that it was foolishness. It had to have been someone seated at the table, participating in the game. Unfortunately, Maddie had been concentrating too much on her own description of Mr. Frawley to pay much attention to what the others seemed to be writing. It had occurred to her that they might have everyone write something, and then compare the handwriting, but the partygoers had clearly not been interested in conducting any kind of serious investigation. Tretham had been upset by it, of course, but he had recovered as soon as Mrs. Frawley set about soothing his ruffled feathers.

Come to think of it, Maddie thought, remembering how Mrs. Frawley had run her finger down Tretham's arm in a terribly suggestive fashion, perhaps she did understand why the parties Lady Emily held were considered so scandalous. Especially since that lady's husband had been sitting a mere foot away.

Their hostess herself, once informed of the matter, had been the most upset by the accusation against Tretham. Though she hadn't moved to touch that gentleman, or to offer him more than a simple apology that he'd suffered such an indignity in her home, something Maddie could not name had passed between them. Some undercurrent of emotion that she was unable to understand. It had been far more complex than the interaction between Tretham and Mrs. Frawley. That had been simple lust, she had surmised. But the look Tretham had given Lady Emily had been almost one of apology. Though why he should apologize for something he had nothing to do with, Maddie could not say.

To be truthful, the various threads of conversation, the undercurrents of emotion, and her own awareness of Christian sitting beside her had made the whole evening an exhausting one. Closing her eyes, she leaned her head back against the squabs of the carriage, and tried to clear her mind of the noisy thoughts that swirled around there.

As soon as her lids closed, however, she found herself reliving that moment when Christian's lips had touched hers. What did it mean that the one man she found fascinating was the same man whose high-handedness maddened her? Shaking her head, she tried once again to clear her mind. This time she was interrupted by the carriage stopping abruptly. So abruptly that she nearly found herself tumbling to the carriage floor.

Thinking that there must be some sort of obstruction in the road, Maddie peered out the window into the darkened street.

"Here now!" she heard the coachman shout, and a shiver ran through her. Checking the side compartment, she was relieved to see that Christian, like her father, was in the habit of keeping a pistol in the carriage. Even if it wasn't loaded, she thought, removing the gun from its hiding place, at least it might frighten off whoever had called a halt to the carriage's progress. A gun in the hand of a lady had a way of sending even the bravest fellow into a lather of panic.

But when the carriage door opened, it was only the coachman she saw.

"What's amiss, Bolton?" she asked, lowering the gun with relief.

The taciturn Mr. Bolton said only, "Young feller said to give ye this." Thrusting a carefully folded note toward her, the man waited for her to take it, then made to shut the door. Only the way was blocked, as Christian climbed past him into the interior of the carriage.

"What on earth are you doing?" she demanded as the carriage was once more under way. "I thought it was too scandalous for us to be alone in a closed carriage."

"It would be even more scandalous if you were to be killed by ruffians while riding in my closed carriage at night," he retorted. "What's in the note?"

"I don't know yet," Maddie said, trying to settle her elevated heartbeat a bit. His proximity after all the excitements of the evening gave her a rush. Rather like the first bite of an ice from Gunter's.

"It will have something to do with that business at Lady Emily's," he said with conviction. "I would have gone after the urchin who delivered it but he had left long before I even reached the carriage."

"How were you so close in the first place?" Maddie demanded, distracted by his solid presence in the seat before her. "I thought the whole purpose of my riding in the closed carriage alone was so that we aren't linked together. Which can hardly be accomplished if you were following just behind."

"Do not rip up at me for ensuring your safety, Maddie," he said, rubbing the bridge of his nose. "It could hardly be remarked upon if we were traveling down the same streets in Mayfair of an evening. And this way I could ensure that you went unmolested."

"Ah, yes," she said with a roll of her eyes, "I see how well that plan worked."

"Well, how was I to anticipate that a small boy would leap from the shadows and accost the carriage?"

he retorted. "I was anticipating grown ruffians, not childish ones. Besides, he was hardly tall enough to climb into the carriage, much less get to you inside of it."

"I shall have to wait until I am home to read the note," Maddie said, turning the tightly folded page in her hands. "I do not like to light the carriage lamps when we are not supposed to be seen together."

His only response was a grunt, and that, she supposed, was that. No longer feeling the least bit tired, she reflected on how different the air in the carriage felt with him in it. As if someone had lit an invisible flame in the darkness of the carriage that emanated heat without light. Now that he was here, her thoughts returned again to the kiss. Her hands fisted in her lap, and the crumple of the note in her hand reminded Maddie that more was at stake than just kisses. With a pang of guilt, she forced herself to concentrate on the search for Tinker's killer and what she'd learned tonight.

The carriage arrived in the mews behind Essex House before too long. Silently, Gresham leaped down from the vehicle, let down the steps, and handed her from it to the ground. Ignoring the tingle in her sides where his hands had touched her as he assisted her to her feet, Maddie said simply, "Thank you for an interesting evening, my lord. I will contact you with any information I might glean from the note."

In the dim moonlight, Maddie thought she saw him frown, but perhaps that was just a trick of the light.

"Good night, Maddie," he said, taking her hand in his and kissing it. He gave a slight bow, and turned back to the carriage.

She was somewhat disappointed by his lackluster farewell considering the kiss they'd shared earlier, but she supposed he did not wish to agitate her further.

The note still clutched in her hand, she slipped into the back garden of the house and made her way to the kitchen door, which had been left unlocked for her by her maid.

Maddie was relieved to find that no one in Essex House had realized she'd gone out. Slipping into her bedchamber, then her dressing room, she allowed her maid to help her remove her gown, then sent the obviously exhausted young woman to bed. Slipping into a night rail, she washed her face and took care of her other needs before stepping back into her bedchamber.

She was removing the pins from her hair as she moved toward her dressing table, when an arm snaked around her midsection and a hand clamped over her mouth. A jolt of fear assailed her as she twisted and tried to wrest herself from her captor's grasp.

"Shh," a voice whispered in her ear as she wriggled, "it's me, Maddie. It's me!"

She had just recognized the voice as Christian's when she landed an elbow to his midsection. No longer intent upon screaming down the house, Maddie took advantage of his momentary distraction and whirled around. It was indeed Lord Gresham standing before her, holding one hand up in surrender while the other rubbed his wounded stomach.

"What on earth are you thinking?" she hissed, still gasping for breath as she tried to calm her nerves. "What are you doing here? How did you get in here?"

Indicating with a raised finger that he would not be able to speak for a minute, they stood there, scowling at one another until he regained his breath. "I didn't mean to startle you," Christian said at last. "I decided that I could not wait to hear what the note contained and I climbed the trellis outside your window."

"You climbed the . . . ?" Maddie was stunned. She and Linton had used the trellis to sneak friends into their bedchambers as children, but it had been years since anyone had actually used it to gain access to the house. "What were you thinking, you lunatic? You might have been killed! Not to mention that you might have chosen the wrong room!"

Thrusting a hand into his light brown hair, Monteith shrugged. "It is a perfectly sturdy trellis. And I have friends whose house is built on similar lines a few doors down. The master suites face the square. Since Linton is from town, I figured I would either find your room first or a guest room. Fortunately for me, it was yours. The light still burning helped, of course."

Now that she was over the first shock of it, Maddie felt her heart beat faster for a different reason. Having Christian here in her own personal chamber, with her bed just steps away, was exciting. She didn't bother denying it to herself. Even so, she still thought he was foolishness personified for taking such a risk.

"If my father found you here, he would have no choice but to call you out," she said, shaking her head. "Is that what you want?"

"He might also demand that I marry you," Christian said, his eyes not wavering from hers.

Maddie felt her stomach flip, as if she'd just spurred her horse over a particularly tall hedge. "Yes," she answered, feeling his gaze drop to her mouth as she nervously licked her lips. "He might."

With effort, Christian looked away from her mouth. "I came to see what the note said," he said, feeling like a dolt even as he said it. But he could hardly tell her the truth, that he simply hadn't wanted to bid her good night.

That there was something so addictive about being in her presence, something he hadn't felt for a woman in such a long while, that he had been reluctant to end their evening together. So he'd rationalized that he was only sneaking into her room in order to discuss the case. Now, of course, in her inner sanctum, which smelled of peonies and that inexpressible essence that was Maddie, he was nearly overcome with a longing to gather her into his arms and finish what they'd started earlier in the evening in Lady Emily's drawing room.

A flash of disappointment crossed Maddie's face before she said, "The note is over here. I suppose you'd best make yourself at home." She gestured him into a surprisingly lush armchair before the fire.

Retrieving the note, she followed him to the fire and took the chair opposite his.

Leaning forward to rest his elbows on his knees, Christian waited as she unfolded the letter and began to read.

" '*You do not know the full story,*' " she read aloud. " '*Ask your brother about what really happened to Lord Fielding. Ask him what he and Tretham and Tinker did.*' "

Christian waited for more, but there apparently was none. "That's it?" he asked, frustration humming through him. He sat back in the chair.

"That's it," Maddie said, her eyes thoughtful. "Though it is illuminating. It tells us that the reason for killing Tinker had nothing to do with gambling debts, as we thought, but is linked with Lord Fielding's death."

"And it very well might be," Christian said with a frown. He couldn't reveal to her the Home Office's suspicions about Tinker's involvement with the Citizen's

Liberation Society, and their plot to further the Bonapartist agenda, of course. But if the Bonapartists had something to do with Fielding's death then that would make his own reasons for investigating the matter easier to conceal from her. "What do we know about Fielding's death, anyway?"

"Not much," Maddie reflected, handing the note to Christian. He took it, the brush of her fingers on his sending a rush of blood southward. "At least, not much about what actually happened. There is conjecture, of course. And what Lord Fielding's parents believe. A short version is that Lord Fielding challenged my brother, Tinker, and Tretham to a curricle race from London to Bath. And at some point just before they reached Bath, Lord Fielding crashed his curricle into a tree by the roadside and was killed."

Willing himself to concentrate on the matter at hand, rather than what he wanted to do with his hands, Christian said, "I was on the Continent at the time so I only know what I heard about the matter later." He recalled one of his men reading a letter from home about it, and how annoyed he'd been at the news. Here he was, mourning the loss of his men who had died honorably fighting for their country, while some young idiots were foolishly squandering their own lives in ridiculous sporting pursuits. Of course there had been plenty of his men who had pronounced Fielding to be a fine fellow, but it hadn't made him feel any less bitter about it. Aloud he said, "Did your brother ever talk to you about it?"

"Not directly," Maddie said with a shake of her golden curls. "He was upset, of course, at the loss of his friend, but he never spoke directly about what happened. And Mama forbid me to discuss it, of course. So that was the end of it."

"I should like to discuss the matter with Tretham," Christian said thoughtfully. He had sensed the other man had wanted to say something more in his defense earlier that evening, but had thought better of it. Perhaps over a drink or two at White's he could get the man to confide in him.

"I think that would be wise," Maddie said. "I do wish Linton hadn't left town. I would very much like to encourage him to assist us in clearing his name. I do not like to say such a thing about my own brother, but . . ." Christian watched her hesitation and cursed Linton for putting her in this position. "It seems rather craven of him to leave town while all of this suspicion is swirling around him."

Christian could see that it was a difficult admission for her to make, and felt a pang of admiration for her. "You are quite loyal to him, aren't you?" he asked quietly.

"He is my baby brother," she said simply. "Though he is male and the heir and so is therefore more valued by my parents. When we were small we were quite close. And I suppose I cannot forget that."

"It bothers you a great deal?" Christian asked, sincerely wanting to know. To understand what was at the root of her frustration with women's lot in life, as well as her unexplained devotion to her brother. "Do your parents not cherish you, as well?"

"It drives me to distraction," she admitted wryly. "Despite Linton's constant gaming and drinking and God knows what else, he is still afforded more respect from my parents than I am. There is nothing quite so infuriating as being told that you are automatically less trustworthy, less intelligent, and less capable simply because you had the unhappy misfortune to be born the wrong sex."

Christian bit back a laugh. "I, for one," he said, "am quite pleased you were born a woman."

He watched her eyes darken speculatively at his admission. "Are you?" she asked softly, her hand gently gliding up the curve of her breast. Damned if she wasn't tempting him on purpose, Christian thought wryly

Perhaps it was time to call her bluff.

Standing, he extended his hand. "I am quite glad you were born a woman." She took it, and stood before him, her hand in his, her eyes shadowed in the firelight. "Definitely," he added, unable to stop himself from looking his fill of her, standing there in her night rail and dressing gown, both made transparent by the fire.

Slowly, she stepped toward him. Dropping his hand to slide both of hers up to cup his face. To slip down and around his neck, pulling his face down to hers. "Me, too," she whispered as she brought her mouth up to meet his.

He let her take the lead. Knowing instinctively that she wanted to be the one to control things now. In this moment.

The artlessness of it—at first hesitant, as she nibbled his lower lip, then stroked the tip of her tongue along the seam of his mouth—was devastating. Opening his mouth, he felt her grow more sure of herself, and unable to hold back, he met her stroke for stroke. Her diffidence turned to confidence, as she learned the rhythm of the kiss, and took what she wanted from him. The press of her warm, curvy, deliciously female body against his growing arousal was torturous but he had enough control to stop himself from mindlessly grinding against her. Just enough.

"I would like very much for you to show me the rest of it," she said finally, pulling back to drag her teeth over, then kiss, his chin.

Christian, having lost a considerable amount of brain power due to blood heading elsewhere, blinked. "The rest of it?" he asked dumbly. Then her words sank in and he straightened up a bit. "Ah," he said knowingly, "the rest of it."

She nodded solemnly, and Christian, having regained use of his faculties, took her hand in his again.

"It will mean marriage," he said firmly, half expecting her to balk at the demand. But he was a gentleman and there were some things one did not negotiate about.

"I know," she said, pulling him by the hand toward her bed. "I am not so forward-thinking as to wish to live in complete defiance of the rules of society. And I would not wish to harm your reputation."

He stopped short.

"*My* reputation?" he demanded. "You wish to protect my reputation by marrying me?"

"If you'll have me," she said with a slight shrug.

Was it his imagination, or did he not see a slight tremor running through her? He lifted a hand and touched her lightly on the shoulder. Yes, definitely a tremor.

With a shake of his head, and before she could even protest, he lifted her bodily into his arms.

"What are you doing?" she demanded in a high-pitched squeak.

"Carrying you to bed," Christian said, kissing her on the nose. "Isn't that what you wanted?"

"Yes, but . . ." She looked away, blinking.

He stopped beside the bed. "But what?"

"I don't know," Maddie said, snuggling her head into the crook of his neck. "I just didn't realize I would feel so . . . relieved."

Gently, he lowered her onto the bed. Sitting there, in the glow of the candle that burned beside the bed, she was breathtaking. Her hair, which tumbled down around her shoulders, glinted gold, and the smooth expanse of skin revealed by her night rail called out for his mouth. But it was her face that made his chest tighten. He'd never seen Maddie, *his* Maddie, look so vulnerable before.

He sat down beside her, and gathered her against him. "Why relieved?" he asked. "Didn't you think I'd agree?"

"I thought you probably would, but I didn't *know*." She toyed with the bit of ribbon at the neck of her night rail. "It never occurred to me just how difficult it must be for a man to make himself vulnerable in that way. I have a newfound respect for your sex, I think."

"Well, I *was* the one to mention marriage first," he said, removing her hands from the ribbon and untying it himself. He leaned back and helped her lower her head and shoulders down on the pillows. "I think that deserves some sort of reward." Unable to resist, he dipped down and kissed the vee of exposed flesh above her bosom.

"Perhaps," she said, threading her fingers into his hair. "Though you did not ask. You simply stated your expectations. Just like a man."

"Hmm," he said, licking the indentation above her breastbone. "Perhaps you would like to state your own expectations, now. Just to make things fair."

She moaned slightly as he moved his mouth upward and kissed just below her ear. He filed away the knowledge of her sensitivity there for later.

"I expect that you are wearing far too many clothes," she said as he took her earlobe between his teeth. "Take them off."

Never one to deny a lady, Christian pulled back, and complied.

Maddie had never felt this combination of giddiness and excitement before.

From the moment that Christian had revealed his presence in her bedchamber she'd known that tonight would change her life irrevocably. And she was glad of it.

By the light of the candle, she watched as he shrugged out of his coats, unraveled his neckcloth, and made haste to untuck his shirt and pull it unceremoniously over his head. She drank in the sight of his muscled chest, and well-defined arms, as they emerged from beneath his clothing. She had felt those muscles herself, but seeing them was a far different experience.

He sat on the edge of the bed, revealing his broad, and deliciously naked, back as he went to work removing his boots. Unable to resist, she sat up and ran a finger down his spine.

And nearly made him leap out of his skin.

"Sorry," he muttered, returning to his boots as she continued to explore his body. "Wasn't expecting that. And I'm strung tighter than a drum thanks to those wandering hands of yours."

Maddie smiled to herself at the knowledge she was responsible for his skittishness. This interlude with Christian was educational on many levels. She slid an experimental finger around to tickle his ribs and was rewarded by another leap.

Turning to face her, he raised a brow. "If you want me to get these blasted boots off you have to stop interrupting me."

"Spoilsport," she said without rancor, propping herself up on one arm to watch him.

When he was finally finished with his boots, Christian turned and stretched out alongside her on the bed. She'd never thought her bedchamber was particularly small, but with a large male body in it, it felt like the tiny room of a doll's house.

"So," he said, a half grin quirking his lips as he faced her. Backlit by the candle, his light brown hair's blond highlights shone like a halo around his head. "Where were we?" he asked, slipping a hand over the curve of her hip.

His mouth when it touched hers was soft and hot and utterly devastating. Knowing that she could take the lead when she wished, now she welcomed the mastery of his kiss. Gave herself up to the thrill of possession. She snaked a hand over his naked chest, feeling the warmth of his hot skin beneath her fingers, the rough texture of the hair there. The hair that led a path straight from his chest to disappear into his breeches. Her heart beating faster, she felt the coil of desire well deep in her belly as she stroked him, sending tendrils of need into that aching spot between her thighs.

As if sensing her impatience, Christian reached down to draw the silk of her gown up her body, growling slightly in frustration as it became stuck beneath her hips. Wanting to feel his skin against hers in the most desperate way, Maddie sat up and lifted the gown over her head, tossing it to the floor. As one they came back together, and Maddie nearly wept at the pleasure of feeling his powerful chest pressed against her breasts.

Moving down her body, Christian took the peak of her breast into his mouth, the slight tug of his sucking sending a jolt straight to her center, where a gnawing emptiness made her hips lift in frustration.

Answering her silent plea, he slipped a hand between them, and still toying with her nipple, he stroked his fingers over her wetness. Maddie gasped at the pleasure of it and rocked against his hand, as he slipped a finger into her.

A cry tore from her before Maddie felt Christian cover her mouth with his hand. "Shhhh," he whispered into her ear, even as he filled her with a second finger. "We don't want to wake the house." But the fullness within her was heaven, and unable to stop herself, Maddie moved her restless hips against his hand, begging silently for more.

Kissing her on the mouth, Christian continued to thrust his fingers into her, then when she felt as if she would burst with the euphoria of it, he stroked his thumb over the spot above where he pressed inside her, and Maddie shrieked beneath his hand. Her body, out of her control, convulsed around his fingers, her hips rocked back and forth of their own volition as she felt herself disappear into a world where only pleasure existed.

When she came back to herself, it was to find Christian watching her with an almost pained expression. His hand clasped her buttock, and she felt the press of his arousal against her. Wanting to bring him the pleasure that he'd just given her, she slipped her hands between them and began to fumble with the fastenings of his breeches.

He kissed her, and removed her hands. "Faster if I do it," he said, his voice hoarse as he shucked his breeches and drawers in one motion and came back to press her back into the softness of the mattress.

She gasped at the delicious heaviness of his body against hers. Even with him braced above her on his hands, the sensation of being overpowered by him was oddly intoxicating. And the center of her came alive again, pulsing with need as she felt the press of his erection against her stomach.

"Might hurt at first," he said with an apologetic smile. "But I'll make it good for you, Mads. I promise."

"I know," she said, lifting up to kiss him. "I know."

Closing her eyes, she felt the slide of his hands up her sides, and down again, over her hips. This was what she'd been craving from him. This possession. Instinctively, she opened her legs and drew her knees up to rest on either side of his hips, inviting him in.

Tentatively, he guided the tip of his arousal to her, and though she was braced for a sharp pain, Maddie felt only fullness and a strange restlessness as he pressed into her. When he was fully seated, she closed her eyes at the stretching sensation. She leaned up to kiss him, and he looked down at her with an intensity that made her heart leap up within her.

"Madeline," he whispered against her mouth, flexing his hips to pull slowly back from her. Unable to stop herself, she pressed her hips up to meet him. "I can't go slow," he breathed. "I'm sorry." She answered him by grabbing hold of his taut buttocks and pulling him closer.

With a muttered curse, Christian let go. Thrusting into her again and again, as Maddie rose up to meet him. The delicious friction between their bodies vibrating through her like a chorus without words. Unable to look away, she watched the harsh, beautiful planes of his face in the candlelight. He was at once the man she'd known these past months, and another, darker version of himself. The lover she'd never known she needed. But she knew it now. Knew she craved him. Knew the building tension within her could only be slaked by this man and his body, his soul joining with hers.

"Christian," she breathed, murmuring words she barely undersood as she felt the madness climbing higher, lifting her to the cliff's edge as he drove into her, their naked bodies gliding against one another.

Mindlessly, she gripped his shoulders, held on for dear life as she felt the first quakes of orgasm rippling through her.

"Maddie," he said, kissing her, driving into her mouth in a mimicry of where their bodies joined below. "You're mine."

Her eyes flew open as she went over, the waves of pleasure bowing back, jerking her hips in a mindless frenzy as Christian found his release. As if from far away, she heard him cry out, felt the warmth of his release flood within her, bucked against him as the last throbs of her abandon urged her on.

When Maddie came back to herself, she was acutely aware of the very large, very male body pressing her into the mattress.

"Sorry," he muttered against her neck, still a bit breathless. Kissing her tenderly, he withdrew, turned over onto his back and pulled her with him to settle against his chest. Though she was glad to breathe again, she felt bereft at the loss of their joining. "I didn't mean to crush you."

"You weren't," she said, snuggling into him, liking the feel of his arm around her, of his hard male body at rest. "I rather liked it."

"Did you?" he asked, his eyes closed as he absently stroked her naked back.

"I did," she confirmed, turning over onto her stomach so that she could look at him, this man who had just had his wicked way with her.

He was always ready with a quip or a joke, despite his very serious military career and work for Whitehall, but Maddie had come to realize that there was much more to him than those things. He had shown himself to be protective of her in a way she wasn't quite sure she'd ever felt. Even from her own family. Christian might disapprove of her becoming involved in the search for Tinker's murderer, but instead of forbidding her to do so, he'd simply insisted upon helping her. Or at least following her to ensure she didn't come to harm. In fact, he—

"I can feel you staring at me," he said, not opening his eyes. "I just made you see stars. You should be collapsed in a heap of sated bliss. Instead you are plotting."

Maddie kissed his chin. "I am not plotting," she said. "I am simply thinking of our next step in the search for Tinker's killer."

Christian sighed and opened one eye. "That can wait until after the wedding."

"Wedding?" Maddie squeaked. "I hadn't thought that far ahead."

"That's because you aren't the one who will be facing a pistol at dawn thanks to our thoroughly delightful time together tonight," he said, opening both eyes. He arched a light brown brow. "I, however, have it all planned."

He did?

"You do?"

"Absolutely," he said, neatly flipping her onto her back and kissing her as if he hadn't just spent the last hour doing so.

"In fact," Christian murmured, kissing a line down her chin to her neck, "I think it should take place before the week is out."

"Oh." Maddie sighed as he reached out to lave the tip of her breast with his tongue. "Do you really think so?"

"Definitely."

Maddie felt the muscles in her stomach leap as he moved his mouth downward, over the slight curve of her belly, to slide his hands over the outside of her thighs.

"Wh-what are you doing down there?" she asked, watching the top of his head as she allowed him to pull her knees wide. "Are you . . . are you *looking* at me?"

He glanced up from his study of her, his eyes dark with desire. "You were looking at me," he said with a sly grin. "What's good for the goose . . ."

"But that's not the same as . . ." But when he leaned forward to kiss her there, Maddie lost the ability to think coherently.

The feel of his hot mouth on her most private place, which was still sensitive from their lovemaking, made her inner muscles clench with desire. As if he knew just what her body craved, Christian thrust two fingers inside her. Overwhelmed with sensation, needing to hold on to something, Maddie threaded her fingers into his hair, holding him as he pleasured her.

But the ache she felt demanded more. "I need you," she gasped, lifting her hips in time with his fingers. "Please," she begged. "Please."

To her relief, she felt him lift his head, his soft hair tickling her belly. "As you wish," he said roughly, kissing his way up her body to her mouth, where she tasted herself.

Sliding a hand down his back to grasp his buttocks, she was impatient to feel him inside her.

Mindless with need, Maddie felt him grasp her by the knees and push them up to her chest. The position left her completely open to him, and as she tilted her pelvis upward she was relieved to feel his hardness against her exposed thigh.

"Is this what you need?" Christian asked, pressing into her with a slowness that was devastating. Once, twice, Maddie felt her body clench around him, as if pulling him into the heart of her. Fully seated, Christian gave a slight groan as he kissed her, then began to move. His thrusts sure and controlled and not at all what Maddie wanted. Unable to move her body to angle into his movements, she lifted up to kiss him. "Let go," she whispered against his mouth. "Let go of your control and feel me."

Christian stopped moving. He looked into her eyes, and with a quick kiss, he unleashed whatever had been holding him back. His powerful arms bracketed her, holding his weight off her while he allowed himself to slide into her with the full force of his passion. Again and again he drove into her; hard, strong, and unrelenting. Her body alive with the delicious friction between their bodies, Maddie held on to him for dear life, taking each and every inch of him into her.

Finally, it was too much for them both. Christian's movements became wild, erratic, and Maddie felt herself hurtling toward the bliss she knew they both wanted. Needed. Crying out, she felt her body pulse around him as she lost herself. At the same time, she felt his back bow and he gave a guttural cry, spilling himself into her and lowering his body onto hers.

They lay panting together for several seconds as they got their bearings.

"Did it again," he muttered against her neck. "Sorry." Pushing himself to his arms, he kissed her gently and then turned onto his back, pulling her with him so that she lay atop him.

"Better?" he asked, squinting into her slitted eyes.

She tucked her head under his chin. "I suppose," she said. Then promptly fell asleep.

Much later, Maddie watched as Christian rose from the bed and dressed hastily, tying his cravat in a casual fashion that would have Deveril *tsk*ing.

"I'll be by in the morning to talk to your father," he said, kissing her one last time. "Don't marry anyone else in the meantime."

"You are an absurd man," she said, shaking her head as she sat up in the bed, clutching the sheet to her bosom.

As she watched, he slipped out of the window and stepped out onto the trellis beyond.

"But I'm your absurd man," he said, disappearing down the side of the house.

"Yes, you are," Maddie said to the open window.

Twelve

*I*t was nearly noon when Christian strode into White's, in search of coffee and perhaps a bit of low-key conversation. He had arrived home before dawn, but just barely. And after so much time spent with Maddie, he found that his mind was filled with thoughts of her. And so was his body, which was not sated despite the activities in her bed last night. He wasn't quite sure what to make of that. He'd never found himself in the position of aching for a woman he'd already had. It was a new experience for him, and since he planned to marry her as soon as humanly possible, it boded well for their future together.

But before he could face Maddie's father, he needed strong coffee, and perhaps a bit of advice from his friends. He was pleased to find Winterson ensconced in a corner with a pot of coffee and a tableful of newspapers.

"Good morning, old chap," he said, lowering himself to a chair opposite his friend.

"Why are you in such a good mood?" Winterson, a dark brow raised in suspicion, looked up from his newspaper. "You look as if you didn't sleep at all. But you're whistling. Odd, that."

"I don't know what you mean." Christian indicated to the waiter that he would like coffee as well. "Can a man not be in a good mood without prompting suspicion? If so, you will have to turn your eagle eye upon yourself, for I believe you have been in an annoyingly good mood for weeks now."

The duke leaned back in his chair and surveyed his friend. "Interesting," he said finally, then picked up his paper and continued reading.

They were silent as Christian waited for his coffee, and to see if his friend would extrapolate upon his one-word pronouncement. But after a prolonged silence, in which Winterson continued to read silently, he could stand it no more. "What the devil is that supposed to mean? 'Interesting.'"

When his coffee arrived, he absently took a large mouthful and swore as the hot liquid singed his tongue. Lowering the paper to stare at his friend, Winterson raised his brows in inquiry. "Just what it usually means," he said. "I find it interesting that you came into White's this morning, without having slept, your cravat a mess, your shirt rumpled, and rumors abounding about how you spent last evening."

A peal of warning sounded in Christian's chest. "What rumors?" he asked, his good mood waning.

"What rumors, he asks," Winterson said, shaking his head in exasperation. "The rumors that you kissed Lady Madeline Essex in Lady Emily Fielding's drawing room last night. Which, I might add, has been corroborated by three people in attendance at her little card party."

Damn it. "I had hoped that our engagement would quash the rumors before they even made the rounds."

"So," Winterson said with deceptive calm, "the rumors are true and you plan to marry her?"

"Yes," Christian responded, not fooled by his friend's calm demeanor. As a male relative—even by marriage—of Maddie, Winterson would not hestitate to protect her reputation. Even if that meant crossing swords with his best friend. "And, of course. Have no doubt on that score."

The duke's shoulders relaxed slightly and he grinned. "I am happy to hear it. I must admit that when Cecily first suggested the idea to me I thought she was cracked."

"What does Cecily know of it?" Christian demanded. "I didn't know for sure myself until last night."

"She is a woman, Gresham. Their minds leap from acquaintance to marriage in the space of a moment. Even the ones whose minds are also filled with ancient languages and such."

Christian thrust a hand into his carefully arranged locks. "I dislike being the object of such scrutiny," he said, feeling harassed. "If I'd known she was watching us so closely I might never have . . ." He paused, rethinking the wisdom of admitting last night's encounter *after* Lady Emily's soiree to his friend. "Never mind."

"If it makes you feel any better," Winterson said reassuringly, "Deveril was quite convinced that she wouldn't have you. In fact, let me know when you plan to announce the engagement. I want to be the one to tell him. He owes me a pony!"

Christian's mouth dropped open. "He bet against me? The bastard!"

"Don't be too hard on him, Gresh," the duke said, leaning back in his chair. "Deveril's view of you is colored by the less than crisp nature of your shirt points."

"But yours is not?" the other man demanded wryly.

Winterson shrugged. "To be perfectly honest, I wasn't so sure you'd manage the thing, either. But I reckoned Cecily would reward me for having faith in my friend.

"Which," he continued with a wink, "she did."

Christian shook his head in disgust. "I cannot believe that I have nursed such—"

"I believe the saying is 'vipers in the bosom,'" Winterson offered helpfully.

"Vipers in my bosom," Christian agreed, sipping his coffee. "I can only imagine what mischief you would have got up to if it were a love match."

This erased Winterson's grin. "You mean it isn't a love match?"

"Hardly," Christian replied, shifting uncomfortably in his chair. "I am fond of her, of course. And we are compatible in . . . other ways." He didn't feel right discussing what he'd shared with Maddie last night. It was private. Between them. "I think we will rub along tolerably together."

Folding his arms over his chest, Winterson frowned. "I know it's not always fashionable, but there is something intoxicating about being married to a woman you love."

Since Winterson had married, Christian had seen a change in his friend. And it was one for the better. The duke seemed more settled. More grounded. And happy in a way Christian had never seen him. But it was hardly possible for everyone to replicate the Duke and Duchess of Winterson's happiness.

"The circumstances that brought about your marriage are not so different from mine with Maddie" he said, treading carefully.

The duke paused, his frown deepening. "What circumstances?" he asked silkily.

Christian felt his face color. "Just that it started as a

hastily arranged affair," he said, hastening to add, "As ours will be. That's all I mean."

"Are you saying you compromised the girl more thoroughly than with a kiss, Christian?"

Damn. Winterson hadn't called him by his given name since Eton at least.

Still, he would not allow the other man to cow him. He was hardly Maddie's father. And though he appreciated his friend's protectiveness, he was the one who would be looking after Madeline from now on.

"That is none of your affair," he said, a hint of steel in his tone. "Suffice it to say that we will be married as soon as possible, and that I will endeavor to make the young lady happy."

The two men stared at one another for a moment, then, nodding his approval, Winterson reached out to cuff Christian on the shoulder.

"Congratulations," he said. "She's a fine, if spirited, lady. I wish you every happiness."

"Thanks," said Christian wryly. "But what I need is advice on how to approach her father."

Winterson grinned, and rubbed his hands together in anticipation. "Excellent! As you know I love strategizing."

Relieved that this first hurdle had been cleared successfully, Christian set himself to the task at hand.

Maddie awoke the next morning with the feeling that something was different, but was unable to place what it was. Then the memories of last night came rushing back, and panicking, she reached down to ensure she'd put her night rail back on since she heard her maid stirring about the room.

"Good morning, Lady Madeline," her maid, Landers, said, pulling back the curtains. "You've got a visitor in the blue sitting room."

Thinking that Christian must have already spoken to her father, Maddie swung her legs over the side of the bed and rose.

"I hope he hasn't been waiting long," she said, moving to her dressing table to pull a brush through her tangled locks.

"Oh, it isn't a gentleman, my lady," Landers said, bustling about the room. "It's a Miss Snowe."

Maddie paused, the brush halfway through a knot. "Miss Snowe?" she demanded. "Miss Amelia Snowe?"

When the maid assured her that it was indeed Amelia, Maddie debated for a moment whether she should see her. Amelia was hardly a dear friend who would be expected to call. However, the very fact that the other lady had called was remarkable enough that she couldn't possibly resist receiving her.

Dressed in a pale pink sprig muslin morning gown that she adored—it was important to one's confidence she'd found of late to wear something one loved when facing a difficult task—Maddie entered the blue sitting room a bare half hour later to find that Landers had been correct. Seated there on Maddie's favorite chaise for reading was Miss Amelia Snowe.

"Good morning, Miss Snowe," Maddie said, approaching the other woman as if she were a coiled cobra preparing to strike, and curtsying just enough to be polite. "To what do I owe the honor of your visit?"

Amelia stood and offered her own abbreviated curtsy. "Lady Madeline," she said, her china-blue eyes narrow with dislike. "I have come on a matter of some delicacy."

That brought Maddie up short. What could Amelia possibly have to discuss with her that might be called delicate?

Waving for the other girl to continue, Maddie took a seat in a chintz chair opposite the chaise.

Returning to her seat, Miss Snowe said bluntly, "I received an anonymous note this morning informing me of the fact that you and Lord Gresham shared a very public kiss last night at the home of Lady Emily Fielding."

What the . . . ? Maddie felt her spine stiffen. "That's ridiculous."

"I do not know, nor do I care, about the truth or falsity of the matter," Amelia said with a frown. "What you do with Lord Gresham is your affair." She colored slightly. "I will admit that I have not harbored the most . . . friendly of feelings toward you and your cousins. In fact, I have taken you in active dislike. But whoever sent this note to me thinks that I am the sort of person who would spread the type of rumor that could ruin a young lady. I am not pleased that they thought this of me."

Maddie felt her eyes widen. "You mean to say that you do not intend to spread this tale? Despite your dislike of me?"

She was astonished. Not by Amelia's declaration that she disliked Maddie and her cousins. That was obvious to anyone. What surprised her was the other young lady's decision to keep the potentially ruinous bit of gossip about Maddie to herself. Next she'd be cooing at small animals and chucking babies under the chin.

"No," Amelia said, her lips tight. "Not because I do not think it's true. But because I do not wish my reputation to be further sullied by the notion that I am an ill-tempered shrew who will stop at nothing to ruin her social enemies."

When it was stated in that light, Maddie felt the world tilt back to its normal axis. This was the Amelia she'd come to know and despise. She was somewhat relieved. It would have been quite difficult to adapt to the notion of Amelia as a kind, upstanding young lady.

"I suppose thanks are in order?" Maddie said, unsure how to proceed.

Amelia thrust a folded letter toward her. "Here it is. I thought perhaps you might wish to see it, to determine who sent it. I did try myself, but since I assume this is someone who wishes you ill—and that number could be legion—I decided that you might do a better job of investigating the matter."

Taking the note, Maddie read the scrawled lines:

> *Lady Madeline Essex kissed Lord Gresham before an audience last night at Lady Emily Fielding's card party. I'm sure you won't be able to keep this all to yourself.*
>
> *A friend.*

"What I dislike the most is that this person assumes I am a gossip," Amelia said tightly. "It is infuriating."

"I can see why you'd feel that way," Maddie said, unsure of whether she should try for commiseration or condemnation.

Amelia stood. "I will leave you now. I feel sure that you have licentious lords to kiss, or some other mischief to get up to."

With that, Amelia walked from the room and left Maddie staring after her.

Dumbfounded.

But when her puzzlement lifted, she realized that there was something more at stake than her continuing war with Amelia.

Someone had purposely set out to ruin her reputation. Someone who must have been there at Lady Emily's last night and seen her kiss with Christian.

A chill ran over her as she wondered who would do such a thing. And more importantly, why? Could it be that she was getting too close to whomever had murdered Tinker?

Christian arrived on the front steps of Essex House feeling slightly nauseous at the idea of making his case to Madeline's father, and clutching a posy of spring roses. It wasn't that he was afraid. Exactly. It was just that he'd never proposed marriage before. And remembering his discussion in the park with Lord Essex about the suspicions surrounding Linton, he wasn't quite sure that the man would view him as a suitable choice for his daughter's hand.

Of course whether Essex saw him as suitable or not had lost all meaning when Christian had sneaked into the fellow's house the night before and seduced his only daughter. Running a finger under his suddenly too tight cravat, Christian applied the door knocker.

"The Earl of Gresham to see Lord Essex," he said to the butler before the man had barely opened the door.

Surveying him and the bouquet he carried, the majordomo looked surprised, but ushered Christian in. "I'll just see if Lord Essex is receiving today, my lord."

Stepping into the entryway of the town house, Christian was surprised to hear a low-level hum, not unlike that of the card room at the club, or the crowd at a prize fight.

"Is Lord Essex having a meeting of some sort?" he asked the footman who stood near the door. He hadn't counted on pulling the other man away from a gathering. It would draw undue attention to his visit. Not that he thought the reason for it would remain a secret forever.

"Oh, no, my lord," the footman said with a smile. "That's just the fellas who came to bring posies to Lady Madeline this morning."

Christian froze. "And how many of these fellows are there?" he demanded. When he'd told Maddie not to marry anyone else while he was away, he hadn't actually thought there was a possibility of it happening.

"Oh, perhaps two dozen or so," the footman said, blithely unaware of the jealous rage he'd lit aflame in the man before him. "First time for everything, I s'pose. Lady Madeline has never seemed to inspire so many gentleman callers before, but something must have changed them."

Abandoning his plan to see Lord Essex, Christian strode past the footman and up the stairs, following the sound of male conversation until he reached an open doorway. Stepping inside, he saw the two dozen men the footman had promised, milling about chatting with one another, and presumably waiting to pay their respects to their hostess.

Maddie herself was surrounded by at least six men who all vied for her attention. Laughing merrily at something one of the men had just said, she looked more beautiful than he'd ever seen her. And Christian was swept with a wave of possessiveness that nearly had him striding forward and telling the men surrounding her to go to the devil.

"Good afternoon, Gresham." A female voice punctured the haze of his jealousy.

Turning, he saw Juliet, Deveril's viscountess, and Maddie's cousin. "You look ready to slay the room at large," she said with a barely suppressed smile. "You needn't look so murderous. She is merely enjoying the experience of being the center of attention for a change. I have no doubt that as soon as she realizes you are here she'll send them packing."

Christian wondered if that was the case. He had left Maddie last night assured of their affection for one another, but perhaps he'd overestimated her attachment to him. After all, she had barely received much male attention at all before he seduced her. Perhaps she wished to determine if some other man might be a more suitable match for her. He suppressed a growl. She would simply have to understand that she was stuck with him. Last night had changed everything and he was damned if he'd sit by while she searched for his replacement.

Excusing himself to Juliet, he strode forward, intending to stake his claim before the halflings and drones buzzing around Maddie managed to turn her head.

"Here's another bouquet, Lady Madeline," the second footman, Tom, said, approaching her with another posy. This one was the simplest of the lot. Fresh spring roses in the palest shade of pink that matched her gown perfectly.

Shaking her head in renewed surprise, she buried her nose in the blooms. She would no more have imagined herself in the midst of a crowd of eligible young men than she would have said the moon would come calling for tea, but as soon as the hour arrived when it would be proper to pay calls, the knocker of Essex House had begun sounding and it showed no signs of stopping.

"Thank you," she told the footman and rose to put them with the others. "Who sent them, Tom?"

"They are from me," Christian said, looking every inch the nobleman as he strode toward her, scattering the other gentlemen like a cat among the pigeons.

Unbidden, the memory of his face limned in candlelight the night before as he stroked powerfully into her sent a wave of heat through her. As if he could read her thoughts, Christian met her gaze.

Burying her nose in the flowers gave Maddie a moment to regain her composure. Unfortunately it also gave her other gentlemen callers, oblivious to the death looks Christian was sending them, time to regroup around her.

"I chose wildflowers for you, Lady Madeline," Lord Philip Thompson said, eyeing Christian jealously, "because I thought they best suited your personality."

"That was very thoughtful of you, my lord," she said brightly.

"Lady Madeline," Christian said in a voice loud enough for the room at large to hear. "I wonder if I might have a word?"

Having grown tired of the senseless chatter of the men surrounding her, Maddie leaped at the chance to leave them. "Of course, my lord."

"Madeline," Lady Essex said, abandoning her conversation with Cecily and Juliet and approaching Maddie. "It would be highly improper for you to leave the room just now. Especially when you have so many visitors."

Christian was in no mood to be gainsaid, however. "I beg your pardon, ma'am," he said with a bow. "I assure you that I will be speaking with Lord Essex shortly after I have a word with Lady Madeline."

The implication of his statement was crystal clear.

The room that had been loud with chatter quieted.

"I say, Gresham," Mr. George Vinson said with a touch of annoyance, "do you mean to cut the rest of us out that easily? Not sporting of you. Not a bit."

A chorus of agreement rose up among the other young men.

Their objections, however, held no weight with Lady Essex, who dismissed them with a wave of her hand. "I will allow my daughter to speak with you, my lord," she said to Christian, "though I will have your word that you will speak to Lord Essex before you quit this house."

Christian bowed to Maddie's mother. "You have my word."

To Maddie, she said, her eyes broadcasting her wishes, "My dear, please do be sure to listen to Lord Gresham's speech most carefully."

Maddie reflected that if Lady Essex were aware of the intimacies she'd shared with Christian last night she would be demanding that her daughter listen to the man's proposal, rather than requesting.

Nodding to her mother, Maddie put her hand lightly on Christian's arm as he led her down the hallway to the sitting room where she'd met with Amelia earlier.

He'd left the door open slightly, as was proper, though Maddie thought it rather foolish. But such was the way of proprieties. They really did little to ensure that the lines between good behavior and bad were never crossed.

"Come," he said quietly, reaching for her arm and pulling her toward him. "Are you well?" he asked, looking into her face, as if trying to determine her mind before she spoke.

"Quite well," she said, ducking her head with a blush. She was finding it rather more difficult to look him in the eye in the light of day than it had been last night. "And you?"

The corner of his mouth quirked up. "I am well, as well. Also. Too."

"You are a silly, silly man," she said, though she meant it with affection. She had come to appreciate his sense of the absurd as much as his strength and loyalty. Who would wish to be tied to a man who never laughed? she wondered, leaping ahead to what she knew this interview was truly about. Not their well-being or their absurdity, but their marriage.

"I am," he said solemnly, pulling her closer, "but I'll be your silly man if you'll have me."

The confirmation that they were of one mind made Maddie's heart beat faster. How dreadful it would be to tie him to her if he did not wish it, she thought. She risked a glance up at his eyes. "Are you sure?" she asked, knowing that if he said no she would be wretched for a long time to come.

"I rather think that is what I'm supposed to ask you," he said seriously. Lifting a hand to stroke her cheek, he said, "Will you have me, Maddie? If so, are you sure?"

Unable to speak around the lump in her throat, Maddie, who had long been the most outspoken of her cousins, nodded, hoping that he understood that she was answering yes to both.

"Then there's nothing for it but to do the thing properly," Christian said with a grin, dropping to one knee and taking possession of her hands again.

"Lady Madeline Essex," he asked, looking at her with such affection and something else that looked suspiciously like love, that she nearly dropped his hands. "Will you do me the great honor of becoming the Countess of Gresham, and not inconsequentially, my wife?"

"Of course I will, you great gudgeon," she said, pulling him to his feet and embracing him so that he wouldn't see her tears. "Of course I will."

He took her by the shoulders and held her away from him. "What's this, Maddie? Tears?" Christian leaned in and kissed first her eyes, and then traced the path of a tear down her cheek to her mouth.

But his lips had no sooner met Maddie's than the sound of a throat clearing made them leap apart.

"Am I to take this display of ardor to mean that you have accepted his lordship's proposal, Madeline?" Lady Essex, accompanied by a less than pleased looking Lord Essex, said from the doorway.

"Hypothetically," Maddie said with a smile.

Her mother was not amused. "What do you mean, hypothetically? My lord, I was given to understand that your proposal was sincere."

"Indeed it was, your ladyship," Christian said, with a warning glance at Maddie. "I fear Lady Madeline was simply referring to the fact that I have not yet spoken to her father."

"Then let me put your minds at rest," Lord Essex said firmly. "You have my permission to wed my daughter, Gresham. Just as soon as we can arrange it."

Maddie frowned. Her parents couldn't know about the need for them to wed in haste. She had planned to work up to telling them of the necessity.

Christian squeezed her hand. "My lord," he began, "it's not that I do not wholeheartedly agree that we should marry before the week ends, but is there a particular reason why *you* think we should?"

The earl's jaw clenched. "I had not meant to discuss the matter in front of the ladies, Gresham," he said curtly, "but as you have brought up the subject, I suppose we may as well get it out in the open."

Turning to pace before the fireplace, Lord Essex stopped and faced them. "I have heard talk this morning that you were seen kissing my daughter during a card party at Lady Emily Fielding's home last evening."

"Oh, Papa, it's not—" Maddie began, feeling shamed to the roots of her hair by the look on her father's face.

"Do not tell me what it is not, young lady," the earl snapped. "You were behaving like the veriest lightskirt before an audience last night. Emulating that Fielding widow, no doubt. And bringing censure down on the family while you were at it."

Maddie would have objected, but Christian was there before her.

"I must ask that you keep a civil tongue in your head when you are speaking with my future wife, Lord Essex," he said, his hand firm and warm in hers. "It is true that we kissed at Lady Fielding's last night, but it's over and done now and there's nothing to be done about it. And I must respectfully tell you that if you ever refer to Lady Madeline in such vile terms again I will not hesitate to defend her to you on the field of honor."

Maddie's eyes widened at Christian's threat to meet her father over his insult. She'd known that if society learned of the incident at Lady Emily's, there would be some price to pay—and she supposed that their betrothal was a payment against that bill—but she had to admit that she hadn't thought through the ramifications of the scandal on her reputation with her family. It was a jarring realization, and hearing her father's insult followed by Christian's defense of her emphasized just how serious the matter was.

She was surprised that rather than standing up to Christian, her father instead seemed to diminish before the other man's ire. It was the first time Maddie had seen her father as something other than the brusque patriarch she'd known since late childhood. She was at once grateful for Christian's championship and a little saddened by her father's quick dismissal of her.

"You are welcome to her," Lord Essex said gruffly. "She's always been a difficult one to manage and I wish you good luck with her."

Realizing that her husband's ill temper might ruin what she herself saw as the best match she could have dreamed of for her daughter, Lady Essex laughed off the exchange. "Oh, you men with your harsh words," she said with forced gaiety. "I vow that you will be sharing drinks together at the wedding breakfast."

Turning to Maddie and Christian, she said, "We'll leave you two lovebirds alone for a few minutes. Then we must set about planning the wedding, Madeline. And you, my lord, must secure a special license at once. If you have any trouble there, I can ask the archbishop himself. He owes me a favor."

And then, as quickly as they'd been interrupted, they were alone again.

"Are you all right?" Christian asked, looking intently into Maddie's face.

She nodded, and stood up on her tiptoes to kiss his cheek. "Thank you for standing up to my father for me. I could have handled him, but I must admit I don't think he would have backed down as easily for me."

Christian's jaw hardened. "I shouldn't have needed to do so," he said grimly. "I wish you'd told me that he was so disrespectful to you. I thought you said that he'd become a better man since giving up drink."

"I said he was more rational," she said wryly. "He is still a rather unpleasant sort of person. But he is my father."

Slipping a hand into his coat, Christian said more cheerfully, "I almost forgot to give you this."

He extended his hand, which had a rather large sapphire ring resting in it.

Maddie gasped. "For me?"

His raised brow drew a giggle. "Of course for me," she said with a smile. "Will you put it on?"

Nodding, Christian took her left hand in his and removed her glove, slipping the sapphire onto her ring finger. It was a perfect fit.

"It was my great-grandmother's," he said. "The setting is a bit archaic, but I thought it suited you."

He leaned down and kissed her, then. Maddie welcomed him into her mouth, trying to say with her kiss all those things she was too afraid to say aloud.

Thirteen

A betrothed man had no business at a brothel three days before the wedding, Christian thought, tossing Galahad's reins to an urchin loitering in the street before the Hidden Pearl. But the note he'd tucked away in his coat pocket, and its promise to disclose information relating to the death of John Tinker, had made it imperative that he do so.

Besides, he thought, Maddie was busy with wedding plans today and need never know.

"My lord," the beefy man at the door said, extending a very large arm in welcome. Christian had little doubt that the fellow served both as butler and muscle for those occasions when clients of the establishment became a bit overzealous for the club's liberal tastes. "The rest of the gents are in the parlor. You can take your pick there, or if you've got a particular girl you'd like to see—"

"I'm here to see Mrs. Pettigrew," Christian said before the big man could finish the thought. "We have an appointment, I believe."

The other man's brows rose but he did not argue, directing Christian into a surprisingly comfortable sitting room that might have been found in any respectable home in bourgeois London.

He couldn't help pacing. He felt as nervous as a mouse in a cat house cooling his heels in this place. All he needed was one person to see him and take the news back to Maddie and he would have a great deal of explaining to do. She would doubtless understand upon hearing his reasons for being here, but he'd just as soon skip the conversation altogether.

"Lord Gresham," a sultry voice whispered from the doorway. "What a delightful surprise."

Turning, Christian surveyed the woman in the doorway. She was not attractive in the conventional way, but what she'd been born with—a large bosom and a slender figure—she'd put to good use. He had little difficulty imagining she kept her clientele happy.

"It can hardly be a surprise," he said, kissing the air above her hand, "when you issued such an intriguing invitation."

She laughed. It was a sultry, throaty sound. "Leighton said that you were a bright one."

Moving farther into the room, she took a seat on a plush settee before the fire.

"So, it was Leighton who directed you my way?" he asked, moving to stand with his back to the mantel. "You've worked for him in the past, I suppose."

"In a manner of speaking," she said with a wink. Then straightening a bit, she fingered the diamond necklace at her throat. "I have, in my profession, been privy to information that my country often finds to be of use. Lord Leighton and I have met on more than one occasion when I thought the information warranted his attention."

"And what information have you gleaned this time?" Christian asked warily. He was well aware that Leighton gathered bits of news from a variety of sources, but he wasn't quite sure that the madam before him could be judged a reliable source.

"All business, aren't you?" she asked, not bothering to hide her amusement at his discomfort. When he raised an imperative brow, she rolled her eyes and said, "All right, all right. I'll get to it, then.

"I have an occasional customer," Mrs. Pettigrew said, dropping the pretense at seduction. "He is a member of a certain group that you've been looking into."

"The Citizen's Liberation Society," he said flatly.

Mrs. Pettigrew nodded. "I've cultivated the relationship because he often tells me of his exploits with the group after a good—"

"I get the idea," Christian interrupted. "Go on."

"Well," she continued, "he isn't very powerful in the group, or I've little doubt your lot would have snatched him up. And his tattle sometimes leads to bigger fish."

He wasn't surprised to learn that the government had let the man go unfettered. Sometimes a braggart on a lower rung of the organizational ladder could be a wealth of information about those at the top.

"And?"

"And night before last he told me about another one of his lot who had been killed in a gaming hell."

Christian's senses went on alert. "Did he name this person?"

"No," Mrs. Pettigrew said, "though he did tell me that the hell was a place run by a Mrs. Bailey."

He clenched his jaw to keep from cheering. "And what did he have to say about the killing?"

She met his gaze. "He said that the group was puzzled, because they couldn't figure out who would have killed him."

"So you're saying that they were not responsible for the man's death?"

Mrs. Pettigrew nodded. "According to him, they don't know who killed him or why."

Christian thought for a moment. Since the incident at Lady Emily's when Tretham was accused of the murder, Christian had suspected that the society was not responsible for Tinker's death, but this news was proof of it. Which meant that he would no longer need to investigate the matter for the Home Office, and that the runners would have to be called in.

Unfortunately, it also meant that Viscount Linton was once more a suspect, along with Tretham and the rest of them. And that Maddie had likely been correct in assuming that the killer was one of those in Linton's set. For Maddie's sake, he would do what he could to ensure that the case didn't get turned over to the magistrate just yet. If he could not use his political influence on behalf of his near brother-in-law, then of what use was it?

"Thank you for sharing your information with me," he told Mrs. Pettigrew, taking his leave of her.

"No problem, guv," she said with a grin. "Think of it as a wedding present."

A present he would definitely *not* be sharing with his bride until after the wedding, Christian thought as he tossed a coin at the lad who'd looked after Galahad.

And maybe not even then.

"What a delightful gown, Lady Madeline," Mr. Frederick Staines said, bowing so low over Maddie's hand that she was able to see just where his hair had been carefully combed over his bald spot.

Thanking the gentleman for the compliment, she let her mind, and her gaze, wander.

She spied Christian on the other side of the room, chatting with Winterson and Deveril. He looked handsome in his evening clothes. And since their encounter in her bedchamber, she knew he looked just as well out of them.

They had decided to stay apart from one another until the announcement of their betrothal later in the evening. Neither of them wished to add fuel to the rumors circulating about the reasons for their betrothal by appearing to live in one another's pockets. Lord Essex, despite his consent to the match, had continued to disapprove of the way it came about, and when Cecily's stepmama had offered the Hurstons' home for the betrothal ball, Maddie and Christian had accepted with alacrity.

So far she had spent the bulk of the evening being paraded around the Hurston ballroom by her mama, who wished to prove that Maddie was quite capable of behaving with propriety in the presence of her betrothed. It galled Maddie that she was the one who had to prove her modesty, but it was just another reason why she so disliked the inequality of the social strictures of the *ton*.

Adding to her annoyance was the fact that she was now expected to spend the bulk of the evening talking to people—like Mr. Staines—who had very little of interest to say. If this was what she'd been missing during her years with the other wallflowers, then she had been well out of it. Cecily and Juliet had remained by her side for a while tonight, but even they had absconded when Mr. Staines approached.

"And then I said 'Of course he don't understand you, Francis! He's a dog!' " Mr. Staines said, laughing as if he had told the funniest tale imaginable, rather than a not-so-witty witticism about a conversation between his horse and his dog. "Are you an animal lover, Lady Madeline?"

"Why, yes, I do like animals, Mr. Staines," she said

cautiously, fearing that her affirmative would bring forth another deluge of animal stories. Then, spotting a familiar face coming near, she all but shouted with relief. "Lady Emily, how delightful to see you again."

Her expression revealing that she had summed up Maddie's situation and decided to offer a conversational rescue, Lady Emily Fielding stepped forward, saying, "A delight to see you, as well, Lady Madeline. And Mr. Staines! I believe I heard my father telling Lord Reardon about your Flossie's new litter. You must hurry over at once lest he offer up the wrong details. I know no one as meticulous as you are when it comes to bloodlines."

Puffing up like a peacock, Mr. Staines quickly excused himself with a blush at being singled out by Lady Emily.

"You do not know how much I appreciate your assistance, my lady," Maddie told the other woman. "I was beginning to despair of his ever moving along to share his expertise with someone else."

The dark-haired widow smiled. "He is a harmless enough fellow, but long-winded, it's true. I'm glad I could be of service to you, Lady Madeline. Especially since I am to understand you were given a bit of a fright at my home earlier in the week."

Maddie was not surprised to hear her refer to the accusation of murder against Tretham and not the scandalous kiss she'd shared with Christian. For someone like Lady Emily the gossip surrounding their indiscretion and the subsequent repercussions would hardly be worth mentioning.

"Yes, it was a bit frightening to hear talk of murder," Maddie said, "but I can assure you it was hardly as frightening as that night when Mr. Tinker was killed. I daresay Lord Tretham was more disturbed than I."

"I believe he was quite worried by the accusation," Lady Emily said tersely. "But, nonetheless, I do not like hearing that one of my guests was foolish enough to make such an accusation in so public a venue. And certainly not in the presence of the very woman who bore witness to poor Tinker's demise. My sincerest apologies."

Maddie sensed that Lady Emily was more disturbed by the accusation taking place in her home than over the accusation itself. Still, she accepted the apology and tried to turn the subject. "I thank you for the invitation to your home, nevertheless. It was an intriguing evening despite the unpleasantness."

At that Lady Emily smiled and Maddie was reminded of how stunning she was. "I am pleased that you enjoyed yourself. If I'm not mistaken you enjoyed the company you brought with you as much as any of the other guests I invited."

Maddie felt a blush creep into her cheeks. "Yes, I fear you are correct. Though I did enjoy getting to know some of my brother's friends better. I had wondered what it was that attracted Linton so to your little set, but now I understand."

At the mention of Linton, Lady Emily's expression sobered. "Lady Madeline," she said, "I wonder if we might converse in a more private location? There is something I need to tell you about your brother. And I do not wish to do so in such an open setting."

Maddie's gaze sharpened. "Yes, of course," she said, trying not to show how eager she was to hear the other woman's disclosure. Linton had sent word by messenger yesterday that he was safely hidden away—she guessed in Scotland at the family hunting box—but that didn't mean that her fears for him had dissipated. It was bad enough that he would miss her wedding, but if he were to be hanged for murder the family would never recover. "I believe there is an antechamber off the long gallery where we can be private."

Scanning the room for her mother or her cousins, Maddie was disappointed to see that none of them were near enough for her to tell them where she was bound. Reasoning that Lady Emily was unlikely to be a danger, she beckoned the other woman to follow her, and wound her way through the crowd to the door leading to the long gallery. The faint strains of the musicians filtered into the empty hallway as they entered the room where her aunt Violet kept her household office.

Pushing the heavy oak door, Maddie was relieved to see that the chamber was empty. Gesturing that Lady Emily should be seated in one of the high-backed chairs facing the fire, Maddie remained standing, her nerves too much on edge to allow her to rest.

"Now that we are here, I don't even know where to begin," Lady Emily said, for the first time in Maddie's presence appearing nervous.

"I believe the beginning is often the accepted place to start," Maddie said, not unkindly. There was more to the widow than she'd previously guessed, she realized, watching as she visibly prepared herself to speak.

Finally, taking a deep breath, Lady Emily said, "I believe you know already that I was married at a very young age."

At Maddie's nod, she continued, "What you may not know is that my husband, Charles Fielding, was a brute." She said the words quickly, as if the faster they left her mouth the less damage they could do her.

"We began our married lives together quite happily," she went on matter-of-factly, "I was smitten. And though my father was not in favor of the match, I was persuasive enough that it took me very little effort to convince him to allow our marriage."

Maddie said nothing, knowing instinctively that the other woman needed to relay the tale in her own time, in her own way.

"We had been married nearly three months before he hit me," she continued. "I do not even recall what set him off. It was likely something foolish like a forgotten engagement, or a failure to inform him that I was going out. As the daughter of a duke I was used to doing as I pleased—within reason, of course—and it took me a little while to realize that Charles would not be as lenient as my father had been.

"He characterized his strictness as the result of worry. It worried him to have me out of his sight, he said. It worried him to have me neglect him by forgetting to tell cook he disliked green peas. No matter how trivial the offense, he was beset with worry over my every transgression."

Maddie tried to imagine living with such surveillance, and could not. Even at his worst her father had never been so demanding.

"After a few such incidents," Lady Emily went on, staring off into space as she spoke, "I began to realize that it had very little to do with worry and a great deal to do with control."

"What did you do?" Maddie asked, her stomach tight with tension at the thought of how suffocating Lady Emily's life must have been.

"What could I do?" the other woman asked, turning to look at Maddie. "He was my husband. Under English law a wife is simply one more possession."

That was true enough, Maddie knew. It was one, among many, concerns she had about entering the wedded state herself. Though she had little doubt that if Christian were to mistreat her in any way he would face the wrath of her cousins and their husbands, but if he truly wished to do so the law would be on his side.

"I will not bore you with the details of my five years of marriage," Lady Emily continued, "but you will understand, I think, that his death was something which afforded me some degree of relief."

"I do not doubt it," Maddie said. "But what has this to do with my brother? Or for that matter, with the accusation of murder against Lord Tretham?"

"Patience," Lady Emily said with a twisted smile. "You know already that my husband, your brother, Tretham, and Tinker were all good friends. Until, that is, Tretham, your brother, and Tinker walked in on Charles hitting me one afternoon. They did not cut his acquaintance, of course. They could not do so without revealing the reason for it, and I did not wish it to be known to the *ton* at large that I was subjected to such indignities."

"But they let you continue living with him?" Maddie felt ill.

"My dear Lady Madeline," the widow said sharply, "you must have more faith in your brother. He and Lord Tretham threatened my husband within an inch of his life if he laid another hand on me. And for whatever reason, it worked. Charles and I continued to live together until his death."

"Then what of your husband's death?" Maddie demanded. "Was it an accident as it was claimed?"

Lady Emily shook her head in disappointment. "They had no hand in Charles's death if that's what worries you. It was his own fault. Too much drink before he embarked on a cross-country race. He was lucky he killed no one but himself."

"So, if we are agreed that your husband's death was a happy accident," Maddie said carefully, "then what is the problem?"

The other woman's mouth tightened with tension. "I'm afraid that someone, thinking that the accident was not an accident at all, has elected himself to be my husband's champion," Lady Emily said, her hands clenching in her lap. "And Mr. Tinker was the first victim."

Before Lady Emily could explain herself further, they were interrupted by a sharp knock on the door as Christian stepped into the room.

"Ladies, I apologize for the interruption, but I'm afraid you're needed in the ballroom, Lady Madeline."

Maddie met Christian's gaze and noted the question there. She gave a slight shake of her head to indicate that she was all right.

"I hope you will excuse me for just a few moments longer," she said, touching him on the arm. "I have a few more things to discuss with Lady Emily."

"Place the blame at my door, Lord Gresham," Lady Emily said, rising. "I rather foolishly requested Lady Madeline's assistance in a personal matter."

Her stomach sinking, Maddie turned to the other woman. "Please don't go. I can spare a few moments longer."

But Lady Emily was already stepping away. "I have said what I came here to say, my dear." She took Maddie's hand in hers and squeezed it. "I will trust you to do with the information what you wish."

Maddie nodded, her mind racing at the implications of Lady Emily's revelation. If someone were avenging what they saw as Lord Fielding's murder at the hands of his friends, then they would have no compunction about harming her brother or Lord Tretham. Especially now that Mr. Tinker had been dispatched.

Her reverie was interrupted by Lady Emily's conversation with Christian.

"I wish the two of you every happiness, my lord," the older woman was saying. "You have chosen a very resourceful bride. I hope you will not object to it if I continue to count her among my friends."

Maddie's jaw dropped. "How on earth did you guess? We were going to announce the engagement tonight."

Lady Emily smiled knowingly. "You'll forgive me for saying it, but a person would have to be utterly blind not to notice the attachment between the two of you. Besides, after the scandal you created at my little party, it was inevitable."

And before Maddie could say anything further, she was gone.

"What was that all about?" Christian demanded, his brow furrowed with concern. "We've been searching the whole house for you. I was afraid you had decided to cry off."

Maddie felt her heart constrict as she saw that this last was only half said in jest. "I apologize," she said, leaning up to kiss his cheek. "There was no one about to tell where I was going, and I had the feeling that if she were put off, Lady Emily might not make the effort to find me again."

"Well?" he asked impatiently. "You don't think I'm going back into the ballroom without hearing what she had to say, surely?"

She bit her lip in indecision. On the one hand, telling Christian would convince him once and for all that her brother was not responsible for Mr. Tinker's death. And that news would mean that he could be removed from the watch of the Home Office once and for all. On the other hand, she had little doubt that the news that someone was trying to kill both her brother and Lord Tretham would make him work doubly hard to keep her from involving herself in the matter.

"You may as well tell me, Maddie," Christian said after a few beats of silence. "I can almost hear the gears turning in your head as you weigh the options."

"I want to tell you," she said, finally. "But you must first promise that you will not forbid me from assisting you with the investigation into Tinker's death. If I tell you what Lady Emily said, that is."

She watched his face harden with annoyance. He didn't want to make the promise, that much was visible in the pinch of his nose and the furrow between his brows. Finally, with a muttered curse, he said, "All right. I promise, but you must also promise that if I tell you to stand down, or that something is too dangerous for you to handle, you will do as I say."

It went against Maddie's better judgment to agree to such restrictions, but since she needed him to perform those investigative tasks that she, as a woman, could not, she nodded. "I promise," she said.

Indicating she was ready to return to the ballroom, she said, "It's a complicated tale, most of which I will save for later. For now, however, suffice it to say that my brother and Lord Tretham are in very grave danger."

"May I have your attention, please?"

Lady Hurston was tiny, but she had a voice that carried, and the lull in the dancing coupled with the cessation of the music helped. "I know that when I originally planned this ball it was to celebrate my husband's recovering health . . ." At this, she reached out to take Lord Hurston's hand as he remained seated in a place of honor next to her. "However, I am delighted to use this entertainment to celebrate another happy occasion."

Christian shifted from one foot to the other while he watched the assembled guests hang on Lady Hurston's every word. Winterson and Deveril had escaped having their matches announced in so public a manner, which he envied them. A gathering of men he would gladly speak before without qualm. But a society ball filled with everyone from turbaned matrons to green debutantes was enough to send him into a panic.

He also could not shake the pall that Lady Emily's revelation to Maddie had cast over him. Coupled with what he'd learned from Mrs. Pettigrew, the news that someone was killing off the men who had been involved in Lord Fielding's death was troubling. A killer was, it would seem, walking among them. And though he had narrowed the field down to those who were present that night at Mrs. Bailey's, it was not beyond the realm of possibility that someone had entered and left the establishment without being seen. As an ex-soldier, he was quite comfortable with facing an enemy he could see. But this business, which pitted him against someone who was essentially hiding in plain sight, was the very devil.

His attention was diverted from his worries by Lord and Lady Essex stepping forward.

He hadn't exchanged a word with Lord Essex since the day he proposed to Maddie. Her father's condemnation of Maddie had filled Christian with a rage he had not thought himself capable of feeling. His years in the army had taught him to control his emotions. A commander with a hair-trigger temper was more dangerous than the enemy's bullet. However, that day in the Essexes' little parlor, he had used every ounce of his self-control to keep from slamming his fists into the older man's face. Was this the sort of condemnation Clarissa had faced when that son of a bitch Selford had ruined her? The thought of Maddie being subject to the sort of self-recrmination that his sister had explained in her suicide note was almost more than Christian could bear. He would do just about anything to ensure that she never felt that kind of shame. Especially when he was equally at fault for their present situation.

Truth be told, he was glad that they'd arrived at this betrothal, no matter what route had led them here.

So, when she grabbed him by the arm and pulled him forward, he went willingly.

"It has been no secret," Lady Essex began, "that my daughter has not been the most . . . docile of young ladies."

This drew a laugh from the crowd, and Christian felt Maddie's grip tighten on his hand.

"Like her cousins, Cecily and Juliet, now the Duchess of Winterson and the Viscountess Deveril," Maddie's mother continued, "Madeline has often preferred her books to her dance lessons."

"I wish she would stop cataloguing my faults and simply make the announcement," Maddie said in a low voice.

"Patience, my dear," Christian whispered, though he, too, wished that Lady Essex would speed things up.

"But it gives us great pleasure," Lady Essex continued, "to announce that our daughter, Lady Madeline Essex, has just accepted a marriage proposal from the Earl of Gresham."

A chorus of cheers reverberated through the ballroom, and Christian was pounded on the back by Winterson and Deveril and, for appearances' sake, his future father-in-law. Beside him, Maddie was embraced by her cousins, their husbands, and her aunts and uncles. Even the prickly Lady Rose Shelby. During the announcement, footmen had been moving efficiently through the room handing out glasses of champagne to the guests. Seeing that Maddie already had her own glass, Christian took one for himself and prepared to be toasted.

"I hope that you will all join us in a toast to my niece and her betrothed," Lady Hurston said. "To Lady Madeline—"

But Maddie's aunt was forestalled from continuing by a to-do on the other side of the room.

"No!" shouted a female voice from somewhere near the terrace doors. Conveniently a path opened up, revealing a very angry Miss Amelia Snowe as she shouted at her mother. "I will not toast Madeline Essex! It's not fair! She isn't half so beautiful as I am! I am the toast! I should be the one whose engagement is being announced! I should be the—"

And, as often seems to happen just when it's too late to take the words back, Amelia seemed to sense at last that the room had become deathly silent for the latter part of her tirade. As Christian watched, Amelia's face flushed an unbecoming shade of red.

Covering her mouth with her hand, as if that might recall the words she'd just uttered, Amelia stared at Maddie and Christian at the head of the room. And Maddie and Christian, nearly as surprised as she was, stared back.

With a sound that seemed suspiciously like a sob, Amelia turned on her heel and fled out the terrace doors.

The room hung in uneasy silence for a moment, then someone coughed, and as if awakening from a momentary sleep, Lady Hurston continued her toast. "To Lady Madeline and Lord Gresham!"

Fourteen

Oh, dear," Maddie said with a mixture of sympathy and amusement as she sipped her champagne. She and her cousins were huddled in a corner talking among themselves as the crowd in the ballroom drank champagne and made merry. "I knew Amelia disliked me, but I had no idea just how much until now."

"It's not just you," Cecily said with a shake of her dark head. "It's all of us. Imagine what she would do if she knew about the . . ." She leaned in and whispered in a low voice, "The dance card."

"I know!" Juliet said, also keeping her voice hushed. "If it weren't for the dance card I would never have gotten the courage to dance with Alec."

"And I know I wouldn't have made the push to speak to Winterson," Cecily agreed. "Indeed, though Maddie seems to have sent Amelia over the edge, she is the one who has needed the you-know-what the least. After all, she snagged Gresham without it. And they are just as besotted as we are."

"Don't," Maddie said before she could stop herself.

"Don't what?" Cecily asked, puzzled. "Don't talk about the dance card?"

"No," Maddie said impatiently, "don't speak about my relationship with Gresham as if it is the same as yours with Winterson, or Juliet's with Deveril."

"Whatever are you talking about, Maddie?" Juliet asked, wrapping an arm around her cousin. "Of course it's the same."

"No," Maddie insisted, "it isn't. You two are blissfully in love with your husbands. Whereas Christian and I are . . . well, I'm not sure what we are, but I know we aren't blissfully in love."

Cecily and Juliet exchanged a look.

"So," Cecily said quietly, "he loves you but you don't love him. Like I was with Winterson."

"Not necessarily," Juliet interjected. "They could be like Alec and me. She could love him but he doesn't love her. Yet."

"Is that it, Maddie?" Cecily asked.

"No," Maddie said impatiently. "You both have it all wrong. Christian and I are marrying because it's known we kissed publicly at Lady Emily Fielding's card party. I am compromised and he is marrying me to save my reputation. What is left of it, I mean."

"Oh, I see," Cecily said her voice heavy with irony. "You are right, that's nothing like my match with Winterson."

"You don't understand," Maddie said impatiently. "You were overcome by the heat of the moment. The passion. When Christian climbed the trellis into my bedchamber—"

"Madeline Honoria Essex!" Juliet hissed. "Never say that you have anticipated your vows!" She held a mocking hand to her chest. "I, for one, am shocked! Shocked!"

"Forget about being shocked," Cecily said. "I want details!"

Maddie felt herself blush. "Of course I won't go into detail," she said impatiently. "What I was trying to say is that our match is not the product of irresistible attraction. It is the result of a scandalous situation and a bit of gallantry on his part."

"Gallantry?" Cecily asked. "My dear, a man does not marry out of a sense of gallantry. Yes, a gentleman will marry a young lady whose reputation he has compromised, but I hardly think that is *all* there is between you."

"I've seen the way he looks at you, Maddie," Juliet said softly. "When you aren't watching. He is fond of you. He may well love you."

Maddie looked at the floor. "I know he holds me in some affection. As I do him. But we are not hopelessly in love as you two are with your own husbands. True, there is passion. But from what I can tell, that is possible even when there is no affection at all."

Impulsively, Cecily hugged her. "I know you think it's different for you. And perhaps it is. But do not set yourself up for failure before you've even said the vows. What would one of the heroines of your novels do? Surely she would not resign herself to a loveless marriage."

A half smile quirking her lips, Maddie conceded the point. "You are right. She would not."

"Show a bit of the spirit you are known for, Mads," Juliet said, hugging her as well. "If he doesn't love you already then you need to demand that he do so at once!"

At the mental image of Christian's face should she tell him such a thing, Maddie bit back a laugh. Perhaps she did need to look at this marriage business from a different perspective. After all, she and Christian were friends. Surely they could find their way to love along that path. Her match was different from her cousins', true, but that did not mean that it must necessarily be inferior.

"All right," she told her cousins, drawing strength from their support. "I will not give up on the idea of finding love in my marriage just yet."

"Good girl," Cecily said with a grin. "Just remember to tell him plainly what you want."

"And," Juliet added with a wink, "a whisper-thin night rail might not come amiss, either."

The morning of the day before his wedding dawned cold and gray. Late spring in London, Christian reflected as he navigated the streets of the city on Galahad, making his way to his sister's grave.

As a suicide, she was technically not allowed to be buried in consecrated ground, but Christian's uncle the archbishop had arranged for Clarissa to be interred in the Bunhill Fields Cemetery north of London, in Islington. The site of burials for a large number of dissenters and members of other faiths than the Church of England thanks to its unconsecrated grounds, Bunhill Fields was open to the burial of anyone who could pay the fees.

Tethering his horse to the fence surrounding the graveyard, he stepped through the gates and wended his way toward the east corner of the cemetery where a small, unprepossessing headstone marked the last resting place of the sister that Christian had adored.

Kneeling, he brushed a climbing vine from the stone, in a gesture reminiscent of the teasing way he used to brush her hair from her eyes.

It had been months since he'd come here. He knew well enough that the remains buried here were no longer Clarissa. And when he'd first returned from the Continent he had avoided coming here for that very reason. Haunting a dead sister's graveside would hardly bring her back, or right the wrong that had driven her to this place.

Still, on this, the day before he would wed the girl whose own brother had abandoned her to her fate, Christian had felt the urge to confide in Clarissa. As he had done when they were children together. Before she succumbed to the melancholia that had ultimately killed her.

He had come here to talk about Madeline, but it was his sister who filled his thoughts now. "Clarey," he said aloud, feeling foolish, but needing to vent the feelings that threatened to overwhelm him. "Why could you not wait for me? You know I would have set things right. Like I always did. Why couldn't you wait?"

Turning, he saw a straight-backed older lady approaching. Her light brown hair, so like his own, was escaping its pins, hinting at a liberality that did not, unfortunately, apply to her personality.

"So," Mrs. Elizabeth Monteith said, approaching her son, "you are as unwilling to accept her guilt as ever, I see."

Christian bit back the curse that threatened to escape him as he watched his mother approach. It was an old argument between them. Going even as far back as his childhood when he had watched his mother castigate Clarissa for some meaningless infraction. For some reason, she had never been able to give her youngest daughter the benefit of the doubt. She saw Clarissa's moods and melancholy as a weakness. And weakness was something Elizabeth could not, would not, tolerate.

"I am surprised that you are here," he said finally,

noting with amazement that his mother carried a posy of violets, which had been Clarissa's favorite flower. "I thought you were in Scotland with Deirdre and Eleanor."

His mother looked down at the bouquet and then up at Christian.

"Just because I am able to admit that she did this to herself does not mean that I don't mourn her, Gresham." Her words were chiding, but Christian saw genuine emotion in her eyes. "I do. Every day."

"You'll excuse me for not recognizing your constant criticism of my sister as motherly devotion," he said bitterly. "It's a wonder she lasted to the ripe old age of twenty-five before she threw herself into the arms of the first bounder she could find."

"That is unworthy of you," his mother said curtly. "She was ill, Gresham. Perhaps it was too late before I realized it. I do not claim that my handling of her was always the most effective. Clearly it was not, or she'd be here to argue her own case. But I did love her. As I love all my children."

She paused and met his gaze. "Even the ones who call me everything but a murderer."

Turning away, Christian pinched the bridge of his nose. He was probably being unfair to her, had known as much for some time now. But he was so damned racked with guilt at the thought of Clarissa thinking that a bottle of laudanum was the answer to her predicament. If he'd not been on the Continent he could have been here to stop her.

"She knew you loved her, Christian," his mother said, diffidently laying her hand on his bowed back. "She did not blame you for your absensce. She was proud of you. So proud. I sometimes thought that the only time she smiled was when she spoke of you and your heroism during the war."

"I should have been here, Mama," he said, staring down at the grave marker. "I should have been here to stop her from getting caught up in that business with Selford."

He would have been up on murder charges himself if Lord Selford hadn't left for America shortly after Clarissa's death. Christian had been told by the man's solicitor that he had done so primarily out of fear for what his abandoned lover's brother the war hero might do on his return.

"She was unpersuadable on the matter, my dear," his mother said quietly. "She was in love. Or thought she was. He was handsome enough. And had manners that fooled even me for a while."

Christian turned to frown at her. "Really?" he asked, unable to keep the surprise from his voice. "I thought you forbade her from seeing him."

"That was after I found him trying to bribe her maid to leave the back door of the house unlocked for him."

Thinking of his own trip up the trellis at Essex House, Christian felt a pang of guilt. The difference, however, was that he was prepared to marry Maddie. Selford had seduced then abandoned Clarissa. Leaving her with child and a broken heart. And a volatile temperament and an impulsive nature that was almost guaranteed to lead to a bad outcome.

"I doubt you could have done much to stop them," he said with a heavy sigh. "Clarey was hardly a biddable daughter. And once she'd decided to have him, she would probably have done anything to see him."

"Still," she said quietly, "I should have tried harder. I should have seen through his charming manners to the man underneath."

Silently, he took his mother's hand, and they stood thus for a moment, in a rare bit of solidarity.

"From what I've heard," Mrs. Monteith said, "Clarissa would have liked your Lady Madeline."

Christian turned to look at her quizzically. "What do you know of her?" he asked.

"Only what I've heard from the bit of gossip that reaches Edinburgh," she said with a slight shrug. "That she is a most determined young lady who refuses to be cowed by the strictures of the *ton*."

He smiled at the description. "You don't know the half of it," he said with a grin. "She is all that and more."

"Do you love her?"

Christian felt his ears redden. "Well, I . . . that is to say . . . I have . . ."

His mother's laugh rang out in the empty churchyard. "I am only raking you over the coals a bit, Gresham. What you feel for the young lady is your own affair."

He relaxed a bit. "Thank you for that, at least." Whatever it was he felt for Maddie, it wasn't something he was comfortable discussing with his mother.

Reminded of the wedding, he turned to her. "Why are you in town? You cannot have gotten word of my betrothal." Despite his anger with her over his sister's death, he had sent a note to his mother in Scotland informing her of his pending marriage earlier in the week. But there was no way the missive had already reached her. They'd probably crossed paths on the road.

"No," she said, her eyes keen. "I only learned of that when I arrived at your aunt Harrison's this morning. And was rather surprised, I might add."

"By the circumstances?" he asked.

"By the circumstances," she affirmed, "and by the fact of it. I had no idea you were looking to marry."

Christian stared at the toe of his boot. "I wasn't, but

things have changed. And I am fond of Lady Madeline," he offered.

"So I guessed," his mother said, smiling. "I hope that you will allow me to attend the wedding."

This last she added almost as an afterthought. Christian wondered for a moment if his mother, whom he'd always thought of as invincible, was feeling shy. The notion made him feel like a churl for his earlier temper at her. But she doubtless understood that the strong emotions they both felt over the manner of Clarissa's death was what had caused his outburst.

"I would like very much for you to attend the wedding, Mama," he said. "And for you to meet Lady Madeline."

"Thank you," she said. "I would like that."

"So, why are you in town?" he asked again.

She looked down at Clarissa's headstone. "It was time," she said, bending to smooth a gloved hand over the curve of the stone's top. "I've hidden myself away for long enough."

Reflecting that he'd misjudged her on many counts, Christian slipped an arm around his mother and walked her back to her waiting carriage.

Fifteen

The week of Maddie's wedding was spent in a whirl-wind of activity as she, Cecily, Juliet, and Lady Essex set about putting the preparations in place. Not only was there a new wardrobe to order but also the packing and moving of Maddie's belongings to the Gresham town house in Berkeley Square. As a result, by the time the actual wedding arrived, Maddie was exhausted, and doubted her ability to remain awake when she was finally afforded the opportunity to stand still. Which, as it happened, was in the church standing before the archbishop.

The wedding itself was a small affair, with only Maddie's cousins, their husbands, her parents, and Christian's mother, whom she'd met just yesterday, in attendance. She'd been in St. George's Hanover Square countless times for countless weddings, but when she arrived there for her own, it seemed wholly new. As if the edifice itself had been reborn just for the occasion.

She spied Christian at the front of the church as soon as she stepped into the sanctuary. She'd recognize those broad shoulders and his slightly messy light brown locks anywhere. And when he turned and met her gaze, she felt a chord of harmony thrum through her, as if she were a tuning fork suddenly striking the perfect note. His slightly crooked smile, and the warmth in his eyes, spoke to her more eloquently than a library full of poetry would have done.

"Hello there," he whispered, as she stepped up beside him, and took her hand in his. "Fancy seeing you here."

"You are absurd," she said with a smile that softened the tartness of her words. "Utterly so."

"You are beautiful," he said, his eyes catching hers and holding her gaze until Maddie felt the tickle of incipient tears.

"My lord," the archbishop said with a benevolent smile—he was Christian's uncle, so he was a bit more lenient than he might have been with someone who wasn't family. "Might we get started?"

"Absolutely," Christian told the clergyman. And just like that, Maddie's playful companion was replaced with a businesslike bridegroom.

The ceremony itself was all too brief. Maddie and Christian spoke their vows clearly and evenly. And despite another moment of near tearfulness, Maddie made it through the rite with her sensibilities intact.

"What God has joined together," the archbishop intoned, "let no man put asunder."

And with that, Lady Madeline Essex and Christian Gerard Monteith, Lord Gresham, became the Earl and Countess of Gresham.

"Dearest, I am so deliciously pleased for you," Cecily said, gathering Maddie into a fierce embrace. "And for you as well, Gresham," she said, moving on to embrace the bridegroom while Winterson kissed the bride.

"Welcome to the club, old fellow," Winterson said, cuffing his friend on the shoulder.

"I wish so much happiness for you, Maddie," said Juliet, her tight hug nearly robbing Maddie of breath. "I just know you are going to be blissful. I can feel it."

Thinking back to their conversation at the betrothal ball, Maddie hoped that her cousin's feeling was right. If they did not find happiness together, she vowed silently that it would not be because she hadn't tried her best to make it so.

"Just let us know if this fellow gives you any trouble, Maddie," Deveril said with a wink. "I'm more than happy to keep him in line for you."

"So you say," Christian retorted. "I think if it meant risking your lace cuffs or your cravat you'd turn craven and hie off in the other direction."

"Mock all you wish, Gresham," Deveril responded, "but at least I can tell the difference between the two."

"Gentlemen, really," Juliet scolded, "now is not the time or the place for your brangling."

"No, the time and place is at Essex House during the wedding breakfast," Maddie said with a laugh. "Come, husband, let's be on our way."

"Married five minutes and already you're ordering me about," Christian complained, as they led the others down the main aisle of the church and to the waiting carriage.

Her senses heightened by the proximity of her new husband, Maddie felt her heart beat faster as she hurried up the carriage steps. As soon as the door shut behind them and Maddie was seated, Christian leaned forward and plucked her neatly from her perch and onto his lap.

"There, that's better," he said, wrapping his arms around her. "You have no notion of how difficult it was for me to maintain my composure during the ceremony. It was all I could do to keep from mauling you right there in front of all those people."

"That would have been embarrassing for them," Maddie said with a smothered laugh as she offered her neck for his delectation. "I can only imagine what your uncle's response would have been."

"Uncle Cedric was quite the ladies' man before he married," her new husband informed her, dragging his teeth over her earlobe. "I suspect he's seen much worse in his day."

Ignoring the flash of just how much worse the archbishop could have seen, Maddie tried to push back a little. The drive from the church to her parents' house was hardly long enough to facilitate the sort of dallying Christian seemed intent upon.

"This is highly improper," she reminded him. "I sincerely doubt that this is the sort of thing one is supposed to get up to in a carriage."

Christian pulled back to stare into her face. "I had thought that being a writer would mean that you were possessed of an advanced imagination," he said. "Obviously I shall be forced to teach you the error of your thoughts on this matter."

"But not just now, I hope," Maddie said, stopping his hand as it began to lift her skirt and bringing it to her lips. "I would die of embarrassment if anyone were to guess what we'd been up to in here."

With a sigh of mock dejection, Christian settled back into the squabs and contented himself with lacing their fingers together. "I would not like to see you embarrassed, my dear," he told her, tucking her head under his chin. "I will attempt to leash my ravening beast within until we are alone in a proper bedroom.

"But," he added, "I will make no promises as to what will happen then. I may have to punish you with kisses for forcing me to curb myself."

Maddie suppressed a shiver at the notion, but agreed.

Changing the subject to one that would spare her blushes, she said, "Have you contacted Lord Tretham or my brother about the possible threats against them?"

Linton had not been able to make it back to London in time for the wedding, and though Maddie had been disappointed, she had been more than willing to have him remain away if it kept him from danger.

At the mention of the mystery, Christian heaved a great sigh, which Maddie felt in the rise and fall of his chest. "I had hoped that we might save talk of the investigation until tomorrow at least, my dear. After all, even the Lord took a day to rest."

Maddie felt her face flood with color and tried to pull away from him to remove herself to the opposite side of the carriage.

"I am sorry if it bothers you, my lord," she said stiffly, "that I am concerned for my brother's safety, but I have just gone through the marriage ceremony without having him there to witness it. I can hardly be expected to forget about the potential danger he finds himself in simply because of a church ritual."

Christian, however, clamped his arms more firmly around her and would not let her go.

"Don't get your back up, madam wife," he said in a soothing tone. "I did not think of the fact that you might be missing Viscount Linton today. I apologize for my thoughtlessness."

Somewhat mollified, Maddie relaxed a bit, but the easy camaraderie they'd shared before she mentioned her brother and Tretham seemed to have dissipated.

"To answer your question," Christian continued, "I have sent a special messenger to Scotland to warn your brother to stay put until he hears from me again."

Maddie breathed a sigh of relief. "Thank you," she said sincerely. "Ever since I spoke with Lady Emily

I've been worried that Linton might try to return, putting himself in more danger."

"Of course," he said simply, though Maddie knew that there was no "of course" about it. He could easily have left Linton to fend for himself. "As for Tretham," he continued, "I did try to call on him, but he appears to have left town as well. I even attempted to get his servants to tell me where he's gone but they were unpersuadable."

Maddie shrugged. "Tretham can take care of himself," she said, leaning back. "I do not mind telling you that knowing my brother knows to remain hidden relieves my mind greatly."

He stilled. "I know that," he said finally. Maddie sensed that he was not thinking about Linton at all. Attempting to change the subject to something more cheerful, she said, "I was pleased that your mother was able to come. I thought she would have to miss it, since she was so lately in Scotland with your sisters."

There was a question there, and Christian did Maddie the courtesy of answering it. "Yes, she was here for another reason and so was able to attend. I doubt, however, that we will see her at the breakfast."

"I hadn't realized that you were estranged from your family," she said with a gentle smile. "It is sometimes difficult for me to remember that you have a family at all," she admitted. "You seem so self-sufficient."

"You think I sprang from the head of my father like Athena?" Christian asked, stroking her arm. "Much as I enjoy the comparison to a god, I am a mere mortal."

"Does it have something to do with your sister?" she asked, stroking the back of his hand with her thumb, not meeting his eyes. "Your estrangement, I mean."

Christian sighed. Maddie had been so open with him about her relationship with Linton. Had bared her soul about how she felt about her parents' attitude toward her. He owed her the same kind of honesty. But how could he mar the joy of this day, of all days, with the melancholy of his sister's death?

He felt Maddie withdraw a little. It was only a slight shift of her body away from him, but he noticed it. "I'm sorry," she said with diffidence. "I shouldn't pry. Mama always did say that an overabundance of curiosity would be my downfall."

She was nervous, he guessed. Pulling her back to sit flush against him, he murmured, "Don't apologize. You should know. About this, and the whole sordid mess." He leaned his head back against the squabs of the carriage. "I just don't want to dwell on so much unhappiness today. Do you understand?"

Maddie relaxed against him. "I do understand," she said, "but I am your wife now, and a part of your family. You can tell me anything."

His heart constricted. How the devil had he been so lucky to find a woman like her? How could he possibly have missed seeing this generosity of hers for the past weeks of their friendship?

"You are," he said, leaning down to kiss her properly. "And I will tell you. I promise. Just not right now."

The slowing of the carriage punctuated his words.

"Very well," Maddie said, "but do not try to protect me from the truth. I am strong enough to accept it no matter how melancholy it might be."

"I know," he said, squeezing her hand. "Believe me. I do."

While Maddie was almost immediately swept away into a group of women that included her cousins and aunts—doubtless to be interrogated about her plans for the redecoration of Gresham House or some such female occupation—Christian found himself alone in the entryway of Essex House with his new papa-in-law.

Since Maddie's father had made his displeasure about the match known on the day Christian had asked for her hand, there had been little opportunity for the two men to exchange more than a few polite words. Though if he weren't bound by propriety and a desire to keep Maddie from becoming upset, he would have told the older man exactly what he thought of him.

Perhaps also remembering their previous altercation, Essex cleared his throat. "It was wrong of me," Lord Essex said curtly. "What I said before about Madeline's behavior. I was overset by the situation but that is really no excuse."

Christian, who had been carefully studying the watch fob at his waist, looked up in surprise. He had expected this meeting to be awkward, of course, but he hadn't expected this.

"I have a problem," Essex continued, not able to meet Christian's eyes. "Always have had the devil of a temper, you see. And when Linton and Madeline were children I stopped mixing it with drink. But, while I no longer rail drunkenly, I still have a tendency to rail. And this business with Linton has overset me, I don't mind telling you."

"It is hardly surprising," Christian offered diplomatically. He wasn't sure that the stress of Linton's situation was enough of an excuse for what Lord Essex had said to Maddie, but he was making an effort. That was beyond most men with similar temperament issues. "Having your son and heir under suspicion for murder must be quite oversetting."

Finally looking up, Lord Essex nodded. "It is. But what I said to Madeline. Accusing her of being no better than a common sl—" He stopped, clearly unable to say the words. "Well, it was wrong of me. I know she's headstrong, but she's never been one to behave in a wanton matter. I overreacted to the situation, and I insulted you both."

He went on, "I hope you'll find it in yourself to forgive me."

The older man's eyes were intent as he waited to hear what Christian would say. Christian knew it must have taken a great deal of courage for a man who was accustomed to giving orders and commanding attention to humble himself before a man he had insulted.

Nodding briskly, Christian said, "I will forgive you, but I'm afraid it's a conditional forgiveness."

Essex's graying brows furrowed. "And what is that condition?"

"That you apologize to Madeline," Christian said firmly. "With all due respect, I don't give a hang about your insult to me. My anger that day was about the way you treated your daughter, my lord."

Lord Essex pursed his lips, but did not disagree.

"Make things right with your daughter," Christian told him, "and that will right things between us."

Of course, he had no idea what Maddie's response would be to her father's apology. But there would be no amity between them if Lord Essex didn't make the effort. For both their sakes, Christian hoped that they were able to reconcile in the event that something untoward happened to Lord Linton. Because if something occurred to harm the heir to the Essex earldom, the entire family would need to pull together.

Maddie was on her way upstairs to her bedchamber to ensure she'd left nothing behind, when a feminine cough from a little-used parlor door drew her attention.

To her surprise she saw Miss Amelia Snowe hovering there.

"May I help you?" Maddie asked, not quite sure what to say. After the other girl's outburst at her betrothal ball, Maddie had put the blond beauty out of her thoughts. She'd been busy with wedding plans and the like. Her erstwhile nemesis hadn't really figured into that.

At least the other girl had the grace to blush, Maddie thought wryly.

"I apologize for intruding upon your wedding breakfast," Amelia said, looking a bit sheepish. "I did tell the footman that I could wait if necessary."

She looked about the small room. "I have a suspicion he put me here and forgot about me."

"The servants are quite busy today," Maddie said with a slight inclination of her head. Then, not wishing to prolong the interview, she got to the heart of the matter. "What brings you here, Amelia? We are hardly friends enough to warrant your coming here to wish me happy."

To Maddie's relief, Amelia seemed to appreciate her plain speaking. "You are correct, of course, Lady . . . Gresham," she said, pausing to remember her new title. "Especially after my outburst at your betrothal ball."

Maddie was rather shocked the other girl would bring it up, but she supposed it was brave in its way.

"Think nothing of it," she said, feeling magnanimous. "We all have days where we wish a large hole would open up in the ground and swallow us up."

Amelia looked relieved. "You are more kind than I deserve," she said quietly. "I've been perfectly wretched to you and your cousins. I have little excuse for it, except to say that I feel a great deal of unease about my own position in society. After all, I haven't your titled family, or the knowledge that my mother was once considered the toast of London."

She went on, "In any event, I do wish you to know that I am sorry for my ill behavior. And I hope that even if you cannot find it in yourself to forgive me, you will at least allow me to tell you what I've come here to say."

At Maddie's nod, her blue eyes looked troubled. "I acknowledge that today is perhaps not the best of days to reveal this to you. I wish I'd known yesterday so that you might have been able to take action before the wedding, but I cannot help that now."

Feeling a shiver of fear slide down her spine, Maddie turned and shut the door of the little chamber.

"What is it you wish to tell me, Miss Snowe?" If the other girl had something to say that might affect her marriage, she wished to know it sooner rather than later.

"Lady Gresham," Amelia said, for once looking sincere, "I dislike being the bearer of such tidings, but it has come to my attention that your new husband, Lord Gresham, was seen visiting a . . . a house of ill repute earlier this week."

Maddie felt the color drain from her cheeks. "How do you know such a thing?" she demanded of Amelia. After all, young ladies were hardly in the habit of loitering in the neighborhoods where brothels plied their trade.

Amelia looked at the floor. "I overheard my brother mentioning it to one of his male friends."

Maddie's ears began to ring. "And do you know which establishment my husband is said to have visited?" she demanded, trying like mad to keep her voice from breaking.

The thought that Christian might have gone from her bed to a mistress would have been bad enough. But a brothel was even worse than that. At least if he kept a mistress she might be able to rationalize that he was using the visit to break things off. With a brothel, there would not be the sort of arrangement as one had with a mistress. She felt her stomach lurch at the thought.

"I think my brother said it was the Hidden Pearl," Amelia said, looking ill herself. "I remember because I thought it an eloquent name for such a vile place."

The Hidden Pearl? Maddie thought back. She could have sworn she'd heard someone speak about the place before. Someone not related to Christian. She searched her memory, desperate to make the connection. The only other men she was around were her father and her brother. Both of whom were . . . Wait. She suddenly remembered that she'd overheard Tretham and one of the other men at Lady Emily's card party discussing the place.

Put together with her gut instinct that told her that despite his flaws, Christian would not be so crass as to visit a brothel for the usual reasons so soon after taking her virginity, the information made Maddie angry for another reason altogether.

The devious man was investigating the case without her. And had not bothered to share whatever he'd learned with her.

Still annoyed, but not heartbroken as she'd felt when Amelia first disclosed her awful news, Maddie turned back to her unwelcome visitor.

"Miss Snowe," she said, her anger giving her a resolve she'd not been feeling earlier in the day. "I must thank you for informing me of this. If you only knew how much this helps me."

Amelia looked confused. "H-helps?" she asked hesitantly.

"Why, yes," Maddie said grimly. "This is information

that I most certainly needed to know. And I would never have learned it without your help. I have little doubt that my husband would not have told me." The bounder.

"I suppose not," Amelia said, looking at Maddie as if she'd just voiced a thirst for human blood. "I'll just leave you to your . . ." She paused, as if searching for the right word. "Event," she finally settled on before hurrying from the room.

Alone, Maddie reflected on how she would approach her new husband with the news that he'd been found out.

Sixteen

When Christian handed Maddie down from the carriage in front of the Gresham town house, he couldn't help but notice just how quickly she pulled back from his grasp. Perhaps she was feeling a bit of nerves over the night to come, he thought.

"My lord, my lady," his butler, Yeats, said with as much of a smile as Christian had ever seen him muster. "May I offer you the congratulations of the household. And may I welcome you to your new home, my lady."

Maddie's stiffness disappeared at the welcome. "Thank you so much, Mr. Yeats," she said warmly. "I look forward to learning more about the house and about you and the other people who make it run so smoothly."

The old man all but blushed. Directing her forward into the entryway, he indicated the line of servants waiting to bid her welcome.

Christian watched, fascinated, as his new wife moved down the line of servants, repeating their names back to them as if attempting to memorize them, and taking care to make some comment to each of them. She would make them an excellent mistress, he concluded. He was somewhat surprised because he had never considered her the domestic sort.

When they'd finished the introductions, Maddie turned back to Christian, and he could almost feel the air around her cool. He'd put her earlier distance down to nerves, but there was very clearly something on her mind.

"Will you show me to my chamber so that I might rest a bit before dinner?" she asked. Her tone was friendly enough, he thought, but nothing like the easy tone she'd used with him that morning between the church and the wedding breakfast.

"Of course," he said, trying to remember if he'd done or said something that would have changed her manner toward him in the course of the afternoon.

Silently they made their way upstairs, down corridors, until finally they reached the hallway outside their bedchambers.

Opening a door between them, he ushered her in. "This is the sitting room that joins our two chambers," he said, stepping behind her into the room, where a fire was lit to ward off the chill of the overcast day. "To the left is the door to my dressing room and the bedchamber beyond," he said, nodding in that direction. "And to the right, you will find your own dressing room and bedchamber."

He stepped closer to take her hand and lead her toward her rooms. But to his surprise, she pulled her hand from his. "I'm sorry, my lord," she said coolly. "I'm afraid I am fatigued from the day's events. I would like nothing more than to have a nice long nap."

If she weren't bristling with anger, Christian might have allowed her to retire to her chamber and a refreshing sleep. But she was obviously angry with him over something and he was dashed if he'd start his marriage with a quarrel between them.

He looked at her for a long moment as she waited for

him to respond. Her eyes were wary, and her nostrils flared a little, as if she were smelling something bad.

"What have I done?" he asked, finally. He couldn't think of any transgression he might have committed in the past few hours, but obviously something had happened to set her back up.

"I don't know what you're talking about," she said, her mouth tight.

Women.

"Obviously something has happened to overset you," he said, thrusting a hand through his hair. The windswept style his valet had so slaved over that morning had at least lasted this long, he thought wryly. "On our way to the breakfast things were fine, and then after the breakfast you grew distant. Did I do something during the gathering that gave you a disgust of me?"

He saw her inward debate as she stared at him for a long moment.

Finally, she gave a slight shrug. "All right, my lord," she said tersely. "I will tell you. I had a visit from Miss Amelia Snowe during the wedding breakfast."

What the . . . ? "Why the devil would she call on you?" he demanded. He'd never been a great fan of the chit. She was pretty enough, but had the disposition of a sour apple. "You are hardly such friends that she would have come to offer her felicitations, I think."

"She was not making a social call," Maddie said, her spine ramrod straight. "Though she did apologize for her outburst at the betrothal ball."

"Are you angry with me because of something I've said to her, then?" Christian demanded, trying to understand what the devil Amelia Snowe might have to do with Maddie's present state of rage.

"Of course not," she said, waving away his suggestion with an impatient flick of her hand. "Amelia came to inform me of something. Something she would have liked to tell me before the wedding, but that she only just learned."

Christian felt the prickle of unease between his shoulders. If Maddie were speaking in terms of before the wedding—as in, before the wedding so that she might be able to cry off—this was serious business, indeed.

"And?" he prompted.

"And," Maddie said with disgust, "she told me that you were seen departing from an establishment called the Hidden Pearl earlier this week."

Christian pinched the bridge of his nose, struggling to think of how best to explain that visit without digging himself into a deeper hole.

"Well, my lord?" she demanded, crossing her arms over her chest. One small foot tapped impatiently on the Aubusson carpet. "Have you an excuse? A denial? I have little doubt that most men are adept at issuing denials for any number of transgressions. Trips to brothels mere days before their weddings included."

"It's not what you think," he said, knowing that he sounded like every bloody husband who had ever been caught out indulging in an affair. Which made the situation even more unfair, since he hadn't been indulging in an affair. "I mean, I wasn't there for what you think I was there for."

She only raised one blond brow. Her eyes were like blue flint. This would take some finesse, he thought.

He thought about approaching her, maybe taking her hands in his. But Christian knew the unspoken language of the body and Maddie's clearly said, "Do not approach."

"Maddie," he tried again, his voice croaking a little. "I am not the sort of man who would go from your bed to that of a wh—woman of ill repute—in the space of a few days. First of all, I hold you in far too great esteem to do such a thing to you. And secondly, I was quite thoroughly contented by our encounter, and if I were feeling the need to . . ."—He paused, searching for a delicate term—"see a woman, I would just have come to you."

That was hardly something he liked to admit. Not that he was embarrassed by his needs, but he was somewhat abashed at just how much he needed her. Ever since their night together he'd found himself aching to get his hands on her again. Right now he should be peeling her out of that curve-enhancing gown and licking her from head to toe. Instead he was defending a visit to a brothel that he'd undertaken on behalf of saving her scapegrace brother.

To his surprise, however, his admission only seemed to make her more angry.

"Must you be such a *man*?" Maddie demanded, pronouncing the word as if it were a vile epithet. "Do you not think I have the intelligence to know that you were not there for the typical reasons one visits a brothel? Really, Gresham, credit me with a bit of sense."

Christian stared. She couldn't know why he'd actually gone there. Could she?

Apparently, she could.

"I know you were there because of something having to do with Tinker's murder, Christian," she said acidly. "That is why I am so angry."

She was the damnedest woman.

"Let me make sure I understand you," he said, his hands on his hips. "Amelia Snowe told you I'd been seen at a brothel just days after I—very ably, I might add—took your virginity. And you are angry not because you thought I'd gone there to whore, but because you know I went there to investigate Tinker's death? Do I have that right?"

Maddie twisted her lips in disgust. "When you put it that way it sounds foolish," she said with frustration. "How could you, Christian? We promised to work together! You were going to keep me informed of developments in our investigation."

"And I did," he said, almost shouting. "You have been a bit busy these past few days, have you not? When was I supposed to tell you about this? When you were being pinned to death by seamstresses? Or maybe when you and your cousins were closeted together deciding which of your gowns you would be bringing with you to Gresham House?"

"You could have found a way," she said, striding toward him, stopping when their toes touched. "Why didn't you tell me?" she demanded, poking him in the chest with an accusing finger.

"Because I was trying to keep you safe, damn it," he all but roared. "Because I was trying to ensure that you did not suffer any more on behalf of your damned brother! And because the thought of you in that vile place was enough to set my teeth on edge!"

Unable to stop himself, he took her by the shoulders, and crushed his mouth to hers.

One minute they were arguing, and the next they were kissing as if they hadn't seen one another in ten years. All the anger she'd been holding back as the day progressed was suddenly transformed into a frenetic sensual energy, as Maddie gave as good as she got.

Opening her mouth under his, she pressed as close as she could get to every muscular inch of him. Grasping blindly, she held on for dear life to his coat, his shirt, his cravat—whatever she could get her hands on. She felt Christian's hands move restlessly over her, one sliding up to bury itself in her hair, the other clasping her buttocks and pressing her against his growing erection.

"Maddie," she felt him mutter against her mouth, as she stroked a restless hand under his coat, then waistcoat to feel the warmth of his skin through the lawn of his shirt. "My God," he said again, moving down her chin with his lips as she used her other hand to roughly caress him through the placket of his breeches.

"Don't," he said with a strangled cry as she grasped him. "Don't, damn it," he said again when she ignored him. "I want this to last more than a minute," he hissed. But rather than feeling cowed by his admonition, Maddie hid a grin. A grin that disappeared when she felt him press her against the wall of the sitting room, and bend his knees so that he could pull up her skirt.

She gave a little gasp as she felt him run a hand over the silk stockings covering her right calf and up over her thigh to slip along the exposed skin over her garters. Lifting her chin and pressing her head back against the wall, she bit back a squeak as she felt him move up to caress the hot wetness between her legs. At the same time, he deftly pulled down the bosom of her gown and took her nipple in his mouth and sucked. The onslaught of sensation stole Maddie's breath as she felt her pelvis thrust up to meet his hand.

"Ah, God," he said, slipping first one finger, then another into her throbbing passage, moving them in a slowly building rhythm that almost made her weep.

Though she was almost mindless from his ministrations, Maddie reached down again and caressed him through his pants. This time, unable to resist her, Christian thrust himself against her hand, never losing the steady pace of his fingers sliding into her.

It was at once a rekindling of the passion they'd experienced in Maddie's bedchamber, but it was also something more. Something mad and uncontrollable. Maddie felt as if she were going to split apart into a million bits if he didn't give her what she craved.

Unable to keep still, she felt the pleasure build within her as again and again he pressed into her, bringing her closer and closer to the edge. She fumbled to grasp him again, but when Christian touched that spot above where he thrust into her with his thumb, she felt herself convulse and cry out.

Moving uncontrollably until she finally flew over the precipice, she was dimly aware of Christian unbuckling his breeches, and shifting her, lifting her against the wall.

"Wrap your legs around my waist," he said in a tight voice, her body braced between the wall and his arms. Maddie complied, almost instinctively, and when his hardness nudged against her, she felt the languor that had flooded her moments before dissipate to be replaced by excitement.

Wordlessly, Christian held her there with one arm, and bending his knees slightly, guided himself into her. Opening her eyes, Maddie found her gaze locked with his as inch by excruciating inch, he breached the entrance of her and pressed inexorably inside.

Suddenly the haste of their earlier loveplay was replaced by a connection that frightened her with its intensity. Christian did not look away as, fully seated now, he kept one arm beneath her buttocks and began to move within her. Coupled with their shared gaze, the friction of his motions was devastating.

Reveling in the strength of his arms around her, and in the knowledge that this man loving her was not just her lover, but her husband, Maddie was almost overcome with emotion. The urgency built within her as she rocked into him, opening herself wider for him as again and again he pressed her into the wall. All of her senses were hypersensitive to the moment, to the sounds, the smells, the tastes of their coupling.

On an upstroke, he leaned forward and took her mouth with his. The thrust of his tongue into her mouth mimicked the motions of their lower bodies as he continued to move in and out of her heat. Each stroke sent her closer and closer to that place where she would lose herself in bliss.

Suddenly, he began to move faster, plunge higher and harder into her. And Maddie felt her breath quicken and her own movements grow erratic. Pinned against the wall, she felt the crisis come upon her, lifting her higher and higher into the ether until she lost control and began to fly. She was aware of Christian thrusting wildly into her until he, too, found bliss, and she felt the flood of his release within her.

As she came back to herself, she felt him panting as he pressed his forehead against the wall beside her, and slowly he allowed her to unwrap her legs from his waist and slide down the wall.

Wordlessly, he took her hand and led her into his bedchamber, where they both removed their clothing, and climbed into his enormous bed.

And slept.

When Christian roused some hours later, it was to find a lush, naked female body pressed up against him. Maddie's body, he thought with some degree of satisfaction. He might not have foreseen marrying her at the beginning of the season, but now that the deed was done, he was quite happy with the situation. Not only because of the passion between them, which was unlike anything he'd experienced, but also because it quite simply felt right.

He was a logical sort of man. For all of his appreciation of instinct, he had never thought to choose a wife based on it. Like most men with a succession to secure, he had thought to make a rational choice from among a carefully selected assortment of potential brides. But somehow he'd been drawn into Maddie's web, and rather than fighting to free himself, he'd allowed himself to be captured, with nary a protest.

He hadn't intended to behave like such a brute on their first time together as man and wife, he reflected, idly skimming a finger over her soft breast. But he could not deny that the lovemaking had been intense. And, recalling the way she'd held his gaze as he thrust into her, it had been one of the most intimate moments of his life. Their bodies had remained clothed, but through their eyes, their souls had been laid bare.

As his body responded typically to the memory, he felt his new wife stretch luxuriantly in his arms before turning neatly in his arms and kissing him on the chin.

"Hello," she said, her voice still a bit rough with sleep. "Fancy meeting you here."

Sliding his hands down her back and cupping her backside, he kissed her properly. "I am often to be found here," he said, drawing back to kiss the end of her nose. "Most nights, in fact."

Her mouth opened to respond, but her response was forestalled by a very loud rumble of hunger from her stomach. "Oh, dear," she said, coloring a little. "I'm afraid I was unable to eat much at the breakfast. What with nerves and Amelia and all."

"Then I will simply have to feed you," Christian said, tossing the bedclothes off them and lifting her into his arms. At her squeal of protest, he shushed her. "You are as light as a feather."

"A nine-stone feather," she said wryly, clasping him around the neck as he headed through the dressing room and into the sitting room between their suites. At the sight of a small table there, laden with covered dishes and wine and fruit, Maddie gasped. "How lovely," she said as Christian deposited her on her feet, and helped her into the dressing gown draped over her chair.

Watching her lift the covers to determine what savories awaited them, he covered his nakedness with the banyan that had been draped over his own chair. He could quite easily have gone without clothing for the meal, but he suspected that though she'd never admit it, Maddie was not quite that adventurous.

Yet.

They served themselves, Christian pouring the wine, and Maddie filling both their plates with a selection from such delicacies as thinly sliced ham, aspic, strawberries, and sharp cheese.

One of the things that Christian appreciated most about Maddie was her unabashed enthusiasm. Watching her tuck into the meal before her, he couldn't help but contrast her shameless appreciation for a good meal with the women he'd seen pick delicately at their food like so many birds.

As if by mutual consent, they discussed subjects that were not likely to cause discord between them. Christian told amusing stories from his childhood with three sisters, and Maddie related tales of her own exploits with her brother. Their easy camaraderie reminded him of just how much he genuinely *liked* her and enjoyed watching her respond to the world around her.

When they were both finished with the meal, Christian

drew Maddie's hand into his and stood. "I would like for you to come with me," he said, drawing her to her feet.

A slight furrow appeared between her brows. "Why?" she demanded suspiciously.

"It's a surprise," he said, drawing their linked hands up so that he could kiss the back of her hand. "You must trust me and come along."

Her eyes watching him to determine the sincerity of his words, she gave a quick nod and allowed Christian to lead her toward the door opening into the hall. Once outside the sitting room, he led her toward the back of the house, facing the back garden. Finally, he stopped before one door in particular, and put his hand on the doorknob.

"Close your eyes," he said gently, waiting for her to comply. It was clear she wished to protest, but also clear she wished to learn what the devil he was about.

Finally, after opening the door and ushering her through into the chamber beyond, he squeezed her hand.

"Open them," he demanded, watching as she at first peeked out from beneath her lashes, then fully opened her gaze to take in her surroundings.

"Good heavens!" she exhaled, raising a hand to her chest in wonder. "Christian, what on earth is this?"

Seventeen

Maddie gazed about the little office in surprise. The finely turned rosewood desk, which was not so insubstantial as to be ineffective, but not so bulky as to be impractical for a lady, was covered with neatly arranged trays of paper, ink pots, quills, and anything else a writer might need to transport words from the mind to the page.

Behind the desk, and indeed along every wall of the little room, bookshelves ranged from floor to ceiling. Maddie recognized some of her own favorite novels among the rows of neatly arranged tomes. Indeed, if she were not mistaken, they were her very own copies, brought here from her bedchamber at Essex House.

She took it all in, feeling Christian standing tensely behind her. As if waiting for her to approve or disapprove.

"I thought perhaps you might use this room for your writing," he said diffidently, adopting the age-old male posture for hiding vulnerability, his hands thrust into the pockets of his dressing gown. "If you wish," he added, clearly trying to indicate that if she chose not to use the room it was no matter to him.

Turning, Maddie watched as he waited for her response. His body might project indifference, but his eyes told a different story.

"I love it," she said, going up on tiptoes to kiss him. "No one has ever given me a more precious gift."

She saw flags of red appear in his cheeks. "Wasn't much of anything, really," he said, almost shyly. "I simply directed the servants to move your own books in here. And perhaps ordered a few of the novels from Felsham's that the fellow said you'd been waiting for. I used to go there to buy books for . . . to buy books."

Maddie heard the hesitation in his words, but was unable to keep from looking at all the lovely books. She surveyed the shelves behind the desk, reaching up to touch the spines of the books there. "You bought it!" she breathed. "I've been desperate for this one for weeks," she said excitedly, pulling the first volume of the three-volume set down so that she could examine it more closely.

Upon closer inspection she realized that the pages had already been cut. "This one has already been read," she said, turning to look at him with something akin to awe. "Did you read this book already, Christian?"

He shrugged. "I've read a great many of the books in this room," he said, wandering over to run a hand over the spines himself. "When I returned from the war, I read a great deal."

She frowned. "Why specifically then?"

He did not turn to look at her. "I suppose you have no way of knowing, but many soldiers who return from battle have difficulty sleeping. Or rather, staying asleep. I developed the trick during my years of campaigning of being able to fall asleep anywhere. When one is bivouacing wherever is convenient, one cannot afford the luxury of waiting for comfort to grab a bit of sleep. But when I returned, the comfortable bed with a roof over my head actually made staying asleep difficult. With the luxury of time," he went on, "I suppose my brain decided to mull over all those memories that I had suppressed while on the battlefield. As a result, I can rarely sleep for longer than a few hours without being awakened by nightmares."

Maddie watched his elegant fingers, smoothing the spines, ensuring that the books were orderly on the shelf. She imagined how difficult it must have been for him to admit his problem to her. And all the affection and passion and friendship she'd been feeling for the man coalesced right there and then into something that felt suspiciously like love.

"So," he said, turning back to face her, the good-humored mask that she now realized was simply that—a mask—firmly in place once again. "Yes, I did read some of your books before giving them to you. But if it is any consolation, I can vouch for them being quite entertaining."

Stepping closer to him, Maddie reached up and linked her hands behind his neck. "Christian," she said sweetly, gazing up into his familiar face.

At his questioning brow, she leaned up and stopped just short of pressing her lips to his. "Shut up and kiss me," she said.

Much later, when they were sprawled out together in bed, Christian felt Maddie watching him.

"What is it?" he asked, spying at her from half-closed lids. "I can all but feel you preparing to ask me something."

Though his tone was lighthearted, he had a feeling that her question would not be. He had not missed the sharpening of her eyes when he'd stumbled over his words earlier.

"You used to buy books for Clarissa at Felsham's, didn't you?" she asked, slipping her arm about his waist. "That's how you knew to go there."

Pulling her against him, he decided that it was time to debride the wound. "Yes," he admitted. "She was a great lover of books. And all things fanciful."

"Tell me about her," Maddie said softly. Her arm tucked protectively around him gave him a degree of courage he hadn't realized he'd needed.

"We were twins," he began, for the first time in a long while allowing the wall he'd built around memories of his sister to fall away. "She was the eldest by twenty minutes, but when we were small you would have thought it was twenty years."

"Bossy, eh?" Maddie asked with a smile.

"You should know," he said, poking her in the ribs. "You remind me of her at times. Or at least Clarissa before the melancholia set in."

"What caused it?"

"She had her first episode not very long after my father died," Christian said. "We were fifteen. Mama and Clarissa's governess thought it was simply a young girl taking advantage of the situation to indulge in a bit of dramatics."

"But it wasn't." It was a statement.

"No," Christian said curtly, remembering his terror when he'd found Clarey standing on the bridge over the Ouse, her hand gripped around a very large rock. "No, it was not the dramatics of a willful girl. It was a sickness."

"She moved past the episode, though, didn't she?" Maddie asked, kissing his shoulder.

"Yes," he said harshly. "She moved past it. She

didn't suffer any more episodes for several years. My mother, thinking that a change of scenery might keep them at bay, sent her to live with our elder sister in Scotland. She'd married recently and welcomed Clarey into her home.

"I had bought my commission by that point, and was not able to see my sister as often as I would have liked," he continued, "but she seemed happy enough when I came home on leave. She came to town for the season each spring. And when I was here, I'd buy novels for her at Felsham's."

He smiled, "You would have liked her, I think, Maddie." He hugged her to him. "And I know she would have adored you. And most especially your writing."

"I wish I'd been able to meet her," Maddie said. "I know you must have loved her very much."

"She was my twin," he said simply. "I would have done anything for her."

"What happened?" Maddie's voice was strained. She knew how the story ended, after all. She knew that there would be no happily ever after for Clarissa, who had so enjoyed reading about them.

"It came back." Christian could not keep the bitterness from his voice. "The fog, as she called it, came back for her. Four years she'd gone without a spell of melancholy, and then in the middle of the season, she fell in love."

He still couldn't quite understand how something that should have made his sister happy had ended up causing her so much misery.

"Selford was a blackguard of the worst sort," Christian continued. "If I'd known he was anywhere near Clarissa I'd have beaten him to a bloody pulp."

"But you were away."

He nodded. "As it was, I didn't even hear about the

affair until it was over. And Clarissa was gone." His voice broke on the last word.

He felt Maddie rise up, kissing him on the face. To his shame, he felt his own tears there as well.

"I should have been there," he said harshly, trying to smother his sadness with anger. "I should have known what was happening to her."

"Hush now," Maddie said, smoothing her hand over his face. "You cannot have known. You were doing a very difficult job that most men would flee from. You are only one man, Christian. You cannot be two places at once."

They were all things he'd told himself before, but somehow hearing them from Maddie made them feel more true. As if her endorsement of them were more valid than his own. And perhaps it was.

"She was gone before I could even cross the Channel," he said, a great fatigue washing over him. "I had a letter from Mama telling me that she was very ill. I didn't know at the time that the illness was because she was with child."

Maddie froze beside him. "Oh, my dear," she murmured against his chest, where she lay, holding him in her arms. "I am so sorry. Why did this Selford not marry her?"

"He was after her inheritance. Which my mother saw fit to protect not very long after the fellow began seeing Clarissa. But it was too late by then. He'd already seduced her. And when he learned that he would not have access to her funds, he abandoned her."

"Bastard."

"Yes," he agreed, needing to tell the rest of the story. To get it all out. "Clarissa was despondent, of course. Her fog came back with a vengeance.

"Mama knew that in those moods Clarey was not to

be trusted alone," he continued. "She saw to it that a maid was with her at all times. But she could hardly keep her a prisoner. Somehow—we think when the maid was sleeping that night—she left her bedchamber and found a bottle of laudanum.

"She drank the whole bottle," he finished. "The maid found her the next morning."

Maddie's arms tightened around him. "Christian," she said, tears streaming down her face, "I am so very sorry. Oh, my dear. I am so sorry."

He could not speak. Now that the story was told, he felt broken. Clasping Maddie to his chest, he felt a sob rise up in his throat. Giving in to his grief for the first time since he'd buried Clarissa, he wept for the sister he'd loved so dearly. And for the life, the happiness, that she would never know.

Happiness like he'd found with the proud, brave woman he held in his arms, who grieved with him for someone she'd never even met.

Maddie knew exactly where she was when she awoke the next morning. Naked. Alone. Aching in places she'd never ached before.

The evening before had been a revelation in terms of just what was possible between a husband and wife. Or a man and woman, come to think of it. Though Maddie could not imagine giving herself to someone when there was the possibility that he might go away from her and never return.

Christian had been gentle at times, fierce at others. And Maddie had always been conscious that he was making himself just as vulnerable to her as she was to him. That was something that no one ever spoke of when they discussed intimacy—not that polite society discussed such things in anything other than a round-about way. It was just that she'd always heard sexual congress described as something that could make or break a woman. Pregnancy had a way of doing that, she supposed. But she remembered her new husband's gentleness, and the way that he'd allowed her to see him, to share his grief at the death of his sister, to see beneath all the masks and poses that one necessarily donned to face the outside world. She knew that she had been given a rare gift. And she vowed to herself that she would keep his vulnerabilities safe in her heart.

Stretching in the soft sheets and rumpled bedclothes, she glanced at the clock on the mantel and gave a start. It was long past time she was up and dressed. Ringing the bell beside her bed, she was soon washing and dressing and headed downstairs to the breakfast room. To her disappointment, Christian wasn't there, but she had only just been seated when a footman brought her a hastily scrawled note from him telling her that he'd been called to the Home Office and would be back in the afternoon. It was unfortunate but, she supposed, to be expected. Since when had the government had any concern with the wishes of new wives?

As she finished her breakfast, she decided to spend some time in her new writing room. Asking for some tea to be brought up to her, Maddie slipped into the chamber, and set about looking through every cubby and drawer to take inventory and to see what supplies she needed. She was adding sealing wax to the list when a footman intruded with a card on a tray.

Glancing at it, Maddie was surprised to see Lady Emily's name. Telling the servant to show her in, she asked the housekeeper to bring fresh tea and waited for her visitor. But as soon as she saw the other woman, she suspected she might need something a bit stronger than tea.

"I do beg your pardon, Countess," Lady Emily said, her eyes puffy from weeping and her skin paler than Maddie had ever seen it. "But I was unsure of where to go. And you have always seemed so eminently . . . sensible."

Leaping up from her chair, Maddie wrapped a comforting arm around the other woman's shoulders. "Make no apologies, my dear. Just come have a seat and soon we'll have a nice cup of tea and you can tell me all about it."

To her horror, the other woman began to weep. Whatever it was that troubled her, then it must be serious, indeed, Maddie decided, for she did not think Lady Emily was the sort to indulge in public displays of emotion. Could it be something to do with Tinker's death, Maddie wondered, or was it something more personal?

"I am so sorry," Emily said, dabbing at her eyes with a handkerchief. "I cannot seem to stop blubbering. It really is not all that serious."

"I have little doubt that it is serious to you, my dear," Maddie said wryly. To her relief, the housekeeper arrived with a tea tray and a plate of macaroons. "Ah, here we are," she said, pouring out a cup for the other lady.

Thanking her, Lady Emily took the tea and to Maddie's relief did seem to find some comfort in holding the warm cup in her hands. When she had taken several sips, and seemed to be more in control of herself, Maddie said gently, "Now, then, why don't you tell me what it is that has you so upset."

Staring into the amber liquid for a moment, no doubt getting her bearings, Lady Emily was silent. When so much time had passed that Maddie feared the need to repeat the question, her guest looked up. "I need your assistance in finding your brother, my lady. Do you know where he has gone?"

Maddie was silent. She did know, of course, where Linton had gone, but she wasn't quite sure if the woman seated next to her should be informed of where he was. Though Lady Emily had been the one to inform Maddie of the threats against Linton, Tretham, and Tinker, she could very well have disclosed that information because she knew it would become public knowledge soon anyway. And surely if Linton had wished for Lady Emily to know his whereabouts he would have told her himself.

Aloud, she said, "May I ask why?"

Setting her teacup down, Lady Emily took a deep breath. "Lady Gresham," she began, "Madeline. I am not sure that your brother would wish me to tell you."

Maddie frowned. "Since my brother is not here to tell me that himself," she said reasonably, "and since he is currently in hiding because of threats against his life, I believe that I will have to insist upon knowing what it is that you need to tell him before I decide whether to tell you where to find him."

Seeing the other woman's frown, Maddie continued, "Or, perhaps you can write him a note and I will see that it is delivered to him."

"How can I be sure of confidentiality?" Lady Emily demanded, her nostrils flaring with pique. "I must be sure that no one will be privy to what I must tell him."

The other woman's show of temper only reinforced Maddie's feeling that it might be best not to share Linton's whereabouts with her. "I apologize," she said, "but if my word is not enough for you, then I am unsure of what to tell you. I feel certain if my brother wished for you to know his direction he would have told you before he left town."

"He would not have done so because he is the most pigheaded fellow in Christendom," Lady Emily said with exasperation, all traces of her tears gone now. "The bloody fool thought that he was protecting me, but in fact he has simply made things more difficult. Especially in the current circumstances."

"Protecting you from the threat against him? And Tretham?" Maddie asked, wondering if there were more of a relationship between James and Lady Emily than she had at first thought. She had never even considered such a thing though she supposed she should have done so. Thinking back over her conversations with the woman on earlier occasions, she felt some pieces of the puzzle snap into place.

"Among other things," Lady Emily said with a shrug, "I believe he was worried that whoever made the threats against him and the others would take it into his head to add me to the list of suspects in my husband's death. Who better to accuse of murder than the wife, after all? Especially when she is carrying on with her deceased husband's best friend?"

At the confirmation of her suspicion, Maddie nodded. "So, you are lovers," she said. "That explains much."

"I should imagine it does," Lady Emily said wryly. "So now you will understand that what I wish to tell him is of a very private nature."

"You are with child?" Maddie asked quietly. It was the only explanation that made sense. Especially given the other woman's tears.

"Yes," Lady Emily said with a tight-lipped smile. "I had thought that since my marriage to Fielding was unfruitful that I was barren, but it seems not to be the case."

Maddie's mind raced as she thought of the impact such news might have on both her brother's safety—for he would no doubt make the unsafe decision to return to London as soon as he learned of it—and on his current quarrel with Lord Essex.

"You are sure?" she asked the other woman.

"As sure as one can be in such situations," Lady Emily said with a shrug. "So you see now that my wish to contact him is not some attempt on my part to put him in danger. But I do really need to give him the chance to put our case before your father one more time."

Maddie frowned. "You mean Linton has tried to convince my father to allow a match between you before?"

"Of course," Lady Emily said. "In fact, it's been over a year since he first approached Lord Essex. But I'm afraid your father does not think me a suitable match for his son and heir. Not by half."

She should not have been surprised by the news, but Maddie was. It wasn't so much that she didn't believe her father would do such a thing. It took only a glance at his condemnation of her match with Christian to know that he cared little for his childrens' happiness and everything for appearances. But she had always thought Linton's scandalous reputation to be primarily the result of his own recklessness, with only a bit of the blame laid at their father's door. Now she saw that in this instance, at least, her brother had tried to do the right thing, and been prevented from doing so by their father. Who would doubtless condemn her brother for the scandal of a quick marriage to the mother of his unborn child.

Not commenting on her father's role in Lady Emily's current situation, Maddie took the other woman's hand. "I will see what I can do."

Eighteen

*I*t had been hard as hell to slip out of Maddie's arms, dress, and head to White's, but when he found Leighton seated in the coffee room, frowning over the papers, Christian knew he'd done the right thing. His superior looked as if he hadn't slept in days, and his eyes beneath his spectacles were red rimmed and tired.

"Thank you for agreeing to meet me," Leighton said, the courtesy itself putting Gresham on further alert. "I know today of all days is the worst time possible to interrupt your sleep, but I knew that you needed to hear this as soon as possible."

Immediately, Christian felt his whole body go on alert. "What is it?" he demanded.

"It's Viscount Linton, I'm afraid," the other man said curtly. "He is missing."

Christian swore.

"I had word this morning that Gunning and Hedley lost him," Leighton continued. "As far as they could tell, he was snug as a bug two nights ago in the hunting lodge where he decided to take refuge. They retired to the inn where they'd been staying, and sometime in the night, the whole town was roused to help douse a fire in a local house."

"The hunting lodge," Monteith guessed, his jaw tightening. He could have argued with Leighton over the wisdom of Gunning and Hedley not taking turns watching the lodge, instead of both retiring to their beds at the same bloody time, but it was clearly too late for such niceties now. "Was there no sign of him in the house? No body?"

Leighton shook his head. "Nothing that they were able to see. Of course they aren't sure if Essex himself set the fire, or if someone else set it hoping to kill him in the ensuing blaze. The important thing is that he was not found in the ruins of the lodge, so there is every hope that he is alive and well, and simply hiding."

Christian rubbed a hand over his forehead. "Yes, it is good that he is not obviously murdered, I suppose."

"Yes," Leighton said. "And though I had the men watching Linton out of an abundance of caution lest he become the target of the Bonapartists, I agree with you that Tinker's murder was likely the work of someone who blamed him for Fielding's death. The threats against Tretham and Linton seem far more credible a reason for his murder than his involvement with the Bonapartists."

"It does seem unlikely that the Citizen's Liberation Society would kill Tinker and then pass up the opportunity to use it to promote their cause," Christian said with a sigh. "And there has been no mention of them in the press since the murder."

He rubbed his chin. "It is possible, however, that the CLS was involved in the death in some other way."

"Could it be that Tinker killed Fielding because Fielding learned of his involvement with the society?" Leighton asked, his eyes losing some of their fatigue. "It would be easy enough to spook a horse along the road to Bath. There are any number of places to hide. And accidents like that happen all the time."

Christian leaned back in his chair and thought it over. "I suppose it is possible," he said. "Tinker would most likely not be pleased to have his affiliation with them known. And a loose fish like Fielding would hardly be the sort you'd trust with a secret like that. And, since he wasn't involved in the race, Tinker would find it easy enough to tamper wth the curricle in hopes that it would crash in the middle of the race."

"Any of them would," Leighton said with a nod. "Whoever Fielding's avenger is blames all of them— Tinker, Tretham, and Linton—equally. And perhaps killed Tinker first as a warning to the other two."

"It makes sense," Christian said. "I just wish we'd known about the threats against Linton and Tretham sooner. We might have connected this business to Fielding's death and avoided a lot of false trails."

Leaning forward to rest his forearms on the table, he asked, "What do we do now that Linton is missing again? Do Gunning and Hedley have any notion of which direction he might have been headed? Or who might be responsible for the fire? Was anyone seen in the village who might have set it?"

"They set out in different directions as soon as they informed me he was gone," Leighton said reassuringly. "The lodge itself isn't terribly far from the Great North Road, so he might be headed north or to the coast."

"He might be headed anywhere, then," Christian said with frustration. He knew as well as anyone that unless they had some sort of information about where Linton might have gone, he could disappear quite easily. The only thing working in their favor was that Linton did not have military experience, and so was unlikely to think as strategically as he might have done otherwise.

"Indeed," Leighton agreed, drinking up the dregs of his coffee. "Which is why I knew I had to inform you as quickly as possible. My thanks for your agreement to meet me. I know it might not have been altogether agreeable for your new wife to let you go so soon."

Christian didn't disagree with the other man, though Maddie had been fast asleep when he left her that morning. "You'll let me know when you hear from your men."

The other man nodded, rising. "I'll send for you as soon as I know something."

Watching the older man stride away, Christian cursed inwardly at the situation. He did not relish telling Maddie that her brother was missing. Again.

"I shouldn't have to tell you this, old fellow," Winterson interrupted, taking the seat that Leighton had just vacated, "but you are allowed to sleep in on the day after your wedding. In fact, it's sort of de rigueur. Like breeches at Almack's and cant at Jackson's."

"Linton has flown the coop," Christian said curtly.

Winterson whistled. "Damnation. When you have problems, you have problems."

Christian nodded. "I'm at an impasse," he said, after explaining the particulars of his brother-in-law's disappearance from the hunting lodge. "I cannot simply leave town and go off in search of Linton. I just married Maddie yesterday, for God's sake. She is a reasonable woman, but no woman is that reasonable. Even if it is her own brother."

He did not add that he knew without a doubt that she would insist upon accompanying him. A possibility that filled him with dread.

"And you would need to tell her how you know her brother is missing. That her brother was being watched by men from Whitehall who were not quite sure if he was a traitor to the crown or not. Which could lead to some marital tension, I would guess," Winterson said, pouring himself some coffee from the nearly empty pot.

"We did not really think him a traitor," Christian said, knowing he was splitting hairs. "It was more that we hadn't ruled out the possibility that he knew of Tinker's involvement with the Bonapartists. It's a fine distinction, but it's there. We were protecting him, for God's sake."

"Yes, and you see how well that's worked out," Winterson said, brows raised. Then, not unkindly, he said, "She doesn't need to know everything, you know. After all, you are her husband, and are under no particular requirement to tell her about every aspect of your work for the government. In fact, you could say that you were not allowed to tell her. Which is true enough."

"Are you familiar with my new wife, Winterson?" Christian demanded. "For that matter, have you met your own wife? Neither of them would take kindly to being deceived. Even if it meant the choice between duty to one's country and duty to one's wife."

Winterson sighed. "You are correct, of course. They are a headstrong pair, our wives. So what do you mean to do about it? If you cannot go haring across the country in search of your brother-in-law, then there must be some way to find him."

"I suppose I will wait a couple of days to see if he doesn't turn up in town," Christian said glumly. "He does seem to have a remarkable way of landing on his feet. So I shall tell my wife, despite the danger to my person such a confession will engender."

"I cannot say that I would wish to trade places with you for that conversation," Winterson said. "Come on, then, I've got an idea of where we might find your little termagant. And if you're going to tell her, you may as well get it over with."

Following Winterson out of White's, Christian settled his hat upon his head, took up his walking stick, and prepared himself to break the news of her brother's disappearance to his new wife.

"And then what did you say?" Juliet asked, her eyes wide as she reached for another tea cake.

The three cousins were ensconced in Cecily's private sitting room, conversing over yet another tea tray, though Juliet had argued strenuously for something a bit stronger. That notion had been vetoed by Cecily who said that they needed their wits about them if they were to find some solution to Maddie's latest trouble.

"I told her that I would forward her note to James and that he could decide whether or not to return to London," Maddie said, rubbing a finger over her brow. "I must say, she took it rather well. Though I don't suppose she had much choice. What was she to do? Break a teacup and threaten me with the broken crockery? It just troubles me to know that my brother would behave in such a ramshackle fashion. Though I suppose he did leave town for his own safety."

"I know that you are worried for your brother," Cecily said, "but perhaps he really has some affection for Lady Emily and left town, and her, reluctantly."

"You are certainly looking at the situation with a romantic eye, Cecily," Juliet said with a frown. "I know none of us wishes to think of Linton in this way, but it is quite possible that he was simply doing what gentlemen do . . ." She paused, blushing a bit. "What I mean to say is that perhaps he was simply having an affair without any thought to the possible consequences."

"But Lady Emily said that he wished to marry her,"

Maddie said, setting her teacup down. "I do not believe he trifled with her affections. He is not always the most circumspect of men, but my brother is a gentleman after all."

Her cousins nodded, though she wasn't quite sure they agreed with her. It was so difficult to tell sometimes. Still, she was glad to have talked the matter over with them. When Lady Emily had left, her first thought had been to send for Christian, but she refused to become one of those wives who could not make the slightest decision without consulting her lord and master.

Reminded of her new bridegroom, she said, "I am afraid that the news came as a shock to me, in part because of my own situation."

"What do you mean, dearest?" Juliet asked, grabbing her cousin's hand.

"Never say you married Monteith because you are *enceinte*," Cecily said, her mouth slightly agape. "I would never have—"

"No!" Maddie interrupted. "Not at all. It's just that after last night's . . . er . . . activities"—she did not meet her cousins' eyes and knew without consulting a glass that she was blushing furiously—"I cannot help but think that it takes quite a bit of . . . trust . . . to indulge in such intimacies. And I cannot think that Lady Emily, or my brother, would do so without some degree of care for the other person."

"Winterson says that men are much different about such things than we are," Cecily said with a matter-of-fact tone. "They see it as a sort of physical release. Like fisticuffs or a vigorous gallop in the park."

"Good God," Maddie said, "so ladies are no more important to gentlemen than their horses?"

"I know quite a few gentlemen who think rather more highly of their horses than they do of any ladies of their acquaintance," Juliet quipped. "George Vinson, for instance."

The three ladies laughed, but then Cecily continued, "It is not so much that they see ladies as less important. It simply depends upon the lady. And it is simply not as . . . risky for men to indulge themselves in carnal acts. After all, they cannot become with child, and if they are well informed, they have ways of preventing disease."

"It is true," Juliet said with a nod. "And those ways can also be used to prevent pregnancy."

"Really?" Maddie was fascinated despite her embarrassment. She really needed to confide in her cousins more often.

Now it was Juliet's turn to blush. "Since we have little Alice in our household, we are not quite ready for a child of our own. And given my fears about how my infirmity will affect my ability to carry a child, we have used French letters, yes."

"But I thought only—" Maddie stopped, not wanting to insult her cousin, but curious in spite of herself. "Are ladies able to use such things?"

"Of course," Juliet said firmly. "It really isn't all that difficult. Though Alec is not overly fond of them. But he knows that it isn't forever. And he loves me and does not wish me to conceive before I am ready."

"Well," Maddie said with a shake of her head. "I had no idea. I wonder if Christian knows of such things."

"Maddie," Cecily said kindly, "he was a solider. He knows about French letters."

"But Winterson was a soldier as well," Maddie said, frowning. "Why didn't you two . . . ?"

"Because we were not anticipating . . . that is to say, we were . . ." Cecily blushed, making both Maddie and Juliet giggle. "Oh, do be quiet, you two."

After their laughter died down, Maddie returned to the subject that brought them to such scandalous topics. "I sincerely hope that Linton loves Lady Emily as she says. For the sake of the child at the least. But I also hope that he will not come to town before the danger to his life has passed. It is all well and good to do his duty by his child's mother, but it will do neither of them any good if he is killed before he can marry her.

"If," Maddie went on, "he intends to marry her. It will be very hard on them if Papa continues to oppose the match. Linton relies upon him for his allowance, and I would not be shocked if Papa cut him off for marrying her against his wishes."

Further discussion of the matter was forestalled by a brisk knock on the door of Cecily's sitting room. Winterson, followed closely by Christian, stepped into the chamber.

"I found this fellow wandering Mayfair in search of his wife, and took pity on him and brought him in for a drink," Winterson said. "Imagine my shock when I discovered his wife to be here all the time!"

He leaned down and kissed Cecily on the cheek. "See there, old fellow," he said to Christian, who stood diffidently near the door, "I told you we'd find her."

Maddie met her husband's eyes to ensure that he was not so worried as Winterson said he was. To her relief he seemed to be none the worse for wear. "I do not wish to interrupt your visit," he said. Though Maddie found to her surprise that rather than being annoyed at being hunted down, she was ready to leave with him. It had been quite a while since she'd nestled in his arms in the wee hours of the morning.

"We are quite finished," she said aloud. Rising, she slipped her arm into his and they made their farewells. Soon enough, they were in the carriage on their way home. Rather than leaving her to sit decorously across from him, however, Christian pulled Maddie unceremoniously onto his lap and kissed her passionately.

"Good afternoon, wife," he said, once they broke away for breath. Maddie nestled her face into his neck, inhaling that potent combination of sandalwood, bayberry, and Christian. She arched her back a bit as he ran a hand down her back.

"I've missed you," she said softly, dragging her teeth over his earlobe.

She felt a rumble of laughter in his chest. "I've missed you, too, Madeline. But if this is how you greet me when I return then I shall have to leave you more often."

Christian hated to disturb the amity between them, but he knew that keeping the news about her brother from her would only make her angry. Inhaling the fragrant scent of her hair, and sliding a comforting hand over her back, he began, "Maddie, I'm afraid I have some bad news."

She stiffened in his arms. As he might have predicted. "I'm afraid your brother has gone missing."

Quickly he explained to her what had happened at the hunting lodge, not mentioning the fact that the men the Home Office had sent to look after Linton had bungled things. Badly.

But Maddie's response was not what he'd been expecting. Rather than speculating about where he might have gone, or gasping aloud at how close he came to death in the fire, she merely nodded, and laid her head back down on his shoulder. His suspicions raised, Christian grasped her shoulders and looked into her face, only partially lit in the dimness of the carriage.

"You know something." It was a statement, not a question. He should have known better than to try to keep something from his intrepid wife.

Her only response was an eloquent shrug.

Resisting the urge to shake her, he said, "Maddie, tell me what you know. This is not some scheme that you and your cousins have concocted to outsmart the *ton*. This is serious. Your brother's life could be in danger."

"Don't you think I know that?" Maddie retorted, her face flushed with pique. "I was there for Mr. Tinker's dying breath, Christian. I know how deadly serious this business is. Do not do me the disservice of thinking that I am a silly society lady with nothing on my mind but hats and gowns."

He acknowledged the truth of her words, but was still unable to relax. "You are right," he admitted. "I apologize for dismissing your concerns that way. But this business is not for the faint of heart. Tell me where you think he is."

She was clearly weighing the advisability of telling him. Though it was just as likely that her hunch was wrong, Christian knew all too well how discerning Maddie could be. And she knew her brother and his habits better than Christian or anyone with the Home Office did. He was willing to risk the loss of time it would take the see if Maddie was correct.

Removing herself from his lap, Maddie slid into the seat beside him, plucking at the folds of her gown. "There is a town house that our father once owned."

"His mistress's house, do you mean?" Christian was surprised Maddie knew such a woman existed, much less that she knew where she lived.

"Papa used to take us with him when he visited her," Maddie said softly. "He thought Mama would be less suspicious of his whereabouts if he took us with him."

"Good God." He was appalled. He didn't hold Maddie's father in the highest of esteem, but he had taken Lord Essex's attempt at apology at their wedding at face value. But the very idea that the man would bring his children with him to visit his mistress was shocking. "So, you and your brother were acquainted with this . . ."

"Mrs. Hendricks," Maddie said softly. "Yes, we were. She was actually quite lovely to us. And those afternoons weren't lascivious at all. We would visit one of the less public parks, or play with her children—our half brothers and sisters. And she and Papa would just talk quietly."

"But if he had this other family," Christian said, struggling to understand what could have motivated Essex to marry one woman and maintain a separate household with another, "why did he marry your mother?"

Maddie shrugged. "We were never able to figure it out. Of course, we could hardly ask Mama. But she always spoke of their courtship as if she saw him and set her cap for him immediately. And however ineligible Mama and her sisters were, they were at least wellborn, despite their poverty. Mrs. Hendricks is the daughter of a butcher. It's quite sad when you think of it."

It was at that, Christian thought, marveling at her philosophical acceptance of the matter. Realizing that the issue at hand was not his approval or disapproval of Lord Essex's actions, he asked, "So, you suspect that your brother has gone to this Mrs. Hendricks?"

She nodded. "I think it likely, yes. He actually ran away to her once. When he was around ten years old. Mama had forbidden him from doing something, riding his pony alone in the park, I think. And he simply disappeared for a day. Mama and Papa were frantic. Finally, Mrs. Hendricks escorted him home."

He felt his mouth fall open. "To your parents' house in Mayfair?" He tried to imagine what his own mama's response to the arrival of her husband's mistress on her doorstep would have been. It wasn't a pretty picture. "That must have been . . ." He struggled to find the right word.

"Distressing?" Maddie volunteered. "My mother was actually quite calm about it. Now, of course, I know what a shock it must have been, but at the time, I was just glad to see Hennie. And James, of course."

Turning his mind from the turmoil of the Essex household, Christian focused on the here and now. "So, you think that your brother might be there now? With this Hennie?"

"I think it likely," Maddie said. "He has always been fond of her despite my mother's forbidding us to see her. Papa never took us there again, but James and I both visited her upon occasion over the years. Hennie did try to dissuade us, but we knew how much Papa loved her. And then there were the children. Our sisters and brothers. We could hardly just ignore them."

"Can we go there now?" Christian asked, still somewhat stunned by the tale. Nevertheless, he was glad enough to know where they might find Linton now. He just hoped to hell that no one else knew of this Hennie and her unconventional household.

"Yes," Maddie said. "It would likely take my brother a couple of days to reach Richmond from the hunting box, but I believe he could make it there if he had a fast enough horse."

Rapping on the ceiling of the carriage, when the vehicle drew to a halt, Christian informed the driver of their change of direction.

In different circumstances he might have found a pleasant enough way to pass the time on their journey outside the city into Richmond, but both Maddie and Christian were lost in thought for most of the trip. When the carriage finally drew to a stop before a neat row house, they were both eager to exit it.

When Maddie made to follow him, however, Christian frowned up at her from his position outside the carriage door. "I do not think it wise for you to come inside, my dear," he said firmly. "Your brother has been through a great deal, and even though we do not know that he was followed here, there is still every chance that he is being watched. Besides, there is also the matter of Mrs. Hendricks's relationship with your father."

"Oh, really, Christian, do not preach propriety at me," she snapped. "You are hardly the most circumspect of creatures. Besides which, I have known Hennie since I was a child. She is hardly going to taint me at this point. And I wish to see my brother. Now kindly assist me from the carriage or I shall be forced to leap out onto you. And I do not wish to get this gown dirty."

Shaking his head at his wife's stubbornness, Christian reluctantly assisted her down to the pavement.

Offering her his arm, he led her up the three steps to the door, which was opened by a very proper-looking butler. When the fellow inquired what they wished, Maddie spoke up. "Newman! Do you not recognize me all grown-up?"

The butler's wizened features broke out in a smile. "Why, Lady Madeline, why didn't you say so? I can see it now. All grown-up, but I'll bet with just the same love for macaroons."

"Of course!" she responded. "How could anyone not love macaroons? They are quite the best biscuits imaginable." She presented Christian to the old man. "This is my husband, Newman, the Earl of Gresham. I was wondering if I might present him to Hennie?"

A shadow passed over the old man's visage, but he nodded, welcoming them inside the small entrance hall. "I shall inform my mistress that you are here. I know she'll be pleased as punch to see you."

"Thank you, Newman," Maddie said with a smile. "And please say hello to Mrs. Newman for me."

"You shall do so yourself before you go, my lady," the old man said. "She'll be that angry if you do not introduce her to your man."

"If there is time, I shall," Maddie said, gripping Christian's hand in hers.

They watched as the old man left the room. Left alone, Christian glanced about the parlor, which might have been in any fashionable house in London. It certainly didn't look like the inner sanctum of a kept woman. But then again, it seemed that Mrs. Hendricks was not like any kept woman he'd ever met.

Nineteen

The room was unchanged from all those years ago when she and her father and brother had first entered it, Maddie reflected, pacing restlessly before the fire. She wondered what Christian saw when he looked around the chamber. She had seen how shocked he'd been to hear that her father had brought her and her brother to Hennie's house. She supposed it was scandalous, but as a child she'd had little notion of the impropriety of the visits. She'd simply looked forward to seeing her friends Mary and Henrietta and their brothers, John and Henry. There had been no more visits after Hennie's visit to return Linton to Essex House, of course. She supposed now that her mother had put her foot down, but at the time Maddie had blamed her brother for the curtailment of their outings with their father.

It didn't surprise her that he'd chosen this of all places to hide from the men who wished him harm. He'd always shared a special kinship with Hennie. Perhaps because Hennie had understood her brother's thirst for adventure in a way that Lady Poppy Essex had not. Maddie felt a pang of sympathy for her mother now that she understood what it would be like to lose a husband's affection to another woman. She suspected

that her father and Hennie had been in love long before
Poppy came on the scene, however, so she doubted her
mother had ever stood a chance. What a ridiculous social system, Maddie reflected, that would make it impossible for two people who loved one another and
wished to live together to do so without social stigma.
Still, she supposed if there had been a different system
in place, she would not have been born, so she was
grateful for that at least.

"Do you really think he's here?" Christian asked
from near the window. Maddie turned to see him peer-
ing out into the back garden. Whether he was simply
looking or was ensuring that her brother did not escape
out the back she couldn't say.

Maddie shrugged. "I think it's as possible as anything else we've hit upon," she said. "I am hardly the
most knowledgeable about my brother's habits." She
thought again of what Lady Emily had informed her
this morning. She could not before today have imagined her brother carrying on an affair with someone
like Lady Emily, his best friend's widow, with a less
than pristine reputation.

"You are as knowledgeable as anyone," a new voice
said from the doorway. Maddie looked up to see Linton
there, haggard, and looking as if he hadn't slept in
days.

Without a word she flung herself across the room and
into his arms.

"Easy, Mads," her brother said with an awkward
embrace. "I am, as you can see, in one piece."

"We've been rather worried about you, Linton,"
Maddie heard Christian say from behind her. Realizing
that she was making a scene, she pulled back from her
brother and surreptitiously dabbed at her eyes. She had
been as surprised as they were by the burst of emotion

she'd felt upon hearing her brother's voice. She supposed she'd been more worried about him than she'd thought.

"I can see that," Linton said, his gaze looking Christian up and down. "I understand congratulations are in order."

Maddie looked from one to the other of them, sensing an undercurrent of hostility between the men. "Indeed," Christian said coolly. "We were sorry you could not make it to the wedding."

"I was sorry to miss it," Linton said, inclining his head. "But there was no time."

Christian acknowledged the truth of this with a slight nod.

"What happened, Linton?" Maddie demanded, tiring of their posturing. She was ready for all of this nonsense to end so that they could all get on with their lives. "I mean to the lodge. Did you burn it down or was the fire set by someone else?"

Stepping farther into the room, the viscount indicated that they should be seated, and Maddie realized that her brother must be exhausted. "Of course," she said, stepping forward to take the seat nearest the fire. "So, tell us."

"I was there at the hunting lodge for a couple of weeks without incident," Linton said. "Of course, I knew that Punch and Judy were there watching me."

Maddie hid a grin at his nickname for the Home Office operatives. She sneaked a glance at her husband and found that he was less amused.

"I can't explain how I knew someone else had come along," James said, fiddling with the tassel on his boot. "But I just sensed it. I felt like I was being watched, and it wasn't in a benign way, either. That night, I was working out whether I should head north or west to the coast when I heard something in the wood just outside the lodge. I lay there, still, listening, when I smelled the smoke. I knew as soon as I scented it that I had to leave."

"And you came here," Christian said, his brow raised. Clearly, he didn't think that her brother's decision had been a wise one. "Why not keep running?"

Linton reddened. "I . . . there is a lady in London . . ."

"Lady Emily Fielding," Christian said, surprising Maddie. "What?" he asked, taking in her astonishment. "Is it such a secret?"

Maddie shook her head. "No, but I only discovered it this morning. I had no idea you had suspicions of a romance."

"It is hardly romantic to suspect that one's brother-in-law is carrying on an affair with his best friend's widow," Christian said dryly.

Linton stood, swaying on his feet, but remaining upright. "It's not like that, Gresham. Do not be so damned lascivious."

"Dearest," Maddie said, moving to her brother's side, bracing him with an arm of support. "I think you'd better sit back down. You are unwell."

She glared at her husband. "Now, then, Linton," she said, once he was seated again, with her sitting opposite, watching him. "Tell us about your relationship with Lady Emily. She is quite beautiful."

"Yes," Christian said, ignoring Maddie's glares. "Tell us about your 'relationship' with Lady Emily."

"Damn it, Gresham," Linton spat out. "If you weren't married to my sister I'd draw your cork for that. Lady Emily is not a tart for you to malign."

"My apologies, Linton," Christian said, not sounding apologetic to Maddie in the least, "but I needed to ascertain just how you feel about the lady. Especially given that you risked your own life and that of your hostess to get back to her."

Maddie watched as her brother deflated a bit. "I know," he said, dragging his hands down over his face. "I shouldn't have come here and put Hennie in danger. But I could think of nowhere else to go. My own rooms are being watched. Our parents' house is hardly safe. And I dare not go to Emily."

"Where is Hennie?" Maddie asked, realizing that their hostess hadn't come to greet them at all. "Has something happened to her?"

She saw her brother stiffen, his expression pained. "What, Jamie? What's happened?"

"It's not what you think, Mads," he said quickly, taking her hand in his. "But Hennie did not wish to see you."

A silence fell over the room. Maddie felt a constriction in the region of her heart.

"Why?" she asked softly. "Have I done something?"

She felt her brother squeeze her hand. "No, it's nothing like that. She won't see you for your own sake. She says that she will not put your reputation at risk by being in the same room with you."

Maddie put a hand up to her mouth. "But that's absurd," she said finally, frowning at the notion. "I am not so high in the instep that I would refuse to see her. Why, we came here to her house, after all."

"Yes, and so long as the servants and I are able to vouch for the fact that you were never in Hennie's company you are safe."

"Wait," Maddie said, "you sound as if you agree with her."

Linton shrugged. "It's not as if my reputation will suffer any for being seen with her. But you are a lady, for all you try your damnedest not to be. And it would take little enough for the wagging tongues of the *ton* to ruin you."

She turned to Christian. "Do you agree with him?" she demanded.

But her husband was unwilling to enter into the argument. He threw up his hands in surrender. "I know better than to tell you whom to see and not see, my dear. I can see your brother and Mrs. Hendricks's point, but I can also see yours. Besides which, I suspect you have been seen in worse company over the years."

Maddie shook her head in disgust. "So I suppose she's left the house altogether," she said, resting her arms akimbo on her hips. "I am so annoyed I could spit. I can, of course, believe it of Hennie. She has always been far too worried about her effect on my reputation. But when you, James, who have fathered a child out of wedlock, preach propriety at me, then that is the very—"

She stopped speaking as soon as she realized what she'd said. Dash it all, she'd intended to break the news to him in a more gentle manner. Work up to it so that he wasn't more surprised than absolutely necessary.

"What did you say?" Linton demanded, grabbing his sister by the arms. "What do you mean, 'fathered a child out of wedlock'?"

"Easy there, Linton," Christian said, removing her brother's hands from Maddie's arms. "That's my wife you're manhandling."

"Maddie, what did you mean by it?" her brother asked again, thrusting his hands through his hair. "Have you spoken to Emily?"

Seeing that she would have to reveal all, Maddie laid her hand on her brother's arm. "Yes, dearest. I have spoken to Lady Emily. She came to me because she needed to find you. To send word to you. About . . . the baby."

She watched in trepidation as her brother shook his head as if unable to believe what he'd just heard. "A child. I can hardly believe it."

He frowned. "Is she ill? I know that ladies are sometimes ill when they are with child. Did she seem well to you? Is this why you came to find me? That was good of you to do so. We must depart at once so that I can see her. I will go get my things."

Before either Maddie or Christian could respond, Viscount Linton was gone, presumably to gather his things.

"When were you going to tell me about this, Maddie?" Christian asked, his face deceptively calm. "And how long have you known?"

"Just since this morning," Maddie said in an attempt to placate him. "I forgot about it when you told me of my brother's disappearance."

"We rode all the way out to Richmond in near silence," her husband said, his frustration seeping into his tone. "Mightn't you have remembered along the way?"

"Darling," Maddie said, leaning up to kiss him. "I was overset. I was worried about my brother and I could hardly tell you before I told him."

She saw him open his mouth to argue, but Maddie was relieved when he just shook his head. It had been bad of her to keep the news from him. But she had been telling the truth when she said she would not have wished him to know before her brother did. Besides, Lady Emily had told her the news in confidence. And though Maddie would have told Christian eventually, she felt better having kept the secret to herself until she could tell her brother.

"I suppose we should call for the carriage," Christian said, kissing her on the nose. "But I want you to remember that the next time you fail to tell me something that I need to know—especially when it pertains to this investigation, there will be consequences."

But if he wished for her to be cowed, her husband was doomed to disappointment. Maddie grinned up at him. "Consequences. Why, Lord Gresham. What a hard case you are."

With a sigh, Christian led her toward the entrance hall.

When they returned to London, Christian had to argue vociferously to prevent Linton from setting out immediately to see Lady Emily. He was saved the need of bodily preventing his brother-in-law from leaving Gresham House by Linton's own body, which, having transported him from the hunting lodge to Richmond, was finally pressed beyond its capacity and refused to budge a step further. As soon as the viscount stepped from the carriage, he collapsed into a heap on the front stoop.

"Oh, dear," Maddie said, leaping down without assistance to lean over her brother's inert form. "Do you suppose he's been poisoned?" she asked, worry in her eyes as she looked up at her husband.

"I think it more likely that he is either exhausted or ill. He has been on the run for days now. Even a man in the best of health will find himself at the point of exhaustion after such a journey. And I do not believe your brother has been in the best of health."

Maddie nodded, making Christian wish he could erase the lines of worry from her eyes. But he knew that she was, at heart, a realist. And she must know that her brother had been pushing himself beyond his capacity for some time now.

Leaning down, he gestured to the waiting footmen to bring a litter to carry his brother-in-law into the house. He didn't like the notion of having James under their roof while he was still under threat of death from persons unknown. But he could hardly leave the man to lie in the streets. And besides, they might be able to flush out the person responsible for the threats against Tretham and Linton by luring them here. Perhaps he could convince Maddie to go stay with Winterson and Cecily or Deveril and Juliet until they found the culprit. Watching her follow the footmen carrying her brother into the house, barking orders at them, and telling the housekeeper to follow her, he knew that getting her out of the house would be impossible. She would no more abandon her brother to his care than she would leave a newborn babe on the roadside.

Speaking of babies, he thought, hurrying up the steps himself, he turned over the news that Maddie had blurted out at Mrs. Hendrick's house. It was not difficult to believe, of course, given the fact that Linton had been carrying on with Lady Emily for some time now. But there was something about the timing of the lady's announcement that aroused his suspicions. Not only because it was as likely a ruse as he could imagine to convince Maddie to tell Lady Emily of her brother's whereabouts. But also because it was just so damned coincidental. He would need to speak to the woman himself, and soon. Perhaps when she came, as was inevitable now, to visit her lover's bedside.

He was just removing his hat and overcoat when a brisk knock sounded at the door. It was too soon for the physician to have arrived, he thought. Hanging back a bit to see who the butler opened the door to, he was shocked to see Tretham. Stepping forward, and nodding to the butler to indicate that he would see the visitor,

Christian led the other man farther into the house toward his study. Whatever it was that had brought the other man to him, it had him spooked. Christian could see it in Tretham's eyes.

"Drink?" he asked, stepping toward the sideboard where he kept a decanter of brandy. At Tretham's nod, he poured them both enough to be more than medicinal.

"So," he asked, lowering himself into the large desk chair. "What's amiss?"

Not bothering to disabuse him of the notion, Tretham took a gulp of the brandy before replying. "I have received another threat," he said, his face pale. "It says that if I do not meet this person at the Hidden Pearl tomorrow night he will see to it that my parents will be killed."

Christian hid his surprise. But he was, indeed, surprised. This didn't sound like the same person who had threatened the three men before. First of all, the earlier threats had been against their own lives. True, it would harm their families if they themselves were killed, but it would hardly do the same sort of damage to them if their loved ones were killed in their place.

"Does he ask you to bring anything to the Pearl?" Christian asked. "Money? Some proof that you didn't kill Fielding?"

"Oh," Tretham said, reaching into his pocket, "here is the note. Read it for yourself. He asks me to bring twenty guineas. And here's the oddest part. He asks for a note of apology."

"Probably wants the note to use for blackmail later," Christian said, skimming the note. The handwriting was the same as the first note, so he did not doubt the note's authenticity. But it was odd that the person had changed their motivation. Perhaps blackmail had been the goal all along, rather than terror? Still, remembering what had happened to Tinker, he couldn't help but feel that neither Tretham nor Linton were out of danger. Just because their tormentor had realized he might use their fear to extract funds from them before he ultimately killed them did not mean that he did not still, indeed, intend to take their lives. "May I keep this?" he asked the other man, noticing that Tretham, too, was beginning to look the worse for wear.

"Of course," Tretham said with a dismissive wave. "I have no need of it. I've memorized the bloody thing."

"Logic says that this person wants your money and not your life," Christian told the other man. "You can hardly hand over your funds if you are no longer among the living. And yet, there is an escalation of violence here that I cannot like."

Tretham shrugged. "I do not worry for myself but my parents are elderly and do not deserve to be put in danger because of some foolishness on my part." He thrust both hands through his already disordered hair. "If I could go back and undo that wretched race with Fielding I would do so. A hundred times over. Nothing good came of it. Now both Fielding and Tinker are dead and Linton and I are both in the sights of a killer. All for what? Some drunken foolishness."

"That doesn't sound like you," Christian said, frowning. "What happened to your refusal to let the bastard get you down?"

"That was before the bastard threatened my family, Gresham," the other man said with a defeated sigh. "I have never been a particularly moral fellow, you know. I have debauched and whored for years as if I were attempting to outpace death. But I do not mind telling you that this business frightens me. Not on my own behalf—my life is worth little enough—but on my family's. They do not deserve to be tarred with the brush of my ill behavior."

"What do you mean to do about it?" Christian asked, knowing that Tretham would not be speaking so if he didn't have a plan in place.

"I mean to find the villain at the Hidden Pearl," Tretham said, not bothering to hide his plans. "I will go there with the money and with a few choice words, and I shall kill or be killed."

"I have another idea, Tretham." Leaning back in his chair, Christian surveyed the other man through his steepled fingers. "Why not let me go in your stead?"

This must not have been what Tretham was expecting. "Are you mad? You've got a brand-new wife. And a reputation for fair play that I certainly never had. Why the hell would you put that at risk by being seen in a hellhole like the Pearl?"

"Because I wish to ensure that whoever is threatening you, and my brother-in-law by the way," Christian said curtly, "is captured before he does the same to anyone else. And because I believe that he will set a trap there for you that he doesn't mean for you to escape."

"And what of you?" Tretham asked again. "Will you be able to escape the trap so easily?"

"I have some idea of what sort of trap this person has in mind," Christian said calmly. "And I have years of battle experience. Which you, regretfully, do not."

He didn't bother telling Tretham that he was familiar with the Hidden Pearl and that he thought he might be able to persuade the proprietress to tell him who sent the note.

Tretham looked as if he would say more, but finally just leaned back into his chair and shook his head. "If you really wish to go in my stead then there is little enough I can do to stop you," he said. "Besides, you always have been a lucky devil."

"True enough," Christian said. "And I hope to keep it that way."

Maddie brushed a wayward lock of hair from her brow as she hurried toward Christian's study to update him on her brother's condition. She'd sent round a note to Lady Emily and as Linton seemed to be suffering only from exhaustion there was no danger of contagion.

As she neared the door of her husband's inner sanctum, she heard voices. She had just lifted her fist to knock when she heard Lord Tretham's voice saying, "I mean to find the villain at the Hidden Pearl. I will go there with the money and with a few choice words, and I shall kill or be killed." This stopped her cold. The Hidden Pearl was the place Amelia had told her about. The place where Christian had gone to get information about Linton's situation.

It sounded from Tretham's words as if he'd received another threat. A threat which required him to visit the Hidden Pearl with money. Her mind was already leaping ahead to ways that she and Christian could go along with Tretham. Her husband's words confirmed that he was thinking along the same lines. "I have another idea, Tretham. Why not let me go in your stead?"

She felt a pang of affection, and if she were completely honest with herself, something far more dangerous, for her husband. At the beginning of the season she would no more have dreamed that she and Christian could be so like-minded than she would have guessed that Lady Jersey took snuff and wore breeches. But, somehow, over these past few days she'd come to wish that her marriage was a marriage in the truest sense.

She had looked at her cousins' marriages and despaired of ever having that sort of love for herself, but

Maddie was quite certain now that her affection for Christian, and his for her, was every bit as powerful as Cecily's for Winterson or Juliet's for Deveril. For a lady who had spent the past years despairing of ever finding a gentleman she could find worthy of her affection, it was a heady realization.

Deciding to leave Christian to his discussion with Tretham, as he would doubtless tell her about the trip to the Hidden Pearl when they were finished, she hurried to her room to change her clothes and wash up a bit before she went to look in on her brother.

When she returned to the bedchamber where they had put Linton, she found Lady Emily seated by his bedside, her hand clasping his while he slept thanks to a sleeping powder the physician had administered. At Maddie's entrance, she looked up, startled. It was evident from the puffiness of her eyes that she'd been weeping, but her words to Maddie were of gratitude. "Lady Madeline, thank you for sending for me. I know that James would not have done so on his own." She kept her voice low so as not to disturb the sleeping man.

"I knew you would wish to know," Maddie said simply. Feeling a pang of conscience, she went on, "Lady Emily, I regret to say that I inadvertently . . . that is to say, I . . ."

The other woman laughed softly. "I know you informed him of the happy event," she said, her joy evident in her face. "He told me before he drifted off to sleep. I do not blame you. I should have a difficult time keeping such news to myself as well." Her eyes softened as she looked down on James's sleeping form. "You shall be the first to congratulate me. We are to be married just as soon as James is recovered. With or without your father's consent."

Maddie hurried forward to clasp the other woman's hand. "I am so pleased for you both," she said, taking care not to speak too loudly. "This is wonderful news. I hope that my father will be able to be persuaded on the matter. Especially when he learns that the succession will be secured."

Lady Emily blushed. "I hope you are right. I do not wish for James to lose his family because of me."

Maddie shook her head. "I think his relationship with Papa has been fraught with or without your being in the picture. This marriage actually might be something that will persuade Papa to relent. Especially once he hears about the child." She took in the glow of happiness that suffused Lady Emily in spite of her obvious fatigue. She imagined how it would feel to know that she was carrying the child of the man she loved and knew that she would be just as elated. "Before I forget," she said, "I wish that you will call me 'Maddie.' We are to be sisters, after all."

Lady Emily looked up, surprised, but pleased. "I would be honored. And you must call me 'Emily.' I have always wished for a sister."

"And so have I," Maddie said warmly. "Now I will leave you to look over the patient. Please let me know if you wish to stay with us while he is recovering. It would be little enough trouble to have a room readied for you."

"I should like that," Emily said, though she did not look up at Maddie. Her attention had already been drawn back to the man she loved.

When she retraced her steps to Christian's study, Maddie was relieved to find that he was alone. He was seated behind his desk, scribbling something on a paper. When she stepped inside, he looked up. Though he seemed tired, his eyes warmed as he gestured for her to come farther into the room. Rising, he took her by the arms and drew her down to sit in his lap.

"Is your brother all settled?" he asked. "What did the physician say?"

Briefly she told him about Linton's condition, and informed him that Lady Emily would be staying with them for the time being. If she'd been expecting him to cut up rough at the news, she was to be disappointed. "That is sensible," he said, kissing the top of her head. "In her condition, she should not be hurrying back and forth between her own home and ours. When is the wedding?"

Maddie leaned back to look at him. "What makes you think there will be a wedding?" she teased.

"My dear, it is as obvious as anything that your brother is besotted. And now that she is to have his child, a wedding is inevitable."

She snuggled up against his chest again. "True enough. I believe they will wait until Linton is back on his feet. Of course our parents will need to be informed of it, but I shall leave that to my brother."

When Christian did not respond, Maddie looked up at him. "You are preoccupied," she stated. Then, remembering his visitor, she asked, careful not to reveal that she'd overheard them, "What did Lord Tretham have to say?"

Was it her imagination, or did he stiffen momentarily? He seemed relaxed enough when he spoke, however. "Oh, he wished to know what we'd learned so far about the threats. Nothing of particular interest."

She felt a stab of pain somewhere in the vicinity of her heart. Far from revealing the details of his meeting with Tretham, he had instead tried to fob her off with some story about Tretham asking for a progress report. Was she really so untrustworthy that he would keep such news from her?

Aloud she said, "Ah, well then. I think I will go have a bit of a lie-down before dinner." Disentangling herself from his arms, she was surprised when he pulled her down for a kiss before she stood.

But she wasn't as good at keeping her feelings to herself as she'd hoped. "What is it, Maddie?" Christian asked, keeping hold of her hand as she stood.

"Nothing," she said, turning so that she didn't have to meet his eyes. "I am tired, that's all. It has been a busy day."

Hurrying out, she shut the door behind her, and leaned back against it briefly. It was true that she was tired. She felt as exhausted as her brother looked. But she would need to find some way to mask her disappointment in Christian's refusal to confide in her. If for no other reason than to keep him from guessing that she knew about his plans to visit the Hidden Pearl. And intended to go along with him whether he wished it or not.

Her backbone straight, her will resolute, she headed for her chamber. A small nap would not go amiss, she reflected. Especially if she were to spend the next day preparing for her debut as a gentleman.

Twenty

 $\mathcal{W}$ ill I do?" Maddie asked, twirling slightly before her cousin Juliet's pier glass.

When she'd decided to embark upon this latest scheme, she had known it would be impossible to pull off without Deveril's help. Juliet had been forced to cozen him into helping Maddie—he was quite convinced that Gresham would frown upon her little escapade—but he'd finally relented. After promising on pain of sleeping alone that he would not go straight to Gresham and tell him her plans.

"Though it goes against every bit of my better judgment, Maddie," he said sternly, his arms folded over his chest. "I think you would be better off simply telling Gresham about this plan of yours. Then you might at least go into the Pearl with him at your side and he can protect you."

But Maddie had insisted. "There is no way that he will allow me to enter such a place, with him or without him. And I think it says quite clearly what he thinks of my ability to assist him in this manner that he did not even bother to tell me about this latest note to Tretham."

"You do not know that he doesn't trust you," Juliet

argued. "It is quite likely that he simply didn't tell you because he knows that you would force him to bring you along."

"Whose side are you on in this anyway?" Maddie demanded of her cousin. They were in Juliet's little music room where she spent much of her free time. Deveril had joined them when Juliet sent for him and had thus far proved to be more reasonable than Maddie would have expected. Without waiting for Juliet to answer, she turned to Deveril. "Do you think it will be possible for me to get into the Pearl without calling undue attention to myself? I do not wish to put myself in danger."

"I suppose I will have to take you there myself," Deveril said with a sigh. It was clear that he had no liking for this scheme, but because he'd given his word, Maddie knew that he would follow through with the thing. "I have little doubt that Mrs. Pettigrew will put the most perverted construction possible on our arrival together, but I think that should be outweighed by the fact that we are visiting her establishment."

Maddie would have asked what he meant about Mrs. Pettigrew, but Deveril forestalled her question with a staying hand. "Do not ask, I beg of you. I already fear that this will irrevocably harm my friendship with your husband. If he hears that I have also explained the nature of same-sex relationships to you as well, I fear he will simply put period to my existence altogether. And I have a wife to think of now."

Juliet wound her arms around her husband's neck and kissed him. "You are the sweetest husband imaginable. Thank you so much for agreeing to help Maddie."

"I fear that you are the only wife in London who would thank her husband for agreeing to visit a brothel, my dear," Alec said, returning the kiss.

Maddie felt decidedly de trop, and to her horror, a bit jealous as well. The sting of tears behind her eyes made her turn away so that Juliet wouldn't see. She would go to Mrs. Pettigrew's and show Christian that she was quite capable of taking care of herself. And she would prove to him that far from needing to be sheltered from such places, she could enter them and emerge with her sensibilities intact. He would be so ashamed, she decided, that he would get down on his knees and beg her forgiveness for not taking her into his confidence.

That fantasy of Christian's abject apology still fresh in her mind's eye, Maddie stood gazing at her disguise in Juliet's dressing room. Deveril stood back and surveyed her. "You still look like a lady in disguise as a gentleman to me," he said with a frown. "But I suspect that unless someone is expecting you to be a lady in disguise they will simply think you're a very small man."

"I think you look splendid, Mads," Juliet said, though her worried eyes told their own tale. "Though I do wish you'd reconsider. Perhaps we could just go to Winterson House and trick Cecily with your disguise."

But Maddie was not to be deterred. "I am quite determined to see this through, Juliet. I must. I wish to find this person who has been threatening my brother so that he and Lady Emily can embark upon their life together without fearing for their lives at every turn."

"Then I suppose we'd best be on our way," Deveril said with a frown. Maddie could tell that he was not best pleased with their plan, but she would have to fret about her cousin's husband's feelings later. For now, she was giddy with the knowledge that she was about to embark upon an adventure. And though she was somewhat ashamed to feel such excitement, she decided to take it as one of the good things about the endeavor. There would be time enough for laments later when she faced Christian's wrath.

"Lord Gresham," Mrs. Pettigrew said to Christian as he greeted her for the second time in as many weeks. "Dare I hope you have come to sample our wares? Your little wife is hardly up to the standards of a strapping fellow like yourself."

"You have found me out," Christian said easily, though the words pained him to say. He was doing this for Maddie's sake as much as anything, he reminded himself, bowing to kiss the brothelkeeper's hand. "I find that my new bride is not as fond of the bridal bed as one would wish. But enough of that. Now I am in need of some diversion."

He felt the woman's assessing gaze upon him. Doubtless she was trying to determine just how long he might be kept in thrall to one of her girls, and was wondering just how deep his pockets were.

"We've got diversions aplenty, my lord," she cooed. "Don't you worry about that, love." She snapped her fingers, and as if by magic two young women, one a blonde and one a redhead, appeared at his side. Their bosoms were just barely contained by the feebly constructed bodices of their gowns. And without asking whether he might wish it, they wound themselves around him like two particularly winsome snakes.

"Mariah, Desiree," Mrs. Pettigrew said, her voice as commanding as any general in the field, "take Lord Gresham to the green room." She turned her eye to Christian, "Unless o'course you wish for something a bit . . . different. Though I'll warn ye that too much different and we charge extra."

Christian kept his face impassive. "I assure you, Mrs. P., I still like it the old-fashioned way."

"It's a shame, love," the madam lamented, "a real shame. I got quite a few girls that could change your mind if given 'alf a chance. Why, my Nellie has a way with a whip that could bring tears to your eyes."

He coughed into his hand. "I'll keep that in mind," he said. Then, as if he were just remembering it, when in fact he'd thought of little else since he stepped inside, "I was to meet a friend here tonight. A Mr. Sinclair. Has he perhaps arrived yet?" The note Tretham had shown him gave the name Sinclair, but Christian assumed it was an alias.

The old woman shook her head. "No one by that name here yet, love. I'll send him along to the games room to you as soon as he arrives."

Thanking the madam, he allowed Mariah and Desiree to lead him to the green room. Which was also called the games room, in honor of the naughty parlor games that could be had there on any given evening.

The chamber was a rather large, well-lit room, which, in another sort of house, might have been called a drawing room. There was a large mantel with a merry fire in the fireplace below. And a number of settees and sofas were strewn about the room, occupied by couples in various states of undress. Christian didn't look too closely because he did not wish to draw attention to himself. But he spotted various gentlemen of the *ton* and several well-known businessmen engaged in lascivious activities. Here a leader in the Lords, there a member of the Commons who was known for his stirring oratories. Reaching down to grope the bottoms of his fair companions, he dropped onto a settee where he pulled Desiree onto his knee.

He could not have described how wrong it all felt,

even if a gun were held to his head. It simply was. He
felt ill pawing these women when he had sweet, loving
Maddie waiting for him at home. What was surprising
about it was that six months ago he would have been
able to undertake an assignment like this without so
much as batting an eyelid. He was good at his work for
the Home Office. He had been able to blend seamlessly
into those masculine haunts that drew both the respectable and the depraved. And he had been able to do so
without much damage to his reputation. It was one of
the things that made him so respected by Leighton. But
now, thanks to Maddie and their marriage, he was
hard-pressed not to run screaming from the Pearl like a
virgin at her first sight of a naked man.

"My lord," Mariah said, massaging his shoulders,
then running her hands through his hair, "I think you
are too overconcerned with the cares of the world. Let
Mariah and Desiree relieve you of your tensions."

Desiree, not to be outdone by her companion,
slipped her hand up to his neck, and before Christian
knew what had happened his cravat was dangling loose
around his neck, her hand slipped into the open neck of
his shirt. "Here, milord," she said, wiggling on his lap,
much to the amusement of his cock, which cared not
who touched it so long as it was touched. "Let us make
you feel better. It's that sad to see a big, strong man like
yerself unable to take his relief."

He was debating how long he would have to endure
the caresses of the prostitutes when he heard a cough
above him.

An oddly dressed man stood before him. He was
short. And though his attire was cut well enough, the
way it fit the fellow was . . . odd. His high shirt points
marked the fellow as a dandy. So did the precision with
which his neck cloth was tied. In fact, Christian

doubted even Deveril could find fault with the thing.
But it was the man's eyes, which were slightly shadowed by the rakishly set hat, that drew his gaze. The
eyes were a bright blue. And they were . . . well, there
was no other way to put it. They were looking daggers
at him.

He looked the fellow up and down again, noting the
slight curve of the man's hips. The smallness of his
hands. The point of the chin above the shirt points.

He did not remove his hands from the persons of the
women draped over him. He couldn't because he felt as
if he were made of lead.

The man standing before him, glaring at him with
all the scorn of a wronged husband, was quite within
his rights to be so angry. Because the man before him,
who looked as if he'd like to draw Christian's cork,
was, in fact, his wife.

"What a surprise to see you here, uh, Mr. . . . ?" Christian looked up to see Deveril hovering behind Maddie,
his face set in lines of annoyance. Christian had little
doubt that Maddie had somehow convinced him to assist her with her attire. Even so, he was going to have
some very sharp words with the fellow before too much
time had passed. He knew well enough that his wife
could convince a tiger to hand over his stripes, but even
so, Deveril was a man of sense and should be able to
resist Maddie, even at her most persuasive, with little
difficulty.

"Femane," Maddie finished for him, speaking in a
gruff voice that did little to disguise her sex. "Mr.
Femane." She bowed, careful not to let her hat fall from
her head. Which was smart, since he assumed she had
pinned up her long hair beneath it. "I had not thought

to see you here, Lord Gresham. I thought you were newly wed."

That brought a tinkle of laughter from Mariah. "Oh, Lord, if I had a farthing for every newly wed fellow we've seen in 'ere. Don't make no difference to most of 'em, sir. No difference a'tall."

"Yes, well," Maddie said, "I had not thought Lord Gresham to be one of those chaps. But I suppose I was mistaken."

Before Christian could respond, Desiree crooked her finger to beckon Deveril. "Come over here and join us, milord. I don't think Lord Gresham minds sharing."

But Lord Deveril, having delivered his charge, was evidently not planning to remain. "Mr. Femane, I believe I have fulfilled the terms of our bargain. I shall leave you to it, then."

With a slight bow, he disappeared into the crowd of the green room. Christian watched in amusement as Maddie tried to figure out what to do next. She had clearly not thought beyond infiltrating the brothel and finding him. Which served her right, he thought with uncharacteristic malice. She knew better than to enter a place like the Hidden Pearl. No matter how annoyed she was that he'd not told her about the note Tretham had received. He'd done it to protect her, for God's sake. Still, he could not help feeling a pang of tenderness for her as she stood there, decked out in her male garb that did little to disguise her feminine curves.

"Mr. Femane," he said, disentangling himself from Mariah and Desiree, "I should like to have a word with you. Desiree, is there some room where we might be private?"

He knew the moment that it occurred to the prostitutes that he and Femane might not be as interested in them as they'd hoped. Both women's eyes grew round with surprise, and Mariah shook her head. "'Tis a pity, milord. A right pity."

If Maddie had any notion of what the women thought about her relationship with him, she didn't let on. Christian gave a small lament for his damaged reputation, but decided it was hardly worth the thought. He was quite content to live out the rest of his days with only his wife to warm his bed. After he delivered a towering scold for this latest scrape, of course.

Wordlessly, he and Maddie followed the girls to a small room, which was dominated by a large bed. And a painting hanging above it which depicted an orgy in some Grecian locale.

"Don't worry, you two," Desiree said just before she shut the door. "Mrs. Pettigrew is that discreet. We won't tell yer secret."

When the door closed behind her, Christian took Maddie by the shoulders and resisted the urge to shake her. "What in God's name were you thinking coming here dressed like that?"

"I could hardly come dressed for an evening party," Maddie said hotly. "I should think you would be grateful that I chose to come in disguise. At least this way, my reputation remains intact."

"I would have been more grateful if you'd not come at all," he retorted. "Maddie, what on earth has gotten into you?"

"I wished to come and confront the man who threatened Lord Tretham and my brother," Maddie said, her anger bringing rosy color to her cheeks. "I might have trusted you to do it and then inform me of the results later, but since you did not even bother to tell me about the lastest threat to Lord Tretham, you can understand why I was not so convinced that you would do so."

"Because I did not wish for you to tempt me into

bringing you along," he said, unable to keep the frustration from his voice. "Good God, woman! You have me so wrapped around your little finger that I don't know whether I'm coming or going. Is it any wonder that I would doubt my ability to remain firm with you? If I loved you less, then perhaps I might be able to tell you no, but—"

Seeing her gaping mouth, he suddenly realized what he'd just blurted out. He supposed Maddie wasn't the only impulsive one in the family.

"What did you just say?" she asked, her blue eyes wide. "What did you say to me?"

Unable to face the rejection in her face, he dropped her arms and turned to stare, unseeing, at a painting of a satyr ravishing a maiden. He had begun the day with no intention whatsoever of declaring himself to his wife, much less in a brothel. "Forget it," he said, his voice tight. "It was nothing. I simply wished to tell you my reasons for not telling you about the note for Tretham. Now that you're here, we should go back into the green room to see if Mr. Sinclair is here."

To his alarm, he felt her step up behind him, felt her hand on his shoulder. "Christian," she said, her voice low, "turn around. Look at me."

Reluctantly, he did so, careful to keep his face impassive. But what he saw in her expression wasn't the derision he'd expected. Of course, this was Maddie, whose inherent sweetness would not allow her to hear a declaration of love with scorn. She would be kind. Which, on closer thought, was perhaps worse than scorn.

"My love," she said, throwing her arms around his neck. Her hat fell off in her enthusiasm, and almost of their own accord Christian's arms slipped around her, holding her close. The kiss that she bestowed upon him was clumsy because of her enthusiasm, but he didn't mind. "My own love," she repeated. "I was so afraid that your refusal to include me meant that you didn't care for me. I should have known it was just the opposite."

"The extreme opposite," Christian said, unable to take his eyes away from hers. "Maddie, if something were to happen to you, I don't know what I'd do. I should go mad, I think. That was why I didn't tell you. Because I know how determined you are to avenge Tinker and to discover who threatened your brother. But I cannot, knowing how much you mean to me, let you risk your life like that."

She looked guilty. "And I mucked things up by sneaking here against your wishes," she said, her genuine remorse evident in her gaze. "I am sorry, my love. But I am with you, so there is no chance of me getting hurt. I trust you to protect me as I trust no one else."

He shook his head at her trust, so freely given, so determined to put him on a pedestal. "You are foolish to put so much trust in me, Maddie," he said, reluctantly pulling away from her.

"Do not say that, Christian," she said, her voice sharp. "You are the bravest man I know. You were commended by the king for it."

This brought him up short. "Maddie, I am not this hero you think I am. I am a man. I fought the French and looked after my men, true. But what good is all that when I cannot save my own sister?"

Now she touched him, and though he flinched, she refused to be cowed by his resistance. She placed her hands on either side of his face and looked into his eyes. "You are a brave man, Christian. You will not convince me otherwise. And I won't have you speak out against the man I love like this."

He saw the conviction in her eyes, and was unable to bear it. Stopping her pleas the only way he knew how, he kissed her.

Twenty-one

$\mathcal{M}$addie allowed him to take her mouth, knowing that she hadn't convinced him, but also knowing that he now understood she was serious about her love for him.

He'd just begun to unbutton her waistcoat when a pounding on the door made them both jump.

"Gresham!" cried a voice from the other side of the door just before it flew in, rocking on its hinges.

Her hair tumbling down her back, Maddie stared as Lord Tretham burst into the room, a gun trained on them both. On seeing Maddie his expression turned from one of annoyance to one very much like the cat who'd got into the cream.

"Well, well, well," he said, closing the door behind him. Maddie had never been overly fond of Tretham. She had often suspected him of deliberately leading her brother into vice. Now, feeling his lascivious gaze upon her feminine curves made more evident by the breeches, she had little doubt of it. She also had little doubt of who it had been that killed Tinker. "Imagine my surprise when little Desiree, after I paid her, of course, told me that the great war hero was holed up in the green room with another gentleman. But of course the upright Lord Gresham would never be so inappropriate as to be infatuated with another man. How boring to see that it is merely your lady wife you're preparing to tup, Gresham. Just when I'd begun to think you had a bit of imagination."

"I'll thank you not to speak of my wife like that, Tretham," Christian said coldly. "I assume that this unexpected visit from you indicates that you are the one who has been threatening Linton. Clever of you to include yourself in the threats. Really. Well done."

Tretham gave a mocking bow. "I thought that was rather brilliant on my part as well. It occurred to me not long after Fielding died. Now there was a man who was badly in need of some brilliance. Were you acquainted with the man?"

When Christian shook his head, Tretham continued, "Well, the fellow was not gifted in the brainbox, let me tell you. He was so determined to race from London to Bath. No amount of persuasion from Linton or Tinker or myself could dissuade him. So, I decided to use it as a means of removing him from the field altogether. I'd had my eye on the beautiful Lady Emily for some time, and as she was unwilling to be unfaithful to the bastard, I had to get a bit creative. That the brunt of the blame for the blighter's death fell upon Linton was simply a bonus."

"But she fell in love with my brother before you could woo her," Maddie said, so many of the puzzle pieces beginning to fall into place. "That must have infuriated you."

"My dear Lady Madeline," Tretham said, leaning back against the door, "you have no idea. And then there was Tinker with his troublesome questions and unfortunate Bonapartist leanings."

"So you knew about his involvement in the Citizen's Liberation Society," Christian said.

"Of course I did," Tretham said with a laugh. "A more inept spy I've never seen. Though I was grateful for Tinker's dealings with the spies because it led Home Office suspicion firmly away from me. I have little doubt that you lot thought it much more likely that he was killed because of his treasonous activities than over his foolish decision to look a bit too closely into my affairs."

"And Linton?" Maddie demanded, trying to determine how her brother fit into the scheme. "You simply wanted to get rid of him because he was a rival for Lady Emily's affections?"

"That," Tretham agreed, "and the fact that it was just so much fun to torment him. Give me a man in love to toy with every time. There is just something so deliciously heartfelt about them and their determination to protect their ladies from harm."

Maddie felt her heart clench. She had a very good notion of how Tretham planned to make Christian pay for his investigations into the other man's crimes. If she could find a way to remove that threat from her husband, she would do so.

"Well, then, you will be disappointed to see before you two of the most unhappily married persons in London."

Tretham rolled his eyes at her words. "Do not, I pray you, Lady Madeline, attempt to convince me that you two are not disgustingly, blissfully wed. It will not do. You are fairly dripping with honey, you're so sweet on one another. I do not mind telling you that it fair turns my stomach."

Stepping forward, he reached out and took Maddie by the arm. "Now then, my dear," he said, pulling her to the other side of the room, his gun steadily trained on Christian the entire time. "I ask you to remove that handsomely tied cravat—really, you must have done it yourself since I know that Gresham isn't capable of a so perfectly tied knot—and indeed, just remove all of your clothes. I find myself quite intrigued to see what sort of body lurks beneath your mannish attire."

When Christian took a step forward, Tretham waved him back against the wall. "Stay over there, thanks, old chap. I believe I'll use your lady wife's cravat to ensure that your protective impulses are kept at bay." Suiting his actions to his words, he took the cravat from Maddie's hands and made Christian turn around to face the wall.

Maddie searched the room with her gaze, unable to see anything that might be put to good use as a weapon. There was a strange umbrella stand in the corner but there was no way she could get past Tretham to reach it. Still, thinking she might be able to take him by surprise, she crept up behind Tretham. Unfortuntely, he must have felt her, because he swiftly turned around and smacked her across the face.

Christian said a foul word and threatened to do something to their captor that Maddie was quite sure was not anatomically possible.

"Get down on the bed," he said curtly, ignoring Christian's curses. "And take off your damned clothes. I do not mean to tell you again. Really, Gresham, you have done an appalling job of training your wife. If this is how you trained your men it's a shock to me that you survived the war at all."

He finished securing Christian's hands, and wandered over to the umbrella stand and removed what turned out to be a whip from it. "Well, well, well," Tretham said gaily, "I think you and I will have a delightful time together, Lady Madeline. I have little doubt that your dear husband hasn't shown you the joys of discipline. Indeed, that is doubtless why you are so temperamental. I look forward to showing you the error of your ways."

Maddie, who had been untucking her shirt from her breeches, felt bile rise in her throat.

"Tretham," Christian spat out, "I will enjoy killing you with my bare hands. In fact, I shall use that very whip to make my point clear."

"Oh, Gresham," the other man said with a laugh, "you did always have a fine sense of humor. I only regret that you will soon be too dead to continue your amusing repartee. Of course, I will enjoy your wife first. While you watch. I think you should be able to see one beautiful thing before you depart the earth, don't you?"

Maddie, unable to stand the anguish on Christian's face, called Tretham's attention back to her. "My lord, I shall need some help removing my boots," she said, trying to make her voice sound husky.

Turning to look at her, Tretham's eyes darkened with lust as he saw that she had removed her shirt. The binding that she'd used to hide her breasts was still in place, but she still felt quite naked.

"Of course, my dear," he said with a leer. "Never let it be said that I would say no to a lady."

Maddie lifted her booted foot to his hands and then, with all her might, shoved hard at him, managing to kick him in the chin.

"You little bitch," Tretham snarled, backhanding Maddie just before Christian, his hands still tied, butted him in the head.

Unfortunately, Tretham still had hold of the pistol, which, upon the blow from Christian, he fired wildly. In horror, Maddie looked on as a red patch appeared on Christian's arm.

Unable to stop herself, Maddie threw herself at Tretham, slapping, hitting, biting, doing whatever it took to bring him down.

Thanks to the sound of the gunshot, the door to the chamber flew open and Mrs. Pettigrew and two very large men burst in. "Here now!" she shouted, as a whip flew through the air. "This is a respectable house!"

"This couple has assaulted me," Tretham said shrilly. "I demand that you call the authorities."

"Is that what you seen through the peephole, Toby?" Mrs. Pettigrew asked a young lad just inside the door.

"Not by 'alf. This cove were plannin' to 'ave 'is way wif 'er. And not wif this bloke's by-yer-leave, neither." He wiped his nose with his shirtsleeve, for emphasis.

Maddie paid no heed to any of them, having knelt down beside Christian and untied his hands. Using the cravat, she made a pad and pressed it against his arm, which was bleeding profusely now. "It's just a flesh wound," Christian assured her, though his pallor said otherwise. "I've had much worse in the war."

Her hands shaking, Maddie kept her hand over the wound. "I do not doubt you did," she said, "but humor me."

"I'm sorry, Mads," Christian said, sitting up, and holding the makeshift bandage against his arm. "For all of it. I would not be alive if you hadn't come here today. Tretham would have killed me as soon as he saw me."

"You can't know that," Maddie said, brushing a lock of honey-brown hair from his brow. "You were right about the danger. I should have listened. But I am glad I did not."

"Me, too," Christian said, kissing her.

They watched as the two bruisers Mrs. Pettigrew had brought into the room lifted Tretham by the arms.

"Mrs. Pettigrew," Maddie said, "you should call the watch. This man is responsible for two murders."

"Don't you worry, dearie," the madam said with a frown. "Toby saw the whole thing. He heard everything."

"Then why the devil didn't you come to help us sooner?" Christian demanded, his anger giving him a burst of strength despite the blood loss. "We might have been killed."

"Well, now," Mrs. Pettigrew said with a sheepish look. "How was we to know you didn't like having a gun trained on ye? Gents like some strange things these days. But I don't hold with shooting in my 'ouse. So then we decided to come in whether ye liked it or no'."

"I demand that you let me go at once," Tretham ordered the two bruisers. "Do you know who I am? Do you?"

But they ignored him as they carried him bodily from the room.

Christian got to his feet and swayed a little.

"Dearest," Maddie said, wrapping an arm around him, "you should sit down for a bit. Your shoulder has bled quite a lot."

"It's just a flesh wound, Mads," he said again, handing her the shirt she'd abandoned. "Put this on so that we can get the devil out of here."

Maddie pulled the shirt on over her head, and retrieved her waistcoat and coat, putting them on over it. "I have rather a fondness for this little room," she said, looking around her. "You told me you loved me, here."

Christian's eyes darkened as he pulled her into his arms. "I thought I would go mad when Tretham put his hands on you. Do not ever put yourself in danger like that again. Please, Mads, it's not good for my health."

She kissed him. "I promise not to put myself in danger if you promise not to keep things from me."

"Only if you promise not to keep things from me."

"I promise," she said, not letting her gaze waver from his.

"I should have told you, I see it now," he said. "But I was so afraid that you would figure out how much I loved you. And I was convinced that you could never love me as much as I love you."

"Silly man," she said, tucking her head beneath his chin. "How could I not love you?"

Reaching down, he grabbed her hat and set it upon her head. "Now, Mr. Femane, let us go home."

And arm in arm, Lord and Lady Gresham walked quite happily out of the Hidden Pearl.

Much to the scandalized delight of everyone who saw them.

Twenty-two

I cannot believe you did it," Cecily said with wonder, sipping a cup of sweet tea in Maddie's writing room.

The cousins had chosen to meet at the Gresham town house for a change so that Maddie could show them her new room dedicated to her writing. After Cecily and Juliet pronounced the chamber the loveliest thing they'd ever seen, and the best wedding present Gresham might have given her, they settled down in the cozy corner space where Maddie often enjoyed tea and biscuits of an afternoon.

"It took more daring than even I knew I had," Maddie said, biting into a macaroon. "Though it was strangely liberating to venture into a space where no proper lady had dared go before."

"We have always been good at breaking down those kinds of barriers," Juliet said, lifting her teacup. "I am quite proud of all we've accomplished this season."

Maddie and Cecily clinked their teacups with Juliet in a toast of sorts.

"When will Linton and Lady Emily return from their wedding trip?" Cecily asked, leaning back and touching her ever-so-slightly protruding belly. "I cannot imagine embarking on a carriage trip in this condition. It's all I can manage not to cast up my accounts the short distance from Grosvenor Square to Berkeley Square."

Maddie frowned in sympathy. "I believe they are due to return next week. Now that Papa has consented to the match, I think their way forward will be much smoother. Plus, Mama has begun to speak in reverent tones of the expected heir."

Her brother and Lady Emily had married by special license as soon as Linton was able to leave his sickbed. Only Maddie, Christian, and Lord and Lady Essex had been in attendance. None of Linton's or Lady Emily's former cronies had been invited and they were not missed by either the bride or the groom.

"I still cannot believe Tretham was responsible for both Lord Fielding's and Tinker's murders," Juliet said, shaking her red curls. "I never did like him much, but I thought he was a decent enough gentleman, at the very least."

"I thought the same," Maddie said. "I thought I simply disliked him because of his relationship with my brother. And I told myself that the feeling was unfair to Tretham, since my brother's behavior was his own. Now I will know better than to discount my first instinct."

"So, it was Tretham you overheard threatening Linton on the night of the Marchford ball?" Cecily asked. "How did he disappear like that?"

"There's a secret passage in the fireplace," Maddie said with a shrug. "I asked Lady Marchford about it last week and she said her son and Tretham used to play there as children."

"It seems a shame that one man could be responsible for so much death and unhappiness," Juliet said with a sigh. "I suppose we all know now how easy it is for a single person to damage many lives."

"Which is why I am so grateful that we are all of us safe and happy at last," Maddie said, taking her cousins' hands in hers. "I am so thankful for you both. Without your excellent examples I might not have had the courage to fall in love with Gresham."

Cecily raised a dark brow. "I am grateful for you, too, Maddie, but we must give credit where credit is due. Without Amelia's dance card, none of us would be sitting here, disgustingly happy and contemplating a happy future."

Remembering something, Maddie leaped up and hurried over to her desk. Opening a drawer, she slipped in her hand and brought the fan-shaped dance card over to her cousins.

Before she could speak a sharp knock sounded on the door to the writing room.

"My lady," Yeats intoned, "your guest is here. Shall I send her up?"

"What's this, Maddie?" Cecily demanded.

"You didn't," Juliet said, raising a hand to cover her mouth. Her eyes widened as Maddie nodded her head in confirmation. "You did!"

"Miss Amelia Snowe," Yeats said, opening the door to usher Amelia into Maddie's inner sanctum.

Her eyes narrowed, the beauty looked at the three cousins, seated so carelessly around the tea table. "Lady Gresham," she said, offering a slight curtsy. "To what do I owe the very surprising invitation?"

Maddie stood and waved her guest over to the table, pulling a chair over from the other side of the room for her. Once Amelia was seated, Maddie picked up the dance card from the table.

"I believe this belongs to you," Maddie said, proffering the mother-of-pearl-and-gold fan to her.

Amelia reached out and took it from her. Opening

the card like a fan, she looked at the names scrawled on the ivory petals in pencil. And turned it over, frowning as she read the admonition to: *smile, bat, tilt.*

"I found it in the retiring room at the Bewle ball," Cecily said carefully. "I believe you dropped it."

"We've been meaning to get it back to you this age," Juliet said casually, as if she were discussing a missing glove.

Amelia looked up at them. She looked . . . confused.

"This isn't mine," she said finally, setting it back on the table.

"Of course it is," Maddie said with a strained laugh. "Who else could it belong to?"

"I have no idea, Lady Gresham," Amelia said, for the first time in Maddie's memory showing genuine emotion. "I do have one like it."

She pulled open the drawstring of her reticule and pulled out a dance card identical to the one on the table. "You see?" She held it out to her and Maddie took it. Sure enough, when she unfurled it like a fan, the petals were empty of names. As it would be if Amelia had planned to use it again before the end of the season.

Amelia laughed. "I must admit, I was quite puzzled when you asked me to call on you, Lady Gresham. Though I had hoped that we might have gotten past our earlier . . . enmity."

"You mean when you shrieked like a banshee at Maddie's betrothal ball?" Cecily asked casually. "I would call that enmity."

Maddie shushed her cousin. "That's all behind us, Cecily. Miss Snowe and I came to an understanding. She's the one who told me about Gresham's trip to the Hidden Pearl."

Juliet choked on her tea. "I hadn't realized that."

"Oh, yes," Maddie said seriously. "She did me a great service. Without that news I might not have known of the threats against my brother and Lord Tretham. So thank you, Miss Snowe."

Amelia looked at the floor. "I perhaps didn't have the best motives for that visit, Lady Gresham." She looked up, her cornflower-blue eyes shadowed with remorse. "I was so angry, you see. That the three of you had all managed to get husbands before the end of the season while my prospects just seemed to dwindle with every day that passed. And when I overheard my brother talking about Gresham at the Hidden Pearl, I decided to tell you. In an effort to destroy your marriage."

She looked up. "I am sorry, now. I've done a number of things this season that I am not particularly proud of." She turned to Juliet. "Like mocking your limp. And worse when the truth of your injury became known." Now she turned to Cecily. "I was simply horrid to you as well."

Maddie watched as the young lady who had gossiped and harangued and in general made her and her cousins' lives difficult over the past few years sat before them. It would be easy to dismiss her now. To tell her that she had burned her bridges with them and would never be allowed the luxury of their forgiveness.

But that would be the wrong thing to do. In her heart she knew it. Remembering how she and Juliet had spilled punch on Amelia's gown at the Bewle ball, she realized that she and her cousins had been just as awful in their own way to Amelia as she had been to them.

It was time for all that nonsense to stop.

"I forgive you," Maddie said, catching her cousins' startled eyes and willing them to follow her lead. "We all forgive you. For everything. But only if you'll forgive us for our own bad behavior."

"Yes," Cecily said with a slight shrug. "We were hardly innocents."

"I suppose I can forgive the cruel remarks about my limp," Juliet said carefully.

Perhaps sensing that Juliet's case might be the most difficult to navigate, Amelia reached across the table to touch Juliet's hand. "I am so sorry, Lady Deveril. It was horrible what I said and did to you. I am ashamed to admit it, but I was so desperately jealous that you'd caught Lord Deveril's eye. I said the first thing that I could think of that would put you in your place and would keep me on my pedestal.

"But it was lonely there on that pedestal," Amelia continued. "With only Felicia for comfort. Do you know how awful she is?"

"I have some idea," Juliet said wryly. "Perhaps you've been punished already."

They all laughed together at that.

"Peace, then, Amelia?" Maddie asked.

The other girl smiled, and for the first time since she'd met her, Maddie thought that Amelia was actually quite as pretty as she was rumored to be.

They had settled back down with their teacups when a soft mewl sounded from the other side of the room.

Cecily sat bolt upright. "I almost forgot!"

Rushing over to the table where the basket she'd brought with her sat, she picked it up and hurried over to the cozy corner. "We had the most shocking surprise last week," she said over the noises coming from the basket. "You'll never guess."

Opening the lid, she revealed her cat, Ginger, who was nursing three kittens. One black, one tabby, and one snow white.

"Ginger's a girl!" Juliet cried, leaning over to get a better look at the kittens. "How marvelous."

"We didn't know until we found him with the kittens," Cecily said, shaking her head. "I thought he was finally growing up. He was small when Winterson gave him to me, but I thought that was because he was still a kitten. Instead he was small because he was a female."

"I want the black one," Maddie said, lifting out the tiny mewling baby and snuggling him to her ear. "I've always wanted a black cat."

"I would love to have the white one," Juliet said, slipping a gentle hand down to remove that one from the basket.

Amelia peered over the edge of the basket, looking in wonder at the ginger-haired tabby who moved toward the side of the basket and began to climb out.

"You shall have the ginger, Amelia," Cecily said, lifting him to put him in her outstretched hand. "He likes you."

The ginger kitten, not knowing that he was being held by the most reviled beauty in London, began licking her palm with his tiny sandpaper tongue. Amelia laughed.

The cousins exchanged a look. None of them had ever heard her laugh.

"May I?" Amelia asked, her eyes filling with tears. "I've never had a pet before. Mama forbids them. But I think I could keep him hidden in my bedchamber."

"Of course," Cecily said, lifting out her own Ginger from the basket and cuddling her close.

The four ladies sat playing with the kittens and Ginger for some time.

Like friends.

Epilogue

"How long has it been since the last report?" Winterson demanded, his hair sticking up at all angles while he paced the Aubusson rug in his study.

"Only an hour, old man," Deveril said, putting an arm over the other man's shoulder and drawing him to the leather sofa.

"How about a drink?" Gresham asked from the sideboard where he poured out three glasses of brandy.

As married ladies, Juliet and Maddie had been allowed into the bedchamber where Cecily labored to bring the next generation of Wintersons into the world. Though Maddie had confided to him that she was not quite prepared for the realities of the birthing process, Christian had known that when the time came she'd not be kept away from her cousin's bedside. She was a brave girl, his Maddie. And come next summer, she'd be going through the whole business herself, so he knew she was taking mental notes.

"Babies are born all the time," Deveril offered, taking the drink from Gresham. "Cecily will be right as rain. You'll see."

"Spoken like a man whose wife hasn't gone through

the process," Winterson growled, getting up to pace again.

A brisk knock on the door had them all turning. Smiling, despite the tears coursing down her cheeks, Maddie stepped in.

"It's a boy!" she cried, rushing over to hug the duke, who was looking suspiciously close to tears himself.

"Cecily is well?" he demanded. "Tell me, Maddie. I can handle it."

Maddie laughed. "Of course she is," she told him. "She wishes to see you as soon as you are avail . . ." She trailed off as Winterson sped out of the room and up the stairs.

Deveril excused himself to go find Juliet, and Maddie and Christian were left alone.

Wordlessly, she stepped into the circle of his arms.

"Well?" he asked. "Was it as terrifying as you expected?"

She thought about it. "Yes and no. It was amazing. And I will no longer doubt that Cecily is the strongest woman I've ever known. But it was quite natural in its way."

"Will you be able to endure it, do you think?" Maddie felt the tension in his body and smiled. He was frightened on her behalf, the dear man.

"I think so," she said, lifting up to kiss him. "Though I think I should like for you to be there with me."

She felt the terror course through him. But all he said was, "If you wish it."

That was one of the million things she loved about him. Despite his own fear, despite his own natural inclination, Christian would walk on water if she asked it of him. Because he trusted that if she asked there was a darn good reason for it.

"I do," she said, leading him to the leather sofa. "Because I cannot imagine bringing your child into the world without your being there to meet him."

He squeezed her hand. "I might pass out, you know."

"And so might I," she said, leaning her head on his shoulder.

"Love you," he said, holding her close.

"Not as much as I love you," she said.

And they both knew that it was enough.

Coming soon...

WHY DUKES SAY I DO
Available in August 2013

And don't miss these other novels in
Manda Collins's dazzling series

HOW TO DANCE WITH A DUKE
HOW TO ROMANCE A RAKE

Available from St. Martin's Paperbacks